My Last

Hope

Also by Katie Richard

Destiny

Into The Storm

My Last Hope

Katie Richard

Katie Richard LLC

My Last Hope

Published by Katie Richard LLC

www.katierichard.com

Printed in the United States of America for Worldwide Distribution

ISBN: 978-1-7371453-9-4

For those of you who have faced trauma or abuse, you're not alone. Keep fighting, keep surviving. Don't let your abuser take more from you. Don't let them continue to rob you of life after you've separated yourself from the situation.

Fuck them. You deserve happiness and love.

This book may not be suitable for all readers. Mature themes within have a recommended audience of 18 years old and above. Read at your own discretion.

Scenes in this book may include but are not limited to:

~ physical and emotional abuse

~ violence, death, and grief

~ hostage/ kidnapping

~ mention of suicide (not an actual one)

~ substance abuse

~ sexual scenes

Chapter One

Abby

"Honey, I'm home!" Frank belts out from the doorway, making me smile as I put the final layer of cheese on top of the lasagna. Opening the oven, I get a burst of hot air in the face. Squinting from the heat, I shove the casserole dish on the center rack.

The construction company Frank works for landed a big contract for the local hospital today. His crew will build a new inpatient wing on the west side. It's nice to see Dillon, our hometown in Montana, finally get some needed upgrades. Living in such a small town, Frank found the funding sources are limited, unlike East Point, which is about an hour away. They're a level-one trauma center, meaning they get all the fancy stuff. I wanted to help him celebrate by making his favorite dish with my grandmother's recipe.

He comes into the kitchen, tosses his keys in the wooden bowl in the center of the table, and wraps his arms around me from behind. I love how he nestles his chin in the crook of my neck, dragging his nose up and down the side, making me shiver. He knows that my neck has always been one of my most sensitive parts. His mouth twists into a smile as he presses his lips to my skin, where my vein pulses. My lips part as I lean into him while he continues to kiss me there. His rough, calloused hands trail down to my waist and grip me tightly, pressing me against him.

"I missed you today," he says gruffly.

I clear my throat. "I missed you too. Congratulations on landing that contract."

"Thanks. What are you cooking? It smells good in here." He inhales deeply.

"Lasagna," I answer, twisting in his grip and putting my arms around his broad shoulders. I don't mind the drywall mud and paint splatters that cover him. They compliment his dark olive-green eyes. I wipe a chunk of white mud off his eyebrow and grin.

"Mmm. My favorite." Tilting his head, he grins down at me and taps the tip of my nose with his index finger. "Just like you, my favorite person."

I wish it were always like this, the loving couple. I don't answer him back. I can't lie to him and tell him he's my favorite person. He was once, but he's changed too much over time. Instead, I hug him and sigh contently. Times like these make me think there's still hope for us. That we can still go back to the way we were before our current struggles.

He dips his head down and covers my lips with his. I open for him, and his tongue darts inside and caresses my own. As he deepens the kiss, I slide my hands through his short, light brown hair. He abruptly pulls away, leaving my face tingling from his stubble.

"I'm going to go get cleaned up."

"Okay," I say breathlessly, watching him stroll away.

I don't mind him staying in his dirty khaki carpenter pants and the blue sweatshirt with his company's logo on the back. I find it sexy when he's covered in grease and grime from being a blue-collar worker. There's nothing like a hard-working man.

He disappears around the corner and into the hall that leads to the bathroom. Turning back to the stove, I realize I forgot to set the timer. "Shit," I mumble under my breath. I estimate how long I was distracted and set my timer for a few minutes less, just in case. Grandma would curse me from heaven if I burnt one of her recipes. She was a fantastic cook and wrote painstakingly detailed instructions. Even a beginner shouldn't be able to screw up the recipe from inside the pages of what I call my bible.

It doesn't look like anything special. The leather-covered book is cracked from years of use, the binding is fraying at the edges, and there are some spots here and there that I suspect are from food. My mom passed it down to me when I married Frank. Perks of being an only child, I guess.

While waiting for dinner to finish, I start a load of laundry and begin filling the dishwasher before I hear Frank's footsteps. Freshly showered and in clean blue jeans with a white long-sleeve shirt, he takes out a beer from the refrigerator, twists the cover off and tosses it into the open trashcan beside me. I cast my glance back into the dishwasher to hide my disappointment. He's been drinking more and more these days. He hardly goes a night without at least one or two beers.

I still have about twenty-five minutes until I have to check on the lasagna. I grab the paperback out of my purse on the counter and retire to the sofa in the living room to pass the time while Frank watches a football game on the television. I roll my eyes as he shouts commands at the players on the screen. Why is it that most men feel the need to do this? Can't they watch the game in peace? I have a hard time concentrating on the words with all the shouts of, "No! Why did you do that?" and, "Catch the damn ball!"

The timer rings. I sigh loudly, close my book with an audible snap, and set it on the stand. In the kitchen, I find the cheese isn't quite brown enough. I leave it in for a few more minutes. In the meantime, I grab our plates, the same set we got for our wedding shower, white porcelain with a light green ivy pattern circling the rim. I've always loved these plates. After pouring myself a cup of cola and bringing it to the table, I check on dinner again.

"Dinner's ready," I call out to Frank. The sports commentator gets cut off mid-sentence, and Frank comes up next to me in the kitchen. "How hungry are you?" I ask.

"Starving." Right on cue, his stomach growls in protest.

I laugh. "It seems that way."

I scoop out enough to fill his plate to almost overflowing before grabbing about a quarter of the amount for myself. Frank's not a little guy and has the appetite to show for it. At five foot ten, he stands nearly half a foot taller than me. He has a lean muscular build that plows through all the calories I try to feed him.

He takes a few bites of his food before going to the fridge for his second beer. Slipping a forkful into my mouth, I notice it has an odd taste. Weird, I used the same recipe I always do. Maybe it's just me. It's that time of year when viruses love to circulate. As an art teacher, I'm surrounded by elementary students all-day, and we all know how they love to wash their hands whenever they sneeze or blow their little noses. We should earn hazard pay during flu season.

Frank sits back down and takes another bite before scowling. "What's wrong with the lasagna?"

I shrug. "I don't know. I made it the same as always. I thought it was just me."

He tries another forkful before he pushes his plate away. "I can't eat this."

The only thing I can think of that would make it taste off is if the cheese was bad. From the trash, I pull out the food containers. The mozzarella is good for three more months, but the ricotta expired last month.

"God damn it! I'm sorry, Frank, the ricotta I just bought today expired."

"Are you fucking kidding me?" His chair scuffs against the linoleum. "Why can't you get anything right?"

He backhands me hard, sending me flying into the table. Pain cuts into my face, from chin to ear, as if on fire. I fumble for the kitchen table to steady myself, but it's just one of those cheap department store variations and tips over, sending our plates crashing and shattering to the floor. I slam against the wood's edge, knocking the wind from my lungs before landing on my hands and knees. I look up at Frank in shock as my body starts to tremble.

Fury flashes from his green eyes, but the emotion soon morphs into fear. His mouth drops open, and he quickly covers it with a hand. Frank rushes over as I pull my legs against my chest. My breath rasps from my lungs, and I try to shield my face behind my arms.

"I'm so sorry, Abby. Come here. I didn't mean to do that." Frank drops to his knees beside me and kisses the side of my head. My pulse is erratic, and I flinch at his touch. "I promise it won't happen again. I just lost my temper, is all. I love you. I'm sorry, baby."

He pulls me against his chest. My whole body continues to shake. Wetness coats my eyes. He hasn't hit me in a long while, and after every time he's done it, he always feels sorrow and fear that I'll leave him. I know he doesn't mean to. He has anger issues. I could've avoided this if I had just checked the date on the damn ricotta. Why didn't I check the date?

When he starts rubbing circles on my back, I hate how my body still seeks comfort from him. How is it that the one who causes your heart to break is also the one that can put you back together when you fall apart? I hate this yo-yoing of my emotions when it comes to him.

I think I'll leave every time this happens, but I never do. When things are good between us, it's perfect. The few bad instances we've had shouldn't cast a shadow over all the years we've been together, right? The hitting has only been going on for the past year and a half, maybe two. I try to block it all out. We've both been under a lot of stress lately, trying to start a family. He can still change. There's still time for us to fix our marriage.

When I can finally trust my voice, I tell him without turning toward him, "I know you are Frank."

We clean the kitchen without saying another word, but his gaze keeps finding mine. He knows he screwed up again. My side that landed on the table hurts like hell, and my face still burns a little. I haven't dared to look in a mirror. I'm sure his handprint was left behind as a reminder. He fixes us some leftovers from last night, but I can't bring myself to eat now. My stomach is in knots, and I'm afraid that if I eat, it'll come back up. I have to get away from him. We need to put some distance between us.

"I'm going to shower and head to bed," I tell him quietly, barely meeting his gaze. I'm tired of pushing the food around on my plate. I get up from the table before he has a chance to reply.

He nods and hugs his body as I turn away from him. Once in the bathroom, I continue to avoid the mirror. Undressing and stepping under the hot spray, I close my eyes and lean into the shower wall. My throat begins to tighten as unshed tears fight to be free. I don't have the willpower to keep them at bay. Sobs wrack my body as I slide down the wall to sit on the shower's cold floor. Water is raining all around me, washing my tears down the drain. Why do I still love this man? I know I shouldn't. I know it's wrong of me to stay, but I can't bring myself to leave him. He's been my best friend for the better part of ten years. I know we can be happy again if he would stop doing this to me.

I can't stop the barrage of tears. It's as if they're coming from an endless well. One would've thought the aquifer would be dry with how many nights I've washed my salty tears away. Pulling my knees tight to my chest and burying my face behind my forearms makes me feel a little safer. Almost like if I don't leave this shower, no harm can come to me. I still can't believe he struck me like that. It's the hardest he's ever hit me. How can you claim to love somebody so deeply but yet physically hurt them the next day?

Dawson

Bang, bang. Shots ring out behind me, and a chunk of the wall next to me explodes. Pieces of it land on my combat boots before I duck around the corner of the mud brick building. With my back pressed against the rough wall, I crane my neck around to get a look. Where the hell are they? I search the rooftops within my sight, trying to spot who shot at us. The flash of light reflecting off the sniper's scope from the street lamp gives away their position.

"Two tangos, rooftop behind me," I speak into the radio, holding a hand up for my men behind me to wait for the signal.

"On it," Nolan's voice reaches me through the static.

Fucking Murphy really did it this time. My commanding officer was out on recon late last night and never checked in with the base. I told him not to go alone. Me telling him not to do something doesn't hold any water with him. He received some intel that the Taliban were holding two American journalists captive in a building on the north side of town. He was just supposed to check it out, but still, he should have brought other men with him. We're his team for a fucking reason. We're supposed to have each other's backs. He was reckless to go all lone wolf.

Another bullet burst into the wall beside me. "Nolan?"

I originally joined the armed forces as a medic several years ago but switched over to infantry. There's nothing like literally having your life on the line every day. As a medic, I saw many things I wish I hadn't. But out here in the field, this is where I belong. This is where I'm needed. I climbed ranks fast and volunteered for the tour I'm currently on. I'd rather be here risking my life than have somebody with a family take my place. I don't have a wife or girlfriend back home waiting for me. All I have is my sister, Isabelle, and my parents, if you could call them that. They haven't filled the parental role the way they should've. Other than dark hair and blue eyes, my parents and I have nothing in common.

"I got one. I'm just waiting on the other tango to lift his head up again," Nolan replies.

When Lexie, my long-time girlfriend, left me the day I told her I enlisted. They sided with her. My mom told me I'd never be good for any woman if I would rather go to war than have a regular job back in the states. She didn't get it. This is something I felt deep in my bones I needed to do. I'm not heartbroken over Lexie anymore. We were barely eighteen and still figuring out life. I haven't had a serious relationship since her, though. I won't give my heart away again. I can't. My relationship with my parents has always been rocky, but that was when I realized I just don't give a fuck anymore. I'm not chasing their approval, and I don't need it. Bella's all the family I need.

Because all eight guys behind me have family in the states, I have to ensure the team makes it back home. My team's tracking Murphy's location and his ping is coming from the same building the journalists were said to be held in. We're only two blocks out, but this place is crawling with eyes. I feel them like a brand against my skin. My scalp tingles, waiting for the inevitable. I'm sure the captor is already aware of our presence. The sun barely crests the horizon in the east and coats the ground with the first morning rays. The dark of night can no longer be used as our cover. That also means the enemies can't hide from us.

"Both targets neutralized," Nolan's voice comes through the line.

Thank fuck. "Let's go, ladies," I order.

I usher my team in the direction of the building until we're only a block away. Here's where six of my guys branch off. We surround the building on every side while they wait for my command. It's eerily silent. Not even a whisper of wind. It's too quiet. I nod to Emerson before swinging my leg and forcefully breaking the door down. Shards of splintered wood fly into the room as the door teeters on the hinges for a beat before finally crashing to the floor.

"Breached," I give the call letting them know we're in. Now they wait for the squirters to run either out the other exits or straight toward Emerson and I. We'll be ready for them.

The other six wait a couple of minutes before entering the large building from their sides. A few tangos find themselves in front of my gun, pointing their weapons at us. Taking them out quickly, we continue to rush the halls and rooms and raid the building in search of Murphy and the other hostages. Shots ring out from other sections of the building as they dispatch their combatants. Clearing room by room, my team meets in the middle of the building.

One lone room is left, and it's locked. This must be it. There's only one entrance, and we're standing beside that door. By now, they know we're here. We could be walking into a trap.

I kick the door in and step aside, letting the others with their weapons drawn inside first. Picking up the familiar weight of my rifle, a strange sensation comes over me. Something's not quite right. My blood runs cold as soon as the dust settles from the door. There are three Taliban's, each of them standing behind a hostage with a knife at their throat. One is Murphy, and the other two, I presume, are the journalists by their clothing. The one behind Murphy starts to speak in Dari, one of the main languages used in Afghanistan. I only know bits and pieces, but I don't need to know what he's speaking about to know his intentions.

I let my rifle fall to my side on the sling and put my hands up for everyone to stand down and wait. He presses the blade harder against Murphy's neck, creating a small incision that makes blood trickle down his dirt-covered skin. Murphy stays calm, but his deep chestnut-brown eyes betray him by relaying his terror. He knows this could be the end, and he may never see his wife and kids again.

Not if I have anything to do with it. The other two, one male and one female, have dirt-streaked tears across their faces. But so far, their captors hold their blades an inch away from the delicate skin of their necks. I'm glad to see they know who the main threat is. Murphy is a beast of a man with an ego to match. My eyes again meet the older tango behind him; his soulless cocoa-colored eyes narrow into slits. His gray beard reaches chest level, and he continues to spew words I can't translate. But I do know one thing, no matter what we do here, they'll kill them. They'll slice that blade right across their throats. That's what makes them so ruthless; they kill without a conscience. They really don't care who lives or dies.

I make a slight gesture with my hand, not seen by the tangos but immediately fulfilled by my team as shots echo off the mud-caked walls. Before they can act, all three Taliban members drop to the floor with bullet wounds in the center of their foreheads. The knives thud to the floor beside them as dark red blood seeps out and pools around what remains of their skulls. The journalists cry out in panic as my team rushes to pull them away to safety. Taking my Ka-Bar out of the leather sheath at my waist, I begin sawing through the ropes around Murphy's hands and ankles. As soon as he's free, he throws himself at me and hugs me.

"Bloody hell, I thought I would be another layer of dust on the floor. Took you long enough, Connelly," his deep voice booms as he slaps me on the back.

Relief floods through my veins. This could've ended horribly wrong. "We could've avoided this whole mess if you would've listened in the first place and taken us with you." I glare at him as I swing my fist back and punch him in the arm.

He feigns hurt, but then his expression grows serious. "I owe you, man. I owe you my life. Let me know if you need anything when we get out of this dust bowl."

"Noted." I give him a tight-lipped nod. "Now, let's get the fuck out of here. Move out!"

I follow behind my men until we reach the outside, then I retake the lead. Still wary of the possibility of other tangos in the area. It's complete daylight now, but that doesn't mean we won't get ambushed. We slowly make it to our rigs that are parked several blocks away. The ten-mile journey back to base camp went off without incident. I hop out of the Humvee, my boots barely touching the sand before the captain approaches.

"Sergeant Connelly, come with me, please," he says deadpan. His face is one of those resting asshole faces. I can never get a good read on him.

Captain Anderson's another beast of a man, but he worked hard to earn those two silver bars on his collar. I respect the shit out of him. The stories I've heard from his time in the field make him a fucking legend. He's known as the wolf for a reason. After his whole team was captured, he held out the longest. Anderson was the only survivor of the P.O.W. camp the terrorists took him to. The rest of his men were tortured to death. From what I gather, he was knocking on death's door when the rescue team arrived.

"Yes, sir." What the fuck is this about now? I followed protocol. I did everything right. If anything, Murphy should be getting his ass hauled away.

He walks into the barracks and has me follow him to his office before shutting us in. My eyes drift to the wall with maps of the area and the most wanted pictures pinned to it. A few of them have bright-red

X's struck through the center of their face. We're knocking them off slowly. One by one, we'll rid this world of the worst of mankind.

"Take a seat," he says, folding himself into the metal chair behind his desk.

Yup, not good. I sit in the chair across from him, trying to think of why I'm sitting in the hot seat. Zilch, nada, not a fucking clue.

"Some news came in shortly after you left the wire." He scrubs a hand over his chin. "I'm sorry, Connelly, they found your sister dead at her home late last night."

No. This can't be real. Bella can't be gone. My palms are sweaty as I try to rub them on my pants which are still covered in sand dust. No. I don't want to believe it. Loud ringing in my ears drowns out the day-to-day sounds of the barracks behind that door. I swallow the pain crawling up my throat.

"How did she die?" I already know without him answering. Jackson, her piece of shit fiance who beats her, is why she's dead.

He opens his mouth to speak but then closes it. Anderson sighs before answering, "I think you should wait until you're stateside and talk to your family. We're putting you on a bird back home. Wheels up in two hours."

"I need to know, Captain." my voice is as weak as I've ever heard it. But I don't care, that's my sister. She's the person I care the most about in this world, the only person I have left. The muscle in my jaw twitches, awaiting a response. I hold eye contact, and I'm not giving him an out. I need to hear the words. I pray I'm not right and that it was an accident.

Anderson draws in a breath, averting his eyes. He doesn't want to tell me. Meeting my watery gaze again, he informs me, "She was found beaten and strangled to death. They have her fiance in custody."

"No!" I shout, slamming my palms down on his desk, rattling the picture frame so hard it falls over. I fucking knew it! A guttural scream escapes my throat in agony as I drop to my knees on the ground, praying this is all some sick, twisted joke.

I land face-first on the hardwood floor of my bedroom, struggling to breathe and covered in sweat. The yell still burns my throat. "Fuck, not again."

I rub at my temple as the spot begins throbbing. I fling myself back on the bed. I don't know if it's because I've been working at Bella's Safe Haven this week or if it's because Bella's birthday is coming up that my mind likes to replay the worst day of my life while I'm sleeping. Maybe I should start taking those sleeping pills again that the doctor prescribed me a while back. They helped me to have a dreamless sleep, but the side effects made me feel groggy and zombie-like throughout the day. I sit up and lean against the wooden headboard of my bed, still fighting to calm my labored breathing. My fists clench and unclench. The sweat that's covering my body is now cold.

"Why couldn't you just listen to me?" I ask quietly, staring at her picture on my bureau.

It was taken the last time we were together in New Orleans celebrating Mardi Gras two years ago. We're both smiling and wearing more beaded necklaces than I care to admit. She was so happy then. God, I miss her. I was the baby brother who always got into trouble, and she was the angel who always stood up for me against my parents' harsh rules. My life hasn't been the same since she passed, and it never will be.

"I should have done more to protect you." That's a guilt I will forever carry.

Chapter Two

Abby

Beep. Beep. Beep. My shrill alarm drags me out of bed, and I stumble half-awake into the bathroom. Flicking on the bright lights and looking at myself in the mirror, my shoulders sag. My blue eyes are red and puffy from crying, and my lip is fat on the left side. My long blonde hair is frizzy from going to bed with wet hair.

I quietly walk to the kitchen to grab an ice pack to decrease some swelling. After resting it on my eyes until they're so numb they ache, I pull off the pack and look again. Some swelling went down, but not much. There's also a slight bruise on the bottom of my jaw. It seems like it'll be another makeup day. I slap the ice pack down on the counter and cringe at the sound it makes. I'm silent, trying to hear if the noise woke up Frank. No sounds come through the thin wooden door. I let out a shaky breath.

I dress, brush my teeth and hair, then apply my makeup in a way I'm not proud of. I never had to use concealer or foundation before the past year or so. I never thought I would ever be one of those women. I cover the small dark bruise the best I can, thankful I don't have to cover the other bruise on my side. That one is relatively large, about the size of a softball. It still twinges with pain when I move. That one's going to hurt for a while. I grab my coffee in a purple to-go mug decorated with roses and make my way out into the cold winter air. I can't get out of this house fast enough. I'd rather brave the freezing cold than be here for another minute.

Hopping in my little blue Subaru and blaring rock music the entire way to work, I sing along to the song as loud as I can. I park my car in the teacher's lot and steel myself for another day of lying to my friends and colleagues. I plaster on a fake smile as I climb out and dart for the building. That's the thing if you smile, people think everything's okay. It's incredible the amount of pain that can hide behind a smile. It just shows you that you never really know what somebody else is going through. But, if they think I'm okay, it's less I have to lie about.

Sometimes I don't get why I keep covering for him. Some days I wonder if I should go to the police. I keep hoping he'll stay true to his promises of it being the last time. Lately, I've been having a hard time believing that. I try to see the good in people, no matter the circumstance. It's a quality I used to think was one of my best, but it seems it's turned into one of my worst.

"Hey, Abby," Chloe says in a sing-song voice from behind me as I pull the glass door shut, the wind nearly ripping it from my grasp. It's always windy here.

"Hi, Chloe."

As soon as I turn around and she takes in my appearance, her smile falters, and she looks at me with a sadness I've seen too many times. She's the only person who knows even an inkling of what I've been through with Frank. She's my closest friend and the only one I can trust.

Chloe's hazel eyes crinkle at the sides, and her forehead wrinkles. She shakes her head, her dark hair swaying back and forth. "He did it again, didn't he?"

"He didn't mean to. It just kind of happened." I find myself staring down at my black fuzzy-lined boots.

"Yeah, right. Like you accidentally fell into his fist? You deserve much better, Abby." Her eyes flash with anger.

She may be my friend, but I wouldn't say I like her condescending tone. I go to answer her, then snap my mouth shut as Joyce walks by us, her high-heeled boots tapping on the tiled floors.

"Good morning, ladies," Joyce greets us.

"Good morning," we both reply in unison.

Joyce is a nice enough woman and all, but she's nosey. She'll be the first to get the scoop on any drama and tell everybody else. She's the last person I want overhearing anything about my marriage.

"Oh, Abby, what happened to your eyes?" Joyce asks, stopping before me and blocking my way to the classroom.

I grit my teeth as my irritation grows before remembering to smile. "Just allergies."

"Allergies? This time of year?" her voice turns wary. Her eyes feign concern. She's just looking for gossip—typical Joyce fashion.

Yes, I'm aware there's snow on the ground, but people can have allergies at any point of the year. "Yep, I tried some new air fresheners in the house, and apparently, they're too strong." Why do the lies come this easily to me? I hate lying. I hate this whole situation.

"That's too bad, dear. I hope you can clear them soon." She pats me on the shoulder with her glove-covered hand.

"Thank you," I say with a tight smile before she turns on her boots in the opposite direction.

I choose to ignore Chloe's comment and focus on today's assignments. I make sure to tell my students upfront that I have puffy eyes from allergies, and they leave the subject alone for the most part. Some of them even chime in to say they have allergies, too, from pets or plants. My kids prove to be a good distraction once I get that out of the way. Art, for most of them, is fun compared to their other classes. Today is the last day before winter break. To say they're rambunctious would be an understatement. It's good that I love my job and these kids because I sometimes have difficulty reigning them in.

Most of the other teachers are excited about their vacations as well. Me? Not so much. The thought of being stuck at home lately brings me down. I could pick up another part-time job to fill in the days I'm not here. I doubt Frank would go along with that. He already thinks I work too much. That's yet another thing that angers him on the list that never ends. I never had to worry about things that could make him mad before. He always respected my decisions. Now all he seems to want to do is control my life.

The bell rings, signaling the end of the school day and the beginning of nine days off. I felt terrible about picking up expired cheese yesterday. To make up for my lack of date checking and to rule out any errors on my side, I pick up one of those frozen lasagnas you can buy in the grocery store. It's not my grandma's recipe, but it's still lasagna. I hope he's in a better mood. I felt him crawl into bed last night, but he stayed on his own side and gave me space, which I appreciated. Even though we both lay awake for some time, he didn't once try to talk to me.

I usually get home about an hour or two before Frank. I chuck our dinner in the freezer and head to my office. Nine days. What am I going to do for nine days? At least Frank usually only has Sundays off. He's gone a lot. Perks of him being such a hard worker, I guess. I plop down on my daybed by the window and stare at the bookshelves that line my walls. Maybe I'll reorganize my books. That usually brings me a sort of peace. On Saturdays, Chloe and I typically go out to the mall and window shop for a while. She shares my love of books. It doesn't take much to waste away a few hours in the two-story bookstore there. Of course, that means we travel out to East Point because Dillon only has a few small convenience stores and one somewhat large grocery store.

Maybe I can finally finish that painting I started a few weeks ago. I dig out my supplies and line them up the way I like on my tray beside the easel. I put dinner in the oven and remember to set the timer right off this time. I've been trying to paint a lush landscape with a sunset behind it. I take out my phone and look at the picture I took for reference. It was from one of my favorite times with Frank. I smile sadly. We drove all over to find the best picnic spot on one of his days off last summer. We had sandwiches, chips, cut fruit, and wine in the cooler on the backseat of his truck.

I don't even remember where we were, but we came around a sharp corner that opened up into a small clearing surrounded by trees and wildflowers. We both looked at each other simultaneously with identical goofy smiles. We stayed there sprawled out on the blanket until the stars came out. It was beautiful, and it was magical. Those are the memories that I choose to hold on tight to. Not the dark moments we've had. That's the hardest part in painting it, capturing all the magic and happiness when lately I just feel sad and lonely. I want to be happy again like I was when I took that picture. Happiness feels so far out of my reach, like my arms aren't long enough to grasp it.

Gravel crunches outside as the telltale sound of Frank's old truck chugs up the driveway. My shoulders tighten up as I hear the front door open and close. His keys clang together in the wooden bowl with mine. As his footsteps draw near, my heart begins to race. He rounds the corner, and I see a vase of flowers in his hands. Of course, my favorite lilies. All in shades of pink and white with some sprigs of baby's breath mixed in. I used to love seeing a vase full of lilies, but now they only represent the bad times.

He stays rigidly in the archway, and I watch the roll of his throat as he swallows. My eyes raise to his face. His usually luminous green irises are dull, and the surrounding white is bloodshot. His lips slightly pull up at the corner before saying, "I'm really sorry, Abby."

"I know you are," I whisper, and I believe him. I know he's sorry. "We can't keep doing this, though." I don't know how much more I can take. I don't know how to keep picking myself up off that shower floor. I'm afraid I won't have the strength to do it one day.

His eyes turn glassy, and he gives me a curt nod. "I know. I don't know what happens. I've had a lot on my mind, and when I get angry like that." He pauses and runs a hand roughly through his hair. "It's as if somebody else takes over."

Frank turns away from me as he sets the flowers on my desk. He takes a step closer to me and embraces me. I stiffen and rake in a shaky breath. Just like that, I'm right back to last night when he struck me. If he notices the change in me, he doesn't stop. He begins placing kisses from the base of my neck up to my ear. A war rages inside of me, equal parts turned on and terrified. My body craves his touch, but my mind knows he's dangerous. In the end, it's the fear that wins.

"Please stop," I beg him as breaths shudder violently out of my chest, and my hands fist at my sides.

He sighs and runs his hands through his light brown hair several times before turning on his heels and stalking out of the room. I let out a breath and close my eyes. I press my palms into my eye sockets, trying to stop the tears. I'm drawn to the flowers on my desk when I open them again. Walking over, I bring my face down and inhale their sweet mixture. It's always the same pattern. Abuse, flowers, and love for a while, then right back to abuse again. When will it finally be enough for me to smarten up and leave? The thought of walking away from Frank and the love we've shared over the years makes my chest ache more than the bruises on my body. I don't want to leave him even though I know I deserve better. My heart hurts just thinking about walking out that door and never coming back. I don't want to give up on him, on us.

The timer dings dragging me out of my trance. I woodenly walk out to the kitchen and take the lasagne out of the oven. I dish out the same amounts I did the night prior. Sitting at the table, my eyes keep straying to the chunk of drywall missing from when the table was slammed into it. The memory keeps replaying over and over in a relentless loop. Forcefully chewing and swallowing each bite until my plate is empty. I ignore Frank for the rest of our meal. I can't even look at him without seeing the face he wore last night just after he hit me.

Once he's finished, he rinses his plate and disappears from the room. Soon, I overhear the sports commentator in the background. He watches his game, and I go to my office and hide in a book to escape from this life I've found myself in. Or try to anyway. This isn't the life I pictured for us when we wed. Two people who are supposed to love each other are spending their evenings in separate rooms because they can't stand being around each other. Sometimes I wonder why we both even try to make this work between us. There has to be more for us in this life than just this.

Dawson

My cell phone vibrates in my pocket. Pulling it out, I see it's a text from her again.

Addisyn: I miss you.

I sigh and roll my neck back and forth, eliciting a cracking sound. I wish she would take the hint. I broke it off with her over a year ago. She still sends me texts like these every once in a while. I don't reply back. I'm busy at work. While waiting for my last patient to arrive, I finish typing my notes into the computer from this morning's patients before my phone vibrates again. I don't want to look at it, but I also use this phone for work, so I have to.

Addisyn: I'd like to see you.

Me: I've got a lot going on right now between work and Bella's.

My screen lights up with three little dots meaning she's typing a reply. They disappear, then reappear as if she keeps changing her mind about what she wants to say.

Addisyn: Another time, then. Could you text me when you're free?

I tuck it back into my pocket. I won't be texting her when I have free time. We dated for a while, but it was casual. I'm just not into her enough to try to make it into a more meaningful relationship. I haven't felt that way about another woman in a long time. Not since Lexie broke my heart. I won't give another woman a chance to fuck me over like that again. I'm not cold-hearted. I keep my heart out of the equation regarding women. I give them what they want, and they do the same for me, no strings. Until I meet the one that changes that, this is who I am. Addisyn knew that when she got with me. It's on her that she thought she could change me.

Closing out the program and locking the computer, I shuffle out to the waiting room. My final patient of the day should be here by now.

"Gabriel," I call out to the busy waiting room.

The older gentleman struggles to stand with his cane. He drags his left foot across the tile floor. I open the door and let him through. Following behind him, I try to make small talk with him to no avail. His only replies are grunts or one-word answers. Gabriel's one of those typical grumpy older men. I power through his appointment and show him the stretching he's been doing at home needs to be corrected. He didn't like that very much, but I instructed him on the correct way to do it again.

That's the main thing with being a physical therapist; your job is very, very repetitive. Sometimes I miss the sporadic days of being in the field with the military, as crazy as that sounds. I finished my term after Bella's death and didn't reenlist again. I can't even look at my uniform without remembering that day, and I've found a new purpose in life. I want to help victims of domestic abuse to know there are safe options for them to get help.

I don't usually work on Saturdays, but I'm trying to make up my time from last week while I was on vacation. I can't really call it a vacation when I worked at the shelter all week. I never take an actual vacation. I'm too much of a workaholic. Come to find out, the shoddy contractor I hired to do the wiring in the building did a crap job. We had to replace most of it. No wonder he was so cheap. The wires started to arch in the breaker box. We're lucky the breaker tripped, and there wasn't a fire. It could've been worse.

My cell phone vibrates in my pocket again, and I groan. Slowly pulling it out as if it'll bite me, I relax when I notice who the sender is.

Russell: Are we still on for burgers?

Me: You know it.

I met Russell several years ago in between deployments. He owns one of the bars in the city that I frequented when I first got back stateside. He's a no-bullshit type of guy, and we hit it off almost immediately. We get together once a week for a meal. I see him at the gym, too, but that's different. He's going through a painful divorce right now and can use all the guy time he can get. His wife cheated on him, and now she's trying to get half of the bar he built from the ground up before he even met her—all the more reason not to get too involved with the other sex.

I finish my shift and meet him across town at the mall. I don't know why he always wants to drag me here. He claims the food is the best in town. I've had better burgers in a hell of a lot better atmosphere. I think he has the hots for the manager that works here. It's the only logical explanation. We sit on the balcony overlooking the shopping mall's center. I see him surveying the restaurant looking for her. I shrug my dark gray coat off and hang it on my chair. The glass on the balcony is entirely see-through, giving us an unobstructed view of the customers below. This is a good thing because I need to see the exits.

I get anxious if I can't, thanks to fucking PTSD. The foot traffic has slowed down immensely since the holidays have passed.

"Are you ready to order?" a young girl with red curly hair and the annoying trait of snapping her gum asks us.

"I'll take the cheeseburger with a side of fries and a coffee," Russell answers without even looking at the cheap laminated menu he holds out for her to take.

We've been here often enough he could probably recite the menu from memory. I've seen some of the other dishes they've brought out to the tables, and they didn't look too appetizing. I'll stick with the usual too.

"And I'll have the same." I fold up the menu and hand it to her.

She tucks the menus into her black apron. "Alright, the server will be out shortly with the food."

I glance around the dining area. It's fairly large and retro with a black and red theme. The tables are too small to fit any more than four people comfortably. The dance music is constantly pulsing too loud in the overhead speaker and grates on my nerves. I don't care for music that loud when so many people constantly move around me. Call it my training or my experiences, but I'm always hypervigilant. This place sets me on edge. Russell doesn't know that because I haven't had the heart to tell him. He doesn't ask much of me. I can put my shit in a little box deep inside and do this for him.

"Are you going to finally tell me why you always insist on coming here?" I cross my arms over my chest and raise my eyebrows.

He looks taken aback. "I like the food."

I smirk. "Sure, buddy."

"You don't believe me?" He leans forward on the table, but his eyes glance behind me and track somebody.

I turn around in my seat. My eyes land on the manager. Her long dark hair is pulled up in a hair clip. Her dangly earrings reflect the light as they sway from side to side as she talks animatedly to one of the female customers. I face him again.

"I'm not an idiot. You practically salivate every time you see her." I tap my fingers on the table.

He doesn't respond; he just quietly watches her from afar like a stalker. If I didn't know him as well as I do, I'd be worried for her.

"Ask her out," I tell him.

Again, I am still waiting for a response. Giving up on conversation, I begin scrolling through emails on my phone when I hear a female laughing below us. The sound travels through me and straight to my groin. Every nerve ending is standing at attention. I look over the banister, trying to spot her. About ten women are walking around on the first floor. I scan them all, wondering who gave me such a reaction.

"What are you looking for?" A knowing smirk splits his face.

"I thought I heard something," I reply. Now *he* wants to talk?

I continue to scan the crowd. There it is again, that playful laugh sending a shockwave through my body. Is it possible to want somebody just from the sound of their laugh? I spot her with long, straight blonde hair and a navy blue coat. My eyes drift down her slim frame from her skinny jeans hugging that perfect ass to her black boots. Fuck, she's gorgeous. Her dark-haired friend points something out in one of the closed window displays. They both look at each other and laugh again as the blonde bumps her with her hip.

"The brunette or the blonde?" Russell follows my line of sight, leaning over the railing as well.

"The blonde." I don't bother trying to hide it. It's not like I'd go after her anyway. Women that look that good are trouble, and I don't need any of that right now. I got enough shit in my life.

"Go get some." He tilts his head in her direction. "But bring the brunette back for me."

It has been a while since I've gotten laid.

When she bends down and hugs a little boy, something in my chest warms. Minutes later, the boy runs up to a couple, no doubt his parents. Even I can see the relief on their faces from here. The blonde smiles at the trio before turning away. I've always had a soft spot for kids. Seems she does too.

After she strolls further into the mall and past my line of sight, I lean back into my seat and sigh.

"Nah, I don't have time for that right now. And aren't you in enough hot water with women at the moment?"

But I'll be damned if my eyes don't continue looking for her every few minutes. My ears perk up at any female voice, wondering if it could be hers. None of their voices zing through me like that.

"I still have needs, you know," he chuckles and stretches his arms out in front of him.

"How about the manager?" My forehead wrinkles as I wiggle my eyebrows.

"Can't, not yet." He scans the restaurant again.

I shake my head. "And why not?"

"Because Mia slept with her husband." His lips tighten into a thin line, and his eyes narrow at the metal light fixture hanging above our table.

Oh. Well, that explains a lot. Mia was Russell's wife, the hoe who cheated on him. I didn't realize it was to a married man she did it with. What a home wrecker. No wonder he drags me here every week. It's his silent way of getting back at Mia? Before I have a chance to ask, the server arrives.

"Two cheeseburgers, fries, and coffee?" After we nod, the server sets the plates in front of us.

He's not quite as young as the girl who took our orders, but I swear they get younger and younger. That or I keep getting older. I'm still in my mid-thirties. I'm not old yet. The whole time we eat, I keep hoping I'll hear that laugh again. I take my time dipping each fry into the ketchup and chewing more than necessary. I know what I'm doing, the same as what Russell's up to. We're both stalling for time. We both want to catch another glimpse of the women who captured our attention.

"Does she know who you are?" I take a long drink from my coffee mug.

He shakes his head. "No. How can I go up to her and say, you don't know me, but my wife is the tramp that fucked your husband and ruined your marriage too? Wanna have dinner?"

"Well, you don't exactly have to put it that way." I shove the last fry in my mouth and roll my eyes. Russell's always had his own way with words. At least he doesn't sugarcoat anything.

He sighs and leans back in his seat. "Don't ever get married." His face twists in agony before turning away.

"I have no intentions of it."

It's the truth. I almost asked Lexie to marry me. I would've dropped to one knee if she had stayed with me. She couldn't do long distance and would rather dump me than try. I dodged a bullet. Who knows where my life would be if we did get married?

I keep looking for the woman in the blue coat while Russell keeps watching for the manager. What a sad pair of men we make. Both of us want women that are too far out of our reach because of our own fucked up reasons. I continue to look for the blonde even on our way out of the mall. I didn't see her or hear her again. It's a shame. I would've at least liked to know her name.

What kind of name would suit a woman like that? A Brenda? No. Elizabeth? That doesn't sound right, either. Angel, that's the name that comes to me when I picture her. Somebody far too good for this twisted man. I don't even know how to make a woman happy anymore besides in bed. I'll stick to what I'm good at. It's easier that way. Shit gets messy when hearts get tangled up in it.

Chapter Three

Abby

Today is one of those days when I know my life is about to change drastically. I can feel it deep in my bones that some monumental event is going to happen. It's been gnawing at me all day. I'm not a pessimist by nature, but I just haven't had the greatest luck in the past few years. I need something good to happen for a change. I don't know how much longer I can continue to live like this.

I nervously twist my white-gold wedding band around my finger. I hate sitting in this fertility office. The pale pink walls only remind me of what I'm lacking. The pictures hanging on the walls all relate to pregnancy options. I don't have anywhere I can look that doesn't remind me of where I am. Every time we've come here hoping for some good news, we leave more devastated than the last time. If I'm told the eggs didn't take, another piece of me is going to die. Frank and I have been trying to conceive for almost three years now. The first year was on our own with no success, so we turned to in vitro fertilization.

This is our sixth time going through the process of harvesting and implanting the fertilized eggs into my uterus. My periods have never been reliable, and all the hormones I've been taking have made it worse.

Frank's bouncing his leg up and down rapidly. He gets his hopes up every time we have a pregnancy check. Frank wants a child so badly, and I desperately want to give him one. But I don't think I'm pregnant. I think I'd notice some sort of the change in my body within the last six weeks. They took a vial of blood and a urine test when I arrived here about thirty minutes ago, and we've been anxiously waiting for the results.

A knock at the door makes me jump. My nerves are frazzled. I straighten and hold my hands together in my lap as I turn toward the doorway. Dr. Soloman walks in with an easy smile, tucking her long wavy brown hair behind her ear. God, I hate how hard it is to read this woman. Her poker face has no limits. She always wears the same face, never giving anything away. Maybe that's a doctor thing?

"Good morning, Mr. and Mrs. Miller. How are you two today?" Her high heels clack against the tile floor as she walks around us toward her own chair.

"I'm doing well, and you?" My automatic reply to everything lately. Nobody wants to hear the truth anyway.

"I'm okay," Frank grunts.

"I can't complain, it's a beautiful day, and the sun is shining."

Hope starts to bloom in my chest. She said a beautiful day. Does that mean we're pregnant? She wouldn't be this optimistic if she were going to deliver bad news, right? I squeeze my hands together so tight they ache, waiting for her to get on with it—my breath stalls in my chest.

I dare to glance at Frank, who looks as hopeful as I am, a rare smile on his face. I wish he'd smile more. He's handsome when he does. Like the man I fell in love with, not the man he's become. His Ivy League tawny hair is longer than he usually lets it grow. I shake my head to clear the bad stuff I just brought up. It's been seven weeks since the last time he hit me in the kitchen over spoiled ricotta. He can be better. I know it. We need this baby.

She sits opposite us and crosses her legs at the ankles. Her silver anklet shimmers under the lights. "I won't keep you waiting. I know you've been through a lot. I wish I had better news to give you, but unfortunately, the tests are negative. I'm very sorry. We can try again in another two months if you wish?"

My head falls as my eyes water. I can't bear to look at Frank, knowing I failed yet again. The ringing in my ears builds as the muscles in my back tense. I know what happens next. The blame, then the screaming and yelling. Which always leads to hitting. The cycle of my life.

Frank's chair scrapes loudly on the tile floor as he stands abruptly and stomps to the exit. I intake a sharp breath. "I'll be in the truck," he says gruffly before slamming the door on his way out, making me flinch violently.

"Abby, I'm sorry." She reaches out with a pale hand tipped with pink nail polish and pats it.

"Why can't I get pregnant?" I ask her once I'm able to look up again. We've asked before, and it's always the same answer. Maybe it'll be different this time.

"I really don't know." She shakes her head. "I've done all the tests for everything that it could possibly be, but there are no clear answers. The workup from both you and Frank is inconclusive. Sometimes we don't know why." She rubs my knee as if it'll make it all better. Like, I'm a damn dog.

"I need to give him a baby. That's the only thing he's asked of me."

Tears well in my eyes. God, I hate all these hormones I've had to take. They make me more emotional than I've ever been. I feel like all I ever do is cry or try not to cry. If she only knew what this was doing to my marriage. Each time I fail at conceiving a viable pregnancy, it changes him for the worse. He blames me even though we don't know if it could be his genetics playing a role. It's always my fault.

He's not the same man I walked down the aisle to five years ago. He's not the loving husband who comes home from work and asks how my day was anymore. He only asks if I feel any different. That's all he cares about now. At least in the six-week window between the insertion and the pregnancy check, I don't have to worry about him hitting me.

"There are other ways to have a baby. You could do surrogacy or adoption?" she offers, pulling me from my dark thoughts.

I frown. "I've talked to Frank about that, and neither is an option."

He got extremely angry with me the last time when I brought it up; he slapped me across the face for thinking he'd want somebody's throwaways, his words, not mine. If he only knew how many amazing kids are out there without parents. They all deserve a loving home. I could give a child that whether they come from my genes or not.

"Why don't you give me a call when you guys are ready to try again or if you decide on the other avenues." She gives me a thin smile.

She's just doing her job. She's not a therapist sitting here wanting me to tell her all the problems I have to keep hidden from the rest of the world.

"I will, thank you."

I gently get up and walk to the door, careful to shut it quietly behind me. I lean against the wall and close my eyes. I count to five before I start walking toward the exit and to where Frank is waiting for me. I reach the beat-up burgundy truck and climb up. Frank won't even look at me as he turns the key. The engine comes alive with a loud grumble.

"Frank, I'm sorry." I reach for him, but he pulls away as if my touch is toxic.

"Have you been sabotaging your pregnancies?" he asks, his voice deathly quiet, the warning in his voice clear as the window in front of me.

"Why would you think that?" I stare at him. I can't believe he would accuse me of such a thing. Why would I purposefully lose a child?

"I don't think you want this as much as I do." His nostrils flare as his lips tighten.

He finally looks at me, and I almost wish he hadn't. The fury in his green eyes is unmistakable. I press my back against the door, hoping he wouldn't be dumb enough to hit me in a public parking lot surrounded by many other people.

"I do want this, and I've done every goddamn thing I was supposed to do. It's not my fault it's not working," I snap. I've wanted a baby so damn bad too. I've wanted kids for as long as I can remember.

"It's your body that's rejecting our baby, so yeah, it is your fault." He slams his palm on the steering wheel, cursing. My body instantly stiffens as he mumbled to himself. "Why do I get the defective woman whose womb is broken."

I think it would've hurt less if he struck me instead. Tears fall from my eyes as I angrily swipe at them. Doesn't he see the pain that not carrying a baby causes me? As if I don't feel inadequate enough of a woman already, he has to voice it too? What if he's the reason we can't conceive?

"What the fuck are you crying for? You want me to give you a reason to cry?" he snarls, wrapping his hand around the base of my throat.

Shocked, I shake my head. "Maybe you should be with somebody else who can easily give you a child," I say, forcing the words out of my throat against the pressure of his hand.

"You think it's that easy to walk away from me? You're my wife. Are you saying you don't want to be with me?" His fingers tighten around my neck, making it hard to take a breath and daring me to defy him.

"No, that's not what I'm saying." I swallow painfully. "I mean, maybe you're better off without me because I can't do this for you."

His eyes narrow. "You will have my child, or you'll die trying. We're not giving up yet, understood?" He gives my neck a painful jerk.

My stomach turns to ice at his words. What does he mean by 'I'll die trying?' Would he really kill me if I'm unable to have kids? I nod so he'll turn away, releasing me from his iron grip. I've always had a fear of what he could do, but I've never felt this terrified of him. He's never put his hands around my throat before. He's slapped, punched, kicked, and shoved me, but he's never done this. We ride the rest of the way in silence. His anger is palpable in the cab of the truck, suffocating me and making it hard to breathe as if his hands were still there. I dread what's waiting for me when we get home.

He'll pin me to the wall and scream at me until his voice is hoarse. Slapping me or squeezing my arms until my skin is bruised. I can't go back to that again. I was hoping he'd leave me if the tests were negative again today. Just be done with me. I know there's nowhere I can go that would be safe from him. He'll always find me. I can't turn to my parents or Chloe. I'd only put them in a dangerous position.

The rectangular blue sign for our little town in Montana comes into view, along with a crushing amount of panic. We're almost home. My hands start shaking, and my pulse is like a freight train in my ears. I can't go back to that house. I know this time will be so much worse. His violence is escalating to a level I'm fearful of.

"Pull over, please," I manage to choke out.

"Why?" he snaps.

"I need to get out," the words rush out of my mouth.

His angry gaze flicks to mine. "Like hell you are. Your ass is staying right there."

Come on, grow a set and tell him. "Please, Frank. Just let me go," I sob. "I can't do this anymore."

I watch as my words sink in that I want to leave him and that I can't be with him anymore. That I can't endure this suffering any longer. His face morphs into something I don't recognize. There's no sign of my best friend in those features.

"Never," he shouts, "I'm never letting you go."

With that, I know for sure my Frank is gone, and the only way I'm getting out of this alive is by my own hand. I knew the day might come at some point when I would have to act, but I hoped he would change and I wouldn't have to leave him. Without thinking clearly, I lunge for the steering wheel, yanking it toward me. If he won't let me out of this truck, I'll let myself out.

"What the fuck are you doing?" He yells as he tries to keep the truck on the road as it fishtails.

I slam into the dashboard as the truck swings back around. My shoulder hurts like hell from the impact.

"Just let me out," I scream, pulling harder on it. I can't control the panic. All rational thought splinters and there's only the need to escape.

"No. Let go!" He tugs it back again.

I keep my grip on the steering wheel even as the knuckles from Frank's fist slam into my face making pain explode inside my cheek and left eye. He yanks the wheel back to the center, causing the tires to squeal in protest. I give one final tug with every bit of strength left in me, and the tire goes off the side of the road pulling us closer and closer to the ditch. The truck starts to tip on its side, rolling over before colliding with the tree with a loud crunch, and then everything goes black.

No more shouting, no more engine rumbling beneath me, no more heater blasting in my face, just nothing.

Dawson

I pull up to the security fence I had installed at the driveway to Bella's Safe Haven. I punch in my code in order for the gate to swing open for me, and I park the truck in the back of the building. When I bought this place, I extended the driveway to be behind the building. That way, any passersby can't see the vehicles of the guests seeking refuge. I tried to think of everything that could happen. All the ways an abuser would try to find them or get to them. Killing the engine and hopping out, I go around to the back entrance and again punch in a different code to gain access. The lock springs free, and the handle twists in my grasp.

As soon as the door opens, it's as if I'm beaten over the head with a vase of flowers. That's all this place ever smells like. But what did

I expect? It's for women. It can't exactly smell like grease and wood chips. I just got off my shift at the hospital, and I like to swing by here a few times a week. Even if I'm not needed. I know Maggie has everything under control, but control and routine are something I need, according to my shrink.

I believe her because when things feel like they're out of my control, I get anxious, and I don't like surprises. They put me on edge. I had to take anger management courses after I lost my sister and before I opened this place. The last thing these ladies need is me losing a gasket because I dropped a tool or something while fixing it. Because that was the type of man I turned into when she died. I've always had a short fuse, but I'd never lay a hand on a woman, though. That's a line I'd never cross.

I also like to come around frequently enough that any of the women staying here know who I am and that I'm not a threat. Some only stay a matter or a few days, and others a month or more. They're free to stay as long as they need to be able to get back on their feet safely. I'm the only man allowed in this building besides Russell on the off chance I'm away when a repair needs to be fixed. Other than that, it's strictly all female. It's not that I don't trust other men. Most of us aren't like that. I didn't want any added stress here. They've been through enough. They've survived the unthinkable.

"Hey, Dawson, how's it going?" Maggie comes into view as I round the corner to the kitchen. Her auburn hair is tied back in a braid. She leans against the counter sporting a pair of blue jeans and a sunflower shirt.

"Hi, Mags. It's been a day, that's for sure. How about you?" I set my keys and phone down on the slate gray countertop.

"It's actually been a good day. Claire's all moved into her new apartment, and I already have her room cleaned up for the next one." She scratches at the scar on her wrist unconsciously.

"I wish we had more rooms." I rub the back of my neck. It's an awful feeling having to turn away abuse victims. I never realized there were so many. Even in a city this size, the number shouldn't be that large.

"I know. I had to turn away two last week. Of course, they never want to leave their contact information in case one becomes available. Maybe you should buy a hotel." She laughs as if that thought is ridiculous.

"I've thought about it. If I had the funds, I would. Unfortunately, we wouldn't have the money to run it for long." I sigh, wishing I could do more. It never feels like enough. I could pour all my own money into a bigger place, but it still wouldn't make enough of a dent.

"Are we okay?" she whispers, looking over her shoulder and making sure nobody else hears.

"Don't worry. We have plenty of money to run this one. I'm also going to put together another event to get more donations, to be safe long term." I cover a yawn with my palm.

I only have two paid employees, Maggie and Angela. Maggie lives in the upstairs apartment, so there's always somebody here, and Angela covers for Maggie on her days off. I've also covered vacations. Some people donate their time, such as a therapist and a chef from a local restaurant. There are only six bedrooms available for the victims. I dream of growing this even larger, having multiple safe houses across the state. My goal is to never turn anybody away ever again.

"Tired?" she asks, stifling her yawn. "See what you started?"

"Yeah, I haven't been sleeping well lately." I hear that blonde woman's laugh in my sleep, sometimes even when I'm awake. I can't stop thinking about her. I want to know who she is and what her story is. I'm not telling Maggie that, though. I'd sound like a lunatic. Maybe I am.

"Is everything okay?" her voice hitches up on the last word.

Maggie and I grew close when I first started renovating this place. She's like the younger sibling I never had. She has her own troubled past, with abuse stemming from her childhood. When I interviewed her for the manager position, I liked her immediately. I knew she would be a great asset to the women seeking refuge here. She's guarded around men but outgoing and funny with women. It took a while for her to warm up to me like this, and I don't blame her. You can never be too careful. Once you've been hurt, the walls come up to protect what's left.

"I just got a lot on my mind," I answer. It's more like a who.

"I'm here if you need me." Her green eyes soften, and she rinses out her water bottle in the sink.

"I know you are. Thank you." I yawn again. Damn, maybe I should go home and go to sleep. "Is everything running smooth?"

She sighs and rolls her eyes. "I got it all under control. That's what you hired me for, remember? I'll let you know if I need anything."

"Alright, I think I'm gonna head home and try to get some shut-eye."

"Alright, get some sleep." We hug briefly before I walk out.

I only live about ten minutes from here with my roommate Ralph. He's a sales rep for a large pharmaceutical company and travels more than he's at home. He's a decent guy, very clean, and always pays his rent; it could be worse. I pull my truck into my side of the garage. Ralph's silver Mercedes is parked in here as well. It looks like he's home for a change.

I open the fridge, scour through the take-out containers, and find some sliced turkey in the back. Opening the container, I sniff it and shrug. Smells good to me. I make myself a sandwich with the last of the cold meat. I can barely keep my eyes open long enough to scarf it down. The meat is on its last leg. It tastes funky, but it's all that's here. I don't buy many groceries since I'm not usually home that often.

"I'm surprised to see you home, stranger," I say to him as I pass the living room. His black hair nearly blends in with the dark fabric of the couch.

"Not for long. I'm leaving for the East Coast in a few days. They lined up a bunch of conferences and hospitals for me to pitch to." He shrugs his shoulders and sets his cell phone face down on the coffee table.

"You're a hot commodity. You must be doing something right then." I lean against the wall to steady myself.

"I feel like a rockstar on tour without all the perks," he huffs. His hazel eyes do look tired. He's a workaholic like me, never taking any time for himself.

"A least the pays good." Silver linings and all that shit.

"True." He nods and grins at me.

"I'd stay and chat, but I'm exhausted."

"I'm not far behind you." He stands and brings his fast-food bag to the trash can.

I nod and retreat to my bedroom. Stripping to nothing, I crawl into bed and stare at the ceiling. After several minutes of tossing and turning in the sheets, I take one of my sleeping pills. I don't use them often, but I know my functionality will be totally screwed up tomorrow if I don't get a decent amount of z's. While I wait for the medicine to kick in, my gaze falls on the wooden picture frame beside the bed. Her dark hair and eyes stare back at me.

The silver chain hanging off the corner catches the light when my cell phone goes off with an email notification. I sigh. That was her favorite necklace. It's a simple chain with a nickel-sized monarch butterfly dangling off it. She adored butterflies, and because of that, I despise them. I can't even look at a butterfly without having an enormous amount of pain fill every crevice of my body.

I thought the pain would ease by now. In some ways, it has. In others, I swear it's magnified. Through the shelter, I've helped dozens of women. But I wasn't there for the person who needed me the most. I was half a world away, fighting a battle that wasn't ours to fight. My eyelids grow heavy, and as I close them, the last thing I hear is a laugh that brings out a primal need in me to find her.

Chapter Four

Abby

I awake with a gasp, and my whole body feels like it's on fire. I cry out in pain. Frank is unconscious in the driver's seat but looks okay. The truck is tilted on its side, and I'm still buckled against the door. The pain in my leg is intense enough to make me nauseous. I try to pull it up from beneath the caved-in dashboard, but a scream rips through my lungs. My legs stuck. Every time I try to pull it up, it feels like the skin is tearing apart.

"Help!" I yell and stretch my arm up to bang on the windshield, instantly regretting the move. Looking down, I discover a large shard of glass has pierced through my shirt and into my flesh, while blood seeps into my shirt. I don't dare pull it out. We're stuck and not getting out unless somebody helps us. I keep yelling through the pain until I can't anymore. All that comes out of my lungs is a strangled cry.

Frank snaps his head up, and creases form on his forehead. He slowly turns toward me, hatred filling his eyes. The veins bulge in his neck as he snarls, "Look what you did!"

I can't focus as a wave of dizziness drowns out everything around us. His menacing shouts at me drift away quieter and quieter until I'm surrounded by darkness.

"Ma'am, wake up," a soothing voice greets me and nudges my shoulder. "Ma'am."

I drag my eyes open and squint against flashing red and blue lights. I look around and remember what I've done. I did this. I crashed the truck. I groan as another wave of pain threatens to take over any coherent thought. I wanted an out so bad I hurt Frank in the process. I just wanted to get out of the damn truck. Why couldn't he just let me out? Why couldn't he just let me go? Why couldn't he be a better man for me?

"Your leg is crushed by the chassis. I can't pull you out just yet. I'm starting an IV to give you pain meds while we wait for the team with the saw." The young man reaches into the bag beside him on the ground.

The pick of the needle barely registers. My head is throbbing, and the pressure builds and builds in my leg with each pulse of my heart. I dare to look over again at Frank, but the collar around my neck won't let me turn far enough. I knew my pain was bad, but if they're giving me pain meds while I'm still in the vehicle, I must be in terrible shape.

I can't think of that right now. I need to know if Frank's okay.

I open my mouth to speak, but my throat is raw from yelling for help, and nothing comes out but air.

"It's okay. It's just a precaution. Your husband's in another ambulance getting checked out, but he seems alright." He smiles warmly down at me.

A calming sensation spreads across me. It must be the pain meds he spoke of. I'm half aware of the first responders laying some sort of blanket across me. Then a saw cuts through the metal. The noise screeches into my brain. My God, the noise. Worse, the pain from the vibration of metal against metal. It's excruciating. I shudder before blacking out.

Small flashes of my surroundings seep through the darkness. The ambulance ride, the hallway, all the faces hovering above me saying things I can't hear. The ringing in my ears drowns out everything else. The next thing I know, I'm rushed into an operating room and put under anesthesia. The doctor counts backward from ten. Ten, nine, eight, seven, six, five...

The steady thrum of beeping draws my attention. My eyelids are heavy as I struggle to open them. I'm exhausted, and everything hurts. I feel like I got run over by a bus. Where the hell am I?

"She's waking up," a woman's voice reaches me. "Abbigail, can you hear me?"

Who is that?

"Yes," I croak. At least, I think I did. That voice doesn't sound like mine.

"It's okay, hun. Take your time. I'll go grab you some water," the soothing voice reaches me. I want to ask her who she is, but I can't get the words out.

A warm hand wraps around my own. Then I remember the fertility clinic, the parking lot, and the crash. I remember everything.

"I'm here, baby. Wake up."

It's Frank, and it sounds like old Frank, my best friend, the one I fell in love with. The man who wouldn't hurt me, the man who made me laugh until I cried. I want to stay here like this when our love was pure and good. I don't want to wake up yet. My heart aches. Maybe he's changed his ways and still loves me like he used to. Back before my body failed to give him a child.

Finally able to lift my eyelids, I squint against the harsh light. Everything in this room is white, making my vision that much worse. My head is still throbbing, and my leg hurts terribly. I try to sit up to get into a different position, but sharp pain shoots through my side.

"It's okay, I got you," he says soothingly. A drastic change from a few hours ago or however long it's been since we crashed, and he was yelling at me.

Frank gently eases my body forward and places an extra pillow behind me, and that's when I notice it. I rub my eyes thinking I'm wrong, but it's still there when I reopen them. Or, not there, I should say. The blanket is flat against the mattress where my left calf should be. I try to move my leg and wiggle my toes, thinking it must be there, but nothing happens. The blanket doesn't shift or do anything. I reach down with both arms but the stabbing pain in my side stops me. My breath saws in and out of my lungs in short, shallow breaths.

Where's my leg? Where the hell is my leg? What the hell happened?

With one hand, Frank firmly takes my chin, pulls my head to face him and commands softly, "Look at me, Abby."

I drag my gaze back to his bloodshot eyes. His eyes soften with sympathy as he tells me, "I'm sorry, baby. The doctors did everything they could, but they couldn't save your leg. They had to amputate just below the knee."

Couldn't save my leg? Amputate? The words pound over and over in my brain like a jackhammer. Tears fill my eyes and start to fall down my cheeks, dampening the blanket over my lap. I remember the firefighters having to cut the metal from the truck to get me out, but they never said anything about taking my leg.

"It's all my fault." I sniff. "If I hadn't-"

"Shhh. It's okay, not now. Don't say anything about that here. They think I swerved to miss a deer, okay?" He scoots to the edge of his seat.

His eyes beg me to obey him. I nod as I look at my husband, really look at him. How can he be kind and caring after what I did? I could've hurt him badly as well. He gently wraps his arms around me as I sob into his chest. His embrace isn't as comforting to me as before, making me cry harder for the man I lost long ago. Why does fate have to be so cruel? What have I done so wrong in the world to deserve the hand I've been dealt?

Soft footsteps draw near, but Frank continues to hold me. "Welcome back, Abbigail. I'm your nurse Kali, and I got you some water if you're ready for it?" Her kind eyes are a soft shade of hazel, and her dark hair is pulled up into a messy bun.

I nod as I reach for the bottle of water. I place the straw between my chapped lips and take a sip. The cool water coats my raw throat like a balm.

"The surgeon will swing by soon to talk to you, but I'm guessing you already noticed?" She gives me a sad, compassionate smile while leaning against the side of my bed.

"Yes." That's all I can manage to say.

"How's your pain?" She studies the monitors beeping quietly beside me.

"My head hurts a lot, but my leg and my side are unbearable." I hand the water bottle to Frank.

"Okay, we can fix that. I'll put in an order for more pain meds. Is there anything else I can get you?"

"No, thank you."

"Alright, hun, I'll be back shortly. If you need anything, press the call button," she says, lifting the remote attached to the bed and setting it beside me. Kali shuts the door quietly behind her.

Feeling drained, I lean back into the pillows and close my eyes. What am I going to do now? How can I teach a room full of elementary students art if I can't even stand? I can't walk. How can I leave Frank when I couldn't outrun him before? I'm stuck, just like I was back in that truck.

"Frank, were you hurt in the accident?" I ask, holding my breath for his answer.

Even after how many times he's hurt me in the past, I don't want to cause him pain. I'm not wired that way. I don't want revenge. I want to be able to feel safe again, and I'll never be able to feel safe again staying married to him.

"I'm alright, just a concussion." He rubs the side of his face where a small bruise has formed.

"I'm sorry," I whisper. "I never meant to hurt you." Words I don't think he's ever meant when he's told me the same.

He leans back in the small blue chair, crossing his arms. His eyes narrow slightly and his voice grows curt, "It's fine. We'll discuss this when we get home."

He still thinks I want to go back home. I don't. I need to be free. I can't live like that anymore. But where will I go? Especially now that I'm missing a limb. I refuse to go back to my parents. I haven't seen them much these past few years, and I won't burden them with this. I rest my head back on the paper-thin pillows trying to figure a way out of the new mess I've found myself in. Why didn't I walk away sooner, before it got this bad? I should've waited until we got home and then made a run for it.

Kali returns and injects my IV with medications that take the edge off and make me sleepy. I don't remember Frank leaving, but thankfully he's gone when I wake up a few hours later. There's a crystal vase by the window with flowers. I don't have to read a card to know they're from Frank. They're the usual, "I'm sorry I'm such a shitty husband" bouquet of lilies and baby's breath. I swear even the shades of velvety pinks and creamy whites are the same as last time. I wonder if they're a Frank Miller special.

I hate that I love those flowers. Lilies are by far my favorite, but I have a soft spot for all of them. He used to buy me flowers on valentines day and our anniversary but now the only time he thinks to get me anything is when he screws up. I don't expect any gifts from him, but it would be nice to feel like he still cared. He used to pick me up a chocolate bar or something small like that as a surprise when he went to the store, and I'd do the same for him.

When we started having fertility issues and our marriage started to become strained, that's when it all stopped. It's odd how little things like that can mean so much when you no longer have them.

Dawson

Ting. Rolling over and picking up my cell phone off the nightstand, I sit upright. It's a message from the orthopedic surgeon at the hospital I work at. It's not usually a good sign to get a text from him on my day off.

Noah: Just giving you a heads up, I had an emergency below-knee amputation last night. I sent the paperwork to your office, but could you make time in your schedule in the next few days to fit her in?

Me: I can do that. Thanks for the heads up.

Noah: You're the best.

Being a physical therapist and having a specialty in amputees is both a depressing and rewarding job. It's rewarding when the patient can find their independence again, but if they don't do well, those are the hard ones. People generally do good when it comes to losing a leg, but it's an uphill battle to get there. Some give up before they reach the top.

I took some personal days this week because Bella's birthday is today, but I can view and manage my patient schedule from my cell phone. I rub the sleep out of my eyes. Pulling up the app, there's a little wiggle room on Monday. Mondays are always busy, but I can shift some things around. My patients are generally accepting of last-minute changes. It's not like anybody ever plans on losing a limb.

I schedule a block of thirty minutes which is shorter than usual, but it's all I can do last minute. I typically like to spend some time getting to know them and their goals first before we dive in. My gaze falls on the picture on my nightstand of Isabelle. She would have been thirty-eight today. I roll out of bed and throw on the first set of clothes I can find. It's not like the souls in the cemetery will care what I wear. I can't bring myself to eat, but I drink a coffee before heading to the florist.

I always get a bouquet of gerbera daisies to put on her grave. They were her favorite. I try to find the most colorful group that best represents her beautiful personality. Nothing could ever capture the magic that was Bella. She was a kind, loving and compassionate woman with a wild side. Parking on the side of the road, I sling my waterproof blanket over my shoulder and grab the flowers, shot glasses, and a bottle of whiskey. This is where I go when my world goes to shit. I sit by Bella's grave, drinking whiskey and talking to her as if she were still here. Sometimes I wonder if it's healthy for my mental state to do this. My therapist said it's my way of processing the grief, whatever that means.

I'm thankful I don't see my parents' SUV yet. They usually stop by later in the afternoon, and I don't want to see them today. It's hard enough losing her. I can't deal with my mother bashing my lifestyle and begging me to settle down with a "nice woman." My mom doesn't get she's part of why I haven't tried to find a woman I want to settle down with. All of the times she said I wouldn't be a good husband stuck with me, because I chose to enlist in the military and serve my country.

I set my belongings down on the snow-dusted ground and move a few twigs out of the way before spreading my blanket out on the grass. I pour two shots of whiskey before I finally have the nerve to look up at her gravestone. I set one of the glasses on her black granite headstone and press my palm against the butterfly carved just above her name.

The headstone reads, "Isabelle Marie Connelly. Beloved daughter, sister, and friend," along with her birthdate and death date.

It's a beautiful stone, but she'd hate that it wasn't one of those colorful stones you can get. I tried to talk my parents into having one of those for her, but they wouldn't listen to me. They chose this, and all I can do is accept it. One of these days, when I'm able to visit this place without fear of coming apart at the seams, I'll plant some daisies for her. I'll make sure they're every color of the damn rainbow.

"Fuck, it still hurts that you're gone." My throat aches. I feel the pain of losing her all over again.

I don't think there'll ever come a time when her death won't tear me apart. I down the whiskey in one gulp, enjoying how the liquid burns down my throat and all the way to my stomach. Placing the flowers on the ground in front of me, I wrap the blanket around myself to block the wind that's swirling through the trees and pour myself another round.

"You wanna hear some funny shit?" I shake my head. Of course, she would. Bella would always find humor in almost every situation. "I heard a woman laugh at the mall several weeks ago, and now she haunts me. I hear her in my sleep. I even sometimes hear it when I'm awake." I shift and lean against the headstone, careful not to tip the liquor.

"I don't know what it was about the sound of her voice, but it awakened something in me that died when Lexie left me." I pause and take another swig, this time straight from the bottle. Why waste my time with the shot glass? It's not like anybody else is having any. "I didn't even hear her say words, just body-enveloping laughter filling the air."

I shrug. People may look at me and judge me for having a full-blown conversation with my dead sister, but I don't give a fuck. They can think what they want. I can almost hear what she would say back to me. We were that close. She's the only person in this world that gets me. Well, that got me. Russ is a good friend, but there's no replacing Bella. Nobody will ever be able to fill the void left by her absence. She wasn't just my sister. Bella was my best friend. The better part of me died the day we laid her to rest. Because of that, I shut myself off from a lot of feelings. I was numb inside, at least until I heard her laughter.

Bella would reply something like, "That part of you never died. It was just waiting for the right woman."

"And you think that blonde is the right woman?" I sigh and pick at the corner of the label on the glass bottle.

"How do you know unless you try?" she'd say.

I rub at my sternum. "I think I've suffered enough heartache for a lifetime, Bella. I'm good with the way my life is."

"No, you're not. You're lonely," she'd scoff.

"No. I'm not." I shake my head.

"You want kids."

"Who doesn't?" I shoot back as I savagely rip the label from the bottle.

"With the hours you work, you need a wife to help you care for that child or at least a girlfriend. And I want a sister-in-law," she'd say, full of sass and pointing her finger against my chest.

The image cuts deep. I take another hard swig. "But you're not even really here." And you never will be. I'm just sitting here conversing with a ghost who isn't really talking.

"I'm always with you."

I rest my head back against the stone and squeeze my eyes shut.

"I should've done more to save you," I whisper into the wind.

"It was my time to go, D."

Nobody's called me D since she died. That was the nickname she gave me when I was a baby. Bella was only three, and she had a hard time saying Dawson. I couldn't bear to hear D from anyone after that.

"But you didn't have to," I say as a sob rips through my heart and out my throat. It's like reliving that awful day all over again. Every part of my body is in pain. My lungs struggle to take in a cold, ragged breath. The trees are closing in around me, caging me in.

"If I didn't pass away in the manner I did, you wouldn't have found your true purpose." Always the wiser sibling.

"You don't know that." I believe I still would've opened the shelter because of what she went through, even if she lived.

"My death wasn't in vain. You made sure of that. Because I died, you've been able to save several women from the same fate. I'm proud of you."

I swear I can feel her leaning her head against my shoulder. The right amount of pressure and warmth. Or maybe it's just the whiskey.

"Twenty-five years isn't enough of a sentence after what Jackson did to you." I still can't believe that prick didn't get a lethal injection. That bastard doesn't deserve to live after what he's done.

"You need to promise me you won't kill him when he's released," she'd beg me.

She knows me too well to think I'd actually make that promise. I've planned that since day one. He's going to find himself at the bottom of the ocean with a pair of cement shoes. By the time his body surfaces, they won't be able to identify his remains. That son of a bitch is a goner. I don't care what I have to lose to avenge her. Nothing will get in my way.

"Dawson?" she'd warn.

"I can't promise you that, Bella," I grind out.

"Don't let him take more from you, from our family."

After several moments of silence, I ask her, "Am I crazy?"

She'd laugh and say, "Of course you are. The best of humanity usually are. I love you, little brother."

"I love you, my guardian angel."

I wrap myself tighter with the blanket and continue to take swigs of the amber liquid. I'm too far in to stop now. I've drunk too much to drive home. I might as well finish the bottle. I don't care that it's only thirty-five degrees out or ten in the morning. When I sit here beside her grave, it's almost like she's still here with me.

Grief is an awful thing like that. You can be fine one moment, and the next, you can't breathe because it hurts too much to take in air.

Like your heart is on fire, and your lungs are too choked with smoke to expand. Some days I'm okay, but on days like today. I fear the grief will consume me.

I'm sitting in silence, drinking my whiskey. My only companion is the wind that rustles through the leaves when I hear them. Fuck, it's my parents. They're here already. I thought I had more time. As soon as they crest the small hill leading to the back section where I am, they both look at each other and shake their heads in disgust. My father looks similar to me but with sharper features and salt-and-pepper hair. Bella took after my mother with her long wavy dark hair and high cheekbones.

"Don't disgrace your sister's resting place. You should be honoring her life, not getting hammered at her grave," my father says, disappointment lacing every word.

"I am honoring her life. Bella loved whiskey." I hold the bottle up and give it a shake.

He scowls."Your mother doesn't need to see you pissing your life away like this."

"Roger," my mom says condescendingly. "It's a hard day for us all. Leave him be."

She looks like she's aged more in the last two years than she has in the last ten. I get up off the ground and wrap her in a hug. "Hey, Ma."

"My boy, I've missed you."

"I missed you too." I kiss her on the cheek.

"I have something that Isabelle left for you." She reaches into her black leather purse and pulls out a cream-colored envelope. She holds it to her chest for a second before handing it over.

Seeing my sister's handwriting on the front of the envelope makes the emptiness inside me grow. "She left me a letter?"

"I think so. It was sealed when we got it, and I didn't open it." Her eyebrows furrow together.

"How long have you had this?" The envelope looks like it's seen better days. The edges are crumpled, and there's a few scuff marks.

She sighs. "We found it with her will. We didn't give it to you then because you weren't in the right frame of mind." She shifts uncomfortably from one foot to the other.

"So you mean to tell me you've been carrying this letter around with you for nearly two years and didn't think to mention it?" I try to keep my tone neutral, but I can't. This is exactly why we don't get along. They always seem to think they know what's best for me when they don't.

"We were worried we'd lose you too," my father interjects.

"And what if I needed this back then? What if this would've helped me to move on? To find closure?" I bark.

"What if it did the opposite, and we had to bury our last child?" my mom snaps. "Maybe if you'd pick up the phone or come around more often, you would've gotten it sooner."

I can't believe they kept this from me. It doesn't matter. It's in the past. I have her letter in my hands now. "I know. I'm sorry."

We all sat together for a while on the blanket, sharing our favorite stories of Bella. It felt nice to be around the only other family I have, even with my mom hinting around that she wants grandchildren soon. I've always wanted kids, but I don't want to share them with somebody I don't love. If I'm going to be tied to a woman for eighteen-plus years, I need to at least care about her. She can't be a one-night stand I found at the bar.

My mind drifts off to that blonde. I bet she'd make a good mom. Judging by the way I saw her interact with that child. But only she-devils are that hot, though. I bet she's one of those high-maintenance broads with the little purse dogs. There has to be something terribly wrong with her. When they look like that, that's the first red flag. You know to run in the other direction.

Chapter Five

Abby

A knock sounds at the door, drawing my attention away from the soap opera I'm watching but can't really commit to. This hospital doesn't get crap for daytime television. At least the drama of who slept with who provides enough of a distraction from my own predicament. A lot of the pain has subsided, along with the swelling. I still hurt like hell, though.

"Come in," I say, not even looking at the person who walks in.

Not like I have a choice of keeping anyone away. Even if I complain about wanting to be alone, every single staff member ignores me and is flat-out determined to bug me. I've been here for four days, and I'm supposed to be discharged sometime in the next week. Frank's been better since the accident. Almost like he used to be. I'm not dreading going home as much as I was the other day, which surprises me. I never thought I'd look forward to going home again. I won't let my guard down; I know he hasn't changed, and I've made my decision. I've made peace with it. As soon as I'm able to walk again, I'm getting out of there.

"Hello, Abbigail. My name is Dr. Connelly, but you can call me Dawson." A deep grumbly voice snatches my attention.

He holds a large hand out for me to shake, and I'm struck by his dark blue eyes, made even more striking by his emerald green button-up shirt. His easy smile puts me at ease. I place my hand in his firm grip before he lowers himself into the seat next to the gurney I'm on. His broad shoulders taper to a muscular build barely hidden by his dress shirt. He looks far too handsome in a setting like this. Maybe I'm still sleeping, and this is my mind's way of fulfilling the lack of entertainment here. At least then, my mind would be good for something.

"Hi, Dawson. Please call me Abby," I say, surprised by the confidence in my voice. I don't feel confident not in the least. It's a good thing I'm used to hiding behind politeness and a smile. I click the power button on the remote, instantly silencing the television.

He nods. "I'm sorry to hear about your accident."

I look away before replying, "Thank you."

The guilt still hasn't subsided. I'm the one who made our truck crash. Frank hasn't told anybody that, though. At least, that's what he told me. He's back at work already. He took the first few days off and stayed here with me until visitor time was over. Whereas I've been stuck here in this room. At least I can wear normal clothes, as long as they're shorts. That way, the doctors and nurses can check on my dressing.

"I'm a physical therapist specializing in amputees, and I'll be working with you quite a bit over the next few months. Has the surgeon mentioned a prosthetic to you at all?" His gaze is intense on me, and he clasps his large hands together in his lap.

"Yeah. But he said that won't be for a while, though?" I try not to squirm. It feels like he can see right through to my thoughts.

The thought of having this man around for a while is nice. He's perfect eye candy with his dark brown, almost black hair trimmed into a medium fade that's longer on the top. He's a few inches taller than Frank and definitely more muscular. His five o'clock shadow covers a strong jaw.

"We're looking at probably about five to seven weeks before we fit you to one, but we need to get your leg ready to be fitted and strengthen the muscles all around it. Do you mind if I take a look to see how it's healing?"

"Sure, but how do I strengthen the muscles when I'm stuck here in this bed or in a chair?" I raise my eyebrows. "I'm sorry I don't mean to sound bitter. I'm used to keeping busy. Being tied down is really starting to get to me." When I'm not teaching, painting, reading or occupied with something else, all the awful memories of Frank and his fury take over.

I lift the blanket to the side as he stands back up. I stare out the window, unable to look at my leg. If I do, it gives me flashbacks to that day, and I much prefer to block it all out. My anxiety ratchets up as he unwinds the gauze with gentle hands. It makes me really uncomfortable when the staff stare at my stub. I know they're doing their job, but it's like I know people outside of the hospital will only see me for my injury. I hold my breath as the silence stretches on. I watch as the trees gently sway in the breeze, wishing I could also be outside. It's almost springtime, and I'm dying to see my flower garden spring to life again.

"It's fine, trust me, I understand. The amputation area looks like you're healing well, and to answer your question: we'll start with gentle exercises like rolling from side to side, sitting up, standing, and progressing to walking with crutches." He secures the gauze wrap with a new piece of tape.

"Wow, sounds like quite the extensive list. I don't know if I can handle all that." I smirk at him.

He grins back. "We need to start small. Make sure the right muscles are engaging for you before we build up to bigger things. What do you say, wanna give it a shot?" His wide shoulders raise.

"I don't have anything to lose," I admit.

What more can this world take from me? I can't have kids. I have a husband who doesn't love me in a healthy way, and now I've just got the one leg. Why not? I can't continue to feed my depression. Otherwise, I'm liable to spiral into a deeper depression.

"I'm going to lower the headrest to flatten the bed out." Dawson presses the button, and it lowers ever so slowly until he towers over me, making me feel even smaller in his presence. "Alright, the first thing I want you to do is to roll onto your stomach."

Sounds easy enough. I try to scoot back against the other rail, but it's hard to do without your feet to help steady you. Instead, I'm relying on my arms and my one good leg to do most of the work. Thank god I'm not wearing a johnny anymore, or my ass would be hanging out for the world to see. It's one thing for him to see my leg, another thing entirely to see my ass. It's a struggle, but I get there, finally lying on my stomach. The wound from the shard of glass has been healing well. Luckily it didn't hit any organs, but it still stings with the twisting of my skin as the stitches threaten to tear. I turn my head in his direction.

"Good job. How do you feel?" His eyes scan the length of me before settling back on my face.

"Okay, I guess." Should I be proud of doing such a simple task?

He crosses his large arms with an unreadable expression on his face. His jaw locked tight and his fingertips press hard into his biceps. "Now roll onto your back."

Did I say the wrong thing? I question as I do what I'm told. This was actually easier than the other way. My arms didn't have to strain nearly as hard, and my right leg helped to push me up.

"I'm going to have you get back on your stomach again, but this time I'm going to place my hand on your upper abdominals and help you focus on those muscles instead. Are you ready?"

I bite back the sudden fear that springs up at the thought of being touched by a man. "Yes."

My body momentarily tenses as he reaches down toward me, almost in slow motion. My eyes snap to his face as the warmth from his hand flows through the thin fabric of my t-shirt, and heats me from the inside. He sucks in a short breath as he avoids my gaze. I can't remember the last time a man put his hands on me without harming me. I try to take slow even breaths. He's not Frank. Dawson's not here to hurt me. This is a safe place. Everything's going to be okay.

"Tighten your abdominal muscles right here and use them to help take the strain off your arms," he says roughly as he gently presses down with his fingertips.

I worry he can read my fears. The last thing I want to do is make him feel uncomfortable. He finally looks at my face again, but I can't read his expression as I nod. Then I focus on tensing my stomach muscles. As I shift to the side, he removes his hand, and I'm able to maneuver on the bed.

"You see how much easier that was?" He raises a questioning brow.

"On my arms, it was easier, but not so much on my stomach."

He laughs, and the deep sound rumbling from his throat makes my insides flutter. "That's okay. Most of us don't use those muscles when we should. The biggest part of this will be to retrain your body and the correct muscle groups, making those stronger. Once you do that, every movement will become easier for you."

"That makes sense." Being close to him makes me feel self-conscious, but one thing I know is I could listen to him talk all day. His husky voice is sexy as hell.

"Great. Roll onto your back, and we'll try sitting up. Make sure to engage those abdominal muscles again."

All kinds of dirty thoughts float through my mind at his command to roll onto my back. I bite my lip as I feel a flush creep from my neck to my face. Great, just what I need is for him to know what his innocent words are conjuring in my mind. His eyes darken the longer his gaze lingers on me. I'm sure I'm not the first of his patients to find him attractive. After I succeed, I lay on my back and stare at the ceiling, taking a moment to breathe. Moving back to front and back again is making me tired. Clearly, I've gotten lazy by sitting here this long.

"It's harder than it looks, huh?" he says quietly.

"I guess you're going to make me eat my words then?" I laugh and glance in his direction, and he tries to hide his grin with a hand rubbing at his chin. His beautiful eyes take on a mischievous twinkle.

"Nah, you're good." He shakes his head and starts to head for the door. "I'll be back tomorrow to work with you some more. Just continue to do what I showed you, and you'll be back at it in no time."

"Sure thing, boss." I mock salute him.

He makes that stomach-fluttering laugh again. "Have a good night Abby."

"You too," I manage to say.

He walks out, and I can't help but notice that his black jeans make his ass look good too. I smack myself on the forehead. Sure thing, boss? What the hell was I thinking? I'm such an idiot. Why do I say weird things like that? I bet he's wondering what kind of fruit cake he's working with. He tucked his tail and just about ran out of the room. I turn the T.V. back on, hoping I won't die of embarrassment before tomorrow. Or maybe I hope I do because who knows what will fly out of my mouth next time I see that hunk of a man.

Dawson

Maybe it's been far too long without a woman in my bed. Or maybe, I'm just used to patients I'm generally not attracted to, but her? She's the woman I spotted at the mall almost two months ago, the one whose laugh stayed with me and haunted me both while sleeping and awake. Man, I think I'm going to need to have my colleague Sandra work with her instead. I need this job and I can't let my wanting to fuck my patient get in the way.

The way her light blue eyes draw me in, there's a pain hidden in them I know all too well. She's somebody who's gone through a lot in her lifetime. Her agony calls to mine, wanting me to heal her in ways only I know how. I could take it all away for her, at least for a little while.

She did well with everything I threw at her yesterday and once I'm done in the clinic today, I have to stop in to see her and work with her some more. Sandra's on vacation right now and won't be back for another week. I just have to keep myself in check until then. I hit up the gym last night and pounded out some of my frustrations on the speed bag. It only helped a little. Now that I know her name, I feel like I need to know more about her. She's been on my mind almost constantly since I saw her. The image of the high-maintenance woman doesn't fit with what I saw yesterday.

Howard is my last patient of the day and he's always a chore. He expects to get better without putting any work into it and is always a grump.

"Have you been doing the stretching at home?" I ask.

"Of course I am. I should be better by now," Howard rushes the words out.

"It takes time, Howard. You have to work at it every day," I remind him.

I coast through the appointment far too fast. I'm not ready to see her yet. I'm nervous but excited at the same time. I shouldn't be, she's a married woman and she's my patient. I saw the ring on her finger and I've never been one to break up a happy marriage. Not like that's an option for me anyway. She's my patient, a definite off-limits. Personal and professional lives need to stay divided. Of all the women who would lose a limb, why her? It's like Bella's up there pulling strings just to screw with me.

At room 203, I lift my hand to knock, but my hand pauses midair. It was only yesterday I walked into Abby's room. I don't have a choice. I take a deep breath and rap my knuckles on her door.

A set of crutches balance on my arm for her to try today. She said she had a hard time being tied down; I know that feeling all too well. Maybe these will help.

"Come in," her sweet voice runs through me.

I pride myself on being able to be professional at all times while I'm working. I wasn't prepared for a woman like Abby, though. She's smart, funny, and beautiful beyond anyone I've seen before. The moment my hand touched hers yesterday, I felt something pass through me, which was only made worse when I put my hand on her slim stomach. I know she felt it too, because she snapped her gaze to mine. I had to look away to be able to school my features before she saw them. Desire flowed heavily through my veins, making it damn near impossible to do my job.

I open the door and walk in, looking down at my black shoes while I shut us in together and try to get a handle on my crazy reaction to her voice. Finally, I manage to glance up to see her radiant smile, and my breath catches in my throat. She's lying on the bed on her stomach with an open laptop in front of her, completely engulfed in the screen. She's like the sun, drawing me in and lighting up my world. My own personal sunshine that I'll never be able to have. I could never devote enough time to a woman to satisfy them. Between my job, the shelter, and making sure my mental health stays good, it doesn't leave a lot of free time. Her eyes flick to mine and hold my attention for a few seconds before she's back to the screen, only long enough to feed the embers of desire a scrap.

"Okay guys, I gotta go. The doctor's here to make me work." She scrunches her face up and rolls her beautiful light blue eyes like she's not happy I'm here.

A bunch of giggles comes through the speakers and I have to smile. They sound young. Even more of a reason for me to shut down how I feel. She's not only married but they have kids together. I knew she'd be a good mom. That thought hits me hard in the chest.

"Bye, Mrs. Miller!" The children on the other end shout.

"Bye everyone, I'll see you soon. Keep up the good work. I'm so proud of you!" She blows them a kiss and a wave before closing the laptop and setting it aside. She changes position on the bed until she's sitting upright.

Well, maybe not a mom? Doesn't matter. Married. Patient.

"Hi, Dawson. I'm sorry about that."

"Hey, Abby. You don't have to apologize for anything. I take it you're a teacher?"

"The best kind. I teach art to elementary students," she says with a smile that can only be brought on by something that makes one truly happy. A smile that makes it hard for me to breathe. Nobody's ever had this much of an effect on me before.

I clear my throat as I tug at the collar of my shirt. "That's awesome, I always loved art, but I was never any good at it." I shrug as I set the crutches against the wall.

"Everybody's good at art. It's the reflection of your personality. How can somebody judge someone else's work without admitting that each work is a piece of their maker's soul, made just the way it was intended to be portrayed?" She raises her eyebrows.

I contemplate her words. As I thought, she's smart. "Very true. I bet you're a great teacher, and the kids are lucky to have you." I wish I could have her. Where the hell are these thoughts coming from? Fuck, Connelly. Get it together. I'm just grateful I didn't say them out loud.

"Thank you. I miss them even though it hasn't even been a week."

Her lips fall into a sad smile that makes my heart ache for no reason. I need to change the subject. I don't like seeing her sad. It makes that hollow feeling in my chest come back.

"How are you feeling today? Have you been doing the exercises we worked on yesterday?" I take a seat on the chair beside her bed.

"Yes, I have. Every two to three hours I've been trying to do them. I don't exactly have anything better to do." She gestures around the room.

"That's good to hear, and you feel okay?"

"A little tired, but I'm good."

"And your leg?" My fingertips tingle. God, I want to touch her again.

She shrugs with a frown. "It's a little rough today."

I lean forward with my elbows on my knees. "Do you want me to get the nurse so she can give you some more pain medication first?"

"No. I'll be fine. I don't like being on that stuff." She plucks at the sheet by her thigh.

"It's okay if you need it, you know?" She shouldn't feel bad for taking them. In a recovery like this, you need pain killers to help take the edge off.

"I know. I'm okay for now. I'm assuming I get to walk today?" Excitement flashes in her eyes and brings my smile back. I know what it's like to be told you can't do anything but wait. I'm glad I can be the one to make that happen.

"If you're willing to try." I tilt my head to the side.

"Absolutely, I want to get out of this room." She laughs, nearly sending my heart into an arrhythmia. God, that laugh.

Keep your shit together man, she's your patient. "Scoot to the edge of the bed, and I'll help stabilize you when you stand."

She shifts on the bed then stops. I realize she's focusing on clenching her abdominal muscles before moving, just as I showed her. It's nice when they take your advice. After she slides her butt to the edge of the bed, I come to stand in front of her with a set of crutches. I lean them up against the bed and hand them to her one at a time. I lower the bed until her foot, covered by the textured gray sock, is flat on the floor.

"I'm going to hold your sides and when you're ready to stand, then do it." I recall in her file she has a laceration on her right side that I need to be careful of. "But remember, you'll be off balance because you're used to the weight of the other leg. I won't let you fall." I shake my head as I crouch down.

"Okay," she murmurs as I cup my hands on the flare of her hips.

She tenses. I don't know if it's from my touch, but she quickly relaxes. Abby feels perfect under my palms. I can only imagine how she'd feel naked in my bed. She squares her shoulders, tightens her hands on the grips, and pulls herself up to stand. She's shaky, but she's doing it.

"There you go! Just stay like that for a minute."

I have to look up to see her face, which is mere inches above mine. Her soft, feminine floral scent drapes around me. She takes a few steadying breaths before sitting back down, and I release my hold on her hips.

"Good job," I say, hoping she doesn't hear the rawness in my voice.

Being this close to her messes with me like I've never experienced. Ever since I saw her yesterday, I can't get her out of my mind. I'm so proud of her, more proud than I've been of my other patients. She stands back up again, and I place my hands against her sides. I shouldn't notice, but her thin gray linen shorts hug her curves perfectly. Once she's standing and stable, I release my grasp and take a step back. Not too far where I won't be able to help her but far enough for me to think clearly.

She slowly brings the crutches forward and swings her good leg in front of her and loses her balance. I lunge forward and wrap my arms around her waist as she crashes against my chest. Her mouth is close enough to mine that I can feel her warm breath across my lips. She quickly turns her head and swallows thickly.

"I'm sorry. I thought I had it," she says in a breathy whisper after a minute. With every shallow breath she takes, her breasts press against my chest.

Knowing that I have the same effect on her, I feel my cock stir. Maybe she's not so happily married after all. Not like I should care about her personal life. Keep it professional. "It's okay. It takes time for your body to adjust to such a drastic change." My voice wavers only slightly.

I start inching her back to the bed when the door swings open. In my arms, Abby's whole body goes as rigid as a 2x6.

"What the fuck is this?" A male voice barks out just behind me.

I glance up. Fear darkens her eyes before she has a chance to mask it. The same look from my sister's face when Jackson would show up unexpectedly. Fuck. He must be Abby's husband. I fight to stop my fingers from curling into a fist as I help her sit on the bed. My jaw clenches painfully.

"Frank, it's not-" she starts in a trembling voice.

"-Abbigail was trying to take her first few steps but lost her balance. Do you want me to show you how you can help her when she goes home?" I cut her off, barely able to keep the anger out of my words. I won't allow him to terrorize her here. Hell, fucking, no.

I don't want to give him any reason to be mad at her. She's done nothing wrong, even though the image probably wasn't the best to walk in on. I know how these pricks are. They don't need a reason to turn violent. I see it now when I look at her. I knew there was something hidden in the depths of her eyes. I just never imagined it would be that. Of all the fucking things that could be haunting her, it had to be domestic abuse. It's Bella's situation all over again.

"Yeah, that would be nice," he snaps.

With white knuckles, she holds onto the crutches as if they're the only thing she has left. She's quiet and won't look at me. I want to punch him already, and my fingers flex in anticipation. Easing away from Abby, I stand and look at him, taking in his appearance: the blue jeans and a white t-shirt, the multi-color paint splatters on his clothes. He's smaller than I, about five foot ten, maybe. A fierce frown mars his face, but his narrowed eyes, well, you can tell he's an asshole just by looking at him. Breathe, just breathe. He's not Jackson.

"If you stand right here in front of her, place your hands on both sides of her waist and hover just in case she falls." I show him where so he knows why I was touching her. I was just doing my job. My mind, well, that's another beast he doesn't need to know about. "It's hard to balance when you lose close to a tenth of your body weight. You shouldn't be trying to walk without somebody there to assist you, at least in the beginning."

She nods but remains closed off. The smile and laugh are gone. It's like he sucks the life right out of her. Like he's the clouds that block her sunlight. The bruised eye and cheek I assumed were from the crash make me wonder if they're from him. My blood starts to simmer beneath my skin. I take a deep breath and silently count to five on the exhale. I haven't felt the urge this strong to hit another man in a long time. It took me months to be able to control my anger after what happened to Isabelle.

We go over most of the exercises I've shown her, not that I think he'd really help her, but I want to make sure he has time to calm down before I leave. I thought I was going to have Sandra work with her, but not after today. Not after what I witnessed. It doesn't matter how I feel about her; her safety is my main concern. I'll learn to deal with wanting her and knowing she's not mine to have. She's a victim of domestic abuse, and I'm going to do damn well everything I can to make sure she doesn't end up as my sister did. Even if every day is torture, I'll do my best to do right by her.

Knowing she's relatively safe, I leave the room. There's no way to block the window of the door, and most abusers aren't stupid enough to do it in the open like this, especially in a hospital. I'll try to stop by earlier tomorrow. That way, I can gauge her feelings.

A short while later, I meet up with Russell at the gym. I have to burn off some of this anger that's eating away at me. Every time I see a woman getting mistreated, it brings up memories of Bella and how I wasn't there to help her. I wish she would've listened to me when I begged her to leave him. She'd still be alive today if she did.

After changing, I head over to the octagon in the back room of the gym, where Russell is adjusting his headgear. I set my bag on the bench beside me and dig out my hand wraps and headgear. Applying the wrap to my hands doesn't center me at all. Usually, it helps to take the edge off, but not tonight. There's just too much building inside of me. Too much of what I've worked so hard to repress, and it takes one lone woman to bring that beast out again.

"You ready, Dawson?" Russell asks from the other side of the ring.

"Yup." I pad barefoot across the room.

We dance back and forth, throwing a few warm-up punches until the blood is flowing in our veins. I swing hard, and he barely has time to block it. He jabs me in the ribs as my fist meets the side of his headgear. Blocking his next hit, I fake a right and slam him hard with my left in his abdomen, knocking the wind out of him.

"Sorry, man." I step back while he gains control of his breathing.

"What's got your balls in a twist?" He scrunches his face up.

"Nothing." Just leave it alone. I hold my arms in front of me waiting for him to strike.

He shakes his head. "Bullshit, I knew the moment you walked in here you were pissed. I thought you military men were better at hiding your emotions than that."

"Fuck off," I grunt as I block another advance from him.

I hate to admit it, but he's right. I'm usually pretty good at hiding the turmoil raging inside. But, god, something about Abby makes me turn into a hot-headed teen again. It's better Russ is taking the heat from me than who I'd really like to match up with in this ring. Frank, even his fucking name pisses me off.

I put more energy than I intend as I land a blow to the cheek of his mask, knocking him backward. He stumbles but catches his footing and swings at me again, harder this time. My forearm takes the brunt of the force.

"Come on, Dawson. We've been friends for years. What's going on? Is it work?" Again, he tries to pry.

"Yup," I grit out as his strike catches me in the chin slamming my teeth together.

"You gotta give me more than one-word answers," he demands, ducking my fist.

"Fine, it's a patient, okay? Happy now?" Just shut the fuck up and hit me already. I need the pain to remind me why I have to stay here and not track that bastard down.

"A lady patient?" He wiggles his bushy brown eyebrows.

I sigh, knowing he won't stop until I tell him. "Yes, a woman, but she's married, and worse off, I suspect her douche of a husband abuses her."

He freezes, letting it all sink in. He knows about what happened to Bella and the guilt I carry over it. His pause gives me an opening, and I take it. He left his side unguarded. That's on him. I land a hard right hook.

"Shit, that one hurt," he huffs out, clutching his stomach. "What are you going to do?"

"Just talk to her tomorrow and see what's really going on." I block his swing with my forearm. "If he's abusing her, I'm going to try like hell to get her to go to Bella's Safe Haven."

"You don't usually get this worked up over a woman. Is it because she's a definite off-limit that you want her this badly?" He grins.

At my pause, he strikes hard, landing a crushing fist against my face and slamming the headgear into my skin. I may match Abby with a bruised eye in the morning.

"I never said I wanted her," I growl. That's such a lie. I've never wanted another woman more than I crave Abby.

He stops bouncing on his feet and puts his hands up, stopping me from swinging momentarily. "You didn't have to, my friend. It's written all over your face. Go after her, man."

"I can't! She's my patient." I cross my arms over my chest. What about that, doesn't he get?

"Have Sandra take over, and then she won't be. Sweep that little damsel off her feet and show her what a real man is like." His smile broadens.

I roll my eyes at him. My cell phone starts ringing from inside my bag. I jump out of the ring and fish it out. I notice it's Maggie.

"Hey, Maggie," I answer, still somewhat out of breath. I'm thankful for not having to reply to Russell.

"Hi, Dawson. I'm sorry to bother you, but the fridge isn't working. I've tried unplugging it and checking the breaker, but it won't come back on." Background chatter comes through the line.

"You're never a bother, Maggie. I'll be up with my spare fridge from my garage shortly. That'll hold until I can get a replacement."

That fridge has been on the fritz for the past few months. I used the insurance money from my sister's death to invest in a temporary home for abused women. I cut corners on the appliances opting for better security measures instead. I wanted the women to feel safe, as that was my main concern. After I hang up with her, Russell offers to help me after overhearing the conversation. He doesn't let up on the ride about all the ways I can use my charm to try to get Abby away from Frank. And I'll be damned if the wheels in my own head didn't start spinning.

Chapter Six

Abby

"Your wounds are healed enough. If you want to try taking a shower, I can help you," Kali, my favorite nurse says while tying her ebony hair up in a ponytail. She's wearing cute blue scrubs with daisies all over them today.

"Really?" I ask.

"Yes, really." She laughs at my facial expression.

A shower sounds heavenly. After being here for a week, the whole washcloth routine is old. After wrapping my bandages with plastic wrap to keep them dry, she helps me transfer from the wheelchair into the shower and onto the stool.

"I'll be right out here if you need me." She tugs the curtain closed to allow me some privacy.

The warm water cascading down onto my head is wonderful. It feels like ages since I've been able to do something as simple as taking a shower without somebody's help. Mindful of the nurse's time, I wash as quickly as I can and open the curtain once I'm done. Just as I finish getting dressed into new clothes in the bathroom, someone knocks on the main door. God, I hope it isn't Frank. I don't want to see him after the way he was yesterday.

When he walked in thinking he saw me cheating on him, I could feel his anger coming off him in waves. I know he hated the idea of another man touching me in a way he hadn't in some time. Ever since we started having fertility issues, our love life changed from passionate to only fulfilling a basic need, just trying to procreate. I haven't even had sex with him in about four months. Even before that, half the time, I faked an orgasm so he would just get done with it. It's hard to have any pleasure when you fear the person sleeping with you. I squeeze my eyes shut. I just wish we could go back to before we tried having a baby. Back when it didn't hurt this badly to love him.

"Hold on, we're just getting dressed," Kali calls out as she peeks her head out the bathroom door.

"No problem, take your time."

I'll be damned if the sound of Dawson's voice doesn't do things to me. Something I haven't felt in a very long time. Like flowers coming back after the long cold winter, my libido revs up. Just hearing his deep voice makes my insides flutter. As much as I may hate Frank for what he's put me through, I'm still a married woman, and I made a vow. Whether Frank has stuck to the promises he made to me or not, I didn't cheat on him. I can't believe he thought that I'd do something like that. Although, would it be any worse than what he's done to me? To love and to cherish? Not anymore, not for a long time anyway.

Kali gives me a knowing smirk. "He's a good-looking one that Dawson, isn't he?" she whispers.

I smile back and nod, making us both giggle.

"Here, let me get your hair for you." She takes the purple brush in my hand.

"Thank you; you're so sweet."

Standing behind my wheelchair, she gently brushes the snarls out of my hair like my mother used to. I barely recognize the woman staring back at me from the mirror hanging on the wall. Greenish-yellow bruising surrounds my left eye and stains my cheekbone, courtesy of Frank's fist. The stitches and small purple marks on the right side of my forehead are from where my head hit the window in the accident. The smile that used to come easily always looks fake now. I wish I could be genuinely happy again, but I don't think I'll ever be able to get to that point in my life. I look as exhausted as I feel. The dark circles stand out on my pale skin. Too bad I don't have any concealer and foundation; it wouldn't be the first time I've covered bruises with it, and I'm sure it won't be the last. That's a sobering thought. I'm already counting on it happening again. I sigh.

"Are you ready to go out?" Kali whispers.

"I guess so." I wish I could be more presentable, though. I look like I really did get run over by a bus.

She opens the door and wheels me out. As soon as my eyes find Dawson leaning against the far wall, my mouth goes dry as if I swallowed a cup of sand. He's wearing gray trousers with a black polo today. The sleeves of his shirt reveal a pair of large biceps covered in tattoos that wrap down his forearm on one side. I've always been a sucker for muscled biceps. Married or not, I can still appreciate the finer things in life, like how his grin lights up his face when he sees me. I'm surprised there's not a Dr. Connelly fan club following him around the hospital. I can picture it now as a train of women and girls follow his every step, giggling as they go and fainting when he throws them that dazzling smile he's giving me now.

"Good morning, sunshine," he says as he walks over to me.

His calling me sunshine doesn't help to keep the butterflies in check. It feels as though they'll lift me right up.

"Good morning, Dawson."

"I'll check in on you in a bit," Kali says sweetly as she steps out, throwing a wink my way before closing the door. She's relentless.

"I know we're not scheduled until later, but I had a cancellation in the clinic. I thought I'd stop in and see how you're doing?" He uncrosses his arms and walks over to stand beside the chair. His fingers dig into the blue fabric as he pulls it back a few inches.

"I'm well, and you?" I answer.

I have to look up in order to see his face. Thoughts of yesterday drift through my mind and how good it felt to be pressed up against that hard body of his. I sweep my hair off to the side of my shoulder to busy my hands and to distract my wayward thoughts.

"I'm doing okay." He sits in the chair across from me, and I notice there's a dark bruise on his face.

"Oh my god, what happened to your face? Are you okay?" I reach out as if to touch his cheek before pulling my hand back.

He furrows his brows before saying, "Oh, I forgot about that. I like to box in my free time. The guys and I sometimes get a little rough." He laughs it off.

"Oh." That's hot. Sweaty, shirtless men sparring with each other? Yes, please. I reach for my water bottle on the stand and take a sip to try to douse the fire that the image of a shirtless, glistening Dawson lit up within me.

"I wanted to talk to you about something." He pauses. "You can tell me it's none of my business, and I won't pry." His deep blue eyes search mine.

My heart begins to hammer in my chest, threatening to burst out of my shirt. I know what this is about.

"I'm listening," I barely manage to say, not breaking eye contact. I'm struggling to try to remember that I'm supposed to be smiling, acting polite, and most importantly, hiding the truth. Always hiding the truth.

Dawson clears his throat before scratching his stubbly chin and looking out the window. I have a feeling he sensed something off when Frank came in yesterday. It was the way his fingers curled into fists at my side and how he quickly jumped to my aid, explaining why it looked like we were embracing. Everybody always acts weird before they ask me the inevitable. Unfortunately, I've seen it far too many times.

"Are you safe at home?"

Wow, get right to it. Don't even try to ease into the hard questions. I take in a slow, calming breath.

"I'm okay, he's just-" I look away from Dawson. "He thought I was cheating on him." My voice is barely above a whisper. I'm ashamed to admit it out loud. I'm ashamed of the position Frank continually puts me in.

"That's not what I asked, Abby." His voice comes out more strained than the situation calls for. This shouldn't affect him. I'm nobody to this man.

"I'm fine, really. I appreciate your concern." I hope he drops it. I don't want to lie to him. I'm so tired of lying to everybody. I don't think I have it in me to keep up this charade for much longer.

He sighs and points to the side of my face., "Did he do that to you?"

Touching the bruise, I shake my head, not wanting to give voice to the lie I'm giving him. Why is it so hard with Dawson? Anybody else who suspected his abuse, I was able to sway them easily. Maybe

I'm tired of covering for Frank. I clench my fingers together to stop the tears building in my eyes. I won't cry; I can't. Then he'll know the truth.

Dawson leans forward, placing his forearms on his knees, his face only a foot away from me. I swear he can hear the thud of my heartbeat from where he is. Isn't that how lie detectors work, by how fast your heart rate is? I'm screwed if that's the case because mine is out of control.

Dawson peers out the window again as if he's trying to stop himself from saying something, and a pained expression crosses his face. The guilt builds inside me, knowing he's only trying to help me. I can't give him the answer he's looking for. I can't tell him the truth. I can't tell him how I live in fear most days or how my husband's touch scares me.

"I've known men like him; no matter what you do, it's never good enough for them. They always find a way to be angry and take it out on you." His jaw clenches as he continues to stare outside.

I sit there silently, not knowing what to say to that. I know it's the truth. I've known for a while that I needed to leave, but I thought I had more time. I thought there was a chance he'd change. I desperately wanted Frank to change.

"Sometimes they go too far, and you don't expect it to turn that bad. You think they'll get better. That deep down, they love you. If he really loved you, he'd never lay a hand on you." He opens and closes his fists as he works through what he's trying to say. "Trust me, once a woman beater, always a woman beater. There's help for women who feel trapped by their abuser and don't think they have a way out. Have you heard of Bella's Safe Haven?" His voice sounds as if he's gargling broken glass, and he still won't look at me. He's staring down at his hands.

"I have, yes." I look down into my own lap. I've thought about going there on the days it got really bad. I just couldn't bring myself to leave him. I thought my Frank was still in there, buried inside somewhere, smothered by what he's become.

"There's an available room. It's yours if you want it. I can help you get there when you're discharged. You don't have to give me an answer right now; please think about it. If not Bella's, there's other shelters out there. They can help you get back on your feet, and you don't have to rely on Frank. You can walk away." He finally turns toward me. The pain is clear in his eyes.

His pain is too much for me to bear. I turn away. I can't exactly walk away right now. That's the problem. "Thank you, Dawson. You're a good man," I say without looking at him.

He gently cups my cheek with a calloused palm forcing me to turn toward him. I bring my gaze back to his, feeling like I'm stripped of all my armor. He sees through my mask. I don't know how but he does. He's uncovered my secret, and it pains me that I must keep it locked inside.

After Dawson left last night, Frank told me that if I tried to leave him, he'd tell everyone what I did. That I purposely wrecked our truck. He would spin it like I was trying to commit suicide and take him with me and that I'm a danger to others. I can lose my job for that.

I wasn't trying to die; I couldn't find a way to get away from him. Dawson's offering me a way to be free, but I can lose the only thing in this life that makes me happy: teaching. I love everything about teaching. Those kids are the only reason I get out of bed some days. It's easy to forget my depression when surrounded by giggling happy faces all day, at least until I return to a house that no longer feels like home to me.

"Abby, I can't help if you don't let me." Those gorgeous blue eyes beg me to tell him everything.

God, I want him to help me so bad it hurts like there's a cavern torn open in my heart from lying to him and refusing his help. But I have to keep my secret. I won't lose my kids. The moisture builds in my eyes as he gazes at me with concern. I take a shaky breath as a lone, rebellious tear escapes and blazes a hot trail down my cheek. He gently wipes it away with his thumb.

"I can't," I whisper.

"You can." The sincerity in his voice begs me to let him help me.

I shake my head. "You don't understand."

"Then help me to understand," he pleads as he kneels in front of me, putting his hands on the armrests of the wheelchair.

"I'm sorry, I just can't." If I tell him the hell Frank's put me through, he'll be mandated to report it. Then Frank will tell the world I tried to kill both of us, and I'd lose everything. I just need time to figure out how to leave Frank without losing my job and my kids. There has to be a way.

"If you're worried he'll come after you, I can assure you that you'll be safe at Bella's. They have the best security out of all the shelters." His eyebrows draw together. The concern is etched in every feature. He really does care what happens to me, and that makes this that much more painful.

"That's not it." I wish it were that easy.

"Then what is it? What's holding you back from leaving him?"

"I don't want to talk about it." Feeling trapped in this chair as he stares at me, I turn away from him. I'm too close to tearing that wall down and letting him in. If he keeps pushing me, the bricks will crumble down all around me. Once my secret's out there, it's done. I can't undo it. I can't take it back. I won't lose my kids.

"I'm worried about you, Abby."

So am I. Instead, I say, "You don't have to be; I'll be fine."

He rubs the back of his neck like he's frustrated at my lack of a confession. Finally, he stands and walks to the door. Then he pauses with his hand on the door handle and glances over his shoulder.

"I'll be back later for your therapy. If you need me, I'm only a phone call away." He gives me a sad smile like he's disappointed in me.

"Thank you."

Dawson shuts the door leaving me alone with my thoughts. I wish it were that easy to leave. If I hadn't caused the accident, I wouldn't be in this position. The dam I've been holding back during our conversation lets go, and I can't stop the wracking sobs that take over. I'm always alone, and nobody can save me from myself. I should've left Frank the first time he hit me, but I didn't think it would happen again. He was devastated after, or at least I thought he was. Maybe I played right into his hand. I let him get away with it, and I allowed him to keep hurting me. I allowed the monster to grow inside of him, and I'm the one left to pick up the shattered pieces of my life because of the choice I made to stay. I'm just as guilty for allowing it.

Dawson

I stalk to the nearest restroom and lock myself inside. Leaning against the wall and closing my eyes, I do the breathing exercise my counselor taught me to do when I feel like everything is crashing down around me. Why are women so damn stubborn? I could tell she was close to breaking down and telling me Seeing her pain tore me up inside, so I stopped pushing her. I try to calm my nerves. Fuck!

I'm no good for that woman. She deserves somebody who can love and support her. That's not me. All I'm good at is one-night stands or friends with benefits. I'll never be able to be the man she needs. Damn it, I wish I weren't so fucking broken inside. I can't let her in. I won't allow myself to feel those feelings that are trying to claw their way inside me. I refuse to acknowledge what they mean.

I push myself off the wall, scrub my hands over my face and step back out into the hall. Helplessness dogs me, and my mother's cutting words reverberate inside my head as I see three patients after leaving Abby's room. Too soon, it's time for Abby's appointment, and I have no idea if she'll refuse me as a therapist. It's within her rights to request someone else.

But she needs to see that he'll never stop. I can't force her to get help. I can't even report it to the authorities unless she confesses that he hits her. I stand outside her door and peek in through the window. She's lying on her side, facing away from the door. I knock softly before entering.

She doesn't move as I slip inside her room. The blankets are pulled up to her chin. Her eyes are closed, and her breathing is slow and even. She's asleep. I watch her sleep peacefully for a moment before I back out of the room. Rest is as important for healing as physical therapy. Skipping an appointment won't hurt. I know she's been putting the work in. My fingers brush the door handle when the blankets rustle behind me.

"Dawson, wait," she says groggily. "I'm sorry I must've fallen asleep."

Sighing, I pivot on a heel. When she twists around, rubbing at her eyes, it's like a dagger stabs me in the chest. Her eyes are red, and her lids are puffy. Her beautiful face is splotchy. She's been crying, and it's because of me. I know it. I have to get out of here. I can't breathe. There's a boulder sitting on my chest.

"It's okay. You need your sleep. I can come back tomorrow."

"Please don't go," she whispers.

How can I walk away from her after she says that? I look down at the floor, feeling like a piece of shit for making her upset. Reluctantly, I take the chair beside her bed. "Are you okay?"

She nods and avoids looking at my face, "I just have a lot going on right now."

"I didn't mean to upset you earlier. I'm sorry," I say quietly. I lean back in the chair, making the fake leather squawk in protest.

"You were doing the right thing. I understand." She twists her fingers in her hand.

"We don't have to do therapy today. How about some card games? Are you up for that?" Anything to take her mind off the pain I've caused. Crying women have always been a hard thing for me to be around. It's not that I don't care. I just feel helpless.

"That depends. Are you a sore loser?" She cracks a smile. There it is.

"I've been told I'm very... competitive." I grin at her. "I'll be right back. I know they have cards at the nurse's station." I duck out of her room, swipe a deck off the counter, and jog back.

I pull the overbed table close to her and begin shuffling the cards when she says, "I haven't played a card game in a long time. What are we playing?"

"How about an easy one, war?" I ask. This way, we don't really have to think too hard.

"Sure." She pulls the blanket tight around her.

"Are you cold?"

"A little." A shiver shakes her body. She's only wearing a thin t-shirt, and goosebumps pebble her arms.

"I'll go grab a warm blanket." I'm thankful for something I can do for her, even if it's just a blanket.

"No. Really, it's fine." She shakes her head.

I ignore her and step out of the room again to snag one out of the warmer and drape it over her shoulders. When I lean down to wrap it around the front of her, her soft floral-scented shampoo fills my nose. I inhale the sweet scent into my lungs. "Better?"

"Much, thank you." She relaxes into the heat and closes her eyes.

I pass out the cards until there's none left. "So, Mrs. Miller, what do you do when you're not teaching a classroom full of kids?" I set down my first card, a jack.

"I like to read or paint. How about you?" She places down a six.

I'm not surprised by her liking to paint since she's an art teacher. I take both cards, setting them aside. "I work long hours, but other than that, I go to the gym a lot." My, my I sound interesting, work and exercise. Next round, she wins. "A reader, huh? What genres do you read?" I used to love reading mysteries and horror. I never have the time for it now.

"Romance usually." At my smirk, she says, "Well, I gotta get it from somewhere." She briefly squeezes her eyes closed. "I'm sorry, sometimes things like to just fly out, especially when I'm tired."

I laugh. "That's okay. I like the honesty." I wish she were honest about her abusive husband. "Do you want me to leave so you can rest?" I hope not.

She shakes her head. "No. It's nice to have company."

Has she not had company besides her husband? I make a mental note to check the visitor logs. Abusers also like to alienate their victims by keeping them away from everybody else. They don't want to get caught, and the fewer people in the victim's life, the better it is for the abuser. A few rounds go by, and I have to know the answer to my next question. It's been burning in my brain since she slipped.

"Your husband's not much of a romantic, then?" I ask, already regretting bringing him up.

Swallowing, she looks back down at the cards and takes her victory after placing the same cards down. "Not in a while, no."

"That's too bad."

Her eyes flick to mine. I don't know if she took my question as having sex or flowers and chocolate. I bet it's both. She seems like the type of woman who deserves to be treated like a queen. Her husband's an idiot.

"What about you? Got a lucky lady friend?" She bites her lip and places another card down.

I wait until she's looking at me again to answer, "Not in a really long time."

I hold her gaze until she looks away. The air grows thick with awareness. Fuck, this woman messes with my head. All I can think about is pulling that lip between my teeth, easing her down on that bed, and putting my hands and mouth all over her. The pink blush that colors her cheeks, which looks gorgeous on her, makes me think I'm not the only one whose mind went there. She pulls her gaze from mine, but I see the corner of her lips tilt up.

We reach the end of our stack and grab the cards we've already played. We play a few rounds in silence. The tension continues to grow, but I like it. I haven't had this feeling in a long time. I feel alive again.

To be honest, the first time I saw her in that mall, I wanted to know her. I knew she was special even at a distance. I wonder what she's thinking. Maybe about me? Could she be happy I'm not seeing another woman? I glance at the time on my watch. Shit, I have to go.

"I'm gonna have to cut this short. I have another appointment." I count my cards quickly. "Well, it looks like you beat me. I've only got twenty-two. I'll have to come back to win the next one."

She grins and tilts her head as I hand her my cards. "Competitive, I see."

"Oh, you have no idea. You're not scheduled for therapy, but I'll be back tomorrow to whoop you at some point." If I manage to stay away that long. This woman is like a drug to me that I can't get enough of.

She scoffs, "Maybe in your dreams."

Oh, sunshine, you have been in my dreams. Just not playing cards. "I'll see you later." I slip out to the hall. "Oh, one more thing." I poke my head back in. "After you've had a shitty day, what comfort food do you turn to?"

"Uh, I guess I'd say ice cream. Why?" She scrunches her eyebrows together.

I was hoping for something more specific. There are too many flavors to choose from. "No reason. Any particular flavor?" I try to keep my face neutral.

"Are you going to bring in contraband?" Her smile broadens, making my head swell.

"Me? No, never." I pause. Of course I am. I'd do anything to get her to smile. "But if I were, what do you like?" A grin spreads across my face. I can't hold it back anymore. Her smile is contagious.

"Strawberry's my favorite," she says, still smiling.

"Have a good night, sunshine." I wink at her.

"Goodnight, Dawson."

I love the way my name sounds falling from her lips. I shut the door behind me and walk away from her feeling a strange mix of emotions. I enjoy spending time with her. More than I should. I've never snuck food into the hospital for a patient before. But for her, I would. For her, I have a feeling I'd do a lot of things I shouldn't. That tells me to back off. To do the right thing and just be her doctor, but I can't stay away. I haven't even had a taste of her, and I'm already addicted. If I'm being totally honest with myself, the moment I saw her, I knew I could never walk away.

Chapter Seven

Abby

After Dawson left yesterday, I couldn't stop thinking about him. Not even while Frank was here. The way he said, "Not in a really long time," about having a lady friend keeps replaying like a video stuck on repeat. There was something in his expression that I find unnerving. Almost as unsettling as me being drawn to him, like a moth to a flame. I don't understand it, but one thing's for sure... I can't wait to see him today. My stomach has been flip-flopping every time I hear a knock at the door. I try to hide my disappointment every time it's not him. I know I shouldn't feel this way, but I can't help it.

I press the call button on the remote and a nurse with flaming red hair appears in the doorway shortly.

"What's going on Abbigail?" she asks as her gaze sweeps through the room.

"Can I get something for the pain? My leg's been throbbing all morning." The pain is enough to make me nauseous. I keep changing positions but nothing helps.

"Sure thing. I'll be back in a moment."

I've been here six days now, locked in this bleached prison. I can't wait to get out of here, but I don't want to go home. I know I need to leave Frank, but tempting as it may be to take Dawson's help and go to a women's shelter, I have to do this on my own. I have to be able to walk away from Frank without another man's help. I need to be my own damn hero. I think Frank is expecting it at this point. With the way he's been guarding his expression, he knows I've had enough.

I just have to get through the next ten weeks or so until I'm able to walk again. Ten weeks that's seventy days. I can make it another seventy days, knowing my freedom is at the end of it. I estimated high because I don't want to be disappointed if my healing runs longer. They said it would take five to seven weeks until I get fitted for a prosthetic, and then it usually takes two to three weeks to make the device.

It's getting late. The clock says five-thirty. Something must have come up for Dawson not to show. He doesn't seem like the type to flake on someone. By this time, I'm sure he's gone home for the day. Frank will be arriving any minute now anyway, and I don't want to explain the odd relationship I've started to build with Dawson. I don't even know what it is yet. It feels like more than friendship. I feel like my heart knows him, as crazy as that sounds.

Knock, knock.

"Come in." Flip-flop goes my stomach again. Every knock on that door today has made my stomach feel like a roller coaster. The food cart rolls into view, and I sigh. Just my dinner. The worker leaves my tray on the table.

I lift up the metal lid. Turkey and mashed potatoes with a side of green beans. It smells good. I do have to say out of all the hospital food I've eaten since coming here; this one tastes the best. I'm getting tired of the meal, unfortunately. The door swings open, letting the fluorescent light filter through. For a moment, I'm hopeful until I hear the heavy tread of boots. The same boots I've dreaded hearing for far too long.

"Hey." The disappointment is barely hidden in my voice.

"Hi." He comes over and places a kiss on the side of my head. "How are you feeling?"

"I'm pretty sore today. How was work?" I take another bite of the turkey, taking the time to chew, so I don't have to talk as much to him.

I don't miss how his nostrils flare when his gaze lands on my missing leg. Like it's another reminder of the woman he should've married. One whose body doesn't look or act like mine. Ever since we started having fertility issues, I've been self-conscious about my body. Even more so since losing my leg.

He flops into the chair beside the bed. "Exhausting, we're coming to the end of the contract on the hospital, and we still have a lot to do. I don't think I'll get to stop by tomorrow. They're saying it might turn into twelve to fourteen-hour days until we finish.

I try to look like that bothers me, but it doesn't. To be honest, the thought of not seeing him for the rest of the time I'm here makes me happy. Every time I look at him, I remember the day of the accident and how he's physically assaulted me time and again, and I'd rather not keep reliving the memories.

"That's okay, I understand."

"When are they discharging you?" He rubs at his arm, the one he hurt a while back on a job.

I sigh. "Three more days, I believe." I finish eating my food as he continues on about the problems they've been facing at work, nodding along when appropriate. At least he's not in a bad mood tonight. I can tolerate him when he's like this. I can almost forget the pain he's caused, almost.

The nurse comes in to check on me and takes my food tray out of the room. I'm not hooked up to the monitors anymore, but they still poke their heads in when they make their rounds to see if I need anything.

"I better go before they kick me out. I'll call you tomorrow. I love you." He places a kiss on my temple.

"I love you too. Good luck with the project." I hate that it's the truth, that I do still love him. I think a part of me always will, no matter what. It would be so much easier if I were able to hate him, but I can't. I don't think I've ever been able to hate anyone. I think people can always be redeemed for their actions. Most actions, anyway.

It's five of seven, and visiting hours end at seven. Once Frank exits, I pull the table up to the bed and start laying out the cards to play solitaire. Might as well do something other than watch another soap opera.

Another knock, but my excitement has vanished. It wouldn't be Dawson this late, and I'm surprised by how down I feel that he didn't come. I answer with not my usual bubbly personality. "Come in."

"Starting without me?"

That deep voice penetrates through me, driving the butterflies in my stomach wild. I glance up to see Dawson in a pair of worn blue jeans and a charcoal gray button-up shirt, with the sleeves rolled up to his elbows. The ink on his forearm peeks out. A small paper bag is held in his hand. Holy shit, does he look good tonight.

Right, he asked a question. I turn to the clock. It's almost five after seven."I didn't think you were coming."

"Visiting hours don't apply to me." He shrugs and pulls out the chair next to the bed. "Now, what I'm about to do can get me fired. Do you promise to keep this between us? I don't need to get hauled off to contraband court." He holds a very serious expression on his face.

"I promise." I hold my pinky up for him to link his with mine, and he does with a grin.

Dawson uncurls the folded bag and sets two pints of strawberry ice cream on the table, along with napkins and spoons. My heart warms from his gesture. I can't believe he actually did it.

I laugh. "They'll fire you for ice cream?"

"Oh yes, so we better enjoy it. They don't mess around. They'll cuff me and drag me right out," he says with a straight face.

"Thank you. I take it you had a late day today?" I can't hide my smile as I peel the cover off the top and stick my spoon into it. The thought of handcuffs on him sparks a fire low in my belly.

"I got done around six, but you had a visitor. I hung out in the nurse's lounge until he left." He doesn't look at me.

"You didn't have to wait around. You should've gone home." I feel bad now. He has a life, too, and it doesn't revolve around bringing me ice cream. He must've kept it in a freezer while he waited for it not to be melted.

"I wanted to see you." He pauses before quickly adding, "And it's not like I have anything else going on. I told you all I do is work and go to the gym. My roommate Ralph is away on a business trip; I'd just be going back to an empty house." He puts a spoonful in his mouth.

I wanted to see you. I have a feeling this is out of the ordinary for him. I'm not sure how I feel about all of that. It's sad that he would be going back to an empty house. His waiting this late for me and bringing me ice cream makes me begin to feel things for him I shouldn't.

"It's very sweet of you." I take a spoonful of strawberry goodness and close my eyes. It tastes amazing after the crap I've been eating. When I open them back up, he's wearing a boyish grin and watching me intently.

Footsteps stop at my door, and we both freeze and lock eyes. His grin is infectious. Once the footsteps continue past my door, we both burst out laughing. I like this side of Dawson. I have a feeling not many get to witness it. In between spoonfuls, we begin to chat about everything from the weather to other favorite foods. Talking to him like this, without heavy topics, is easy. I really wish we met under different circumstances. When I do leave Frank and can bring myself to trust another man, he's the type I want to find. There has to be more like him out there.

Once the pints are emptied, he shuffles the cards together and deals them out to play war again. Flipping our first cards over, our hands gently brush each other. I pull mine away first but not before awareness floods through me. What I feel when he touches me is like nothing I've ever felt before. I don't know if it's the situation I'm in or just pure Dawson, but holy hell, I want him. I want all of him. I swallow and fiddle with my cards as warmth climbs past my chest and neck before flowing to my face.

I don't raise my eyes until I think my thoughts are hidden from my expression. When I finally meet his gaze, it's as if I'm pinned to the bed I'm sitting on. I can't look away. His dark eyes are impossibly darker. When he looks at me like that, as if nobody else exists, the whole world disappears. It's as if we're the only stars shining in the sky. Nothing else matters. My pain no longer hurts. I'm utterly consumed by him and completely at his mercy.

I know he feels this thing growing between us too. I'm not imagining it, but the things I am imagining would definitely get him fired. And if Frank were to know where my mind is at, he just might take it that far and kill me. Seventy days, only sixty-nine tomorrow. Yeah, I should've left that alone. It didn't help the image in my head at all. Well, shit.

Finally able to pry my gaze from his, I swipe the cards away because I won that round. We carry on quietly, both not mentioning the elephant in the room, thankfully. Our heated gazes keep meeting. I feel like I'm dancing with the devil, each step takes me closer to the edge, but I want this forbidden desire. I haven't felt a connection like this with another man this intensely in my life. Not even with Frank. I think it's a bad idea to be alone with Dawson like this. But I can't bring myself to tell him to go, and I don't want him to.

"What are your plans once you get out of the hospital?" he asks, his voice low and delicious.

"Just go back home and try to make the best of my situation." Until I'm well enough to leave, then I'll have to figure out where to go from there.

"You're not gonna take my offer then?" He sounds disappointed.

"No, but I'm glad it's there if I need it." I can't tell him my plans, or he would know for sure Frank's hit me.

He sighs. "You know he's not gonna stop, right?"

I do know that. But hopefully, I'll be gone before Frank has the chance to do it again. "I'll be okay."

His jaw hardens as he rubs the back of his neck. "I hope so. I'd love for you to prove me wrong about this because I really don't want to be right."

I don't know what to say to that, so I keep silent. We play a few more cards without talking. I flip my last card over, a four.

"Ha! I reign now."

I eye his eight and hide a yawn with the back of my hand. "I believe that makes us tied."

"Hmm. I guess tomorrow will have to be the tie-breaker, then. Whoever wins wears the crown."

"So dramatic." I laugh at him.

The thought of doing this again tomorrow makes me excited. I haven't looked forward to a tomorrow in a long time, and it's a good feeling to have. To be able to be hopeful again. But I've learned the hard way not to trust hope. She loves to dangle the carrot until it's almost in your grasp and then rip it away at the last second.

His smile crinkles the edges of his eyes but then dips. "I should go. It's late. I'll see you tomorrow morning, though, for your appointment."

I yawn again, feeling drained. "Thanks again for bringing me illegal substances."

"Anytime, sunshine. Good night."

"Night."

He shuts off the bright light to the room and closes the door behind him, leaving me alone with my thoughts. What a roller coaster ride the past week has been. Highs and lows, but all of the highs belong to Dawson, and the lows to Frank. What the hell am I going to do? What am I doing with Dawson? I know it could never work out for us because of obvious reasons. He's my doctor for one thing, and another is I haven't been alone in eight years. I feel like I don't even know who I am as a person anymore.

Dawson

I toss and turn in my sheets, trying to get comfortable. Just the fact that we have to sneak around should tell me it's wrong. It feels right, though. Being with her is all I think about when I close my eyes to sleep. I know I shouldn't be visiting her after hours, but I have a hard time staying away. What am I going to do when she goes back home to him? I'm sure her sneaking me in a back door would raise all kinds of red flags.

Staring at the clock on my nightstand, it reads nearly midnight. I pound my fist into my pillow a few times and squeeze my eyes shut again.

I've been trying to fall asleep for at least two hours now. I just keep picturing her face when our hands touched, that blush that colored her pale skin. The way her breathing changed when she met my stare and couldn't look away. She was as turned on as I was. It must be because we both know we can't have the other. I yell a string of curse words into my pillow. I'm a fucking glutton for punishment, must be, because I know damn well I'll be doing the same thing tomorrow night.

Abby's getting discharged on Monday. I'm off this weekend. That only leaves tomorrow, tomorrow night, and Monday morning to talk her into leaving him. I finally turn my mind off enough to catch a few hours of sleep before I have to head to work.

My alarm blares loudly beside the bed, and when I try to turn it off, it falls to the floor, continuing to blast rock music through my pounding, sleep-deprived brain. I reluctantly slide out of bed, turn it off and hop in the shower. I make myself a very strong coffee and drive to work. I drag my sorry ass through the front doors and stifle a yawn when I nearly bump into Sandra in our shared office.

"Shit. Sorry."

"Late night?" Her warm brown eyes shine.

"You could say that." If she only knew how many hours I lay awake thinking about all the dirty things I'd like to do to my patient.

"Buck up, buddy. We have a full schedule today." She elbows me in the side, nearly spilling my drink.

It's going to be one of those days, I see. Sandra's in her early fifties, but she's a wildcard. I enjoy working with her, and every day is different. I've learned to expect the unexpected from her. Her brown hair is dusted with grays, but she wears them proudly. She's earned every one of them by raising six kids.

Pulling up my schedule on the computer, I almost spit my coffee out. I forgot Abby's my first patient, and I'm nowhere near ready to see her. I can still picture her moaning my name as she orgasmed in my dream last night. I let my head fall back and stare up at the ceiling. I want to see her, but at the same time, I don't. It hurts knowing I can't have her. That she'd rather go back home to a husband that beats her than let me help her. Whatever, it's her choice. But I won't stop trying to save her. I'll never stop.

I down the rest of my coffee and amble toward the inpatient rooms. It's not a long walk to where Abby is, but I try my best to clear my head as my footsteps come closer to her door. During these hours, I have to stick to my job. That line can't turn blurry. Her door is open, and I overhear Kali talking to her quietly. I knock anyway to let them know I arrived.

"Good morning, ladies," I greet them both.

"Good morning," they answer. Abby's sitting in the wheelchair by the window, and her eyes shine brighter when they land on me. Kali excuses herself as I draw near.

"Are you ready to work?"

"Sure." She turns the chair to face me. "What are we doing today?"

"We'll work on some stretching, and then I'll have you try to walk again if you're ready?" Thoughts of the last time she tried to walk spring into my mind. How close she was to my lips, the feel of her small body against mine. I catch myself looking at her mouth, and I turn away.

"Yeah, I'm up for that." Abby takes the black hair tie from around her wrist and sweeps her long blonde locks up into a ponytail exposing the slender cream column of her neck.

She's wearing a loose-fitting lilac shirt and matching polka-dot shorts. Seeing her in her pajamas makes me think of her being in a bed, and that's nowhere near where my mind should be. I clear my throat and demonstrate the stretches, which she does seamlessly. She's a fast learner and eager to please. I grab the crutches that were leaning against the wall in the corner and hand them to her one by one.

This time when Abby stands, I'm more comfortable holding onto her waist, maybe because I'd done it before. Or maybe because I want her against me again. I should always want the best for my patient and for them to make progress. It's a horrible thought to want her to lose her balance again, so I have a reason to have her that close to me once more. What can I say? Apparently, when it comes to her, I'm a fucking savage, taking what little scraps I can get my hands on.

I release my grip on her and step back. Standing directly in front of her, I want her to feel steady on her crutches before she tries to walk. I nod, letting her know I'm ready whenever she is. She only comes to my chin when I stand at my full height, and she has to look up into my face. I don't miss how her gaze lands on my mouth before dropping her gaze. She's not making this easy on me at all. I take another step back to put some more space between us. I'm having all I can do to keep my hands to myself. I don't know how I'm going to last the next few months, seeing her every week and not acting on the impulsive desires swirling through me.

Abby brings the crutches forward and swings her leg, and to my wrongful disappointment, lands the step. We spend several minutes not talking but just having her walk around her small hospital room. It's a comfortable silence, not the awkward kind. Her steps start to slow as the fatigue sets in.

"Take a seat." I gesture toward them both, and she chooses the bed. "Do you mind if I check the incision?"

"No, it's fine." She reaches a hand down to her dressing.

"I'll get it." I'll take whatever excuse I can find to have my hands on her.

I pull the chair close and sit in front of her, and slowly begin unwinding the wrap. She's been here for just over a week now. The stitches are probably almost ready to come out. Taking the last of the bandage off. There's still some pink around the edges, but the cut line looks to be sealed. She always looks away when I check her leg. I don't know if it's because she doesn't want to see it or if it's because she wants to avoid my gaze when I'm this close to her. I rest my hand on the side of her knee as I feel around the joint below. Her skin is soft and warm beneath my palm. Her pale eyes finally find mine.

"It looks to be healing well." It feels like something is lodged in my throat, and I try to clear it. "They'll be taking the stitches out soon."

"Uh-huh," she says before swallowing and taking an audible breath.

My fingers itch to go higher, to her sweet spot. Time stands still in this moment. I don't think she'd object to me sliding my hand up her thigh. Her eyes take on a fuck-me sheen the longer she looks at me. This woman is jeopardizing my career in so many ways right now. My back to the door blocks any passerby's looking in and seeing where my hand rests. It's utterly silent, with the only exception of our breathing. I lick my lips in anticipation of tasting her, and her hungry gaze lingers on my mouth. Neither of us makes a move.

A rap at the door snaps me out of it, and I yank my hand back. Holding the gauze in my other hand, I begin putting her bandage back on the amputated leg. Fuck. That was close.

"Hi, Abby. I have a Chloe in the waiting room to see you?" a nurse says from behind me.

At this, I gauge her reaction. At least somebody else is coming by to see her. I checked the visitor's log yesterday, and so far, it's just been Frank.

"Okay. Once we're finished here, you can send her in," she says.

"That's okay." I quickly rise. "I'm on my way out."

I need to leave before I do or say something stupid. From her expression, I can't tell if she wants me to stay or go. If I want to keep my job, I need to leave. But hot damn, those fuck-me eyes nearly did me in. Desire still lingers in her gaze, but not as brightly as they did moments ago.

"I'll see you later, Abby."

"Bye."

Her throaty whisper follows me into the hall. I make a beeline for my office. I have to put as much distance as I can between us. My attraction to her is so fierce the struggle to keep my hands off her is getting harder.

Chapter Eight

Abby

Chloe pokes her head in.

"Hey, Abby." She comes over to where I sit on the bed and wraps her arms around me.

I hold her tight. This is the first time she's stopped in to see me, but I've talked to her every day. Sometimes several times a day. I've missed seeing her. I've missed seeing the kids. Watching them through a screen is nothing like being there in person. I miss their hugs the most.

"No school today?" I ask, a little confused. It's noon, and she should be teaching the class right now.

"Parent-teacher conferences." She shrugs off her dark green coat and sets it on the back of the chair that Dawson just vacated and takes a seat. I notice a thick brown paper bag poking out from the tote bag she sets on the floor.

"Oh, yeah. I can't believe I forgot about the conferences. I'm so out of it being stuck here." I look forward to these every year. I get to share with the parents how much I enjoy having their children in my classroom. Sadness threatens to taint the moment because it's just another thing I'm missing out on because of my injuries.

"I can't imagine. How are you holding up?" Her gaze finds the lilies on the windowsill, and her eyes narrow. She knows what they signify.

"I'm doing as good as I can be, I guess." I don't think everything has sunk in yet.

"Did he hit you?" she seethes.

My heart beat rachets up a notch. "Why would you say that?"

"For one, the bruise on your face, and for two, the flowers. I know Frank only gives them to you when he does." She puts a hand on her hip and gives off a don't bullshit me air.

I can't lie to her. She's the only one that knows about the issues in our marriage. "He did, but I'm okay," I tell her quietly. The door is shut, but I don't want to chance anyone else hearing.

She sighs. "I wish you'd leave him."

She places her hand on my uninjured leg. It's amazing how a touch feels so different, depending on who does it. From her, it's just a friendly, compassionate touch. From him? It's a singeing, I want to rip your clothes off and fuck you like an animal feeling. I squeeze my thighs together and exhale a long breath.

"I'm working on that," I huff.

Her hazel eyes widen. Clearly, she wasn't expecting me to agree with her. "Really?"

I nod. "I've had enough. I can't do it anymore. I just have to get through this, and then I will. I promise you."

"Good. There's a room already with your name on it at my house." Leaning forward with an elbow on her knee, she props her chin on her fist.

A warm smile comes easily to me. "Thank you for always being there for me, even if you didn't understand."

She'll never know how much her support over the past two years has meant to me. Even though she hates Frank, she's always stood by my side through the hardest of it.

"That's what friends do. Whatever you need, I'll be there." She gives me a sad smile.

"I know you will." My gaze falls down to her tote. "What are you hiding in that purse of yours?"

"The kids wanted to make you something." She pulls the bag out and hands it to me.

I gently take the bag and unroll the end. From inside, I pull out a bunch of folded papers with splashes of color. They made me cards! Sadness and happiness both overwhelm me as I slowly flip each one over and admire their beautiful drawings and inspiring words of get well soon and we miss you.

"Thank you. This made my day." I pause. "Week, actually."

"No problem. I'm sorry I couldn't get here sooner. Things have been a little hectic."

"I understand. I'm sorry I left you to deal with everything alone." I feel bad for making her pick up my slack while I'm away.

"That's okay. I don't mind. It does, however, give me a new appreciation for everything that you do behind the scenes. They're big shoes to fill." She widens both hands to show how much.

"I'm sure you're doing great. There's nobody else who could pull it off besides you." She's been my assistant for just over two years, and she's great at it. The kids love her.

We're both quiet for a moment. "You said they're discharging you on Monday, right?"

"Yep." Conflicting emotions flare up inside me. I want to get out of here, but I don't want to go home. The fact I won't be able to see Dawson nearly as much, either, weighs on me too.

"Do you want me to come pick you up when I get off work?"

"No. Frank said he'll do it." I crack the knuckles of my hand.

"Of course he did." She rolls her eyes. "Well, if you need anything. You know where to find me."

"Wrangling small children at the zoo we call work." I giggle at our inside joke.

"I brought you something else." She again reaches into her bag, and I recognize the book as soon as part of it peeks out.

"No, way."

"Yes, way. I stopped by the bookstore on my way here to get it." She grins widely.

She holds out the next novel in the series I've been dying to read. The book was just released this past Tuesday. It's by one of my favorite authors. It doesn't help she always has mouth-watering heroes on the front covers of them all. My thoughts drift to Dawson. He'd look good shirtless on one of these, I bet. I guess I know how I'll be occupying my time over the next few days. Yay, no more soap operas.

"Have I ever told you how much I love you and that you're the best?" I hold my hands out for it.

She laughs and hands it over. "I know I am. Speaking of, do you think you'd still want to go to the mall next Saturday? I imagine you'll have a wheelchair I could push you around in?"

Just her mentioning the mall sends a wave of anxiety through me. My life will never be the same. I blink back sudden tears. I took my body for granted. Every outing is going to have to take some planning. I put on a smile, so she doesn't have to worry about me. She doesn't need to know how much I stress about every little thing that could go wrong.

"Of course, I want to go."

Dawson

I wait in the nurse's lounge again until seven. King douchebag hasn't shown, but I don't want to give him a chance to see me in here. I haven't seen Frank since the first day he walked in while I was helping Abby walk. I've purposely distanced myself from him. He reminds me too much of Jackson, and I'm afraid I'll snap if he treats her like shit in front of me. I'd step in to defend any woman in that situation, but with Abby, it feels different. I'm unhinged when it comes to her, and I don't like it.

I've worked hard to be where I am, and I can't let anyone bring me down. She's the first woman since Lexie that I thought about ripping off this iron cage around my heart for. That scares the hell out of me. No woman should hold that kind of power over me. What happened earlier in her room is exactly why I need to reign myself in. I'm too close to fucking everything up.

At Abby's door, I hesitate before knocking. I debate on just leaving, but this will be the last time we'll have privacy without my work getting involved. It's a dangerous combination. I rap my knuckles softly on the door.

"Come in," her sweetly seductive voice drifts through the thick wooden door and through all my extremities.

Shutting the door quietly, I find her by the window on her crutches. I'm struck by how much more alive she looks, even just since this morning. The bruising on her face is nearly gone, and her coloring isn't as pale. The last bits of sunlight shine through the open curtains casting a shadow behind her.

"Hey, sunshine."

"Hey, Dawson. Are you ready to lose?" she goads, smirking at me.

"I think you should be taking it easy on me. Because, you know." I pull out her favorite ice cream and set it on the table. Her eyes sparkle with her smile. Warmth spreads through my chest.

"I think you like the thought of being cuffed," she says.

"Maybe." I twist my lips up. I think her cuffing me would be the highlight of my life. "Could be fun."

She shakes her head with a smirk. Realizing where I went with that. She sits in the wheelchair this time. Scraping my chair across the floor to bring it closer, our knees almost touch under the table. She's still an inch away, but I can feel her throughout my body, like a hum in my veins. Ripping the lid off my ice cream, I lean back and watch her eat hers. When she takes that first spoonful and closes her eyes, it's almost as if she lets out an inaudible moan. I did that. I gave her that feeling. I try to hide my grin as I shovel a scoop into mine. It's a heady feeling having that effect on a woman.

"How was your day?" I ask.

"Alright, I guess. My friend Chloe stopped by, and I got to go out into the common room for a little while, which was nice to get out of here." She waves her hand around the room.

"I know that feeling all too well. When I got shot on my first tour, they sent me to a hospital in Germany to heal. I couldn't leave my room for a week, which was hell."

She tilts her head up. "Thank you for your service."

I nod. That statement always makes me uncomfortable. I get why they say it, but civilians don't realize everything we give up to keep them safe. And that our battles don't end when we return home.

"It's supposed to be somewhat warm this weekend. If you ask one of the nurses, they might be able to bring you outside."

"They can do that?" She leans forward on her chair.

I only nod. The smile that plastered her face stole my breath away. I should probably tell her I won't be here for the next two days. I bought new appliances for Bella's, which are getting delivered tomorrow. I'll end up spending both days hooking them all up. But she looks happy. I'll wait till I leave to let her know.

"Deep dive here. What are your plans after your recovery?" I skipped a lot of these questions during the first appointment because I was thrown off by her presence.

"Honestly, I haven't thought much further than getting my prosthetic. I want to return to work, but I just don't know how that'll work out for me."

"People do all kinds of things after losing limbs. You'd be surprised how fast your body can adapt. A lot of it's up here." I tap my temple. "If you want something bad enough, you find a way."

"I don't want to have to explain to everybody why I don't have a leg," she says quietly, staring into her pint as if it has the answers to all her burning questions.

I narrow my eyes as my fingers flex in and out of a fist. Is that bastard the reason they crashed? "You don't owe anybody an explanation. They can either accept it or not. It's your life." I pause before asking, "Why don't you want to explain it, though?"

She rubs a thumb up and down her ice cream carton as a frown mars her face. "I don't want to keep reliving one of the worst days of my life."

"I'm sure you don't" I rotate both shoulders. "Have you thought about seeing a counselor?"

"Telling a complete stranger my story scares the shit out of me." She sets her ice cream container aside on the table and tilts her head.

"It did me too, but mine helped me through a lot. I think it might be worth a shot for you." I don't know why I'm telling her this. Very few people know of the struggles I've had since coming back from the war.

"I'll think about it." She shrugs her shoulders. "Do you think people will see me differently because I lost a leg?"

I think about her question for a moment. "I've seen a range of reactions from other people in this line of work. The majority of society is curious as to what led to you missing the limb. But you're still the same woman you were the day before it happened. The only difference is now you have struggles you have to work through that most can't comprehend. If they see you differently because of it, that's on them."

"If you knew me before I lost my leg, would you look at me differently now?" she whispers and picks at her nails.

I can't get a read of her thoughts. The way she's holding her breath and waiting for my answer makes me think she's searching for something. Closure, maybe? "No. I wouldn't."

She gives me a half smile. "Thank you for being you."

"Anytime." I raise my eyebrows as I take the deck off the table and shuffle. "It comes down to this round. Should we make a wager?"

"You have me at a disadvantage here. I don't really have anything to offer." She sighs and twists her fingers together in her lap.

She's wrong about that. She has so much to offer. "Okay, being the king is enough, I guess." I grin.

"We'll see about that." She laughs.

Playing round after round with her and seeing how much more animated she is as she warms up to me makes me wonder if I've made a mistake by doing this. I can feel that cage around my heart slipping farther and farther away from it with every intimate confession, smile, and gaze. It's not just my heart I'm toying with here. It's hers too. If I were a good man, I'd just do my job and nothing else. I can still keep trying to get her help without making things personal between us. Walking away from her is what I should do, but I can't. Not when I've finally found somebody who fills the emptiness inside me.

We talk back and forth and stay on safe topics until I have to break the news to her. "Hey, sunshine?"

"Yeah?" She smacks a king down on my queen with a sultry smile that makes my heart skip a beat.

"I'm not working this weekend, and I won't see you again until Monday morning before you get discharged."

"Oh." Her face falls before she has a chance to mask it. "Okay."

"I'm getting all new appliances delivered, and I'll be pretty busy both days hooking them up. Otherwise, I'd stop in." I can't tell Abby the appliances are for the shelter. I'm not ready to tell her about Isabelle yet.

She glances at me with an inscrutable expression.

"That's okay. I guess I'll have to find another way to occupy my time. Chloe dropped off a new book for me."

She's quiet the rest of the game, and I regret telling her so soon. When I do leave her room a short time later, a heaviness drapes over me and doesn't let up the rest of the night.

I spend all morning at Bella's Safe Haven swapping out the fridge and the oven and then getting rid of the old ones at the dump. Tomorrow I'll be back to do the microwave and the dishwasher. Trying to get Abby out of my thoughts, I stop by the house and get cleaned up before heading out to Russell's bar, Tapped. The loud dance music pulses through the black, ornate wooden doors every time they swing open to let customers in or out. When I step inside, the crowd is already swarming the dance floor, and I find an empty stool at the bar. Russell built a good place to let loose.

"What can I get ya, handsome?" the young bartender, with her black hair pulled up tight in a bun, asks as she saunters over to me. I think her name's Amelia.

"I'll take a bourbon on the rocks." Maybe that'll get Abby out of my head. She nods before she reaches behind the bar for a glass.

"Hey, my man. What brings you here?" Russell comes out from the back room with a dishcloth in his hand. He tucks it into his belt and leans against the epoxy-covered bar. The knots from the slab of wood are perfectly preserved with clear polish.

"Just needed a distraction," I yell over the noise of the crowd, running my finger along the edge of the bar top. I haven't been here in a while.

"She's really got you wrapped, doesn't she?" Not taking the warning of my glare, he continues, "Just stating the obvious."

The bartender returns with my drink. I take a long swig of the sweet amber liquid before answering, "I want one night that I don't lose sleep over her."

He gestures to a spot over my shoulder. "You got a room full of distractions. Take one of them home."

I look over my shoulder at the scantily-clad women gyrating on the dance floor. Some of them are pretty, but they're not Abby. "Maybe." I down the rest of my drink and set it on the bar.

"Another?" she asks.

"Keep 'em coming, sweetheart." It's going to be one of those nights tonight; I can already feel it. The bourbon is going down far too easily.

"You put yourself in this position. You can have her if you wanted her. You just gotta relinquish some of that control." Russell's the only one I trust and knows about the situation I'm in.

"I can't," I grind out. "If she's going back home to that prick, I'll be seeing her only once a week during her appointments. I want far more, but she's made her decision."

He sighs and starts wiping down the bar top. "You're only making it worse on yourself."

"I'm not giving up on her," I snap. Who would I be if I just walk away from her when she needs somebody the most? She'll come around. She has to because I won't stop trying to get her out of an abusive relationship. She deserves a better man, whether that's me or not.

"I never said you had to, but she's aware of your offer. You made it clear you'd help her. You can't force her to leave if she doesn't want to." He pours himself a glass of bourbon and clinks our glasses together before downing his in one gulp.

A few more drinks in, and I start feeling like maybe I should take a woman home. Maybe burying myself inside someone else is exactly what I need to get her out of my head. I twist on the bar stool, scanning the dance floor. None of the ladies here seem to steal my attention for more than a few seconds.

A brunette with skin-tight pants and a low v-neck sits beside me. She's pretty with bright green eyes.

"Is this seat taken?" She flutters her lashes while twirling a strand of curly, shoulder-length hair.

"All yours." I turn back to the bar and set my empty glass down.

"Hey, what's your name?" She trails a wickedly long fingernail down my arm as the bartender gives me a refill.

"Dawson." I meet her gaze. She's wearing far too much makeup, not the type I usually go for.

"Dawson, I'm Cami. Nice to meet you."

"You too." I tip my glass back and set it down on the bar for Amelia to fill once again.

Cami and I flirt back and forth for a while. It's clear she's looking for a hookup. When she leans in close and whispers in my ear, "You wanna get out of here?" I don't tell her no. Abby's married and going back to that piece of shit. She doesn't want me enough to leave him.

I pay my tab and Cami's, grabbing her by the hand and leading her through the throng of people. That's when I realize just how much I drank. My feet feel heavy. I can't drive home like this. We barely make it to the side of my truck when she starts putting her hands all over me. Her lips meet mine, and I close my eyes. It feels good to be wanted, to have a woman's hands run up the length of my chest and around my neck, pulling me against her. I kiss her back hard.

Abby's face flashes in my mind. Ignoring her, I keep kissing Cami. She tastes like stale beer and cigarettes. I bet that's not what Abby's mouth will taste like. I've noticed the watermelon-scented chapstick Abby uses when I get close enough. Fuck! I grab Cami just below her ass and lift her up, pressing her against the driver's side door of the truck. She breaks the kiss to go lower, kissing my jaw and my neck, and still, all I see is Abby. Her light blue eyes blaze with intensity, and her cheeks are rosy from a flush. This isn't going to work for me. What the fuck is wrong with me?

I ease Cami back to the ground, and she frowns up at me, confused. "I'm sorry, Cami. I can't."

"Are you fucking serious right now?" Her face twists in disgust, but I really don't care. I don't blame her for being mad at me.

"I'm going through a lot right now, and this." I point at her. "Is too much. I'm sorry."

"You should be." She turns on her heel and stalks back into the bar, no doubt to find another drunken fool.

Fumbling with my keys in my pocket and dropping them to the ground, I shout in the empty parking lot, "Son of a bitch."

I finally right myself after almost toppling over on the pavement, and I climb into my truck. I lie across the seat as my surroundings swirl around and around. What the fuck is this woman doing to me?

Banging on my door makes me jerk upright. I must've dozed off. I rub my palms into my eyes. It's just Russell. I roll my window down.

"Get in. I'll bring you home." He points to his truck idling behind him.

I stagger out and into his vehicle. The instant the heat from the interior of the car hits me, I start to drift off.

"I don't know what's gotten into you besides that girl, but as your friend, I hate to see you hurting," he says, his tone loud and harsh and nothing like he usually uses with me.

My eyes snap open. "I know. I just can't get her out of my head. It's so much more than protecting her from her husband," I admit to him.

"Maybe she's not meant to leave your head." He turns the heaters down.

I scratch at my five-o-clock shadow. "I don't know what I'm doing, Russ. I've never felt like this before, this out of control. Not even after Bella died, I'm having all I can do not to go back to her right now."

"Give her time. She's probably terrified of what will happen once she leaves him. And you have no idea if the guy is threatening her. All you can do is be there for her. If she's as smart as you say she is, there's a reason she hasn't left yet."

"Everything in me comes alive when I'm with her." I rest my head against the cold glass, and my breath fogs up the window.

"Then keep fighting for her," he demands.

"I don't know if I should," I say quietly. The oncoming traffic in the other lane is zooming by at lightspeed and makes my head spin to where I have to close my eyes.

"Why the hell would you say that?" he snaps as if he's offended.

"Come on, Russell. You know how fucked up I am. And with her being married to king douchebag? She needs someone stable, and not someone seeing a psychiatrist for mental issues." Even if that's all I want is to be whatever she needs. I'd only make her life worse.

He sighs and turns his blinker on before coming to a stop at a red light. "Because you've gone to war for your country and killed people? Or because of Bella?" he asks.

"Both." I don't hesitate.

"Whether you want to admit it or not, I believe you're a hero. Not many men can do what needs to be done like you have." He takes a deep breath before continuing. "As for your sister, that may make you the better man for her. You know what kind of devastation can result from abuse. I mean, hell. Look at all the classes you took before you opened the shelter. If you ask me, you're the perfect man for her. You are what she needs."

"Everything I learned in those classes goes out the window when it comes to her. I can't think straight. A week. That's all it took her to fucking wreck me." I open my eyes again and stare off at nothing.

"Sounds like you're falling in love with her."

I let his words linger in the air before I answer him with a groan, "I think you might be right."

Which terrifies me more than any tangos I've ever gone toe-to-toe with. How did I let her in without realizing it? I thought I had that shit locked up where nobody could ever get to that bruised and beaten organ again.

Chapter Nine

Abby

Ever since Dawson left my room Friday night, I haven't felt right. I know I'll see him today, and it feels like I miss him. He makes me feel things I thought were lost. Frank didn't come Saturday, so I spent most of the day reading, but he was here yesterday. Frank seemed distracted by his phone most of the time. It's my last day here. The last day that I feel somewhat protected from his wrath. Am I an idiot for going back home temporarily? I don't have anywhere else to go besides the shelter, and I'm worried about the repercussions if I choose to go that avenue. He said he'd never let me go. Between losing teaching and worried that he'd track me down, I haven't been sleeping well. I can't take the chance of bringing danger to the other women there.

After spending a week and a half here, I can finally get out of this over-sanitized jail cell. I should be excited to leave the hospital and go back to my house. All I'm doing is just going back to another cage. A beautiful ranch but still a cage nonetheless. Frank has had a few moments where it seemed like the old Frank was coming back to me and making my traitorous heart sing with hope. I hate to think he's gone forever. That's the war raging inside my body. My heart still loves the old him and wants to stay, but my mind tells me to run. To run as fast and as far as I can go. Run? Yeah, not likely. Maybe limp or wheel myself away quickly.

Frank will be here this afternoon to pick me up. I don't have many belongings here with me, just a few outfits and some shower supplies. I'm scared of what will happen once I'm home and not in the relative safety of these walls. He said we'd talk about it when we get home. If he thinks I'm putting my body through another round of hormone therapy and egg placement, he's wrong. As much as I wanted to have a baby, I can't go through that again. Not the anxiety of not knowing if it'll take or afterward when the blame is laid solely at my feet. I can't live with a monster anymore.

There's a squirrel in the tree just outside my window. He's been a frequent visitor, always running up then down and across the small patch of grass to the next tree. It's only just begun to warm up recently. It looks as though he ate well over the winter, though. He's such a cute little guy with his big poofy tail. I watch him frequently, wishing my life was as simple as his.

"Hey sunshine, today's the big day, huh?" I turn as Dawson saunters in as if he owns the place.

"Yeah, I'm getting discharged in a few hours." I'll miss seeing his more handsome-than-he-has-a-right-to-be face. I haven't seen him since Friday night, and I already started to miss him. Seeing him makes the ache in my chest grow even more.

"I heard. How do you feel about going home?" Every day he comes in, he's tried to get me to open up about the abuse, but I won't. I hate that I can't tell him.

"Well, I've missed my bed and my books. I have a feeling I'll have a lot more free time to read now." In between plotting my escape and dodging Frank.

He sighs. I know that's not what he asked. He's far too observant.

"You know what I mean."

"I'll be fine, Dawson."

He stares at me as if waiting for me to change my mind. "You have my personal number on that business card. If you need anything, and I mean anything at all, you call me. I don't care what time it is."

I can think of something I need. Him. I bite my lip to stop myself from saying it. Around Dawson, I seem to like to blurt stuff out without thinking. Surely making love to his patient wasn't included in the "anything at all" category. I doubt he'd like to know where my dirty mind has gone. I blame not having sex in months. How would sex even work for me now? That's a problem for another day.

Instead, I simply say, "Thank you."

He nods. "Let's run through the exercises one last time. After this, I'll only be seeing you once a week, so it's very important if you want to be able to use a prosthetic that you do these multiple times a day."

"Yes, sir." I make a salute to him, which causes his sexy as-hell laugh. I love that sound.

He has no idea how important getting a prosthetic means to me. Only seeing him once a week makes me sad. I know I've grown an unhealthy attachment to him. How could I not with the way he looks at me like I'm the only woman in the world? When our gazes are locked, it doesn't matter that I can't have kids and have lost a limb. At least, that's how it feels. He probably looks at every woman like that.

The session is done too quickly, and he leaves before I say anything stupid. He was completely professional and I should be happy with that. I don't need any more complications in my life.

I distract myself again with the new book that's just starting to get to the good steamy parts when the thud of boots against the floor draws my attention away from the pages. I sigh. Frank's here early. I'm not ready to go even though I've packed the few belongings I have in the large clear bag the nurse provided.

"Are you ready?" he huffs.

"No. I haven't been discharged yet. I told you after two." He's an hour early. What did he expect?

"Well, I got shit to do. I can't be waiting around this fucking place all day," he clips out, crossing his arms over his chest. Great, it seems somebody's in a wonderful mood.

"You didn't have to pick me up. I can have Chloe do it when she's done school." It's not too late for him to just go back to work.

"I'm already here. Page the nurse and see if they can get a move on," he orders.

I sigh, pressing the call button on the remote. A nurse I don't recognize pokes her head in. "Is everything alright?"

"I was wondering how my discharge paperwork was coming along?" I'm embarrassed to be rushing them.

"The doctor is signing off on it right now. It should just be a few more minutes. Anything else?" She looks from me to Frank.

"No. Thank you." I look pointedly at Frank.

My muscles tense as he sits beside me on the bed. How the hell am I going to make it through the following days or even weeks when a minute of his presence has my skin crawling with fear?

Soon after, I'm officially discharged. With my paperwork in hand, Frank wheels me out of the room and down the long corridor. When we round the corner, I catch a glimpse of Dawson leaning against the wall with his arms crossed over his chest. His forearms and biceps are bulging, and his lips are pressed in a firm line. When I meet his eyes briefly, to my surprise, I don't see anger, but hurt. He's upset I'm not taking his help. If only he knew my predicament, he'd understand.

My heart begins to race the closer we get to the parking lot. A parking lot is where he lost it that last time. I wrap my arms around myself and squeeze my forearms, hoping the fear will pass. My throat aches with the memory of his hand wrapped around it. Today is a new day. He may be pissy, but I'm not going to anger him. I won't give him a reason to lash out. I'll be good.

We reach his new burgundy truck, and he helps me climb up before folding my wheelchair and stowing it in the backseat along with my crutches and bag. I can't look at him while he climbs in beside me. It's all just too much, and I try to find anything to latch onto that's different than the last truck. The shape of the vent in front of me has rounded corners instead of the rectangular vents the last truck had. I'll just focus on that. One small thing that's different, that's new.

The drive seems endless. We're coming up on Dillon's welcome sign. My breathing grows shallow and rapid. When I see the scars on the large oak tree, my hands start to shake and grow clammy. The bark is missing from where the truck collided with it. I shut my eyes tight, begging the memory to subside. Sixty-six days left. Sixty-six more days. Sixty-six, sixty-six, sixty-six. I keep repeating that in my mind until we're a ways past where the accident took place.

As he pulls into the gravel drive, I realize my home never felt more like a jail cell than it does now. The place doesn't feel like a house either, just a building that holds all my secrets. I open my door and grasp my crutches, tucking them under my armpits. I slowly slide down off the seat. Frank grabs my bag off the backseat and unlocks the door, letting me in. I walk to the kitchen and sit at the table. Just another place that holds more secrets and lies. What was my last lie at the table? Oh yeah, allergies.

After bringing in my wheelchair, Frank sets my bag down on the table in front of me. "I have to get back to work. Do you need anything before I leave?"

"No, I'm fine." I won't ask him for a damn thing.

"I'll have my phone if you do." He must sense the anxiety within me because he doesn't kiss me or say I love you this time.

I nod, hoping he'll just leave already so I can breathe. I don't relax until the door shuts and he drives away. I sit there at the table for a few minutes before I scrape up the energy to go into my office. Sitting on the daybed in the window, I tug the blanket off the side and over me. I lie there thinking about Dawson and how fucked up my situation is. I can't get over the hurtful look on his face when we went past him in the hall. I hurt even more, knowing I was the reason.

Frank's still not home when I make myself a bowl of cereal around seven. I take my meds and head to my bedroom to go to sleep. I didn't think I'd fall asleep that fast. I thought I'd lie there for a while like I usually do. Maybe I felt safer because he wasn't around.

The following morning when I wake up, Frank's already left for the day. I stretch out in our bed as pain shoots up my thigh. I can't wait to be healed. I've been told phantom limb pain can last a while. I always thought it was just in their heads. I was wrong about that. It seems I've been wrong about a lot of things lately. Sixty-five days left. If Frank keeps working long hours like he is, it might not be so bad. If I only have to see him for a few hours at night and on Sundays, I might be able to avoid most of his temper.

To stay on his good side, I'm going to make dinner for him tonight. Nothing huge, but it seems he's been living off frozen dinners and canned goods while I was away. I drag my phone off my nightstand and pull up my calendar. I sigh. I won't get to see Dawson until Friday, another three days. I connected with him on a level I never had with

Frank. I shouldn't be thinking about him or, well, fantasizing about him. It's better than reflecting on my own life at the moment. I open a grocery store delivery app and add enough food and staples to last us the week.

Later on, that evening, when I manage to dish out supper when he arrives home, a sense of pride fills my chest, even though I'm exhausted having maneuvered around the kitchen with one leg. I can do this. One day at a time, I'll figure out my new life.

"This came out good." Frank twists his fork in the spaghetti.

"Thanks." I won't tell him how incredibly hard it was to cook on crutches for the first time. Each day will get easier as I adjust to the change, but I made enough spaghetti to last a few meals.

"About what happened." He takes another bite.

My throat closes up. I'm not ready to have this conversation with him. I'm trying really hard not to piss him off.

"You will never run us off the road again," his voice is like an ice cube that coats my skin, slithering all over my body.

"I won't," I say quietly, staring at my aloe plant on the windowsill. The light green leaves almost touch the saucer below to catch the water and soil. I'll have to repot it soon. I focus on that instead of him.

"Good," he says with finality.

He doesn't bring up anything else for the rest of the night. We do our usual, he goes into the living room to watch the sports channel, and I lounge in my office reading. Somehow, someway I think this is working out the way I wanted it to.

Dawson

I lay awake for hours last night, wondering if Abby was okay. Wondering if he's abusing her. Wondering if I should've pushed her harder to go to Bella's. I'll never forgive myself if something happens to her. If I don't save her in time.

I've had a shitty day at work today. Nothing is going right. My first patient was a no-call no-show. My next patient was irate. I ended up wearing my second cup of coffee instead of drinking it because my mind was elsewhere when I bumped into a nurse in the hall. This is why I don't have relationships with women, not like you could call what Abby and I share a relationship.

It takes everything in me not to look up Abby's address in the system. It wouldn't be hard, and it's literally only two clicks away. Once I do that, there's no going back. I'd be the creepy stalker doctor going to check on her. And then what? What if I scare her off and lose the chance to get her to safety? Fuck. I rub my hands over my face. The more I stew on it, the blurrier the lines get.

My work day finally comes to a close, and I drive home to an empty house again. When my keys hit the counter, they bump into Bella's letter that I still haven't opened yet. I stare at the envelope as if it could spark a fire in my home. I'm afraid of what it says. What if I'm better off not reading it? It's been sitting there taunting me since I got home on Bella's birthday. I keep flip-flopping on whether or not to open it.

Fuck it. I grab a lowball glass from the cupboard and toss some ice cubes in it before filling the rest with whiskey. Pulling out a bar stool, I flip the envelope back and forth under the light. All I can see is writing on the inside, but I can't make out any of the words. I tear open the corner and slide my finger across the seam. I shake out the folded piece of paper. It's one of those made-to-look old pages from the journals she used to write in. Isabelle was always journaling when she was younger. The edge of the paper is rough from where she must have torn it from the binding. I take a big swig of liquid courage before I carefully unfold it. Seeing her delicate handwriting makes my chest ache with a hollowness I've come to know as where she resides in my heart.

My dearest little brother,

if this letter finds you, I'm truly sorry for leaving you. Be easy on Mom and Dad. I know you guys have your grievances but remember, they lost a child. That's a fate I would never wish on anyone. Almost everything in this life can be forgiven if given the proper time. You need to forgive them. They only wanted what was best for you. They want you to have a good life, as do I.

I can't imagine how much my loss will devastate you because I can't imagine a world without you in it, either. We've always danced to our own music, but it's time you find your own tribe. Know that I'm proud of the man you've become and that I get to call you my brother.

I know you don't want to hear this, but you need to give love a chance again. There's more to life than being deployed all the time. You need to remember the people you're fighting for and the reasons you chose to go to war. I know you did it so Lexie and I will never see a world in which our country falls. But without Lexie or me, who are you still fighting for? Who do you love? I know you closed your heart off, but I'm begging you to let the light back in again. Allow yourself to feel love.

No, Mom didn't put me up to this. I just didn't get around to making you realize this sooner. Life is too short to spend not enjoying every minute of it. If not for Mom, then do it for me. Find that person who steals your breath away and makes life worth living. My wish for you is to be able to live your life with the happiness and love you deserve, D.

And remember, I had a good life, however long or short it was. I have no regrets. Don't waste your time with what-ifs. All they're good for is stealing precious time and stopping you from following your heart.

P.S. Please don't do anything stupid, or I'll find a way to haunt your ass.

I love you and miss you. Until we meet again,

Bella

Well, I wasn't expecting that. This letter would have helped me after she died, but I'm not sure that I would have been as receptive to it as I am now. I reread it to make sure I didn't miss anything.

I tilt my head up to the ceiling. "Abby's your doing, isn't she?" That would be typical of Bella. Haunt my ass. "If so, you could've made it a little easier on me. You know, not throw in domestic abuse and shit."

Let the light back in again. Abby's my sunshine, and she definitely *steals my breath away*. What am I doing? I'm no good for her. If I don't love her already, I know my heart is racing into that terrifying black abyss. I know she wants me. That much is obvious. But love? Not if she's going home to him. I don't know how she could love a man like that. How was he even able to get her to marry him? I take another gulp of the burning drink.

I need her like I need the air in my lungs. It's only a matter of time before I burn the whole fucking world down to get to her. My fingers hover over my phone screen. I need to know if she's okay. It's killing me not knowing. He usually works during the day. Maybe I can sneak away from work for a bit to go see her? Would she be open to that?

Chapter Ten

Abby

Bang. Another cupboard door slams shut and makes me jump. Frank opens another one, sighs, and shuts it hard.

"You really don't have to bring me, Frank. I can call a cab," I say around a spoonful of cereal.

"Why? Is there a reason you don't want me to go?" He stops his search in the kitchen and narrows his eyes at me.

"No." Here we go with this again. I can't wait until I can drive again, one more week. I have to be off all my meds to be able to get behind the wheel. I guess if I had to lose a leg, I'm glad it was my left. I don't have to have my car altered. "I'm just saying, I know you're already behind on your construction deadline, and taking a few hours to bring me to an appointment, isn't necessary."

"It's fine. I already requested the time off." He takes a glass bowl from the cupboard and pours a packet of instant oatmeal into it.

I finish the rest of my cereal quickly. If he's going to be an asshole, I don't want to be around him any longer. I hobble my way into the bathroom and take a hot shower. It's nice now that I can let the water fill the bottom of the bathtub. My incision hasn't healed completely yet, so I still have to keep my leg propped up. I can't wait to take an actual bath. Relax with candles and bubbles, and maybe some music. The whole nine yards.

We arrive at the hospital shortly after and check in with the reception desk. I know I shouldn't be excited to see Dawson, but I am. It's been four days since I've seen him last. This is my first appointment at the clinic. I don't know how much different it'll be here versus back in the other part of the hospital. Frank turns to me as if he's going to say something, but then I hear Dawson's voice and everything and everyone else disappears.

"Abbigail." The sound is like a silk caress around every inch of my body.

Standing up and walking toward Dawson on my crutches, I can feel his eyes roam over me, which heats up my skin. Frank's feet shuffle loudly behind me.

"Sorry, sir. Only patients are allowed back there," Dawson tells him.

"Why?" Frank stops halfway from his seat to the door as he shoves his cell phone into his front pocket.

"For a few different reasons, one, patient privacy, and two, there's not a lot of space back there."

"I just watched somebody else go back there with a patient." He gestures to the door behind me.

God, Frank, why do you have to embarrass me? I can feel the flush spreading up my face as I turn away from the staring faces of the waiting room. Doesn't he see what he looks like to everybody? He's a control freak, not wanting his wife out of his sight. It's a wonder

I didn't see this so clearly before, but he never used to be this bad. I wonder if he feels threatened by Dawson. Good, he should. Dawson's more of a man than Frank will ever be.

"Minors are the exception." Dawson's tone may seem calm, but I notice his hand curl into a fist, while the veins of his forearms stand out.

Frank crosses his arms, a scowl on his face. "I don't believe this. I think you're just making shit up."

I watch as an older couple turn toward each other and share a knowing head shake. Dawson takes a step to the right, closer to me. He points at the blue sign just above his shoulder that says, "Patients only past this point."

"The appointment will be about an hour. You can go down to the cafeteria and get coffee or something while you wait," Dawson says, his voice firm and unyielding. Tension fills the air between the two men.

"I'll wait right here," he says gruffly, unmistakably pissed as he takes the seat he just vacated.

Dawson pushes the large wooden door open, and I follow close behind on my crutches. He pulls out the beige-printed chair for me to sit on. "We can take a seat here, and you can leave your bag on the table."

"Okay," I answer without looking up at him. I'm afraid I'll get flustered or say something stupid again.

"How are you doing, sunshine?" The way he says sunshine makes me feel warm all over.

He probably does this to all of his patients. Finds a way to connect with them and make them feel special. That's what he's doing to me anyways. He makes me feel like everything will be alright.

"I'm sorry Frank was an ass out there." I finally meet his gaze.

I slide my cross-body bag off and set it on the table. This is a fairly large room filled with all sorts of equipment one might find at a gym. There are a few people on the other side of the room working with the machines and some large exercise balls.

He chuckles. "It's not the first time I've dealt with that, and I'm sure it won't be the last." His gaze lingers on my face for a beat before looking away. "How have things been at home?"

"Fine." Beneath his words, I know he's asking if Frank's hit me.

"You look tired." That's not exactly what women want to hear.

There's no point in lying about it. "I am. It's been hard... adjusting to how my life is now."

On the days Frank is working, when I go to bed, I sleep better. But on the days he's home, I struggle to fall asleep. Every night, regardless of whether Frank's there or not, I have nightmares. The hours spent alone in my house make me miss spending the days in the hospital. At least here, I saw people.

"Is there anything I can do to help?" Concern immediately replaces the longing I thought I saw flash in his eyes.

I know what he's really asking. Will I take him up on his offer to help me get away from Frank? I wish I could. I'm not ready to take that chance, though. If I lose teaching, I don't know what I'll do. I'm trying to work through how to leave him.

"I'll manage." I give him what I think is a reassuring smile.

He nods. "Have they taken the stitches out yet?"

His gaze drops to my leg, and I don't know what it is about Dawson, but he doesn't make me feel like less of a woman by not having both of them. Maybe because he told me he wouldn't think differently of me had he known me before, or maybe it's because it's his job. I can't help but remember the last time he had his hands on me. My thighs press together in my Bermuda shorts as I remember the fire that burned between my legs for him. At the time, it looked like he was going to kiss me. I don't know that I would've pulled away from him. No. I take that back. I would have welcomed his kiss.

What would it feel like to be loved by him? I need to think of something else.

"No. I have that appointment right after this one." I can't wait for them to be removed. They itch badly.

We do a lot of core work, and to my dismay, he keeps his hands off me. It's for the best, but I craved having him touch me again, even if it was just guiding me on an exercise. When I walk out of the therapy room, I feel empty and unfulfilled because of it. Frank's brooding stare when I come out warns me to watch what I say or do.

"How did it go?" He falls in step beside me.

"It went alright."

"What did you do back there?" I think a layer of jealousy slides into his voice.

"He showed me some more exercises that I need to do to strengthen my core and help my balance." I look straight ahead.

He doesn't say much after that, and I read my book on the way back home. I don't bother trying to have a conversation with him. Every time we talk, I feel like it's an obstacle course with every word I say. God knows I don't want to make him angry and trigger another attack.

As we drive by the crash site, I tense. I have yet to be able to calm my nerves when we go by the area. If it bothers Frank, he doesn't show any signs.

Dawson

Ding. A new text. The name on the screen makes me sigh. Great. Addisyn. Again. I've been dodging her phone calls and most of her texts. She wants to get back together. I can tell by her veiled hints.

Addisyn: What are you doing tonight?

Me: Hitting the gym, and you?

A few moments go by without any reply as I finish up my paperwork for the day.

Ding. I mutter under my breath.

Addisyn: I think we should talk. How about tomorrow?

Me: Lunch at Mountainside? Say 1 pm?

Addisyn: I'll be there.

Hopefully, with it being lunch, she won't think it's a date. By seeing her face-to-face, I can get through to her that it's over between us. I wasn't in the right mind when I came home after losing my sister. I wasn't ready for anybody, let alone her. She didn't do anything wrong. I want her to move on and be happy. I have. Well, not exactly the happy part, but I'm managing.

After powering down my computer, I head over to the gym. I need to burn off some tension. Seeing Abby today and having to deal with

Frank put me on edge. I had to do everything in my power not to attack him in that waiting room. I could feel him sizing me up and wanting a fight. I almost gave it to him. I toss my bag on the floor of the locker room and change into a pair of shorts and a t-shirt.

I didn't touch Abby once the entire time today. I couldn't. I was afraid if I did, my control would snap, and I'd have her flat on that table below me. Until Abby, I didn't realize how much physical contact I had with my patients. Touching her would have been equivalent to lighting the fuse on a bomb. I wanted to touch her so bad my fingers ached, and the shitty organ behind my breastbone felt as if it would shrivel up and die at the loss of her warmth.

Russ couldn't make it to the gym tonight because Fridays are always one of his busiest nights at the bar. I do several sets with the free weights before moving on to the weight machines. I work my muscles until it burns to do the simplest of moves. I'll be hurting tomorrow. I needed this today. By the end of Abby's appointment, she barely looked at me. I know she could feel me pulling away. I didn't have a choice after what happened the last time I touched her. If that nurse didn't come in when she did, I know I would've crossed that line with her.

As I struggle to sleep for the night, a vision of her pain-filled doe eyes fill my mind's eye. I could tell she was hurt by my aloof behavior, but I had to put a mental distance between us. Maybe I should have her see somebody else because I don't know how to make this work. I'll find a way to get her to the shelter. Then when she gets her life back together, I'll maybe ask her on a date. The thought is ludicrous.

The following day I make my way to the little diner on the outskirts of town and see Addisyn's car already parked. Time to get this over with. Reluctantly I climb out of the truck and walk over to her white sedan. She opens her door before I get there. Painted on blue jeans paired with a white blazer and matching tank top makes her cleavage almost fall out. She is beautiful. I'll give her that. But I'm not attracted to her like I once was.

She wraps her arms around me, hugging me tightly. After a quick embrace, I let her go and step away. I start walking toward the entrance as she keeps pace with me. Every step I take aches from my workout last night. Once we're inside the building and seated, a waitress takes our order. I'm dreading this conversation. I wish she just would've taken the hint.

"How have you been? I haven't heard from you in a while." She tilts her head to the side, studying me.

"Busy as usual between work, gym and Bella's. Are you still pulling long hours with that law firm?"

"I actually made partner. Which, of course, means I'm still doing long days, but at least now my name's on that door too." She taps her long-painted nails on the table.

"That's awesome news. Congratulations." I want to get the hell out. I could have ghosted her, but I'm not that type.

"Thank you. So. Um. I wanted to talk to you about something."

Here we go. "And that is?"

"I think we should give it another shot. I've missed you." She purses her full lips.

"I'm sorry, Addisyn. I'm not trying to be a dick here. I just don't feel the same way anymore."

"Come on, Dawson. We had a lot of fun, didn't we?" She reaches across the table and grasps my hand in hers.

Pulling my hand free, I start drumming my fingers on the table but then stop. "Yes, we did. But it's over now. I've moved on, and so should you."

"But why?" At my silence, she continues. "I think we both know you owe me that."

"I liked you a lot, and we had some good times, but that's all it was. I wish things were different, but I made it clear I wasn't in for anything serious when we first started dating."

The door chimes, announcing someone coming in or out of the restaurant. I glance over to the door. My breath halts. My gaze rakes over her blonde hair, the flowery dress and the crutches. Out of all the places for me to cross paths with her, it would be here. She's chatting with a woman I think I recognize from the mall. Abby looks happy, and it's a good look on her.

"I see," Addisyn says.

I lost track of our conversation momentarily. What did I say? Oh yeah, good times. The waitress brings the two ladies right by my table. When Abby sees me, her step falters.

"Hey, Dawson," she says before noticing Addisyn, and her smile slips.

"Hey Abby, having a girl's day?" I ask. Wow, that sounded stupid. What the fuck am I supposed to say?

"Yep, this is Chloe, my assistant and best friend. Chloe, this is Dawson, my," she hesitates a moment, "Physical therapist."

Chloe grins at the mention of my name. It seems she's told Chloe about me. That's a good sign.

"And this is my *friend*, Addisyn." I intentionally stress the word friend for a reason. I don't want her believing I'm on a date. Oh, hell. There's no mistaking the sadness in her eyes, and date is exactly what she thinks.

"Nice to meet you." She offers her a tight smile, then to me, "I'll see you later."

She takes a seat not too far away from us. Her eyes flick to mine with a sad smile before she disappears behind a menu. I think she's jealous. One side of me hates the idea, but another has me feeling elated.

"It's her, isn't it?" Addisyn says quietly after the waitress delivers our food.

"What?" I ask around a mouthful of greasy cheeseburger.

"The girl on the crutches, she's the reason why you won't try again with me, isn't she?" No anger in her question, just curiosity.

I can't help but look at Abby when she says this. "She's my patient."

"Not for long, I bet." She dips her chicken tenders in the BBQ sauce and takes a bite.

"Why do you say that?" I ask, guarding my expression.

She sighs, then shrugs. "In the six months we were together, you never looked at me like you just looked at her."

This just got awkward as shit. What the hell do I even say to something like that? "I want you to be happy. Unfortunately, that's not with me."

"I know that now." She sighs again.

She continues to eat without any more small talk. My eyes continually drift to Abby's table. She's chatting softly with her friend, but I can spot her fake smile from a mile away. I keep hoping she'll at least glance at me while I'm looking at her but nope. That's not going to happen.

"A piece of advice Dawson." Addisyn stands up once we've finished our meal. "Don't wait too long to go after what you want. It may be too late."

Following behind her on our way out, I peer over my shoulder at Abby. The pained expression that crosses her face before she looks away deflates me like a popped balloon. God, I wish I could go over there and tell her this isn't what it looks like. But that's wrong on so many fronts. I shouldn't care if she thinks this is a date. I need to remember she's my patient. I have to keep it that way until she's safe from her husband. Then and only then will I be comfortable with Sandra taking over. Only then do I think I'll be okay with taking a chance and letting her in.

Chapter Eleven

Abby

I keep rereading the same page. Nothing is sinking in. Books have always been my happy place, but this one just isn't snagging my attention as it should. Looking at the page, all the words blur and swirl into one big inky mess. The two main characters' sappy love story is only making me more pissed off at my own situation. Why couldn't Frank be more like Dawson, a good, honorable man? How the hell did I miss the red flags? Were there even any red flags? I don't recall anything that would've alerted me to the way he's treated me recently. But, I guess you never really know somebody until it's too late.

"Abbigail." Dawson's chest-rumbling voice cuts through the waiting room.

Oh, I'm back to Abbigail now. He's only ever called me that when Frank was around. I hate the way my body reacts to his voice and how just the sound alone awakens everything inside of me. I'm not ready. I snap my book shut with a little more force than I intend and tuck it into my cross-body purse slung in front of me. I avoid looking at him as I cross the waiting room. His spicy, woodsy scent invades my senses as he holds the door open for me to slip by. He strides beside me and opens the next door. The therapy room is quiet, with only two other therapists working with patients. I sit at the table and slide my purse off, and he takes the seat across from me.

"How are you doing, sunshine?" The way he calls me sunshine means way more to me than I bet he wants. The nickname only makes my heart break even more, to where it's about to crumble into dust on the floor beneath me.

I don't know why it hurt so bad to see Dawson with another woman. I felt like my heart was tearing apart while every beat tore more and more flesh away from the muscle. I ate my cheeseburger and onion rings on autopilot and tried to make conversation with Chloe. My heart wasn't in it. I looked forward to that day for a week. Of all the favorite diners Chloe had, of course, it would be the one he brings his lady friends to as well. I'm so stupid. So much for not having a lady friend in a long time. That's probably why he was so distant with me at our last appointment. It makes sense now.

"I'm alright, and you." Always hiding the truth and always covering up the pain. Some things never change.

It shouldn't matter that he has a girlfriend or fuck buddy or whatever the hell she is. Clearly, I'm not even the type he prefers. With the amount of skin that woman was showing, it could've been featured in an R-rated movie. I'm still married to Frank, even though I tried leaving. I'm counting down the days until I can actually leave his ass. It would be kind of hard to run away while still on crutches. Once I have my prosthetic leg, I'm divorcing him. I don't think he'll be able to prove the accident was my fault, and even if he tried, I'll threaten to tell his secret. I don't think they'll take kindly to a man beating his wife. I've heard the boys already locked up take a special liking to men like him. This was part of that lunch date with Chloe. I need her help to pack and leave while he's away at work. I don't think I'll be strong enough to carry the boxes out of the house.

I ended up crying myself to sleep the last few nights, thinking about them two together and wondering if he was kissing her or sleeping with her. If she was waking up in his bed. My chest has felt empty ever since I saw them. I know what it is, but I don't want to say it out loud. I've been slowly falling for a man who I can't have, even if he wanted me. Maybe it was because he's been so kind and caring to me these past few weeks, or maybe it was because I thought something was growing between us. I almost canceled my appointment today, but I won't let anything get in the way of my prosthetic, not even a broken heart.

"I'm okay." He opens his mouth, then closes it. After another pause, he seems to come to terms with what he's about to say. "About the other day, she's just-"

"Don't worry about it, Dawson. You don't have to explain anything. You're allowed to have a life too." I try to laugh, but it comes out too high-pitched. I fidget with the wedding band on my finger.

He tilts his head, studying me. "But I want to. She's my ex, and she's been trying to get back together with me." I really don't want to hear this, but he continues anyway, "I took her to lunch to get her to understand that it's over between us. She wasn't taking the hint through texts or phone calls."

I avoid his gaze as I pick the remaining purple polish off my nail. "I'm sorry if I interrupted your meal. I didn't mean to."

"You didn't. I just wanted you to know it wasn't a date," he says low enough that others can't hear.

I look up at his handsome face. "Why do you care what I think?" My lack of a filter knows no bounds. I shouldn't feel better knowing he's not dating anyone. That's a horribly selfish thing of me to want.

"I shouldn't, but I do." He leans back in the chair. He seems to find interest in the tablet on the desk.

Thump, thump, thump. My heart thuds loudly. I shouldn't get excited. I always read way too much into things. If what he says is true, why did it feel like he was distancing himself from me last time? After every other time we've been around each other, why now?

I blurt the first thing out to dissipate the awkwardness. "I was leaving Frank when we got into the accident." Why would I say that? Why would I admit it? Now he might know the truth.

His dark eyes snap to mine. "And now?"

"I'm still leaving. He just doesn't know it yet." I bite my lip. Frank's going to be furious when he finds out. The only other person I've told is Chloe. Karma can be a real bitch at times.

"What are you waiting for?" He swallows, making his Adam's apple bobble up and down.

I have the sudden urge to kiss him there. My cheeks heat, hoping he doesn't notice me eyeing him like a Thanksgiving dessert.

"It's kind of hard to pack up and run away with only one leg." I gesture to the limb in question.

"I can help you, Abby." He leans forward on the table, a serious expression on his face. "I mean it."

I wish it were that easy. His involvement would only make it that much worse, though. "Thank you, but I need to do this on my own." Well, without a man's help, anyway.

"How did it go the last time you tried to leave?" He searches my face. I wonder if he thinks that's why we got into the accident. It kind of was, but not in the way he thinks. I can't tell him I was the one who caused the crash.

"It'll be different this time. I'm leaving while he's at work. I'm going to stay with my friend Chloe, the one you met, until I can get my own place. He doesn't know where she lives, and he won't be able to find me." I hope he can't, anyway.

"Please, Abby, have someone there with you when you do leave. Men like that snap without warning." He looks away as if lost in thought. He clears his throat. "And about the prosthetic, I can see if they can fit you in within the next week or two to get molded for one. You've been healing so well. I think you're ready."

"Really?" I ask, hating that I'm allowing hope to find a place in my heart. Hope hasn't exactly been kind to me recently.

"Really." He nods with finality.

I've been waiting so long to hear those words. They mean freedom. Freedom to move easier, freedom to be able to go places crutches and wheelchairs can't, freedom to go back to work, but most of all, freedom from Frank and the shackles this life has put on me.

Dawson

I was able to get Abby scheduled for her prosthetic fitting today. She doesn't know I'm tagging along to the appointment with her after having moved some patients around on my schedule. I don't usually have to be present, but I can't pass up the opportunity to get to see her twice this week. I didn't even think to ask if Frank would be coming with her. He hasn't been out in the waiting room during Abby's last few appointments she's had with me.

I scratch at my chin. Fuck, I didn't think this through. This is what I worry about with her. I'm slowly letting her in, and she's completely taken over all available space in my brain. I'm distracted at work, and obviously, I make snap decisions that aren't wise moves. How am I going to play this if he's here? I haven't seen him since our little standoff in the waiting room, and my hate for that man has only grown more each day. This is a big day for her, and I didn't want to miss it. This is the first step in her getting out of that abusive relationship and one step closer to safety. The prosthetist's office is just down the hall from mine. It wouldn't be out of the realm of possibility for me to be hanging around that part. I'll just tuck myself around the corner, and I'll be able to see her walk by to get to the exam room. If Frank does appear, I'll walk away. I won't risk him getting angry at her. There's no denying the ridiculousness of the situation.

Footsteps off in the distance have me holding my breath. The patient comes into view. Dark hair and over six feet. Not Abby. I lean back against the wall and wait some more. I swear I can hear the ticking of the watch on my wrist. I mutter a few choice words under my breath. I'm waiting around like a damn stalker. My finger traces the outline of the clock face. The watch is nothing I'd buy for myself, it's too large for my liking, but it was the last gift Bella ever gave me. It took me a long time to be able to wear it after she passed.

Abby's voice cuts through the chaos in my mind. I close my eyes and let it reverberate through me. She walks by, chatting with the prosthetist, Hudson. I let out a sigh of relief when I realize she's alone. I step out of the hall and jog to catch up to them.

"I hope you don't mind me tagging along, Abby," I ask nonchalantly.

Her head snaps around as she falters with the crutches and fear flashes on her face before she masks it. Apparently, she doesn't like surprises. I shouldn't have spooked her like that.

"No. Not at all," she says politely.

I walk beside her until we reach the casting room. It's a tight fit having all three of us in there, which means I'm sitting closer to Abby than I probably should be. If Hudson notices anything, he doesn't relay that. I'm hyper-aware that she's only inches away in the seat beside me. Hudson explains what to expect for this appointment, but the words are lost on me. The only thing I can focus on is her. The way she's breathing and every little movement of her face or her hands.

My lips squeeze tight when he presses all around on her leg and when he goes higher to feel around the joint, I have everything I can do to hold back the protectiveness. I didn't think seeing another man's hands on her, a medical professional's hands, would do this to me. The only thing keeping my ass rooted to this seat is that he he's not hurting her or affecting her as I do. Her breathing or facial features don't change when he touches her. I don't think I'd hold back if it did.

This is all new territory for me. I've never been the jealous type. If you want to go fuck around with somebody else, go for it but don't come back. Abby, though? That green monster is barely keeping its claws to itself. She scoots forward and pushes her leg closer to him, leaning back in the chair. My jaw clenches painfully as she lays herself out before him until she turns to look at me with a smile.

"Slow day?" she asks.

It takes a minute before I comprehend what she's saying. "Yeah. I thought I'd stop by in case you had any questions for me." I came up with that excuse earlier, just in case. Now that the words are out, they sound stupid.

I hold her gaze as Hudson begins to wind the roll of plaster around her residual limb and up over her knee. Her eyes soften as the earlier tension leaves her face. She turns away from me, and her smile falls. I'd give anything to know what she's thinking right now. Was I wrong for coming here?

"How long does the cast take to dry?" she asks Hudson quietly.

Just as I thought, she can't wait to get away from me. I shouldn't have done this. Glancing at my watch, I debate leaving.

"It should be dry enough for me to cut off in twenty minutes," he tells her.

Hudson dips another roll of plaster into the bucket beside him and squeezes off the excess water. It's pretty cool to see how these are made. Too bad it doesn't distract me from all the thoughts bouncing around in my brain. An uncomfortable silence settles in the room.

"Have you been able to get out of the house much?"

Normally we don't have an issue with making conversation. I don't know if it's because Hudson is listening to every word or if it's because I went too far by inviting myself along.

"I've taken a few drives, and I go to the mall on Saturdays with Chloe." She shifts in her chair. "How about you? Been doing anything fun lately?"

"Punishing myself at the gym," I accidentally slip. I meant just to say going to the gym.

Wrinkles form around her eyes. "Punishing yourself, why?"

I also gained Hudson's focus to my disgust. I clear my throat. "I've been working through a lot of stuff, and it helps relieve some of that stress." Understatement of the year.

She bites her lip and folds her hands over her stomach.

"Alright, the cast is all set. You just need to stay still. I'll be back shortly to remove it, and then you can be on your way."

"Okay, thank you," she replies.

After he walks out and closes the door, I can't hold it in anymore. I need to know if I fucked up already. "Are you upset that I'm here?"

She shakes her head and suddenly looks really tired. "You're not the only one working through stuff."

The hairs on the back of my neck raise. My heart rate picks up. "Did he hit you?"

"No," she says too quickly.

I pinch the bridge of my nose as anger claws its way up my spine. I nearly jump when she places her hand on my bicep. It was unexpected. She's never put her hands on me. They've brushed against me on accident, but that's not what this is. The thin fabric of my button-down does little to stop the electricity flowing between us. I drop my hand from my face, and my gaze sweeps over her, looking for any marks on her skin.

"He didn't, Dawson," she states, making eye contact. She's telling the truth.

I swallow as I ask her, "Does your stuff have to do with me?"

When she doesn't answer right off, I question whether the words actually tumbled from my lips. The look that flashes across her face tells me two things. Yes, she heard, and yes, her stuff does have to do with me.

Saving her from having to answer, I say, "God, I wish things were different."

"Me too," she whispers and looks at her hand still resting on my arm.

I cover her small hand with mine, and she closes her eyes after giving me a sad smile. When the knock sounds at the door, we both jerk our hands back. I know I'm playing with fire here. The more I'm around her, the more my feelings for her grow. If there wasn't the added layer of domestic abuse, she wouldn't still be my patient. I would've passed her off to somebody else because I would've tried to date her. I can tell she's not happy in her marriage, and she already admitted that she's leaving him. There wouldn't be anything holding me back.

Once Hudson removes the cast from her leg, we part ways. I won't see her again for nearly a week. I groan at the thought.

Chapter Twelve

Abby

"We're trying something new today," Dawson tells me as he holds the door open for me to pass through.

"Oh yeah? And what's that?" Please be outside. It's so nice out today. It's nearly fifty degrees which feels warm after the cold weather we've been having.

"I have a generic prosthetic that you'll try just during the appointments. It's not fitted to you, and it won't be as good as it should be, but it'll give you a little practice until they can finish yours. Take a seat here." He points to the chair.

I like it when he's bossy. "Yes, sir."

I place my bag on the table and lower myself into the seat he pulls out for me. I like how much he's been trying to prepare me for a new leg. I don't know if this is how he usually is or if it's because he knows why I need it so badly.

He smirks as he digs through the cupboard beside me and pulls out a clear rectangular bag. "I think this one is small enough. This is the sock you'll have to wear when you use this prosthetic. It'll help with chafing. May I?" he asks, gesturing to my left leg.

"Knock yourself out." I lean back in the chair, trying to pretend his touch doesn't affect me. My heart starts frantically beating against my sternum like a caged animal trying to break free.

His warm fingers slide up the sides of my leg as he pulls the fabric up until it's all the way on, halfway up my thigh. Just a little further and he would be touching me between my legs. I close my eyes as desire unfurls in my belly. I revel in the feel of a man's gentle touch. His touch. It's been too long since a man's touched me sexually. Even though Dawson's being completely professional, I sense something more from him as his hands glide over my skin. I can't stop thinking of having sex with him. With Dawson, it's all I think about. I'm sure he knows how to treat a woman, unlike Frank.

"Good, it's a snug fit. Tight, but not too tight. Just the way we like it," he says before grimacing. I burst out laughing. "I'm sorry that came out wrong."

"I'm sure it is. Mine hasn't been used in a while." I snap my head up and cover my face with my hands feeling the familiar heat climbing up from my chest to my neck and my cheeks. Oh my god, I didn't mean to say that out loud. I'm so embarrassed. What the hell's wrong with me?

He chuckles before coughing. "Hey, it's okay, Abby. Obviously, we both say things we shouldn't. It's just us in here anyway. Nobody else heard."

And clearly, we both have the same thing on our mind with how charged the air is around us. I slowly lower my hands and look around the room, thankful he's turned his back to me. Maybe my face will have time to cool down before he sees it. I can't believe I didn't notice before that nobody else is in here. It's the first time we've been completely alone since I was hospitalized, which is dangerous on so many levels.

"Where is everyone?" I ask him.

"Sandra's out sick today, and Mason's on vacation. It's just me." He turns toward me with a prosthetic in his hand with a few straps dangling down. "This one has straps that I'll have to tighten onto your leg, but the one you'll get works off suction, which is a more natural feel."

He slowly wraps the straps around my leg and tightens them until they don't move. He won't look into my eyes. Maybe what I said has him thinking about making love to me too. I swallow down the sudden lump in my throat as his large, capable hands gently secure the artificial leg. Yeah, he'd be an attentive lover. That just makes this all that much more difficult for me. I wanted him before, but I think I need him now.

"That must make for a long day for you, then?" I try to attempt small talk to make the situation a little easier for us both.

"It's not bad. I like to stay busy. Then I don't have time to think about other stuff." His expression is inscrutable. I know little of his past other than an old girlfriend and being shot in the armed forces. Could he have a bad past like mine, or is he referring to his time in the military? At my casting appointment last week, he said he was working through a lot of stuff. Could it be the same stuff I've been working through? Like how can I make this work between us?

"I understand that." I nod.

He meets my gaze and sparks light deep into my stomach. I could look into those eyes all day. Instead, he stands and reaches a hand down to me.

"Ready?" His hooded eyes beckon me closer.

"Am I ever." In too many ways.

I place my hand in his open palm and press up from the table with my other hand. Slowly I put a little bit of my weight onto the device. It feels weird on the stub to be pushing down on something. I go to take a step on my amputated leg, and it nearly buckles.

"It's okay. Take your time. I'm right here."

He wraps both of his hands around my forearms, which are both covered by my long sleeve shirt. I bite my tongue to hold in my wince. There's a bruise on my left arm from where Frank grabbed me the other day. He was pissed because I spent the day at the mall with Chloe while he "works his ass off all week."

I test move forward again, and within minutes I'm able to take slow steps around the room. Dawson doesn't let me stray too far from the wall. He hasn't let go of me, and I haven't asked him to, even though it hurts a little. I start to get cocky and walk faster.

"Go slow, sunshine," he warns.

But I don't want to. I feel giddy with excitement at walking without crutches for the first time in far too long. I don't heed his advice and continue at the same pace. "Shit." The fake leg twists a different way than I intend, and I trip, falling onto Dawson's chest. Biceps flexing, he steadies my stance with strong, capable arms. I right my feet and start to pull away from him when he tenses.

"What the hell is that from?" he asks after a moment, confusing me.

"What?" I tilt my head up to meet his hard blue eyes.

"The bruise on your arm, Abby."

Oh shit. When I fell into him, my shirt sleeve rode up as he gripped my upper arm to stop me from falling. "I fell."

"Don't lie to me," he growls.

I look away. I hate lying to him. "I'm sorry." I blink back tears that start to well. "I wish you wouldn't ask. Then I wouldn't have to."

He cups my waist and urges me backward until I'm flat against the wall, but he doesn't step away. Dawson slides my sleeve up higher to reveal my bruise. It's an ugly yellow-green, and the grip from all five of Frank's fingers is clear as day. "Does it hurt?"

I shake my head. "Only when it touches something."

"I'm sorry, sunshine. You need to tell me these things. The last thing I want to do is hurt you." His face falls, no doubt remembering that's where he was just holding on to me.

We stand there with locked gazes as we both realize how close we are. The tension builds between us. My lips part as I take in sudden shallow breaths. The things this man does to me by just looking at me.... As I run my tongue across my lips, he closes his eyes and takes a deep breath. When he opens them again, the blue, almost black irises are the darkest shade I've seen in him. Placing my arms across his shoulders, Dawson rests his hand on my hip and the other one on the wall behind my head. His head dips, but he freezes at the last second and pulls away slightly.

"Dawson, make me forget. For one moment, I want to forget," I whisper. My palm cups his stubbly chin, trying to pull him closer.

"Don't tempt me, sunshine. The line I'm dancing on is razor-thin. It could snap at any moment, and I don't think you're ready for that." His rumbly voice makes my insides melt.

"And if I am?" I hold my breath.

He swallows thickly, never taking his eyes off mine. "You don't know what you're asking for."

Oh, but I do. "All I'm asking for is you."

He's silent for several seconds. Then he takes in a shaky breath. "I can't, Abby. You're my patient." He rests his forehead against mine, our breaths mingling together. He's trying to fight the force drawing us together.

"I could see another physical therapist." I'd see anybody else if it meant I could be with him.

He groans. "I need to be able to keep tabs on you. I have to know you're okay, and this is the only way I can do that." He pauses and caresses my cheek with the hand that was on the wall. "For as long as you're in that house, we need to keep things professional. I want this so fucking bad, but I can't lose my job, sunshine. I'm sorry."

I try to fight back tears. I try really freaking hard. His rejection of me feels worse than anything else I've gone through recently. It really sucks wanting something you can't have. No. Not wanting, needing. It feels like the walls are caving in, and there's nowhere for me to go. I guess that's what I get for wearing my heart on my sleeve. Why would he want me anyway when he could have pretty much any woman? Why should he sully himself with a mess like me?

"I should go." My voice cracks as I turn away from him, making his hand fall to his side. I have to get out of here before I break down. I can't let him see me fall apart.

"Abby, wait."

"I need to get out of here, Dawson." My throat feels tight, and the urge to cry is unsurmountable. It takes everything I have not to let the sob out that's clawing its way up.

I hobble over to the table and start pulling at the straps. My vision blurs as tears spill from my lashes. I can't see the damn straps clearly enough to undo them. Dawson is still standing where I left him. I don't dare to look at him. I'm barely holding on as it is.

"Here, let me get that," his voice is rough, as if he, too, is feeling as hurt as I am. He's the one who turned me down. Not the other way around.

As soon as the last strap is undone, I sling my bag over my shoulder and hoist myself up with my crutches without looking back. He calls out to me, but I continue to hobble from the room with the very last bit of dignity I have. I can't believe I just threw myself at him. I should've known better. At least he tried to let me down easily. I only make it to the hallway before the tears start streaming down my face. I keep my head down the whole way and move as fast as I can manage. I can't even swipe at my eyes because of these damn crutches. What a shit show this day has turned into.

Breaking through the exit, my car's in view, and I quickly unlock it. After throwing my bag and crutches in the back, I fumble into the front seat, lock the doors, and then lose it. If there is a god in this world, he must really like punishing me. I've never been a believer. If there was such a force, why would he allow such vile atrocities to occur under his watch? I yank a tissue out of my glovebox and blow my nose. Out of my periphery, a black truck pulls up beside me. I don't think anything of it until somebody raps on my window. Why can't people just leave me alone? I ignore it, but they knock again harder this time. I turn, glaring at the person, until I realize it's Dawson. Yep, punishing me for sure.

Rolling my window down, I ask him, "What?"

"Are you okay to drive?"

I roll my eyes at him and turn away.

"Follow me down the road." He climbs back into his truck without another word.

What the hell was that about? I put the key in and start the engine. He looks at me with an unreadable expression on his face before backing out of the parking space. Confused as ever, I back out and follow him down the road. He pulls into a shopping mall parking lot and parks around the side. I pull in beside him and try to wipe the tears off my face with another tissue.

I unlock the door when he reaches the passenger side. Dawson climbs in and, without warning, takes my face in both of his hands and puts his mouth on mine, slowly licking the seam until I open it for him and thrusting in with his tongue. My hand fists in his hair and he deepens the kiss as he rises on a knee and presses up against me. Every part of me comes alive at his touch. Every nerve ending is on fire as his hand trails from my neck down to my waist and grips me tightly while he continues to devour my mouth. He's more than I thought he would be. I don't understand what's going on here, but I do know one thing, kissing him is like magic.

He breaks the kiss leaving us both breathless and wanting. His hand is still at my waist, but he slides back down into the passenger seat. "I need you to understand the position I'm in here. I can't lose my job, and I'm not giving you up."

"I didn't say you had to."

"I don't think I can be what you need, Abby."

I search his face. "And what is it that you think I need?"

"Somebody who doesn't have all these fucked up things in their head. I've done some bad shit during my time in the service and it messed me up." His intense eyes hold mine prisoner. "I need control and stability, and you're like a fucking hurricane, breathtaking and devastating in the same breath."

I let that sink in. I already figured he had issues from the military between being shot and having to see a counselor. It's nothing we can't work through. It's not like I don't have a mountain of baggage dragging me down as well.

I already know the answer, but I ask anyway. "Will I be safe with you?"

"Always. I'd never hurt you."

"That's all I need, Dawson."

"I hate how I can't get you off my mind. You're all I think about, all I want. I'm losing control around you, breaking rules I thought I'd never break." He takes a breath. "Why can't you leave him now? You can go to your friends, Bella's Safe Haven, or hell, you can come stay with me if you want. I just don't get it. After everything he's put you through."

"And if he comes looking for me? How do you expect me to be able to get away fast enough on crutches?"

"I hate to tell you this, Abby, but you won't be fast on a prosthetic for a while. Bella's has great security measures. You'd be safe there or with me." He tucks a lock of hair behind my ear.

I have no doubt in his ability to keep me safe. But I won't do that to him. This is something I have to do on my own. "It's only what about three weeks until I get my prosthetic?"

"Yeah, something like that."

"I'll manage."

"I want to make him pay for what he's done to you." His hand curls into a fist on his lap. I take his curled fist and interlock my fingers with his. His hand is much larger than mine and calloused but warm and comforting. "What we're doing right now can't happen again until you're no longer my patient. And even then, you need time." He looks down at our hands as he draws circles on my skin with his thumb. "But I'll be here when you're ready."

"You will?" That takes me by surprise. Three more weeks. I'll be counting down.

He nods as his other hand traces my face and stops at my lower lip. This time it's me who leans in and kisses him. He tastes like rain in the desert. Dawson is something I desperately need but can't have yet. He gives me hope for the future, which is something I haven't had in a long time. I kiss him long and slow, trying to draw out the time before he has to leave. I memorize every inch of his mouth, his kiss, his touch. Every feeling and emotion that springs up during this moment. That's what's going to get me through the next few weeks. I wish we could stay in this moment forever. When he kisses me, nothing else in the world matters. He takes away all the pain trapped inside me.

Chapter Thirteen

Abby

Running water pulls me from a fitful sleep. I woke up frequently in the middle of the night in a cold sweat. It's because of the nightmares I keep having. I'm terrified I won't escape before Frank snaps. I was molded for my prosthetic a week ago and should have my leg within the next two weeks. I've been counting down the days in my head, twelve days left. I can make it twelve days. Lately, Frank's anger has been increasing. I've been able to dodge a lot of it by just agreeing with him or trying to stay neutral.

The grinding of the shower knob turns the water off. I wipe the sleep from my eyes and reach for the plush lavender robe I keep next to the bed and throw it on over my nightgown. Sliding my foot into the lone pink slipper on the floor, I hoist myself up with the help of the crutches. Reaching the kitchen, I turn the coffee maker on and pour some water into it. I lean against the cream countertop while the steamy cup is brewing.

The floorboards creak behind me, alerting me to Frank's presence. I don't want to look at him. The vision from my latest nightmare is burned into my eyes. Him standing over me as I take my final breaths, bleeding out on the kitchen floor. The look in his eyes chills me to the bone, and that's all I can picture when my own eyes shut. A shudder rolls down my spine.

"Good morning," he mumbles, reaching around me for his own mug. He's far too close. Just the sound of his voice nearly makes me tremble.

"Good morning," I reply, stifling a yawn and taking a step to my left. The only good thing that calms me is knowing he'll be leaving soon for work. Maybe I'll try painting today. I haven't been in the mood for it in forever. Maybe some art therapy will help get rid of my nightmares.

"Oh, good news. I talked to Dr. Soloman the other day and scheduled for us to meet with her next week."

At this, I smother a sigh, knowing he'll get upset if I reveal how much the idea repels me.

"She said you should be healed enough from the accident to try again."

I swallow a gulp of hot coffee before I answer him. "How about in a couple of weeks? It's still too soon. I'm not fully healed." And it will buy me some time. There's no way I'm going to try to get pregnant with this man.

"Like hell, you aren't. Your leg's fine enough now. It'll be a while before you put on any weight from the baby anyway. Plus, you made me a promise."

"Let's talk about this later, Frank." I turn away from him, silently praying for him to just go to work. I don't have the energy to fight right now, and I'm exhausted. The lack of sleep is starting to get to me.

Frank grabs me by the arm and spins me around to face him. My favorite coffee mug with the little blue butterflies crashes to the floor, shattering and sending hot coffee all across the linoleum.

"Look at what you did, now," he growls, slamming my back up against the counter, sending sharp pain up to my neck and down both legs. My crutches clatter to the floor.

"Frank, please," I plead, grabbing the side of the counter while trying to keep my balance on my right leg.

"You will be going to that appointment, and you will try again." He glares at me.

"I can't." Why doesn't he get what this has been doing to us?

"Why not?" he growls.

My control snaps. I can't hide the bitterness in my voice as I shout at him, "Look at what it's doing to us! Look at what it's turned you into!"

"This is what you made me by denying me a child."

"It's my body, and I said no. I'm not ready." I grit my teeth.

He cages me in with his arms against the cabinets beside my shoulders. My chest rises and falls with quick, shaky breaths. I should've stayed quiet. Exhaustion is making me do things without thinking. I know better. I should've shut up.

"You're my wife, and your body belongs to me!" Frank yells in my face, spit flying from his mouth and landing on me. I shake my head as moisture builds in my eyes, threatening to come out. "It's because of him, isn't it? That fucking doctor is putting all of this in your head."

"What? No, this is me having enough of this shit!" I don't know how much more of this I can take. Twelve more days is a long way away.

Frank's fist collides with the right side of my face with brutal strength. My lip smashes against my teeth. I cry out as my head snaps back. With shaking hands, I claw at the counter for stability and gag at the metallic taste of my own blood filling my mouth. He forcibly yanks my chin with vicious fingers until I'm forced to look at him. His thumb and pointer finger dig deeper into my flesh.

"You made me a promise, and you're going to make good on that," he warns.

I swallow down the vile taste of blood in my mouth. "And what about the promise you made to me, to love and to cherish me? This is neither," I whisper barely above the loud blood pulsing in my ears.

"If you gave me what I ask, I would." My damp palms almost slip on the counter as he twists away from me to make his own coffee. "Be a good wife and clean up your mess."

I spit the remaining blood from my mouth into the sink before wiping my arm across my lips. I grab the roll of paper towels and lower myself to the floor without falling with the support of one leg. The wad of paper seeps up most of the liquid while I scoot myself on the floor to the trash can with the help of my hands. Frank stalks away without another word, and the last thing I hear is the front door slamming shut, rattling the frame and walls, as he storms out. I jump at the noise and slice the meaty part of my palm with a chunk of sharp porcelain.

"Shit."

Blood instantly weeps and trickles from the cut. I press a few clean paper towels to the gash to slow the bleeding. I continue picking up the remaining shards and wiping away the coffee smears. I throw the broken bits into the trash with enough force that they jostle the other pieces inside.

I rest my back against the cupboards and continue to apply pressure to my wound. Everywhere I look in this house fills me with dread. Where did we go so wrong? How has this turned out to be my life? I know he's suffering and wants a family, but that doesn't give him the right to hurt me. Nothing does. I pull the blood-soaked towel back to check if it's still bleeding. The flow slows to where only a bead forms at the wound. I haul myself up to the counter with my crutches and decide to check the damage to my face.

I catch a glimpse of my reflection in the mirror in the bathroom. Blood trickles down my split, fat lip. My chin and cheek are an angry red. It'll turn into just another bruise I have to cover with makeup. I can't hide the lip, though. I was supposed to have another physical therapy appointment with Dawson in a few hours. There's no way I can go looking like this. He won't fall for the whole I slipped and fell routine. The only thing that's been getting me through the past several weeks is seeing Dawson and knowing I'm one step closer to going back to work and getting my freedom back.

I run cold water over my hand before bandaging it up with some gauze and a wrap. I walk into my office, the only remotely safe place I have left. Or at least it feels safe. I take a seat on the daybed by the window and stare out at the flower garden that wraps around this side of the house. The large window offers the perfect view to paint the multitude of flowers and the visiting butterflies and birds.

My painting supplies sit in the corner of the room, collecting dust. I haven't felt the urge to paint in so long that I worry I'll forget how to hold a brush. The last few paintings I made reflected too much of my mood. The colors were subdued and sad, unlike the ones that currently hang on my wall, bright and cheery.

I scan the titles on my floor-to-ceiling bookcases to find a story that calls out to me. Skipping my to-be-read cart, I go for a favorite that I've clung to in times like these. If the crinkled spine is any indication, it's been read a lot over the past few years. It's a romance book, of course, but it's about finding love after loss, which seems to relate to me.

I know I haven't lost Frank. He's still here. But I lost the man I fell in love with a long time ago. The man that wears his skin is nothing like him. I've grieved and mourned the loss of him many times. I don't know why I've chosen to stay for so long. Maybe I'm just too naive and thought things would change. Bringing a baby into this world won't fix anything, and I'll be damned if I bring a child into this world that he thinks he can abuse. No way in hell I'll do that. I don't know why it took me so long to realize a baby wouldn't fix us. Nothing can. We're broken.

I try to relax in the chair, flipping the pages and smelling that familiar scent of worn paper and ink. It just doesn't calm me the way it usually does. I find myself crying more than reading, already knowing the heartache and what the main character goes through after losing her husband to cancer. Only to suffer for nearly three years before she finds somebody that lights a spark in her and pulls her from the darkness of despair.

Dawson has lit a spark in me. Our story is so similar to Amelia's in how simple things can lead to emotional attachments. I went down the rabbit hole and fell in love with him. With my therapist. The first man to show me kindness in years. He doesn't even know he holds my heart in his hands. He has no idea he can break my heart into a million tiny pieces.

I want a future I can't have with Dawson. It's better to think I can't have it than to want it to work as much as I do. What the hell am I going to do? Maybe I should just go to the appointment with Dr. Soloman and ask her to hold off for another month. Then I'll be in the clear. Once I get my prosthetic leg, I'm gone. Twelve more days. Twelve more long ass days. As much as Frank pisses me off, I just need to agree with him to get past this. Then I can be free.

Dawson

I walk out into the waiting room expecting to see Abby's gorgeous face, but she's not there. I frown. That's unlike her. She's never late. Dread builds in my stomach as I walk up to the reception desk. The possibilities are endless. Did Frank find out I kissed her? Did he hit her again? Did he kill her? I can't go there. I won't go there. It's not Isabelle all over again.

"Hey, Harper. Did Abbigail Miller check in yet?" Maybe she's just in the bathroom.

"Oh, no. I'm sorry, Dawson. I meant to tell you earlier, but it's been hectic out here with Clary out sick. She called earlier to cancel and said she wasn't feeling well. It seems there's a lot of viruses going around right now."

Inhale, exhale, inhale, exhale. Don't jump to conclusions. "How did she sound?"

"She sounded fine." Her eyebrows bunch together. "Why is something wrong?"

"I'm not sure. Get me her address and cancel the rest of my appointments for the day." If that son of a bitch laid a hand on her, I'll fucking kill him. My other patients can wait. I'll stay late for the next few days to accommodate them. I have to know if she's alright.

"Oh, okay. Here you go." She scribbles Abby's address on the yellow sticky note.

Taking the paper, I run out to my truck. Praying I'm not too late. I type the address into my GPS and floor it. The bad feeling in my stomach continues to grow the closer I get to her home. I slow down and drive past her driveway, eying the red-trimmed ranch house looking to spot any vehicles. I know Frank has a truck, and there's not one parked where I can see it. Just a Subaru. There isn't a garage for him to park in, either. I pull into the neighbor's driveway and turn around. I drive slowly down her street, looking for any sign of Frank as I park my truck off to the side. Opening the glovebox, I slide my pistol into the back of my pants.

Gravel crunches under my shoes. I knock on the burgundy door a few times and wait. My foot taps on the concrete walkway. At first, I don't hear anything on the other side. My panic rises. I'm fully prepared to kick the door down if I have to. After a few long moments, footsteps draw close, and locks click before the door opens a few inches with the chain still attached. But I see her, my sunshine. Relief floods through me.

"Dawson?" she asks, her eyebrows knitting together.

"Hey, sunshine."

"What are you doing here?" She closes the door to unlatch the chain and opens it wider. I catch a glimpse at her swollen face and lip.

"Abby..." I can't keep the horror from my voice.

She pulls her hair to the side of her face, no doubt trying to cover her bruising. Her eyes dart behind me. "You shouldn't be here. If he comes back and you're here...."

"Where the fuck is he?" I can't help the menacing tone in my voice. My jaw clenches painfully. I'll fucking wreck him for this. Fuck the consequences. He needs to pay for what he's done. What kind of man gets his rocks off by beating women?

"At work," she mumbles.

"Where's work?" I can barely keep the beast caged inside me as I growl those words. Every corded muscle in my body flexes with anticipation.

Her eyes widen and she swallows hard. "I'm not telling you that."

"Well then, can I come in?"

She casts another glance around the front yard before she nods and steps back. She's wearing a long purple house robe that dips low in the front. After shutting the door, she leans against it taking the weight off the crutches under her arms. She looks exhausted. Dark half circles stain her puffy eyes.

"Are you okay?" Stupid question. I know she's not. The fat lip, bruising and red-rimmed eyes tell me that much. My heart aches for her. I want to hold her and take the trauma all away.

"I'm fine." She pulls her robe tighter with a bandaged hand.

"What happened to your hand?" Rage rebuilds inside me, threatening to boil over. I'm reaching my breaking point with this whole situation.

"It's nothing. I cut it on a broken mug," she says quietly as she looks away. "Why are you here?"

I know there's more to it than that. There always is. "I was told you canceled, and I had to make sure you were okay." I can't tell her how terrified I was that she wasn't. That I might never see her again. That I couldn't save her either because then I'd have to admit that I failed Isabelle.

Her light blue eyes meet mine, and so much suffering linger in their depths. I wish I could heal her pain. "I'm okay, but you really shouldn't be here."

"You need to call the police, Abby. This isn't okay."

"Please, don't. There's nothing to report. I fell."

She turns away. Abby can't even look me in the eye as she lies to my face.

"Leave with me. You don't have to live like this. I can protect you. He won't be able to hurt you again." Please listen to me. Stop being so damn stubborn.

"I wish I could, Dawson. But I can't, not yet." She takes a deep breath.

"Why not? Is it because of your leg?" I'll pack her shit and carry her if I have to so I can get her out of here.

"Partly."

"Then what else?"

"I'm scared," she pauses, looking down at the hardwood floor. "I'm worried about what he'll do when I leave." She bites her lip and then winces.

I take a step closer to her, but she flinches. I put my hands up, trying to pretend like that didn't cut me to the bone. She's shied away from me before, but she's never flinched as if I'd hit her.

"I was just offering to give you a hug. It looks like you could use one."

She nods, prompting me to slowly wrap my arms around her as she leans into me. Burying my face in her hair, I tell her, "I meant what I said. I'll protect you. Come home with me. I promise you I'll keep you safe." If Frank ever has the balls big enough to show his face at my home, he'll eat a fucking bullet.

She relaxes in my arms, slips her arms around me and rests her head against my shoulder. I drink in the flowery scent of her hair. She feels so fragile and fits perfectly in my embrace like she's meant to be there. The tension in my muscles starts to dissipate.

"I know you would keep me safe, Dawson, but I won't put you in a dangerous position."

"I don't care what happens to me," I scoff. "I need to know you're safe."

"But I care what happens to you." She pulls her head back to look me in the face. Her gaze lingers on my lips, only inches from hers, before climbing back up to my eyes. "I'll get out of here, I swear. Once I get my prosthetic, I'm gone. The next day while he's at work, my friend Chloe will come to help me. I've already talked to her about it, remember?"

She stiffens briefly as I lean in and kiss her forehead before murmuring, "I wish you'd just leave now."

She clears her throat. "I'll be fine. Today was just a bad day." She rests the side of her head against mine.

"Try to keep away from him as much as you can. Call me, day or night if things get out of hand. I'll come to get you. It's driving me insane knowing what you're going through, and you won't let me help."

Her hot breath fans across my neck, which also makes me go mad at myself. Even with her bruised and battered, I can't help wanting her so fucking badly. Her safety is my number one priority, and if she doesn't leave with me, then I need to leave before Frank finds out I'm here. But I don't want to let her go. Not now, not ever.

"Are you sure you want to stay?" Even I notice the hopeful hint in my voice.

"Just for a little while longer." She places her palm on my chest just above my racing heart. "Thank you for checking on me."

"Can you do something for me?" I ask.

"What is it?"

"I want you to promise me you'll call if you're ever in this situation again." Going back home without her is agony. How the hell will I be able to sleep knowing he's still hurting her?

"I can do that." She shocks me by placing a warm kiss on my cheek, her lips lingering on my skin. "You're a good man, Dawson."

A good man? That's a big hell no. If Abby knew the thoughts I had running through my mind, I doubt she'd be saying that. I want to reach up under this robe and tease her until she begs me to take her up against this door. And I'll keep fucking her until she changes her mind about leaving with me. My cock hardens against her stomach as I think about how sweet her voice would be moaning my name. Once she's fully satiated and limp in my bed, I'll find that piece of shit and beat him to a pulp. When Abby gives me a knowing smirk, I realize she knows what she's doing to me by being this close. I mean, look at her. She's a fucking goddess, for christ's sake. Frank doesn't realize what he has and who he's losing.

"I'll see you in a few days." She leans her head back against the door, a smile lifting her full lips.

At least I managed to lift her spirits a little. "Don't miss another appointment, or I'll come back."

Abby's eyes darken with lust, and she throws me a sexy smile. "I just might forget one, then."

Son of a bitch. This woman is trying to get us killed. I rub my nose from her ear and trail down her neck, causing her to shiver against me. Inhaling her sweet scent along the way until her flowery perfume is all I can smell. My mouth finds that sweet spot where her robe is parted. I give her an open-mouthed kiss just above the swell of her breasts.

Abby's breath hitches as she fists her hand in my shirt and pulls me closer.

"I should go," I say, standing back up. It takes all my willpower to put some space between us. I shouldn't have done that. I keep crossing lines with her.

"You should," she says, but her hooded eyes beg me to stay. She wants me just as much as I want her.

"You could always come with me," I offer one last time. "I can get your stuff and carry that fine ass out of here."

"Goodbye, Dawson." She giggles as she opens the door for me to leave.

Well, I tried. I can't force her to leave. I can only offer to help her. I look back over my shoulder as walk to the end of the driveway. She's still waiting in the doorway. I contemplate running back to her, but I know I can't change her mind. I have half a mind to find Frank and make it so he can't go home to her. Then I know she'd be safe. I wonder how hard it would be to track him down....

Chapter Fourteen

Abby

The day has finally come when I can get my prosthetic. Walking with crutches for nearly eleven weeks has been brutal. The hour-long drive from my house to the hospital Dawson works at is made worse by Frank's brooding in the driver's seat. He insisted on driving me to the appointment, and after our last argument, I thought it best to concede.

The freedom of being able to drive by myself has been exhilarating. Even if I don't go far, just getting out of that house helps. I can breathe easier knowing I have a way to get far from him if I need to. Not like I could really go far, he'd find me or ruin my career. Both weren't options for me. I know I need to get away from him. I'm taking that risk tomorrow.

I sit in the waiting room I've become familiar with. The ticking of the clock seems to echo all around me. Counting down the seconds until I get the key to my freedom. I scroll through emails on my phone, mad at myself for forgetting my book at home. I could really use the distraction right now. At least Frank stayed out in the truck this time and can't embarrass me again. When we got here, his phone rang and he said it was work. The door opens, and Dawson steps through. His face lights up when he sees me, that dazzling smile bringing out his dimples.

"Abby."

I follow him to the backroom and take my usual place at the table. There's a blanket bunched up on top. I set my bag beside me on the floor. The noises from the other workers drift over to us, but I can't take my eyes off his face. He wears a playful expression, and I love this side of him.

"Are you ready, sunshine?" With a grin from ear to ear, he grabs the edges of the red throw blanket.

I nod just before he lifts the blanket off what resembles a skinny version of a terminator's leg. I run my finger down the cold, smooth silver. I've waited so long for this. It doesn't look like much, but I knew this was what my first one would look like.

"It's beautiful."

Dawson tears open a package and holds the sock out to me. "Do you want me to put it on?"

"Sure." I slide forward on my seat as he kneels in front of me. At this level, we're face-to-face.

He glides the soft polypropylene up my leg slowly without pulling his eyes away from mine. My lips part on the exhale as his finger grazes the sensitive skin of my inner thigh. I watch the roll of his throat as he swallows and licks his lips.

"You're gonna get me fired," he whispers, glancing around the room.

"I'm not doing anything. You're the one touching me," I whisper back harshly.

"Well, stop reacting," he warns and steps away from me to position my leg. He angles my limb toward the prosthetic before asking, "You know what this means, right?"

I nod. "Freedom."

"To freedom," he says as he pushes the end against my limb and secures it.

Dawson stands and reaches a hand down to help me up. This is it, the moment I've been waiting for. I take a deep breath and place my hand in his, and he pulls me up to stand. Dawson grips my forearms lightly to steady me. When our eyes meet, he gives me a nod. I take my first step expecting my leg to buckle like the time I tried the other one, but it doesn't. It feels strange, but almost like the device is a part of me now. The prosthetic is much lighter than I anticipated and moves more fluidly than the practice one. After I take several steps around the area, Dawson lets go of me. We walk beside each other making a lap around the room.

"How does it feel?" He shoves one of his hands in his pocket.

"A little weird but good."

"It'll take some getting used to, and you need to break it in slowly. No marathons yet. A few more laps, and then I want to check your leg to make sure it looks okay."

"How long have you worked here?" I ask.

"Just over a year."

He doesn't elaborate, and I don't push. I know what it's like not to want to talk about something. I have a feeling this is one of them. I know he was in the service for a while before. Maybe that led him here. We circle back to the table he uses, and he points for me to take a seat. He shows me how to take it off and put it back on again and has me do it a few times to ensure I got it. He pulls the sock down and inspects my leg before sliding the material back on again. Every touch of his hand burns my skin and lingers after he moves away.

"It looks good. Just break it in slowly and if it hurts, take it off and use crutches. Any redness that doesn't go away within twenty minutes, you should give us a call, and we'll fit you in."

"Sounds like a plan." I sling my bag over my shoulders.

"Abby, before you go, I just wanted to let you know I took tomorrow off. If you want me at your house, I'll come help you." His playful expression disappears with the seriousness of my situation.

Warmth spreads through me, and the ache in my chest eases. "Thank you, but I think me and Chloe got it. I'll text you after I get to her place."

"You better. Please be careful."

"I will. Bye, Dawson." I grin.

"Bye, sunshine." He gives me a lopsided smile that I've come to love.

With the crutches under one arm, just in case I need them, I find walking down the corridor to the exit on my new leg feels amazing but a bit awkward. Coming through the automatic doors, I spot Frank's truck parked where I left him, four rows back from the hospital. He's leaning against the door and talking on his cell phone. Once he spots me, he shakes his head and puts the phone in his pocket. He looks angry. Every muscle in my body tenses, and I try to figure out what's wrong now.

I slow my pace as I approach the truck, going around the front to the passenger side. From the corner of my eye, I catch him closing in on me, my breath stalling in my chest.

"What the fuck is that gonna cost me?"

"My leg?" I squeeze my eyes shut. He can't be serious.

"How much?" he grits out.

"Insurance should take care of most of it, and I'll pay the rest. I go back to work in a month." My short-term disability hasn't covered as much as I'd hoped for. I'm going back just before school lets out, but I agreed to stay on for the summer program too.

"No, you're not." His hot breath on my neck causes a shiver to slither down my spine.

"What do you mean, no, I'm not?" I try to keep the anger out of my voice. One more day. One more fucking day of this bullshit.

"You won't be going back to that place again," he scoffs.

"Why not?" Who the hell does he think he is?

Frank latches onto my upper arm with bruising force and twists me around so fast the crutches fall to the ground with a clang. Pain shoots through me as he slams my back against the truck door, and my bag slaps my thighs hard. He places his hand on the base of my neck, slowly squeezing my throat until it feels as if I can't breathe.

"You will not question what I say, got it?" he warns.

I nod, not trusting my voice.

The last time he put his hand on my throat, he didn't squeeze like this. My head is starting to get fuzzy as I struggle for oxygen. This is what Dawson warned me about, and I should've listened and left sooner.

"Good girl. Now." He swallows, easing the pressure around my neck only slightly. "You won't be returning to that filthy school that puts ideas in your head like running us off the road. You're going to be a good little wife and stay home and carry my child, understood?"

Tears start overflowing from my eyes and dropping to his hand. I struggle against the urge to claw at his hands. Fighting back will only make it worse. I learned that the hard way. I nod again as my vision blurs. I'll tell him whatever he wants to get his grip off my neck. He must know I'm lying.

I'm so focused on Frank I don't see Dawson until his fist smashes into Frank's cheek. The force throws Frank off me, and he stumbles away. I bend over, gasping to get air into my lungs as wracking coughs seize me. For a moment, I glance up. Dawson is pounding the shit out of Frank against the back half of the truck.

"You think you're some tough guy beating your wife? How the fuck do you like it?" Dawson asks as his fists land blow after blow to his face, snapping it this way and that. Frank throws a punch to Dawson's chin, but he doesn't slow down his assault.

"Mind your own business, and stay the fuck out of it," Frank snarls in between hits.

I'm still struggling to breathe. My vision also hasn't cleared as black dots twinkle along my peripheral vision.

Dawson fists the front of Frank's shirt and swings hard with his other hand. A loud crunch, and blood pours from Frank's nose and onto his gray t-shirt.

"Break it up!" A loud booming voice explodes into the air.

Glancing in the direction of the newcomer, I recognize the security guard for the hospital hurrying toward us. Dawson and Frank aren't heeding his warning. Fists keep flying, and Dawson knees him hard in the stomach.

"You two break it up now, or I have to detain you!" he shouts again, jogging toward them.

This time Dawson stops and steps back, putting his hands up. Frank lunges at him as the guard yells at him to stop. My husband stumbles to a stop. I'm surprised he listened. Frank's face is a red mess of blood and swelling is already starting to form. Breathing heavily, Dawson sidesteps directly in front of me, blocking Frank. All I can see is Dawson's wide back and broad shoulders.

"Dr. Connelly?" he asks, shock written across his face. "Is everything alright?"

"We were just leaving," Frank barks out as he tries to step around Dawson.

"If you ever touch her again or even come near her, I will fucking end you. Mark my words, asshole, this is just the tip of what you'll get if you ever lay a finger on Abby," Dawson growls.

"She's already tried to kill me and failed, might I add. Let's go home, Abby."

What? I didn't try to kill him.

"No," I rasp out before another coughing fit shudders through me.

Dawson snaps his head in my direction. Concern etched in every line of his frown. His eyes blaze an even darker shade of blue as they search mine.

"Are you okay?" he asks once I catch my breath.

I nod.

"Get in the goddamn truck, Abby!" Frank bellows, and I flinch. Dawson's jaw hardens.

"She's not going anywhere with you. Leave while you still can," the security guard chimes in.

Dawson reaches behind him to where I stand. His hand meets my elbow as he gently pushes me away from Frank's truck. He never takes his attention off Frank and keeps me safely behind him where Frank's eyes can't land on me.

"This isn't over," Frank threatens, though I'm not sure if it's Dawson he's directing the threat to or me.

At his words, my pulse speeds up. I can't see his face, but I know that tone. It's the tone he used with me before he physically assaulted me.

Frank whips open his door and climbs in but doesn't start the engine. I lean on Dawson's back for support. The heat radiates off from him and feels comforting. I didn't realize I was cold until now, and goosebumps dot my arms as I shiver. I bury my face in his back, just wanting to forget everything.

"Are these your's miss?" The burly security guard's voice is much softer than before.

I clear my throat and swallow before answering in a hoarse voice, "Yes, thank you." I reach for the crutches he offers and hook one under each shaky arm.

"Do you want to get out of here?" Dawson says quietly, still facing Frank's truck.

"I do." Another coughing fit.

"Come on. I'm parked over here." Dawson steadies me with a hand at my lower back. "Do you need me to carry you?"

I shake my head. I don't dare look toward Frank, but I can feel his gaze on me like a hot iron as a sick feeling settles in my gut. He's going to take my kids away from me. I know it. Dawson's blacked-out Chevy is another row back. The walk feels endless. Fatigue weighs me down, and my cough still hasn't completely stopped. He's patient as he walks alongside me, eyeing Frank the entire way. Frank still hasn't started his truck yet. It's a sound I'd recognize anywhere. I dreaded hearing it between the pines that line our driveway.

Dawson opens the passenger door and turns toward me but won't meet my gaze. I know he's offering to help me get in, but I don't want to show Frank any more weakness. Handing the crutches to Dawson, I reach for the handle and pull myself up and into the seat. He tosses the crutches into the backseat, quickly climbs in, and fires up the motor. The tires don't squeal, but he peels out so fast that I throw a hand up on the dash.

"Sorry."

"It's okay," I rasp.

He enters the highway going north. I sneak a glance at Dawson. His jaw is clenched, and his knuckles are white from being wrapped around the steering wheel so tightly. I've never seen him like this. I've seen him angry before because of Frank, but this is so much more. He's furious. The power he held over Frank back there was astonishing. I knew he boxed, but there's a lot more hidden inside that man. I'm not afraid of him, though, even though he towers over me. Even though he's so much stronger than I am, I know no harm will come to me when I'm with him. We ride in silence to I have no idea where until my cell phone pings with a message. Pulling the device from my purse, my blood runs cold.

It's Frank.

Dawson

When I walked behind Abby out of the building, I lingered back a short distance so she wouldn't feel like she was being followed. It just happened to be the end of my shift, and she was the last of my patients. She was already at his truck when I came through the exit. As soon as I saw him stalking her like prey, I knew without a doubt it wasn't going to be good. I took off at a dead run, but I wasn't fast enough.

Seeing that bastard choke her undid me. All the years of training and conditioning went out the window. I should have de-escalated the situation, but I wanted to hurt him. I wanted him to feel the pain he's put her through. I needed him to feel the pain my sister went through. More than that, if it wasn't for Gary intervening, I don't think I would've stopped until his final breath left his body. Not that he didn't deserve it. That prick needs to be in the general population down at county. The boys in there don't take well to woman beaters either. This tiny woman has stormed her way into my closed-off heart, shattering everything else that called it home before her and won't let it go.

Seeing her hurting like that and struggling to breathe after the attack fucking wrecked me. I can't look at her right now. I'm afraid I'll see the fear in her eyes. Fear of me. I went ballistic on that asshole without even thinking of the extra trauma that more violence can put on survivors. I knew that, but I didn't think about any of it. I only thought of getting her justice. When I opened up Bella's Safe Haven, I took many classes so that way I could train myself to react to any situation those women could be put in. I failed them all today, especially my sunshine.

From beside me, Abby's phone buzzes in her purse, and I glance from the corner of my eye as she pulls it out. She sucks in a breath and reaches up to her throat.

"What is it?"

"It's - it's Frank," she croaks.

"What does it say?" I can't help the dread in my voice.

"You can't run from me. If you stop now, it'll be easier," she says barely above a whisper.

"That son of a bitch. Don't reply."

Ting. Another message. "I'm not far behind you. There's no place you can go where I won't find you," she adds, her voice raw.

I step on the gas harder, walking the speedometer up to 75, 80, and 85. "Abby, he won't find you. I'll keep you safe. You have my word." I'll die before he gets close enough to hurt her again. I finally look over at her, and she's rubbing her arms. I reach down and turn the dial up on the heat.

Ting. What's wrong with this guy?

"You think going faster will save you, but it won't. Pull over at the rest stop just ahead."

"Fuck! He's tracking us. Turn off your location settings and then turn off your phone."

She fumbles around with the device. "Okay, I did."

"Good. Now, hold on."

I give her more gas until I reach 100 miles per hour. At this rate, I have to crisscross to get around the slower traffic. I'll be damned if he thinks I'll make it easy on him. The next exit is only about three miles out. At this speed, we'll be exiting the highway in less than two minutes. Coming up to the ramp hidden by the corner and trees, I wait to press on the brakes until we're out of his sight. Careening down to the stop sign, I quickly check for oncoming traffic and take off toward the busier side of the city, backtracking in the opposite direction.

I pull into a gas station about a mile down the road and drive the truck around the back, out of sight of the main road, and put it in park. Abby's been silent since she turned off the phone. I exhale a deep breath before chancing what I think will be there. I twist my body toward her, and she does the same. Her eyes widen as she takes me in.

"Oh my god, I'm so sorry." Her face crumbles.

She reaches for my cheek and searches my features and the cut that's been trickling blood down the left side of my face. I'd be lying if I said her touch didn't take away the pain. I'm thankful to see she's not afraid of me after what I did. Only worry for me clouds her beautiful eyes. I look down at her throat, and a growl escapes my chest. Deep purple bruising already stains her creamy white skin. I wish I could go back and finish him off.

"It's not your fault," I finally say, dragging my gaze back to her face.

"But it is. If it weren't for me, you wouldn't have gotten hurt." She takes her hand away and rubs the back of her neck. "I never meant to bring you into this mess."

"Hey, I would've stepped in to help any woman. Don't blame yourself that he's an asshole. I'm a big boy, and I make my own decisions. Getting you away from him is something I've wanted to do for a while now." Not even just for my own selfish reasons. Her safety has always been number one.

"I know, and I should've listened sooner. I'm such an idiot," she says as she looks away and out the window.

Now it's my turn to grab her chin, so I have her attention. "You're far from an idiot, Abby. Look." I run a hand through my short hair. "You walked away from him. That's something you should be proud of. It takes a lot to do what you did back there." My sister wasn't able to do it.

"Thank you. For everything, Dawson." Her voice is strained.

"You're welcome. I want to check your neck and make sure you don't have to go the ER if that's okay?" I should have done this right off, but I was too worried about getting her out of there and away from him to think clearly.

"Sure. Of course."

"This might get uncomfortable, but I have to make sure you're okay. Let me know if it hurts too much, and I'll stop."

I wait until her eyes meet mine before I begin. I gently run my fingers along her trachea, feeling for abnormalities. "Can you swallow for me?"

She swallows, and everything seems to be okay, but I plan on monitoring her for any changes. These things can change rapidly.

"Does it hurt to swallow or talk?"

"Both."

"Okay, let's get you some cold water. That'll help a little."

"But look at us. We can't go in the store." She gestures at both of our faces.

"Well, somebody has to, and I'm not taking my eyes off you until we get home." I won't let that bastard take her after all this. She can't leave my sight.

"Home?" she asks.

"I live about twenty minutes north of here. You'll be safe there, I promise." I'd rather have her there with me than at any shelter. Shelters would be the first place he'd check.

"I don't want to infringe on you. I can stay at a hotel. You've already done so much for me," she protests.

"I'm sorry, Abby, but no. Guys like him will stop at nothing to find you. You won't be safe at a hotel."

She nods. "Do you have a first aid kit in here?"

"Glovebox."

She pops the compartment open and freezes momentarily at the sight of my pistol before she pulls out the little red box and starts digging around until she finds the antiseptic wipes and rips one open. "Come here."

I turn my face toward the back of the cab so she can see my injury. Her delicate hand rests under my chin as she gently wipes the blood off of my face. Next, she holds a piece of gauze against the wound to slow the bleeding. I lean into her hand as I tuck a chunk of hair that slid into her face behind her ear.

Her eyes are still wide, and her hand shakes against me. I know she's not okay. "How are you holding up?"

"I'll be okay, given time." She checks the wound again before placing a bandaid over it. She tears another packet of wipes open and reaches for my hand.

"I'm fine, Abby. I'll just wash my hands in the store. Are you ready?" Most of the blood is his, anyway.

"Yeah." She wipes the wetness away from her eyes on her shirt.

We make our way into the store, grabbing what we need quickly. The only time Abby leaves my side is when I wash my hands. I'm not going to let anything happen to her ever again. She can stay with me for as long as she needs to. I'd feel safer knowing she's there than at her friend's house.

Chapter Fifteen

Abby

Dawson drives down another side street and slows in front of a gray building with a two-car garage. It's dusk now, but I can still make out the small front yard with a lilac tree in the center. Pressing a button above his rearview mirror, the door on the left opens. Pulling in and killing the engine, he waits until the door is shut completely before getting out and coming around my side to help me into his home.

Once inside, he says, "Make yourself at home, and I'll fix us something to eat."

"You don't have to do that. I'm fine."

He's already done too much. I sit on the bar stool in the kitchen and look around the room. You can tell women don't live here. Nothing is on the walls besides curtains for the windows. It's very modern and sleek.

"I heard the monster in your stomach growl at the store, so by god, I'm going to feed you." He rummages through the fridge and freezer but comes up short.

"My roommate Ralph is away on a business trip, and I don't really spend much time at home. How about takeout? There's Chinese, pizza, and there's a diner nearby that also delivers." He leans against the counter.

"Whatever you want, I'm not picky," I reply in a hoarse voice, wincing at the pain of saying the words aloud. I take another sip of water to coat my throat again.

"Are you feeling worse?" He comes to stand beside me.

I shake my head.

"It's important that you tell me if it does," he says in a stern voice.

"I will." I won't hide things from him like that.

He ended up ordering us some chicken fried rice that we ate while watching some vet show on T.V. It's barely eight o'clock, and I can't stop yawning. I'm exhausted.

"Come on. I'll show you where you can sleep before you pass out on me." He stands and reaches down to help me up.

I follow behind him as he leads me down a narrow hallway and past the bathroom I used earlier. He pushes open the cracked door to reveal a light gray room with a large queen bed in the center. Nothing hanging on the walls here either and very few things on the nightstand and bureau.

"You can sleep here. It's my bed. I'll take the couch." He nods at his bed.

"What? No. I'm not kicking you out of your bed." I struggle to argue. My throat burns. I have to take another sip of water.

"I'm not sending you out to the couch. Sleep here." The finality in his voice stops me from pressing the issue.

Shit, I have nothing to wear to bed, and I'm not going to sleep nude. "Um. Do you have anything I can sleep in?"

"Let me see what I can find." He enters the closet and comes out with a dark gray t-shirt he tosses on the bed. Rummaging through his drawers, he throws a blue and black plaid pair of boxers with it. "I think that's the smallest I have. I can have someone go to the store if you need me to?"

"No, those will work, thank you."

He grabs one of the pillows off the bed. "I'll be right out there if you need anything at all."

Panic bubbles up in my chest. "Please stay," I ask, and he pauses on his way out. I hate how desperate my voice sounds. "I don't want to be alone."

"Are you sure?" When he turns toward me, his face is unreadable.

"Yeah."

I know he'll do everything to keep me safe, but I'm scared Frank will find me somehow. After today who knows what he'd do to me? I grab the clothes he gave me to wear and head to the bathroom to change. The shirt comes down to just below my ass, and the boxers I have to roll up so many times to tighten them they're like short shorts. But they smell like him. I pull the shirt over my nose and inhale his manly scent. I splash some cool water on my face. When I come back, he's already in bed, staring up at the ceiling. When he hears me enter the room, I feel his gaze sweep from my head to my toes, and I shiver. I feel more exposed than I have ever had with him.

Pulling the covers back, I climb into bed next to him and slide the prosthetic off, setting it next to the bed. Lying back on the mattress, I find comfort in having Dawson so close to me that I can feel the heat radiating off from him. The silence that stretches between us is only slightly awkward.

I lie awake for a while, thinking about everything that happened today and thankful Dawson showed up when he did. How far was Frank going to go? What would've happened if Dawson hadn't come out when he did? I finally drift off to sleep with no answers to any of the questions storming my brain.

I awake to the sounds of cars driving by, and I flinch, thinking one of them might have Frank behind the wheel. When a pair of arms tighten around me, I freeze. My hazy mind takes a moment to realize I was asleep on Dawson's chest. His bare, warm, hairless chest. The soft sound of him snoring makes me hold my breath. I don't want to wake him. It feels good to be held, even if he's fast asleep.

He said he'd wait for me, but I bet he didn't expect all this baggage to come along with me. I've already caused enough trouble in his life, and I pray the fight in the parking lot doesn't cost him his job. I drown out all the sounds of the city with the steady beat of his heart beneath my ear. A few more minutes won't hurt. I allow myself to enjoy being in a man's arms again.

When I try to slide out of his grasp, he mumbles, "Don't go." Then he shifts, his arm momentarily tightening around me before he settles and his gentle snores resume. His plea makes me want to stay, but I can't. The longer I stay in his arms, the harder it will be to break free, and the worse it'll be when I leave. Because I have to leave. I need to be able to stand on my own for a while.

I slip out of his bed and shut the door behind me. I search through his cupboards to find a mug and make myself a cup of coffee before settling in at the bar stool in the kitchen. Once I fire up my laptop that was in my bag, I check my emails. I find nothing important, just mainly colleagues checking in. I shoot Chloe a message letting her know not to go to the house today. She was taking the day off to help me escape. I don't want her to show up at my house and find Frank. I can only imagine the mood he'd be in now. I shudder just thinking about it. I've never seen him as angry as he was yesterday, almost as if he was possessed.

Footsteps shuffle down the hallway until Dawson comes into view. Holy shit. A sleepy Dawson with bedhead and nothing on but a pair of navy checkered pajama pants is mouth-watering. I can't help but stare at all those naked abs and lean muscles. The tattoos stretch up into his shoulder and one of his pecs. My fingers beg to run along them all.

"Good morning, sunshine."

And a hoarse, deep voice to go with it? I sigh. I'm like putty sitting in this chair.

"Good morning, Dawson." I finally pull my eyes from his body, up to his face and to that lopsided grin.

"How'd you sleep?" He walks over to the coffee maker and makes himself a cup.

He even has dimples on his lower back. I groan inwardly. I hope he doesn't remember me being on him. "Good. For the most part, you?"

"Same." He takes the seat next to me. His gaze falls to my neck. "How's your throat?"

"A little better," I say. It still aches as if I have strep throat.

"I know you probably don't want to talk about it yet, but I think you should go to the police today and get a restraining order on him." Dawson stretches his arms behind his head, causing the inked muscles to bulge, which makes me remember how it felt to be in those arms.

"Would that even matter, though?" I don't think much would stop Frank. I rub my pounding forehead.

"Whether you press charges or not, at least if he comes within a certain distance of you, he can get arrested. Sometimes that's enough to keep them away." He places his elbow on the counter and rests his head on his open palm.

"And if not?" I blow across my mug before taking a sip. The hot liquid feels good as it slides down my throat.

"Nothing will stop me from protecting you, Abby," he says in a low voice.

A cold chill snakes up my spine with the intense look on his face. I'm sure nothing will be able to stop him, and that's what scares me. I don't want to be a burden on him or have him lose his job, even his life, because of me. Because Frank is dangerous and far deadlier than I could have ever imagined. I only want to add positivity to a person's life, and I think that's part of the reason I haven't told anybody else about the abuse. I know Dawson's right, and I should report Frank's attack, but that doesn't make it any easier.

"Will you go with me?" I hold my breath waiting for his answer. I want him there with me, but at the same time, I don't because he might think the worst of me when he learns how many times it's happened. I'm sure that's a question I'll have to answer.

"If you want me to." He searches my face, and I feel like he knows how conflicted I am. "What is it?"

I'm quiet for a minute before answering, "I just don't want you to think any less of me."

He caresses my cheek. "Nothing could ever make me think less of you."

I lean into his hand and close my eyes. "I'm just ashamed of how long I let it go on. I feel weak because of it," I whisper.

He kisses my forehead, and I tense, not expecting the intimate touch. "Don't ever think your weak for what you did. If anything, it's the opposite. You stayed and hoped it would get better. You chose to show compassion and love when others aren't able to. That makes you strong."

I open my eyes and admit, "I don't even know who I am anymore."

"You have the rest of your life to figure that out."

Dawson

Me: I'll be on my way to your office in about an hour with a domestic abuse victim. I know it's above your pay grade, but is there any way you can free up some time for us?

I send out a quick text and hope Murphy's working today. He's the chief of police, and I'm not putting down any of the others that work there, but with Abby, I won't risk having a rookie doing the paperwork. Everything has to be done correctly. Frank can't get out of it. My phone buzzes on the black countertop.

Murphy: Let me know when you're here. I'll tell the lieutenant to be expecting you.

Me: Thanks, man. There might be footage of the incident. It was at East Point Med in the parking lot. Gary Harrison, the security guard, was also a witness.

Murphy: I'll get on it.

Abby's been in the bathroom for about a half hour. I'm glad she agreed to get a restraining order on Frank. It may not stop him from coming after her, but at least it's a start. I'm sitting at the bar stool, drinking my second cup of coffee and trying to clear the headache that's pulsing at my temples. Frank landed a good one on me, but that's not what's causing it. I can only imagine what Abby felt like to be on the receiving end of his fists. She's holding herself together pretty well, considering the past twenty-four hours.

I woke up to her sliding up next to me last night and putting her head on my chest. I don't know if she remembers it, but I do, clear as day. It's not how I pictured our first night together by a long shot. I don't know what the fuck I'm doing. I'm worried I'll screw this up before we even begin. I rest my pounding head in my hands and let my eyes fall closed. I didn't get much sleep last night. My nerves were in a frenzy, and I'd never felt more out of control in my life than I did yesterday.

The bathroom door opens down the hall, and she walks out wearing the same clothes she wore yesterday. As nice as they are, I really liked seeing her in mine. It made it feel like she was mine too. I stand and stroll past her to take my shower. Our arms barely grazing, I say as I brush by her, "You smell like me."

"I guess it's a good thing I like the way you smell, then." She smirks, taking the blanket off the end of the couch and covering herself up.

I'm still grinning as I walk into the bathroom to clean up. She likes the way I smell. I'm never changing out my shampoo, body wash, deodorant, or cologne ever again.

She's tense during the drive to the police station and doesn't talk much. We arrive at the barracks, and I come around to open her door. She hesitates to stare up at the looming concrete three-story building, looking like she might back out of reporting Frank.

"I'll be with you the whole time, and the officer we're meeting is a good friend of mine. He'll treat you good, I promise," I insist as I wait by the open passenger door of my truck. I don't want to push her, but this is something I feel she needs to do. The attack needs to be documented on the off chance it happens again.

"Okay." She sighs before taking my hand and placing her foot on the sidestep of the truck.

I rest my hand on her lower back and guide her up the concrete steps. She's using her prosthetic right now and decided to leave the crutches in the truck. Pulling open the glass door, I usher her in first. Her steps falter when she takes in the large and open room. Near-constant chatter hums in the air. Several desks, with partial walls, surround the center hub, while a good half of the officers are talking on the phone or hammering away at the keyboard of their computer. I'm sure she's thought about doing this before; coming forward is not a small thing. I walk up to the desk and wait for the young lieutenant to look up from his computer and nod.

"Hi, I'm Dawson Connelly. The chief should be expecting us."

"He is. Right this way, please." He leads us to the elevator. "Third floor. When you exit, talk to Janet at the reception desk."

The elevator dings and we step through. The doors open on the second floor to let other officers on, and Abby edges closer to me. The next stop is us. I talk to Janet, and she calls Murphy's phone to let him know we're here. We don't even have time to sit on the bench she directed us to before he strides through the hallway.

"Well, I'll be damned. It's been a while, Connelly." Murphy slaps me on the back and scans Abby's neck, never missing a beat. "And who's this?"

"Hi, I'm Abby Miller." She transfers her weight from her foot to her prosthetic.

"Come back to my office, and we'll chat in there."

He shuts us in his large modern room, where floor-to-ceiling windows overlook the city of East Point. There's a dark cherry wood desk with a few chairs around the room. The bookcase on the wall where the door is holds several books and trinkets, but I'm drawn to the picture in a plain black frame. I walk over and pick it up. It's a picture from my last tour. Our team of nine is all in there.

"I don't remember this one." I reach into my memory, trying to figure out when it was taken.

"I think that was taken when we first got in the country." He scratches his chin.

I show it to Abby, and she smiles and points to one of the figures. "Is that you?"

"Yeah, and that goofy fucker right there is Murphy," I say, making her laugh.

"Watch it, Connelly. When I got your message this morning, I didn't peg you to be the victim. Mrs. Miller must have quite the swing."

Abby's eyes grow large. "Oh, no, I didn't-"

"It's okay. Just trying to lighten the mood." He gestures to the two gray chairs directly in front of his desk. Once we're seated, he begins, "I was able to get footage from the hospital. I'm sorry that happened, ma'am. What would you like us to do?"

"I um. I want to get a restraining order on him so he can't come near me again." She twists her fingers around inside her hand.

"Do you want to press charges?" He tilts his head to the side.

She looks down and shakes her head. "I just want to be done with it all."

"Did you know the attacker?"

"Yes."

"Was your attacker your husband or boyfriend?" He starts to jot things down in a notebook on his desk.

"My husband," she whispers.

"And his name is?"

"Frank Miller." She crosses her arms, uncrosses them, and crosses them again. She's obviously very uncomfortable. I don't know what the hell to do. I want to comfort her, but I feel like I'd be making the situation worse for her.

"Okay, do you both live together?"

"We did up until yesterday. I was actually going to pack my stuff to leave and stay with a friend today, but his attack happened, so I stayed the night at Dawson's." Her gaze meets mine briefly.

"Does your husband know the friend who you were going to stay with?"

"He knows her but didn't know I was leaving." She shakes her head.

Murphy's forehead wrinkles. "In situations like your own, friends and family are usually the first place the abuser will look for you."

Abby's shoulders slump, and her face falls even more.

"She can stay with me for as long as she needs to," I interject. Murphy looks at me for a beat. I don't know if I'm even supposed to be talking while he questions her.

"Dawson, I'm not going-"

"You're staying. I know you're safe at my house." I'll be damned if that prick comes near her.

"In my opinion, Connelly would be the safer option for you." He nods reassuringly as he sits back farther into his desk chair. "I've known him a long time, and he'll do what's necessary to keep you safe."

She scrubs her hands over her face. "Fine."

I know enough that when a woman says fine, it's not really fine. If she wants to be mad at me for overstepping, she can be. At least I know she'll be okay in the end.

"I'd highly suggest an officer meets you at the residence for you to pack your things." He taps the pen on his notepad.

"Is there any way you could do it?" I ask, respecting his advice. I'll be going with her, and I don't trust other officers to be able to keep me from beating the shit out of him if he starts in with anything.

"I'll pull up my calendar." He types into his computer. "I'm stuck in meetings all day tomorrow, but I can do the day after. Will that work for you guys?"

We both agree.

"Has your husband physically hurt you before yesterday?"

She sighs and runs her hand through her long blonde hair and twirling the ends. "Yes."

"How many times, once, twice, three times?"

"I don't know." She wraps her arms tightly around her and a closed look settles on her face.

"More than three?"

She nods, pulling the sleeves of her shirt down over her hands.

"More than five?"

Another nod.

I see his jaw harden from here before he asks, "More than ten?"

Abby's gaze grows glassy with tears. She looks away and nods again.

Fuck. I had no idea just how bad the situation was. Once is too much, but ten? That son of a bitch. What kind of man can go to sleep at night after physically hurting his wife? My hands flex, wanting to hit him as many times as he's hit her. She should press charges. Send that fucker to prison.

"More than twenty?" Murphy asks, keeping his tone flat. I hold my breath waiting for her answer.

"I don't think so, no." Her voice is raw.

She doesn't think so? I fight the urge to storm out of the room and give that bastard what he deserves. I'm sure this isn't easy for her to do, and that's what keeps me rooted to my chair. I place my hand on the flesh of Abby's thigh and give it a gentle squeeze letting her know I'm here.

"I'm sorry, this is just protocol. Were there ever any witnesses, or have you been treated for any injuries?"

She clears her throat. "No."

"I saw some of the bruises," I speak up.

"And you didn't report it?" He side-eyes me as if I should've.

"She didn't admit to him hitting her and danced around the truth." I hate saying this about her, but it's the truth. She covered for him.

Murphy turns his attention back to Abby. "Is that true? It's okay if it is; I just need a clear picture for the judge to sign off on it."

"Yes, I hid the truth," she says quietly, looking at a spot above Murphy and avoiding both our gazes.

"Okay, I think that's all I have for you. If I need anything else, I'll reach out to you. In the meantime, hang tight, and I'll meet you at the residence at ten am the day after tomorrow. If you could write the address here and then your contact information as well."

We thank him and leave the building. She's silent all the way out to the truck. I knew I'd fuck this up. She still won't even look at me. I have to try to fix this. Before I start the engine, I ask her, "Are you mad at me for what I said in there?"

She finally looks at me with a sad smile. "No, I'm mad at myself for letting it go on for that long."

Abby pulls her seat belt on and leans her head back. Her face is directed toward the window, but I catch a glimpse of her lids closing. I take that as my cue to drop it and get her back home. She doesn't attempt to make conversation the whole ride, which is just as well. My anger has barely calmed down since hearing how often he did this shit to her. My fingers grip the steering wheel tighter as I fight the urge to track him down and give him my own justice.

Chapter Sixteen

Abby

Tipping my mug back, I struggle to let the hot liquid flow down my throat. I can barely drink my coffee because my stomach is such a mess. In less than an hour, I'm going back to what's left of my house to grab my belongings. I don't have much besides clothing, bathroom stuff, art supplies, and my books. My books alone will take up most of the boxes we picked up last night. Dawson said I could store them in his garage for the time being until I can get my own place. I've been with Frank for most of my adult life. I don't know how to live alone, even though I should've left him ages ago.

A short while later, I pull myself up into Dawson's truck. My prosthetic has been rubbing my skin raw these last few days, which makes climbing up into the cab even harder. Russell's truck is idling beside us, waiting for us to lead the way. I twist my fingers in my hands and crack my knuckles, then pat my hair down. Anything to keep my mind off what I'm doing. The chief will be there as well as Frank. Even though I filed for a restraining order on him, he still has a right to be there to make sure I don't take anything of his. Not like I would. Frank can have it all. I don't want anything that reminds me of who he turned into.

"Are you ready?" Dawson says calmly, but he's anything but calm. His locked jaw and clenched fists give him away.

I regret the position I put him in. This isn't his battle to fight, but honestly, I couldn't do it without him. Besides the kids at school, he's been the only bright spot for me for some time now. The only thing that I looked forward to each week.

"I'm ready." I flash him what I hope is a convincing smile, but he only nods stiffly before backing out of the drive.

Twenty-five minutes later, we pull onto my road. I take deep, steadying breaths as we approach my- his driveway. The same officer I saw the other day is standing beside his rig as we park.

"If you want to stay here, I can go in alone," I tell Dawson. I can feel the anger radiating off from him. Having Dawson and Frank in the same house could prove to be a volatile combination.

Dawson snaps his head toward me. "No fucking way. I'm sorry, Abby, but I'm coming in too. Even with Murphy here, I don't trust your husband."

"Okay." I open my door and hop down onto the gravel driveway.

"Good morning, Mrs. Miller," the chief greets me.

"Good morning, Mr. Murphy," I reply, even though it's been anything but a good morning.

Russell and Dawson grab the folded-up boxes from the back of the truck. I follow slowly behind Murphy as he comes to the front door. His stocky body is shielding me until we reach the steps. The little white house with red trim never looked as menacing as it does now.

The policeman raps his knuckles against the burgundy door. My heart is hammering in my chest, and bile seems to want to rear its ugly head. Frank opens the door, and his olive-colored eyes meet mine. I freeze. He's in rough shape, and bluish-purple bruising covers the skin around his eyes and the left part of his jaw. There's a white bandage over his nose. Just as I thought by the amount of blood that came out of it during the fight, Dawson broke Frank's nose. I quickly look down at my feet, waiting for him to let is in. Dawson gently places his hand on my back, calming me. Letting me know he's right there.

"What the hell is he doing here?" Frank snaps, making me jump.

"Your not even supposed to be here, Mr. Miller, so I'd shut your yap," the officer pipes up.

"He's the one who did this to me!" Frank throws his hands into the air.

"I watched the footage myself. If I were him, I would've done the same. You're just lucky Mrs. Miller doesn't want to press charges against you. Let her gather her things in peace, or you can wait outside."

Frank grumbles, then opens the door wide enough to let us pass. I follow on the heels of the cop. I don't want to be close to Frank, and I can't even stand to look at him. He remains in the corner of the living room as I walk quickly past him toward the bedroom, holding my breath the entire way. Opening the door and flicking the light on, I'm flooded with memories. The good, the bad, and the worst. My eyes fall to the bed where he made love to me so many times before he was a monster. Back when he still had a love for me. I bite my lip in an attempt to stop the tears from falling. I just have to pack my shit and get out of here. Then I can move on. One step closer to freedom.

"Where do you want me to start?" Dawson asks quietly as he unfolds one of the boxes and tapes the ends together.

Russell is standing behind him, taking in the room as Dawson prepares more boxes. Today was the first time I met Russell back at Dawson's condo. He seems really nice and has a great sense of humor.

"If you could grab these clothes and toss them in, that would be great." I show him which side as if it's not obvious which side belongs to me.

I head to the master bathroom with a box and shove all my toiletries in there as quickly as I can. Emptying my past out shelf by shelf. Next, my nightstand. I help Dawson finish up with the closet while his friend starts to run boxes out to the truck. Frank is silent and keeping his distance, thank god. We finish the bedroom and head to my office down the hall. Once in there, my hands start to shake as I look at all my books and artwork. The art was a release for me. To be able to put all my pain into something. And my books, well, they were my escape. The one thing Frank let me enjoy. I flip open the last book I was reading. I forgot it that last morning because I was in a rush, but usually, I always carry one with me.

My finger slides down the words of a worn and simple bookmark that has resonated so much with my soul. There's a book floating beside a heart that's cracked. Embossed in silver are the words, "She reads as though the ink can fill the cracks in her shattered heart." Which was exactly what I was trying to do. While reading every book, I didn't live my own life. I became the characters. That was the only way I survived for as long as I did. Every time the main character got their happy ending, I'd make a wish that there was indeed someone out there like that for me. I thought it was Frank. I was very wrong. Snapping the book shut, I set it aside, hoping to finish it later.

"If this is too much, we can take a break." Dawson gives my shoulder a squeeze.

I pinch the bridge of my nose. "No. I'm fine. I just want to get it done."

"When you said you liked to read, I wasn't expecting a full-blown library." He laughs to ease the tension.

"Yeah," I say wistfully.

They've gotten me through a lot. Each one of these books holds memories. With a lot more care than I showed my jewelry and perfumes, I carefully set each of the paperbacks and hardcovers into the boxes. I don't even care about the bookcases. I'll build new ones in my next place. I can vaguely hear mumbled conversation coming from the living room around the corner. I tense, waiting to hear if the voices come closer. It's odd to work side by side with Dawson in this house. I guess, in a way, he was my escape too. Someone I could give my heart to without him ever being the wiser. I'm not stupid. I've seen the way he looks at me sometimes. But it's just lust. He told me that he hasn't been in a relationship for a while. That's all this is. He just wants me safe and that's clouding his judgment.

His cologne keeps drifting over to me every time we're close. It's a heady scent that makes my stomach tighten at the smallest wisp. I never thought wanting somebody could be triggered by how yummy they smell. I find myself wanting Dawson more and more each day. We make a good team, and in about an hour and a half, all the packing is done. Not long at all for me to pack up the last eight years of my life. That's pretty sad. I'm not taking anything else in this house. Even if a lot of the stuff is mine, it's not worth the fight.

When I pause before reaching the archway of the office, a deep sadness washes over me. Dawson notices and wraps his arms around me from behind. I close my eyes and lean into him. His warm body feels right against mine. Like he can take all the pain away from me little by little. I feel safe in his arms, safer than I've felt in a long time.

"I'm right here," he whispers against the shell of my ear, making me shiver against him.

Russell walks back into the room, ruining the moment. "Is that everything?"

"Yes, it is. Thank you for carrying everything for me." I lean my back farther into Dawson's hard chest.

Russell flashes a cocky grin and winks. "Anything for you, doll."

I smirk as Dawson's grip on me tightens.

"Watch it," he warns his friend.

I take a long deep breath before reluctantly stepping out of Dawson's strong arms. There's no point in putting this off any longer. I snake the last book off my desk and tuck it under my arm. Slowly I walk down the narrow hall and into the living room. Frank ceases his pacing when he notices me. Russell keeps walking past me toward the door with the last box. Dawson stays rigid beside me like a viper waiting to strike. I twist off my diamond ring and wedding band and set them on the dark stone mantel. My finger instantly feels naked without their weight.

"Goodbye, Frank," I say quietly as I finally meet his cold hard eyes.

"Wait. Can't we talk about this first?" He uncrosses his arms and takes a step in my direction.

Dawson moves in front of me. "Remember what I said? You touch her, and you'll be six feet under," he growls.

The police chief steps forward and holds a hand up.

"Abby, please stay." Frank's voice cracks on the last word.

I swallow past the lump in my throat. "There's nothing to talk about. It's over, Frank." I look away. Even after the hell he's put me through, it kills me to hurt him.

"I love you, Abby." His voice sounds like sandpaper as his mouth turns into a grim twist.

I close my eyes tightly before I meet his glassy eyes. I don't reply. Instead, I turn away from his sad face. With my heart breaking inside, I walk out the door, not looking back. I meant what I said; it's over. He's not the man I fell in love with, even though he wears his face. I would never have left that Frank.

"Are you sure you're okay to drive?" Dawson asks as he opens the driver's side door, and I don't hesitate to hop in my little blue Subaru. My car is the last of the things I had yet to take with me.

"I'm okay, Dawson. Let's get out of here." I don't meet his eyes. I'm afraid if I do, my frail wall will crumble. I'm barely holding on. My traitorous heart is begging me to run back to Frank.

"I'll have you follow Russell, and I'll be right behind you." He hovers in the opening for another second.

At my nod, he shuts the door and crosses in front of my car to the driver's side of his truck. Once he fires up the diesel, all three of us are off. As I leave the driveway, it's like a weight lifts off my chest, as if I can finally breathe again after being starved of oxygen. I finally did it. I got away, but will Frank tell the police the accident was my fault? Will he try to take the last thing I have from me?

The drive back to Dawson's was a blur. As soon as I got out of my car, I all but ran into Dawson's bedroom. I vaguely recall telling him I wanted to lie down. As if my heart couldn't hurt anymore, it feels as if it was split in two. I thought I'd be happy when I left. I may be free, but I'm devastated. This shouldn't have been our ending. We should've had the matching pair of chairs on the front porch when we were eighty, like we talked about so often.

Dawson

Busying myself with mindless tasks around the house doesn't take my mind off of Abby in the bedroom.

I rack my brain, trying to think of a way to make her feel better. I mean, what can you do for a woman who just left her abusive husband? Thinking back to all of our previous conversations, I place an order through one of those delivery services for some of her favorite things. By the time they arrive, she's still not out of the bedroom. I place my ear against the wooden door, hoping she just fell asleep, but no. She's still crying. I knock softly before entering.

The sight I'm greeted with nearly rips me apart. She's curled up in a ball on her side, sobbing. Her clothes are on the floor beside the bed, and she's wearing my shirt that's a few sizes too big for her small delicate frame. I climb into bed behind her and pull her in close. Her back pressed up against my chest.

"What can I do?" I'd do anything to make her feel better, to make her not hurt this badly.

"Just hold me," she says, her voice thick with emotion.

At some point, Abby's sobs quiet, and she falls asleep. I gently snag the blanket at the foot of the bed and cover us both. Listening to her rhythmic breathing is almost enough to put me to sleep. I don't want to, though. I want to savor the moment of her seeking comfort from me. Abby stretches and presses her body against mine, pushing her ass right into the hard-on I've been trying to hide, making me groan. She stills but doesn't move away. Fuck, this is some sick twisted torture right here. It takes all I have not to grind against her. My breath comes out in little pants as my cock throbs against her.

My hand splays on her hip, holding her there as I back up a little. I can't think clearly when her body is against my cock. She's hurting, and the last thing she needs is me trying to screw her brains out. Neither of us talks. Just the sound of our breathing exists in the room. She's probably thinking all kinds of horrible things about me taking advantage of the situation. That's not at all what I was trying to do. I only wanted to be here for her. She rolls over to face me, and her lips are just inches from mine. I'm waiting for the shoe to drop. For her to tell me she doesn't really want me.

"I'm sorry I'm such a mess." She pulls the covers up to her chin.

I smile at that notion. If she's a mess, she's one hell of a hot mess. "You're not a mess."

"Right, look at me," she huffs as she brushes the tear-soaked hair out of her face.

"I am looking at you, and I've never seen anyone more beautiful," I tell her honestly.

Her red-rimmed eyes flick to my mine before she replies in a whisper, "I think you're handsome."

I lick my lips, drawing her gaze to them. Shit, I'm screwing this all up. "Are you okay?" Dumb question, of course, she's not. What the fuck am I doing? Why do I always ask stupid questions?

She sighs, "I'm alright." Her gaze lands on something behind me and hurt flashes across her face. "I should go."

Thump. And there's the shoe. Where the fuck is this coming from? "What?"

"I don't think I should be here." She plucks at the edge of the blanket.

"Why the hell not?" My heart pounds against my breastbone like a jackhammer. She can't leave yet. It's not safe. How did I fuck this up already? What did I do wrong?

Her beautiful blues flick behind me again before hesitantly meeting my gaze. I roll over to see what could possibly make her think she should leave, and my heart sinks. It's the picture of Bella and me from New Orleans.

"That's my sister."

"Oh." A flush covers her cheeks as she twirls a lock of hair in her fingers.

"You can talk to me, you know? I'll listen." I'm not ready to explain about Bella yet.

She works her jaw back and forth. "I just didn't think it was going to be this hard." She pauses. "In my mind, he left me a while ago. I just wish I could forget the good times, the first years we were together," she says quietly.

I hate everything to do with her ex, but she needs to talk this out. "Tell me about him. I mean, before he was king douchebag."

She grins at my nickname for the prick. "We were together for just over eight years, married for five. He was sweet and thoughtful for most of it, and he was my best friend in college. He kept hounding me for months that we should date, but I kept turning him down. I didn't want to ruin our friendship if it didn't work out." She clears her throat, her brow creasing in memory.

"How did he win you over?" Asking for a friend.

At this, she laughs, the sound almost magical. "He started dating one of the only girls I really, really didn't like on campus. And well, I got jealous, which I didn't expect." She rubs her eyes and stifles a yawn.

"And then what?" I prompt her to keep going.

"Then we started dating and never looked back. It was perfect, everything I wanted. I thought he was the one, you know?" Her smile falls.

I know that feeling well. I thought Lexie was the one. I'm starting to wonder if I should keep prying into her past. "Then what changed?"

She rubs her eyes again. "How much of my medical file did you read?"

What does that have to do with anything? "Just what pertained to your accident and your care afterward. Why?"

She takes a minute before answering. Obviously, whatever she's going to say is uncomfortable for her.

"We've been trying to conceive for over three years. We both wanted a family. For some reason, I just couldn't." Abby takes a deep breath and closes her eyes. "I couldn't get pregnant even with in vitro, and they don't know why."

Shit, that's not what I was expecting. She keeps blinking back tears and looks anywhere but at me.

"I'm sorry, Abby. That must've been really hard on you guys." I splay my hand across her bare thigh.

"It was. Each time we heard the test result was negative, it was as if he lost a piece of the man he was. He started taking it out on me almost two years ago. Blaming me. Each time it got worse. I always hoped that if we got pregnant, it would make him go back to the man I fell in love with. But it never happened. My Frank is gone." She swipes at her eyes.

"Why did you stay?" What would make somebody not leave after all that?

She chews the inside of her cheek before answering, "I felt like I owed it to my best friend. Every once in a while, I'd see him within Frank, but it never lasted for long." She pauses. "I wasn't ready to give up on our marriage."

"What did he mean by you trying to kill him?" This question has been bouncing around in my brain since Frank said it. I can't picture this sweet woman capable of something like that. Knowing the circumstances of their relationship, I wouldn't blame her if she did try to kill him.

No answer.

"Abby?" I ask again.

"I didn't try to kill him." Her body tenses against my palm.

"Okay, I didn't say you did. What did he mean?"

"How about you? Why are you so invested in me? Why do you care so much?" Wow, that changed quickly. I'm not ready to tell her about Isabelle yet. At my silence, she continues, "Well?"

Fuck it. She wants to pry. I'll give her what she wants. "You really want to know? Fine, I actually saw you at the mall about two months before your accident. I was having lunch with Russell, and I heard you laughing with another woman-probably Chloe. I knew you were special even from a distance. I'd hear that seductive laugh in my sleep, calling to me. I didn't even know you then, but I was desperate to have you in my life. I about had a heart attack when I walked into that hospital room and saw you sitting there."

She swallows and licks her lips. "Why didn't you tell me?"

"Honestly, because it sounds crazy to me." I can't believe I told her all that. I should've waited.

"Not to me. It doesn't." Wrinkles stretch across the span of her forehead.

"Well, that's not where it ends. In the beginning, your story reminded me of my sister."

"How so?"

"Her fiance was abusive too, and she wouldn't listen to me. I begged her to leave him. She wouldn't. She thought he'd change. I was overseas when I got the call that it was too late." I rub the stubble along my jaw before revealing the whole fucked up truth. "He beat and strangled her to death."

"Shit Dawson, I'm sorry. What was her name?" She touches her own bruised throat and floods me with memories of Bella's death.

Watching Frank choke Abby made me wonder if that's how it was for Bella when she died. I close my eyes tight before answering, "Isabelle."

When I open them again, I can see the wheels turning in her head. Now she knows why I was so pushy with her to leave Frank.

"Bella's Safe Haven?" Her eyebrows scrunch together.

I nod, fighting the rawness I feel crawling up my throat. She moves closer to me, wrapping her arm around me. It seems she's not the only one seeking comfort tonight. "I inherited her insurance money, and I wanted to help other women like her. Like you. I wanted a safe place they could go."

"How long ago did it happen?"

"Almost two years ago." The same time frame Frank started beating her. A coincidence?

She snuggles in closer to my chest and sighs. I place my arm around her, my hand doing circles on her back. Her back that has no bra strap across it. This woman will be the death of me. I'm trying my hardest to be what she needs right now, and that's not having sex with her. But, damn, she's making this very hard for me.

"Do I need to start sleeping with one eye open, afraid you'll stake me?"

She looks up at me with a sad smile and shakes her head.

"Please, tell me why Frank said that. I won't judge." I try to coax it out of her.

"You're a mandated reporter, just like a teacher, right?"

"On some things, yes, but I'm not working, Abby. Whatever you tell me will stay between us. I promise." I hold my pinky up for her, and she seals the promise.

"The accident was my fault. We just left an appointment with the specialist, and she confirmed yet again that I failed to give him a child. In the truck, he grabbed me by the throat and accused me of sabotaging the embryo." She turns her face away. "The closer we got back home, I knew it was going to be so much worse this time. I could feel it. I couldn't go back to that house again. I asked him to pull over and let me out, but he refused. I felt like I had nowhere else to turn, and I lost it. I grabbed the wheel and fought with him over it. I thought if I made us go off the road, I'd be able to get out. He said he'd never let me go."

My blood turns to ice. He'd never let her go. It was too easy earlier. He's not done with her yet. "Why did you go back home with him after the accident?"

"After my first appointment with you, when Frank walked in on you helping me to walk, he thought I was cheating on him. He said if I left him or cheated, he'd tell the police I tried to commit suicide and take him with me. I'd lose my job. That was the only thing that brought me happiness. I couldn't let him take that away too."

"And now?" That makes sense with how she reacted to me after when I tried pushing her to talk.

"I'm terrified he'll still take that away from me." She pulls the blanket up to her chin.

"I won't let him. I wish you would've told me before. I would've helped you." I could've also saved her from even more abuse if I just would have pushed her harder. I brush the stray hairs out of her face.

"You did, though. Other than my weekly check-ins with my students, you were the only thing I looked forward to." Her voice cracks. "You were my last hope."

I gently pull the blanket down and rub a thumb along her chin. I see the truth in her beautiful blue eyes. Would it be wrong for me to tell her how much I looked forward to seeing her too? She needs time to heal, and I'm still not convinced I'm the right man for her.

"Seeing you was the best and worst part of my day."

Her brows furrow. It seems I can't shut my mouth this morning. "What do you mean?"

"The best because you're like the sun. You light up any room you're in. The worst because-" I stop myself from saying it out loud. Once it's out there, there's no going back.

"Because why Dawson?"

"You make me reckless. I was and still am jeopardizing my career because of my personal attachment to you. I've worked hard to get where I am, but I was ready to burn it all down for you. Abby, there's not much I wouldn't do to try to make you happy, and that scares me."

"Oh."

Silence. My heart thuds loudly in my ear. I think I've said too much.

"What if I feel the same way?" she says.

My heart rate stumbles, and my lungs aren't able to expand. "I'd feel as if I'm taking advantage of the situation. I don't want to hurt you any more than you already are."

"If anything, I'm taking advantage of you. I mean, I am staying at your place right now."

God, I want to kiss her so badly right now. "We'll take it one day at a time. Let's just get you feeling better, okay?"

She nods and rests her head back on my chest.

Chapter Seventeen

Abby

I haven't slept this long throughout the day since I first came out of surgery. I felt so at peace lying in Dawson's arms. Almost as if the past few years never even happened. Unfortunately, my puffy eyes, sore throat, and lost limb are all drastic reminders. I did too much walking the past few days with the new prosthetic. My leg hurts, but I don't want to tell Dawson. He'll start waiting on me hand and foot. I know he would. He's a good man like that. I need to be able to be independent, and he's already done so much for me. I won't be his burden. As it is, he hasn't gone back to work since he fought with Frank. I want to ask if he's in trouble for it, but I'm afraid of the answer. I don't know what I'd do if I cost him his job.

He said he'd start dinner a few minutes ago before he walked out of the bedroom. I grab a comfy pair of yoga pants but decide to keep his shirt on. It smells like him, and I'm not ready to give it up. Slipping the prosthetic onto my left leg, I stand and test the pain. Each step I take rubs my wound even harder. I take small measured steps, exhaling every time I place my fake left foot down until I reach the kitchen. He's standing in front of the stove, giving me a nice view of his behind. It should be against the law to look that good in a faded pair of blue jeans and a black t-shirt.

"What can I help with?"

"Nothing, I got it. Just take a seat." He doesn't turn around, but he motions with his head toward the chairs along the counter.

Big surprise. I pull out a chair and hop up on the bar stool. That's when I notice the flowers, pink lilies sitting in a crystal vase in the center of the table with some ferns in between. They weren't here earlier. Our conversation from before keeps playing through my mind. He has feelings for me. Whether that's lust or more, I still don't know. I do know I've completely fallen for him and have been for a long time. Every time I saw him, he left with yet another piece of my heart. Slowly chipping away at the cement that surrounded it for so long.

I know I shouldn't, but I want him. I want him with everything I have. And I'll be damned if it's not wrong on so many levels. He's my therapist, and I just left Frank. I need time to be alone to find out who I am and not jump into another relationship. But I fucking want him badly.

I bring the vase up to my nose and close my eyes. The sweet and comforting fragrance of my favorite flowers envelopes me before I'm reminded of Frank giving me them every time he hurt me. I open my eyes and find Dawson watching me, a boyish grin on his face.

"Did you get these for me?" I hold the smile in place.

"I did." He's so sweet, and it kills me.

"How did you know they were my favorite?" I raise my eyebrows at him. I don't recall having a conversation about flowers with him.

"Lucky guess, from the paintings in your office, and you had some in the hospital." He puts his hands in his front pockets and leans against the counter.

I did paint a lot of pink lilies. I smile genuinely. "Thank you."

"There it is. Your smile is exactly what I needed to see." He flashes me a cocky grin before turning back to tend to dinner.

I let my smile slip. I hate how I can't even look at lilies without remembering all the abuse. I'd come to expect those flowers after every shove or slap or strike. I won't tell Dawson that. I don't want to tarnish his gift.

"You don't like them, do you?" he asks quietly beside me. I didn't realize he even turned around. Sometimes he's so quiet it's unnerving.

"I love them, Dawson."

He leans on the counter beside me, and a thoughtful frown appears before his eyes grow suddenly intense. "Please don't lie to me. If I did something wrong, you need to tell me so I can fix it."

"You didn't do anything wrong."

"Then why do you look like a puppy just died?" When he comes closer, my body tenses involuntarily. He notices and takes a step back, his voice growing gruff, "Tell me what's wrong."

After everything, he deserves my honesty. "He used to buy me lilies after...." I take a deep breath and pull my fingers in my lap. I can't even look him in the eye. "After every incident."

He sucks in a breath, snatches the flowers off the table, and heads for the trash.

"No, don't!"

He tossed them in the trash. "I won't ever buy you lilies again. I'm sorry, sunshine. Do all flowers remind you of the abuse?"

"No. Just those. You didn't have to throw them away." What a waste of beautiful flowers.

"Yes. I did. I'll buy you different ones."

"You really don't need to."

"I know I don't need to, but I want to."

"Has anybody ever told you that you're stubborn?" I chuckle.

"I could say the same to you." Dawson laughs and starts to take a step toward me before he hesitates and then turns back to the stove.

That's when I notice he was making grilled cheese, another one of my favorites. He reaches up and grabs two wine glasses from the cupboard, and pours us a glass of merlot. I'm on to him now. Three of my favorites? Mister wants to get me feeling better first. Dawson remembers our conversations at the hospital. Over cards, we talked about our favorite foods. His are bourbon and steak.

"Are you trying to win me over?" I ask coyly when he saunters over to me with the glasses.

"That depends. Is it working?" He leans forward on the counter until he's so close that his cologne filters into my nose. That familiar spicy, woodsy scent makes my stomach muscles tighten.

"Maybe," I say, biting my lip as desire flashes in his eyes, making the air around us feel charged.

"Noted," he says, turning around to grab his cell phone while he waits on the food to finish.

I take a moment to catch my breath. When he's around me, all I want him to do is kiss me again. I felt more alive than I ever have when his lips were on mine. I can't imagine what it would be like to sleep with him. The two kisses we shared in my car will never be enough for me. All they did was stoke the fire that burns just for him. I watch him flip the sandwiches over and wonder what I have to do to get him to kiss me again. Whatever the cost, I'll pay it.

He slides a plate over to me and sits beside me. The grilled cheese is perfect, with just the right amount of crispy brown butter. After our meal, Dawson doesn't let me clean up the kitchen. Instead, he orders, actually orders me to sit on the couch so we can watch a movie. He joins me shortly with a soft flannel blanket and sits next to me. As his weight dips the cushions, my body presses against his side. He feels so warm and inviting that I don't move, and he wraps his arm around my shoulders. He clicks through the options with the remote.

"What kind of movie do you like?"

My first choice would be a chick flick, but I'm not in the mood to watch happy couples after everything that's transpired these last few days. "Action?"

"How about this one?"

Looks promising. "Sure."

A few minutes into the movie, the doorbell rings. He grins as he stands, and I watch him curiously as he pulls the door open. I shake my head when he comes through the living room and sets two vases of flowers down on the coffee table. One has red peonies, and the other has various shades of pink and purple dahlias. He disappears to the door again and nudges it closed with his foot before coming back with two more. White roses and yellow tulips. You can't even see the coffee table now. Wetness coats my eyes as I look at him, and I don't know what to say. This is a ridiculous amount of flowers for one person, but I have a feeling he's a go-big or go-home kind of person.

"Is this too much?" he asks warily, eyeing the table.

"Yes, it is. But, I love them all, thank you." I stand up and wrap my arms around him. He hugs me back tightly, and we both stand there holding on to each other for several minutes before settling back on the couch.

I don't even really pay attention to what's on the screen. I rest my head against his shoulder and close my eyes. At some point, he stretches out, and I find myself on his chest. His heart is playing me a lullaby I can't resist. I can't describe the feeling in my chest as he wraps his arms around me and holds me against him. Like I've finally found where I belong. As if I've been drifting out to sea all these years, and he's the anchor I longed for. That I searched for without ever having the conscience thought.

What a day it's been. I still can't believe I finally left Frank. Something tells me I haven't seen the last of him, though.

Dawson

"You know, I can cook too, right?" Abby comes to stand beside me at the stove the next morning.

After giving her a quick glance, I say, "You're my guest, so no."

"Come on, Dawson, I've been here for a few days now. Let me help," she whines.

I'm beginning to like that sound. It means she's getting more comfortable with me, showing me a side of her she usually keeps hidden. I smirk at little miss attitude as she places a hand on her hip.

"What's so funny?" She squeezes my side in an attempt to tickle me.

"Hey, now," I warn as I laugh and shake the spatula at her.

The sexual desire her hands so innocently bring to the surface shocks me every time. If I didn't know any better, I'd say she's flirting with me. She backs away from me and giggles, but she's still got that twinkle in her eye. God, I haven't kissed her in days. I haven't slept with her yet, and I already think I love her. No. I know I do. Just thinking about what her mouth tastes like makes my heart race. The mixture of her and that watermelon chapstick is like nothing I've tasted before. It doesn't help that she's wearing my shirt and a pair of ass-loving yoga pants. She looks so soft and warm beneath the material.

"Fine." Abby reaches above her to the cupboard and takes down two plates, followed by two glasses. "Orange juice?"

"Yes, please." I try really hard not to stare at her ass as she bends over into the fridge. I really tried, but man, that perfect heart-shaped ass is any man's dream.

I'm a horrible person. She's still getting used to her prosthetic, and here I am, too busy taking advantage of her not having mastered how to squat down. I exhale slowly and pull my gaze back to the frying pan. I don't look her way again until the eggs have finished and the toast pops up. I distract myself by buttering the toast as she moves across the kitchen and winces before filling the glasses at the bar.

"Is your prosthetic bothering you?" I ask as I bring our plates over and set them in front of her.

"Only a little, but it's okay."

"Here, let me take a look." I pull the bar stool next to her out and start to kneel down in front of her.

She frowns. "No, really. I'm okay, just getting used to it."

"If it gets worse, let me know." I search her features but feel like she's hiding how bad it is. I want to push her to open up more to me, but I worry if I push too hard, too soon, she'll leave.

"I will. This looks delicious, thank you."

"You're welcome."

We both eat our breakfast quietly. This has been our routine for the past four days. We eat and shower, she works on her laptop, and I work on mine for a while. It's amazing how fast we've settled into a rhythm with each other. Even having my roommate Ralph, this place will feel empty when she leaves. That thought makes the floor come out from my feet. I knew this was temporary, but I don't want her to go. I'm a selfish bastard for wanting her to stay. She needs time to process leaving her asshole husband, time to adjust to everything this world has thrown at her lately. I know firsthand how cruel life can be and how important it is to get your head on straight. I can't stay here watching her eat and counting down the days until she leaves me.

"I'm going to go hop in the shower," I say as I grab my empty plate and head for the sink.

She still has half her meal left. She nods to me before shoving another forkful into her mouth. I stare at my bed when I enter the room. The blankets are still rumpled from when we got up earlier. I think that's the hardest part of all of this. She's sleeping in my bed beside me every single night. Most mornings, I wake up to her on my chest or snuggled in close. As soon as she's awake, she apologizes sheepishly and puts some space between us.

Opening my dresser, I grab a clean pair of jeans, boxer briefs, and socks. I snatch a plain black t-shirt off the hanger in my closet before heading to the bathroom just down the hall. I can barely see Abby from the doorway. She's got her elbows resting on the counter and her chin on her palms. Deep in thought. I wonder what she's thinking about. Before I do something stupid and ask her to join me in the shower, I hurry up and shut the door.

Stepping under the hot spray, I can't stop my mind from conjuring images of her naked in here with me. Fuck, get it together, man. It's been what a year since I've been laid? Maybe that's why this is so fucking hard. I shower quickly. Turning the water off and drying off, I'm painfully aware of the pulsing ache between my legs. After pulling my jeans on and reaching for my shirt, a crashing noise comes through the walls. Shit! He's here. I yank the door open and bolt out of the bathroom and barrel down the hallway, ready to pulverize that son of a bitch. All possibilities run through my mind of what he could be doing to her. No sign of him. I don't see Abby either.

"Abby!" I bellow.

I come to a screeching halt on the edge of the kitchen as the yell leaves my throat. Abby's on the floor picking up pieces of a shattered plate, and she jumps back, startled, and drops the pieces.

"I- I'm so-sorry I didn't mean to. I lost my balance, and it, it fell." Her prosthetic is on the floor beside her. It must've popped off during the fall.

Her normally bright blue eyes are filled with tears as she shrinks away from me as if I'd hit her. That fucking gutted me. It's not her fault. I know that, but it still hurts like hell. That's just another reason why I hate him. Another reason why we need to take things slow. Why I've been trying my damnedest not to kiss her because I know I'll lose control. When her lips are on mine, all of that disappears, and I forget that I need to be careful with her.

"Hey, it's okay. Don't worry about it," I say, kneeling as I start to pick up the jagged pieces of porcelain.

As I get closer to her, she pulls her legs into her chest, hides her face, and sobs quietly. I can't take that. She needs to know I'd never lay a hand on her and that she's safe with me. I place the broken remains of the plate on the counter and crouch beside her.

"Sunshine, look at me."

She slowly peeks her red-rimmed eyes above her arm and takes several deep, long breaths as if to slow her breathing.

"I'm going to help you up now, okay?"

At her nod, I slowly slide one arm behind her lower back and the other under her thighs as she tenses. Picking her up and holding her close to my bare chest, I walk over to the counter and reluctantly set her down on it. She's almost at eye level with me here, standing between her thighs. She wipes the tears away and won't look at me as she apologizes yet again.

"I don't care about the plate. I care about you. Are you cut anywhere?" I ask her quietly as I search her bare skin.

"No, I'm okay."

"We both know that's not true." At my words, her watery gaze finds mine. "You have to know...." I pause and hold my hands up in front of her as my voice grows raw, "these hands will never, ever be used to hurt you." In this lighting, the bruising around her throat stands out in contrast with her light skin. The marks are taking forever to fade. I cup her chin lightly, caressing her cheek with my thumb. "Please tell me you know that?"

"I do." She pulls her lower lip in with her teeth before whispering, "I don't know what's wrong with me. I know you wouldn't."

I rest my forehead on hers and drop my hand to her waist. I sigh. I wish I can take it all away for her. "There's absolutely nothing wrong with you, Abby. It's a normal reaction after what you've been through."

"But I don't want that reaction. Especially not with you." She places her hands on each one of my bare pecs.

My pulse is still thundering in my ears, even with the threat of Frank gone. I'd be surprised if she couldn't feel it beneath her palms. There's nothing in between our skin to diminish it. She swirls her finger around my tattoo. Abby turns her head slightly to the side, our breaths mingling. I close my eyes, willing myself to stop and not kiss her. All the reasons why I shouldn't disappear. Her watermelon-scented chapstick is the only thing on my mind. Her hand burns a trail up my chest to the side of my neck as she pulls me down toward her mouth.

"Abby." I don't know if my plea was for her to stop and push me away or to keep pulling me in to kiss me.

"Dawson." The way my name sounds on her lips breaks the last frayed strings of my will.

My lips crash down on hers as my hold on her hips tightens. She tastes even better than I remembered. Every nerve ending is like a wildfire when her hand blazes down my chest. She grabs my sides and tugs me in until there's no space left between our bodies. I'm aware of her heat pressing against my throbbing cock. She feels as perfect as I thought she'd be. She starts to rub herself against me. Fuck! What I wouldn't give to have her naked underneath me right now. Her fingers thread through my hair and gently pulls on the strands. I slowly run my hands up her body until her head is cradled in them. Heat dances across my back, and awareness floods through me.

I break the kiss and step away from her. I shouldn't have let it get that far. We're both breathing heavily, and my fingers grasp the counter behind me to keep me there when I notice the wetness on the sock of her leg.

"Your leg," I say roughly, edging closer so I can gently slide the thin beige sock off her stump. When she winces in pain, I instantly freeze, not wanting to cause her any more pain.

"It's okay." She places a reassuring hand on my shoulder, prompting me to keep going.

Peeling the sock off, I notice her skin is red, raw and painful looking. It's not bleeding but oozing a clear liquid. The infection has been building for a few days.

"Why didn't you tell me it was this bad?"

She sighs. "I thought it was normal, and you've been so helpful with everything. I just didn't want to burden you any more than I already have."

"You'll never be a burden to me," I tell her seriously and shake my head. Then my voice softens. "I enjoy taking care of you."

I grab the salve I keep in the junk drawer in my kitchen and coat the wound with a thin layer of ointment. I rest my forehead against hers. Now that I've had another taste of her, I crave Abby even more. She starts to tilt her mouth in search of mine. I can't let her kiss me again. I won't be able to stop myself from taking her to my bed. And I can't have sex with her until I know I won't make things worse for her. When I pull back slightly, I see the hurt in her eyes.

"I'm sorry, sunshine. I can't; you're still my patient until we can get you into Sandra's schedule." I latch on to the most logical explanation I can think of as I run my hand down the side of her face.

"Is that all that's stopping you?" She twirls a lock of blonde hair around her fingers.

"No." I make the mistake of looking back down at her sexy mouth.

"Then what?" she whispers the question.

"You're in pain, and you need help. I'm not trying to be an asshole here, but after what you experienced at his hand, I just don't want to fuck this up. You deserve to be happy."

"So, you don't want me because I'm broken?" Her gaze falls to the broken plate on the counter.

I grab her hand and place it on my erection. "I think we can both agree that I want you. I never said you were broken. I said you needed help. Do you know what it does to me to see you flinch away from me? It fucking kills me, but more than that, I don't want that life for you. I don't want you getting triggered constantly. That's not a way for you to live. I'm going to get you the help you need, and then by god, I'm going to fuck that tight little pussy until the only man you remember ever touching you is me." The last few words come out as a growl.

Her eyes widen as she gasps. Yeah, my little sunshine, I did just say all that. Now she knows what's been going on in this head of mine. Right or wrong, it's out there. Sandra can take over her care as long as I can keep tabs on her; hopefully, that'll be here. I wish she'd stay. I think I might need her more than she needs me.

Chapter Eighteen

Dawson

Yesterday, I was able to talk Abby into wearing one of the anklets we offer the women at the shelter. It looks like a dainty chain with a small butterfly, but it actually has a tracker embedded into it. She didn't want to believe Frank would be capable of kidnapping or killing her. Unfortunately, I've seen it happen with one of the women from Bella's. Her boyfriend found her while she was at work and took her when she left late at night. She managed to escape with her life, barely. That's what spawned the idea for these small dainty chains. We would never use them unless it were under dire circumstances. Luckily that hasn't happened often.

Abby wanted to keep up her ritual of going to the mall with Chloe on Saturdays. As much as I hated the thought of her sticking to a routine that Frank could know, it was good to see her with her friend. Of course, that meant I would go with them just in case he decided to show up. I kept my distance for the most part unless Abby started looking for me. I didn't want her to feel like she was smothered. I don't know how Frank was about her friendships, but I'm sure he tried to limit her free time with them. That's something I would never do. Even if we married, she wouldn't be mine to control.

"I don't mind you staying with us, you know?" she'd said earlier when Chloe used the restroom.

"I want to make sure you have your space. It's important for you to have friends like that, she's good to you. I like her," I told her.

"Well, that's good to hear because you're staying with us for the rest of the day." Abby crossed her arms over her chest.

"Oh, I am, am I?" I grinned at her.

"What kind of boyfriend acts like a creep and just follows them around?"

"Boyfriend?" My heart swelled when the word boyfriend left her lips. I didn't care about the creep part. Although it does seem like that's what I did. This was the first time a label came up when it came to our relationship. Boyfriend and girlfriend doesn't seem to fit the connection we share, but I'll take it.

She swallowed and bit the corner of her lip before asking, "I don't know. Is that what we are?"

"I like the sound of that." I pulled her hand up to my mouth so I could kiss each one of her knuckles.

Moments later, the ladies dragged me to their favorite coffee shop located inside the bookstore. Coffee Addict wasn't exactly what I expected to find. It had the usual hustle and bustle of customers getting their daily dose of coffee, which was actually a fairly decent cup. There were plenty of customers who sat at the small square tables and worked from their computers or had a book in their hands.

What I loved most about it, though, was the view. The cafe sat directly in the center of the first floor, and the bookcases went outwards from the center, so I felt comfortable staying at one of the tables while they perused the many shelves of the bookstore. I could see them no matter which aisle they went down as long as they stayed on that floor. Abby seemed lighter and happier today. Almost as if nothing was wrong in her world. I enjoyed watching her from a distance and seeing that beautiful smile grace her face.

Once we get home and have dinner together, I realize Abby's mood has changed, and she seems timid and quiet. "Is everything okay?"

"Yeah, I'm just tired."

"How about after dinner, we go to bed?" The thought of being that close to her so soon makes the tips of my fingers tingle in anticipation.

"It's only five."

"We could watch a movie instead?" I offer.

One she'll probably pass out during as well. She fell asleep not even halfway through the last movie we tried to watch. I didn't mind. She was in my arms. That's all that mattered.

"That sounds good." She takes another bite of her steak.

I love this time of year. When I do cook at home, it's usually on the grill. Steak, chicken, burgers, you name it. My phone interrupts our conversation. It's the ringtone I have set for Maggie. She doesn't call often, and I just replaced all the appliances.

"Hey Maggie, what's up?" I ask, trying to tamp down the unease crawling up my spine.

"Dawson," she cries, instantly putting me on alert. "Our power was cut, and there's a man banging on the door. He already broke the window with a crowbar."

"Son of a bitch! Did you call the police?" I bark out the question.

I jerk to a stand, and the stool screeches across the tile in protest. Abby's fork drops into her plate with a clang.

"Yes. They're on their way. But he's yelling your name," confusion laces her words.

It feels like a bucket of ice water just got dumped on me. It's Frank. It must be. I'll be damned if he thinks terrorizing the other woman will get his way. He must think Abby's in there. "I'll be right there. Get the women to the panic room, and don't come out."

He better not have touched a single hair on any of them. This is low, even for him. Does he really think I would hand over Abby like she's some piece of property? What doesn't he get that he's already lost her?

"We're in there," she says with a sob.

"Stay on the phone with me." To Abby's worried expression, I say, "I'll be right back. You stay here and don't leave this house."

"Why, what's wrong?"

"An emergency at the shelter. I've got to get down there."

"Dawson, promise you'll be careful!"

"Of course." I kiss her on the forehead and grab my pistol from the top of the fridge, tucking my gun into the waistband of my jeans. I don't want to tell her it's Frank. She doesn't need to know. He's over there and not a threat to her here. Swiping my keys, I rush out the door and lock it behind me. My tires squeal on the way out of the driveway. Bella's Safe Haven is only ten minutes out, and that's when I'm not pissed off and driving like a crazed man.

I put my phone on speaker while I drive. The girls are crying on the other line, but I know they're safe in the panic room I had built for this reason. Well, not Frank. But douchebags like him. I wanted a fail-safe if they got past the security gate and the doors that can only be opened by a switch from inside. How the hell did he manage to get through? Catching every damn red light on my way, I throw my hazard lights on and punch my foot on the gas. Angry horns sound as I cut people off. I don't give a fuck, though. They don't realize lives are at stake.

The drive seems endless but, in reality, not long at all. I come to a screeching halt in front of the little white building, with the security fence gaping open. There are still a few hours of daylight left which will help me. No other vehicles are in the yard. I beat the cops here. Slamming my pickup into park, I bolt out of the rig with my gun in my palm. The weight is a familiar feeling in my hands.

"I'm here. Where the fuck are you?" I shout into the wind.

Not a sound. I yell again on my walk up the steps to the entrance. The front door is open by a few inches. I nudge it wider, my hand steady with the pistol. I don't see anyone yet. The front rooms are clear. My phone's in my pocket, and I can't hear the women through the fabric. I inch through the hall, careful of being an open target in case Frank is armed, and check each room one by one. Every single room is empty, and I'm not seeing him anywhere. Furniture's been tossed around, and windows have their glass scattered across the floor. Still no appearance from Frank.

"Where are you motherfucker?" I growl. He wanted me, and he's got me. Now, where is he hiding?

Sirens alert me to the police arriving on the scene. As soon as I hear their boots treading along the wooden floors, I call out to them, announcing who I am. We exchange information and clear the premises for the second time. He's not here. Something's not right. I let the ladies out of the safe room and try to call Abby. No answer. I call again, and still Abby doesn't pick up.

Panic seizes my chest. Realization hits. Getting me out of the house was all a ploy. I gave Frank exactly what he wanted. My scalp tingles as fear takes hold of me. That son of a bitch. I run back to my truck and drive like a madman back to my house. I never said anything to the police. I just bolted. I already lost close to an hour at the shelter. I can't waste another minute explaining to them what's happening.

Come on, Abby. Pick up the damn phone! I keep calling her on repeat as my diesel turns hard on the sharp corners that aren't meant to be taken at the speeds I'm going. Reaching my driveway, I slam on my brakes, nearly sliding into the garage before the big truck stops. Throwing my door open and running across the lawn, I see the window in the front door is broken. Fuck!

"Abby!"

No answer.

Shoving the door open so hard it slams against the wall behind it, I run through the house. "Abby! Frank! Answer me!"

No answer. Nothing but eerie silence greets me. In the kitchen, the bar stools are knocked over, and her dinner is still sitting half-eaten on the counter. A small puddle of blood coats the kitchen floor. I take my phone out. I have a tracker in her anklet that I gave her. The app is taking forever to load. I tap my foot restlessly on the floor.

Loading, loading, tracking. The app is taking far too long to tell me where she is. Standing here just waiting isn't settling well with me. I need action, and I need to do something, anything, to find her. Finally, the tracker emblem disappears. There she is, about five miles out. I rush back to my truck and floor it in the direction the app shows she is.

I can't believe I was that stupid. I should've known better. I should've seen this coming. I knew it was too easy last week. Hold on, sunshine. I'm coming for you. Frank better fucking pray he didn't hurt her.

Abby

Watching Dawson leave in such a hurry really worries me. From his part of the conversation, I can only assume the women at the shelter he owns are in trouble. I push my plate away, suddenly not hungry. Hearing him raise his voice that way sent me right back to my time with Frank. I know he didn't mean to. I could see the guilt in his eyes. He was mad at himself. I wish I weren't such a baby. I know he's not like Frank, and I'm safe with him, but as he said, I need help. I reached out to a therapist several days ago, and I have my first appointment scheduled with her tomorrow.

He won't do more than kiss me until I not only get professional help but switch over to Sandra's care. I already called her too, but she can't fit me into her schedule for nearly two weeks. I don't think I'll last even a week more without Dawson touching me. I know he's holding back, afraid of breaking me more than I already am. I'm not a porcelain doll, and he needs to realize that. Sex with him would be much different than with Frank, the main reason being I don't fear Dawson. I may flinch involuntarily at some of his actions, but it's not him. It's the sudden movements or the loud noises. Sometimes I don't even know what triggers them. But I know one hundred percent. It's not Dawson himself.

As my mind drifts off to all kinds of possibilities the women could be experiencing, tires crunch on the gravel of the driveway. Hmm. Dawson must've forgotten something because he's only been gone for five, maybe ten minutes. I chew the inside of my cheek, trying to figure out a way to apologize for being triggered so easily. Footsteps thud up the stairs on the front porch. Smash. The glass window from the door rains shards down across the living room floor. It's not Dawson! I jump off of the stool and hobble to the side of the kitchen where the knives are stashed. The click of the door being unlocked makes me fumble. Where did I leave my phone?

Bile rises up into my throat. I don't have time to hide, and I wouldn't be fast enough or quiet enough with my leg. Dread builds in the pit of my stomach as I hear the familiar stomp of Frank's rage. I drag in ragged breaths, and sweat forms on my palms. Sure enough, he rounds the corner.

"There you are," he barks.

"Frank, please just leave me alone!" I cry out, hoping the neighbors will hear and call the police. The houses down this stretch of the road are close together.

"I gave you your space. Now you're coming back home with me where you belong," Frank says in a low, menacing voice.

I hold the knife out in front of me and scream so loud my throat burns, "Get out!"

"You won't use that on me." He laughs, the sound grinding on my already frayed nerves.

"I don't want to use it. Just go," I beg him.

My phone is sitting behind him on the counter by my plate. If I could get to it, I can call 911. He reaches for me, and I swipe the knife at him, slicing the meaty part of his palm with the razor-sharp blade. I sidestep around him to get out of his reach.

"Ah! What the fuck?" he yells at me.

As he's distracted by his wound, I dart around him to the other side of the bar. Not quick enough, my fingers brush the edge of the cell phone and push it farther away. He grabs me by the hair and yanks me back from the counter. I stumble, crashing into the bar stool and sending it skittering across the floor along with the knife. My prosthetic pops off as my body lands on the unforgiving tiles with a loud smack. I desperately scramble from him, clawing my way across the floor. With my hands slick with sweat and my prosthetic out of reach, I'm unable to pull myself up to flee.

"Why do you always have to make things so fucking difficult, Abby?" Frank pulls me up to sit, and the smell of alcohol on his breath turns my nose up. Great, he's drunk. He's always worse when he drinks.

"Help!" I scream out as loud as I can. Praying for somebody to hear me.

He slaps his hand over my mouth and reaches above me to the counter where a towel sits. "Shut the fuck up, or this will be even worse for you."

"Please, Frank. If there's any part of my friend left in you, let me go," I plead.

He answers by bringing the towel around my head and making a knot in the front. He tightens the towel, ensuring the knot in my mouth keeps me silent. I try not to gag.

His hand is still trickling blood. He yanks zip ties from his back pocket, and my heart sinks. I shake my head as he tightens them around my wrists. I try to pull my arms back, but he just rakes them behind me, pushing my face down to the floor. The plastic bites into my wrists as they click tighter and tighter.

"You'll pay for what you've done," he snarls against the shell of my ear.

Once my arms are bound behind my back, he pulls me up against him. I stagger and am unable to balance without my prosthetic. He picks me up and throws me over his shoulder like I weigh nothing, knocking the breath out of my lungs. He opens the front door while I squirm and buck in his arms, with a scream locked in my throat because of the gag. Trying to free myself only manages to piss him off even more. He throws me into the truck, and I slam against the passenger side door. I try to pull my hands free, but it's no use. There's no give to the bindings. The action only makes them cut into my skin deeper.

He peels out of the driveway and heads away from the city. I try to recall where we are and what turns we make, but I keep getting jostled around. My face hits the window, and pain explodes behind my eye. I think he took two rights and a left. Or was it three rights and a left? I don't recognize the area we're in. The truck rumbles to a stop in front of a vacant building. The windows are boarded up, and the lawn is almost waist-high with a mixture of grass and weeds. There are no other buildings in sight. We're alone out here.

He's going to kill me. This will be the end of me. I cry out. My breathing comes faster and faster against the knot as I struggle for oxygen. He opens his door, and I kick him with the heel of my right foot, shoving him back against the open truck door.

His eyes widen, and he grits his teeth. Once he rights himself, he pulls a black handgun from his waistband behind his back and pistol whips me on my cheek. Pain rips into my face and blood drips from the wound and onto my shirt. That's not his usual go-to. The way he's looking at me seems almost feral. A chill racks my body. There's something very, very wrong with this man. If I go into that building, there's a good chance I'm not coming back out. I'm not ready to die.

"Try something like that again, and you'll have an extra hole in you. But don't worry, love. I won't shoot to kill you. At least not immediately." He smiles at me. The arch of his lips is almost as unsettling as his eyes.

He plans on torturing me. "What happened to you?" I mumble around the gag, but I'm not sure that he can understand me.

"You did this to me!" He grabs my ankle and yanks me to the edge of the seat as I try to kick him with it. I use my good leg to fight him off—my hands are useless tied behind my back—but he's too strong, and he once again hauls me across his shoulder.

I scream and scream until nothing else comes out. My tears wet the back of his shirt as I'm helplessly carried into the building. It was all a setup. I bet there wasn't an emergency at Bella's Safe Haven. Frank just wanted Dawson out of the house.

My anklet! Dawson said there was a tracker in it. I thought he was crazy at first, but I agreed to wear it all the time. If this came from Frank, it would be controlling but coming from Dawson. I know he wouldn't abuse it. I knew it would make him feel better after the loss he suffered with his sister. I didn't want to admit to myself that this situation could be a possibility. I'm sure Dawson's seen no shortage of messed-up stuff at the shelter. I'm hoping it was all a hoax. If not, he may not notice me missing for hours. And then what? There might not be anything left of me to save.

The rusted metal door creaks open, and it's dark and cold inside. He keeps walking farther and farther into the building. He knows his way around in here. He must have been planning my kidnapping. But for how long? The hairs on my neck raise. How did he even find me? I never turned my old cell phone on at Dawson's place, only at the store where I bought a new one he couldn't trace.

Suddenly, he slams me down onto a metal chair, ripping a gasp from my lungs and snapping my head back from the force. Before I have time to react, he grabs my arms and thrusts them behind the backrest before securing them with more zip ties. He paces in front of me. I watch silently, wondering what his next move is. I've never seen him this far gone. I don't know what to expect or how to prepare myself mentally for whatever is going to happen next.

"Why him?" he nearly spits the words at me.

The question throws me off, and I mutter against the towel. "What?"

Frank lunges toward me and yanks the gag down hard, and I cry out. The towel now rests just below my chin.

"Why did you choose him? Have I not provided for you, cared for you, loved you?"

Are you serious right now? "This isn't love, Frank," I mumble.

"Do not tell me what this is!" He slaps me across the face.

I wince at the pain. "You won't get away with this."

"What makes you so sure?" He tilts his head to the side and crosses his arms across his chest.

"He'll come for me." I lift my chin defiantly. He will. He has to.

"Oh my dear, I'm counting on it. Your knight in shining armor won't look so pretty dead, will he?"

He cocks the gun in his hand, sending my heart crashing against my ribs.

"You don't have to hurt him. He's not part of this. I'll go home with you. Just leave him out of it," I beg.

"I warned you. There's nowhere you can hide where I won't find you."

I swallow down the vomit rising to my mouth, nearly choking on it in the process. I have no way to warn Dawson if he does show up that it's a trap. He'll die not knowing that I love him. I thought I suffered heartache before, but it was nothing like this. My heart feels as if it's shattering into a million sharp little pieces, just like the bookmark back at Dawson's. Every jagged edge cuts deeper and deeper into me, threatening to shatter my soul just as easily.

I can't be the reason Dawson dies. That I know I won't survive. I'd rather die than be that person. I bide my time as Frank asks question after question, each one more bizarre than the last. And then I hear a squeak from the door we entered in from earlier.

Chapter Nineteen

Dawson

"Just fucking meet me there, Murphy!" I shout into the phone before ending the call.

The gap between me and Abby's signal is closing as my truck thunders down the road. I can't be too late. I just can't. I won't fail her as I did Bella. I won't allow him to take her from this world. That douchebag's a dead man. The app leads me to an abandoned warehouse on the outskirts of town. His truck is parked by the door. After hopping out and closing my door with a barely audible click, I press my ear to the door. Mumbled yelling from Frank reaches me. It's hard for me not to rush in, knowing it's Abby, my Abby, my sunshine on the other side of this door. This is where I can't let her affect my judgment. I need to go back to all the experiences I had with hostiles in the military.

She could die if I fuck this up.

I shoulder the door open, and it squeaks in protest. Holding my breath, I wait to see if Frank notices. Nothing but more shouting. "You thought you could leave me that easily? Throw away the last eight years of our lives together? After everything I've done for you, you ungrateful bitch!"

Smack, skin against skin. I cringe as she cries out. My blood is boiling just beneath my skin. He'll fucking pay for that. Edging along the wall of a hallway, until finally getting a peek around a corner at them. She's about thirty feet away, and he has her tied down to a metal chair, a strip of fabric under her chin from a gag. Her tears mingle with the blood from a gash on her cheek.

"Fuck you!" Abby screams.

My heart calls out for her to stay strong for a few more minutes. I don't have a good shot on him; he's behind a steel pillar. I wait as he continues to berate her. She continues to whimper and shakes her head at him. I take a few more steps. Abby notices me and involuntarily stiffens, giving away my presence. I press myself against the wall as his shouts stop. This just got a whole lot harder.

"Is that the hero already? Coming to save the day, are you? Well, not this time," Frank snarls.

"Frank, stop! Please! I'll go with you; just leave him alone. I'm begging you," she cries.

Breathe in, breathe out. Muffled footsteps draw near.

"It's too late for that."

The finality in his voice gives himself away: Abby or I wouldn't be walking out of here. With his obsession with her, most likely, I would be the target. I search for another way around this wall to get to Abby. I don't see one. There's a tin can by my feet. I pick it up and throw it as far as I can. The can rattles as it bounces off the wall and lands on the floor nearly twenty feet away. That'll make him think I'm on the other side of the hall. Sure enough, he stalks right past me and into my crosshairs. Dumbass.

I won't give him a second chance to get to her. He'll never be able to touch her again. Exhaling, I pull the trigger. Bang, the sound rebounds off the walls and echoes across the building. The bullet pierces the back of his skull, and he drops to the floor, the gun falling from his grasp. Blood and brain matter, along with chunks of skin and hair, dot the walls. Abby screams.

"Abby, I'm coming." I kick the gun away from Frank and check his pulse. But I already know. He's gone. He won't be able to hurt anybody ever again. I run to Abby, gently brushing the hair out of her face first.

"Dawson, I thought you were-" she cries out.

"Shhh. It's okay. I'm right here." I kiss her forehead and pull out my knife to work on the rest of her bindings.

"You came for me?" Her forehead wrinkles as if she didn't think I would. I know I've been holding back, but I thought she understood how deeply I care for her.

"I'll always come for you. There's not a force on this Earth strong enough to keep me away, sunshine."

He zip-tied her, and the plastic is cutting into her skin. She flinches as I saw through them, trying my best not to hurt her. I wish I could bring Frank back just to torture him first. As soon as she's free, she wraps her arms around me and clings to me like a lifeline as she sobs into the crook of my neck. Holding her and rubbing her back, I realize just how terrified I was of losing her. My hands shake now that some of the adrenaline has passed. I'm not letting her slip through my fingers unless she wants to. I don't think she does, though.

"Frank?" she asks quietly, pulling her head back while not releasing her grip on me.

I hate having to tell her. "He's gone, Abby."

More tears cascade down her face as she nods. She loved him enough at one point to marry him. I hate that it had to be me that ended his life.

"He won't ever be able to hurt you or anyone else again." It'll kill me if she hates me for this, but if she does, at least I know she's safe. It's an outcome I'll respect. She presses her shaking body closer to me and hides her face in the crook of my shoulder. "I have to call this in."

"I know."

I pull my phone out of my back pocket and call Murphy back while still holding her with my other arm.

"Are they going to arrest you?" Her watery gaze searches mine.

"I don't know. Let's go out to my truck while we wait."

I help her from the chair, and she leans heavily on me. There's no prosthetic or crutches to help her. I block her view of the hallway. She doesn't need to see Frank like that. Once outside, I open the passenger side door and hoist her up so she's still facing me.

"You can't go to jail for this, Dawson. Please, tell them I did it," she whispers. "I don't want you to-"

"Shhh. It's okay. Look at me, sunshine." I place both of my hands on the sides of her head and wait until her teary blue eyes find mine. "If I do end up in prison, it was worth it to know you're safe. I'd do it again without a second thought. As long as you're alive and free, that's all that matters to me. I promise you. I'll be okay." I hold my pinky up for her, but she doesn't link it with her own.

I kiss her on the forehead before she clutches my shirt and holds me close. God, this fucking kills me. I know she'll blame herself if I get arrested. The police arrive moments later without sirens or lights.

"Dawson," she begins, "There's something you should know. I'm in lo-"

"Mr. Connelly, come with us, please," the officer behind me commands. Impeccable timing, as always.

Where the hell is Murphy? "I'll be right back, sunshine."

She jerks her head into a nod.

"Hands up. Any weapons on you?"

"Yes, a gun. Back waistband." I try to reassure Abby with a smile as she silently watches them frisk me.

She tightens her arms around her stomach. The telltale clinking of handcuffs makes my shoulders slump. I should've known they would, but I had hoped, given the circumstances, that they wouldn't.

As soon as Abby sees the cop behind me wrapping the metal cuff around my wrist, she yells at them, "He didn't do anything. Please, you have to let him go!"

She starts to climb down from the truck without her prosthetic or crutches, just the door to hold her up, and another officer charges at her with his gun drawn. She freezes, terror flashing in her eyes. Oh, hell, no.

"Don't come any closer!" the patrolman yells, aiming his pistol at her face a mere fifteen feet from her.

I slam my shoulder into the chin of the officer holding the chain of my handcuffs, and I break free. I lunge in the way of the officer who had the nerve to pull a gun on her in time to block his advance on Abby among all the shouting from behind us.

"Can't you see she's fucking traumatized? Does she look like a threat to you? Leave her the fuck alone!" I growl.

The veins in my neck pulse into my skull. The muscles in my arms strain against the cuffs holding my hands behind me. Cuffed or not, if he touches her, he's going down. The audacity of him to pull a gun not only on an unarmed woman but one who has to hold on to my truck for support. I know their training is better than that.

"Grant, stand down. Clearly, this has gotten out of hand." Thank god, it's Murphy. He'll sort this out. "You two go over there a moment, will you?"

"Yes sir," the officers reply and walk away from us.

"What a shit show you got yourself into here, Connelly." He scrubs his hand on his weathered face before looking behind me. "Mrs. Miller." He nods at her. "It's the protocol that we separate you two for questioning. But I'm sure we'll get this straightened out quickly. The handcuffs weren't necessary." He glares at the officer behind me.

I hurry over and I rest my forehead on Abby's. I'm still breathing heavily from the altercation with the cop. "It's going to be okay, Abby. Just stay here and do what they ask," I beg her. My throat feels tight. I swear I saw my life ending when Grant charged at her.

"Dawson?" She places her hand on my chest, her doe eyes begging me not to take the fall.

"Just tell the truth, Abby. About everything," I whisper. Even if she were the one to pull the trigger, I would still bear the fall for her.

"I will," she whispers back as I place a kiss on her forehead.

The officer grabs my arm and pulls me away from Abby for questioning, but she never takes her eyes off me. A female officer walks over to Abby and starts questioning her. The police take both of our statements when an ambulance rolls into the parking lot. Abby looks away as the coroner wheels past her with Frank in a black body bag. I can't help but feel her sadness from here. I don't know what this means for her, for us. If she could even be with me after this.

Once the ambulance leaves with Frank in the back, I tell Murphy every twisted detail I can remember. Then I walk back up to Abby with a heavy heart. "Are you ready to go home?"

"They're letting us go just like that?" Her eyes widen, and her eyebrows squish together like she doesn't believe me.

"Just like that."

I wrap my arms around her and just hold her for several minutes. Neither of us talk. If she resents me for what I did tonight, I don't know how I'll survive. I love her with every cell in my body. Life without her wouldn't be worth living. I don't think I can live in a world where Abby hates me. The thought alone makes me want to drop to my knees and tell her I'm sorry. Not for killing him because I'll never be sorry for saving her. But I'm sorry for her loss. I want to beg her not to leave me, but I know that's not fair to her.

We arrive home shortly after, and I carry her into the house with her head resting in the crook of my neck. One of her arms is draped around my shoulder, and the other is flat against my chest. One look at her face and how her gaze lands on her crutches, prosthetic leg, and overturned bar stool, and I know she can't stay here tonight.

"Wanna get out of here for a few days?" At her nod, I bring her to the bedroom and set her on the bed. "Tell me what you want me to pack."

"Just that box beside the bed, my shampoo, conditioner, and toothbrush."

After packing my things, we're off. I know just the place to help heal her heart. It's where I went after my sister passed.

Abby

I watch him toss fishing poles into the bed of the truck before hopping in. I haven't fished since I was a kid. To be honest, I haven't really seen my parents in a while either. I worried they knew about the abuse when they started asking questions. And as usual, I was uncomfortable lying to them, so I cut them out of most of my life. Dawson hasn't said much to me since we packed, and I've been trying to process everything that just happened. Frank's dead. Dawson killed him to save me. A hollow feeling fills my chest.

I don't mourn for my husband. I mourn for the man he used to be. My best friend, my partner. We'd been through so much. At the same time, I have a sense of relief and freedom, and I can't help but feel guilty about that. Maybe that's what all these tears are: guilt. If I could've just had a damn baby, none of this would've happened. But then I wouldn't have met Dawson and known what a good man should be. How I didn't deserve to live that way.

After sliding behind the wheel, Dawson's hand rests on the center console. I cover it with my own. He lifts my hand to his mouth, places a soft kiss on my knuckles, and gives me a sad smile. I reach down and turn the music volume up a few notches, letting a rock song drown everything else out. I don't ask where we're going, and to be honest, I don't care.

Stopping at a gas station, Dawson disappears inside. When he climbs back in the truck, he hands me a chapstick. "This should help the cracks from the towel."

It's not the usual watermelon balm I use. This one is an organic unscented tube which would probably be better. I take it and apply it to my mouth. The cracks do hurt, but the chapstick helps to coat my skin.

After driving in silence for a couple of hours, he pulls off the highway into a sleepy little town, takes a few back roads, and eventually, a dirt road leads us to a massive log home. It's nearly midnight, and the sky is dark and clear. Stars shine brightly against the blackness. The sign at the end of the driveway says, "Welcome to Rainbow Lake Lodge."

I've never heard of this place before, but rainbow lake kind of sounds cool. I've always loved rainbows and all the colors that blend together. I am an art teacher, after all. Dawson hops out and comes around the back of the truck. I reach behind me to grab my crutches, but he opens my door with a wheelchair next to it. I give him a grateful smile as he helps me down and into the chair.

It's quiet here. Just the sounds of crickets and water babbling surround us. He wheels me up and through the front doors. We're greeted by an older gentleman with kind eyes and a warm smile.

"How can I help you, folks?" I don't miss the way he stares at my face. I turn away.

"I was hoping you had a room available?" Dawson stands beside me.

"I do. How many nights will you be staying with us?"

Dawson looks down at me as he says, "Two?"

I nod my reply.

"Okay, I'll need you to fill this out. And if you change your mind and want to stay longer, just let me know. Any requests?"

"A jacuzzi suite if one is available."

The concierge types a few things into his computer before answering, "You're in luck. There's one left."

As Dawson fills out the paperwork, I look around at the large open room. All the posts and beams are exposed and decorated with warm white Christmas lights giving it a homey feel. The wood shows all of the knots within. A jacuzzi sounds amazing. The clerk gets my attention and mouths the words, "Do you need help?"

It's good to know there are other good men out there. As I flash him a smile, I silently tell him, "No. But thank you."

"Room 7 is all set for you two. Enjoy your stay, and please let me know if there's anything we can get for you."

"Thank you," we both say.

He pushes me along the wide hallway until we reach our room. Leaning forward to slide the white key card into the slot, I feel exhaustion fill my body. It's been such a long night, and I'm so tired even my soul feels drained of every emotion.

"I'll be right back. I'm just grabbing our stuff." He parks me in the middle of the room and places a kiss on my forehead.

"Okay."

It's a small room but very cozy. The only furniture in the room is a bed, a bureau, a T.V., and a mini fridge along with two nightstands. I close my eyes and just focus on calming breaths. A soft knock on the door.

"It's just me."

Dawson comes in with his bag and my box. Setting them on the end of the bed, he starts to put away our stuff in the wooden drawers. Something about him touching my undies gets me to move.

"I can get those," I say, wheeling myself closer.

He backs away with his hands up, smirking. "I'll go draw you a bath."

"That sounds like heaven."

He disappears from view, but the sounds of water running sound promising. I grab a pair of underwear and a nightgown to sleep in as well as my bathroom stuff, before heading in that direction. My face falls when I notice the tub is too high for me to be able to get in on my own. It's a large beautiful white porcelain encased in white tiles. Maybe if I sit on the edge, I can have enough balance to slide in without falling. Probably not, though. It's really high. Well, this sucks.

"I can help you get in," he says quietly.

Heat rises up to my cheeks.

"I can close my eyes if that makes you feel better?" He laughs as I cover my face with my hands.

"Only if you get in too." My eyes widen at realizing I said it out loud.

"You don't have to tell me twice." He starts to pull his shirt up, and I turn away.

This is so awkward. What the hell was I thinking? His shirt falls to the floor. The clinking of his belt buckle being undone makes me realize we're really doing this. He comes into view as he dumps lilac scented bubble bath into the water. I've seen him with his shirt off before, but damn, watching his muscles ripple as he stands back up. Even in the dim lighting from the small overhead light, he's perfect.

"Abby?" He kneels in front of me. "I don't have to get in if it makes you uncomfortable. I can still help you in, though."

"I have scars, Dawson." I feel so small saying my fear out loud. It's not just the scars, though.

I've only been with Frank for the last eight years, and he hasn't looked at my body the way a husband should in forever. I feel like the body I have now isn't what Dawson would want to see, either. Anxiety bubbles up into my lungs, making it hard to breathe.

His face softens. "We all have scars, sunshine. You wanna see mine?"

Dawson sits on the side of the tub beside me, lifts his right arm, and points with a finger from his left hand to a quarter-sized round mark just below his ribs where the skin is lighter. "I was shot here while on duty in Afghanistan." He turns, "This is where it came out." A four-inch white line with stitch marks goes across the center of a larger round scar. I didn't notice it before.

"I have some here." He points to his forearm. "And quite a few on my legs." He stands and starts to unbutton his pants, and my eyes flick back up to his.

"What are those from?"

"Well." He runs his hands through his short dark brown hair. "I wasn't the greatest when I was younger. As a teenager, me and my buddies thought it was a good idea to climb a barbed wire fence to outrun the cops after a car chase went bad."

I burst out laughing. "No way."

"Yup." He grins before his face turns serious. "Scars can be reminders of your strength, not just what you've survived. It can remind you of how amazing you are. Think of them as stories from faded pictures that you share with others, but only when you're ready.

He turns the faucet off. I sigh, knowing he's right. I still can't get over a younger Dawson being a lawbreaker. Holding the hem of my shirt in my hands, I hesitate before lifting it. Screw it. He's already seen my worst scar, my leg. I drop my shirt to the floor and don't miss the heat that flashes in Dawson's dark blue eyes.

I point to the six-inch pinkish-red scar across my side. "The window broke when the truck rolled before colliding with a tree, and a large piece of glass got lodged in there."

"The scar only makes you more beautiful to me."

My stomach flutters at his words. He always knows what to say. I reach behind me and unclasp my bra, letting it fall on my lap. He turns his head and clears his throat, avoiding looking at me. He's trying so hard to make this easy on me.

"Dawson."

He swallows. "Yeah?"

"Look at me," I coax him.

"I can't," he says in a gravely voice.

My palms grow sweaty. "Why?"

"Because I'm afraid I won't be able to stop...."

"Stop what?"

"Stop myself from loving you," he says in a low timber.

"What if I don't want you to stop?" I whisper.

His sharp intake of breath is the only answer I get. He hesitates before his hungry gaze sweeps over me, and something about the way he looks at me makes me feel like the most gorgeous woman in the world, scars and all.

"God, you're so fucking beautiful it hurts." He leans down and plants a sweet kiss against my lips.

I try to deepen the kiss, needing more of him, but he stops me by pulling away. When I whimper at the loss, he lightly touches the side of my mouth where the gag caused my skin to crack and bleed. I nearly forgot about my pain with his heated gaze and the feel of his lips on mine.

"Let these heal first. You ready to get in?" he asks as he lets his jeans and boxer briefs fall to the floor.

I can't help but stare as he frees himself. He's large and hard and only a foot away from me. I slowly shimmy out of my own underwear and pants as he groans in response. I lick my lips, and his eyes darken.

"Fuck woman, you're going to be the death of me. Just get in the damn tub and cover yourself with bubbles already." He stares up at the ceiling while he waits.

I giggle as I take his outstretched hand and stand. I sit on the edge, and he holds my waist as I turn and slowly sink into the hot water. Leaning into the side of the tub, I pull bubbles up to my chin and smile sweetly at him.

"Finally," he mutters before climbing in on the opposite end.

He stretches his legs out and places them on either side of me as I do the same. Dawson grabs my foot and pulls it up to his stomach, and starts deeply massaging the arch and ball of my foot.

"Oh my god, that feels so good." My eyes close as I lean back against the tub. I haven't had a foot massage in forever.

"I've been waiting so long to hear you say those words."

I splash water at him. "Not fair. You won't even kiss me right now."

"I won't kiss your lips. I never said anything about other places." He looks at me with hooded eyes.

Desire blooms low in my belly as an ache I want him to fill sets in. I'm just about to argue with him about not caring if my mouth hurts when he cuts me off, sensing my impending outburst.

"You need sleep. We both do. We'll relax here for a bit and then go to bed. To sleep." It's almost like he's telling himself this.

"Okay." I lean my head back and close my eyes as he continues to rub and knead my foot.

When exhaustion threatens to make me fall asleep in the water, I unplug the tub, letting the water drain out. After Dawson steps out of the tub, he places a towel on my wheelchair before reaching down to help me up. I stand and sit on the edge. Pulling my leg over while wet is tricky, but I manage to get to my chair with his aid. Feeling far too exposed, I quickly dry myself and slide my nightgown on first before my panties. I wheel myself out of the bathroom and climb onto the bed. The mattress is soft and forms to my body almost immediately.

He throws on a pair of briefs and climbs into bed, scooting over until his body is against mine. Rolling over, I place my head on his chest and my hand on his shoulder, loving how treasured I feel in his arms. Something I haven't experienced in so long that I've forgotten how good it feels. The day's events finally take their toll on me, and I pass out into the dark abyss, knowing Frank will never be able to hurt me again.

Chapter Twenty

Dawson

I'm searching the warehouse Frank took Abby to. I know she's here because of the tracking app. His truck is also parked out front. Entering a dark room, I clear it quickly. I cautiously place my footing around the loose cans and other trash on the floor. I work my way down the corridor and into another large room. There's nobody in here. The small metal chair placed in the middle of the room has a puddle of blood beneath it, but that's not what frightens me the most. The anklet that I used to track Abby sits on the seat with a note that says, "Better luck next time."

"Where the fuck are you?" my shouts echo off the bare walls.

"Dawson!" Abby screams in response.

Bolting in the direction her voice came from, I throw the back door wide open, slamming it against the wall. I glance around behind the building and parking lot. There she is. That son of a bitch has her tied up on the edge of the riverbank. Abby's eyes are large and keep darting back and forth from me to Frank, who stands in front of her with a scowl.

"Frank, stop. Don't do this." I bring my pistol up until he's in my sights. It's too risky of a shot with how close he is to Abby. I won't risk harming her, and it's a bad shot.

"If I can't have her, no one will," his voice trembles as he shifts his weight from side to side.

"I'll walk away, I swear. Just let her live," I plead, tossing my gun down to the ground and raising my hands up. My heart is hammering a frantic beat in my chest, and my body is telling me to run to her.

"It's too late for that. She's already given you her heart," he says sadly.

"Frank, no!" She cries out as he shoves her off the grass-covered bank and into the water below.

"Abby!" I shout.

She tumbles backward and into the river. My feet pound the ground until I reach the water's edge. I don't see her. Fuck! I hold my breath before jumping over and diving into the dark depths. The impact shatters the stillness of the water.

I jolt awake, sitting up and not able to catch my breath. It feels as if I've run a marathon. Looking beside me on the bed, I find Abby's gaze watching me intently.

"Bad dream?" She sits up and stretches her arm out, rubbing my back.

Still not able to catch my breath, I only nod. It felt like I lost her. I didn't get there in time.

"Do you want to talk about it?"

I shake my head. "I just need you, sunshine." I lay back and open my arms for her to come closer.

She leans into me and kisses my chest just above my heart. I don't start breathing better until her small body is pressed against mine, and

I can feel every breath leaving and entering her body. I kiss her forehead and draw circles on the thigh that splays across my legs. If Frank's ghost wants to haunt me, then fine. I don't regret killing him. He'll never be able to hurt her again. I've killed men in combat before, but this was different. I wasn't about to let another person I love die at the hands of domestic abuse.

Abby soon falls back to sleep. I can tell by her breathing pattern. I'm unable to drift off after that nightmare. I lie awake for hours, just holding her, thankful that she's alive and safe. It's early. The sunrise is just starting to peak through the gaps in the curtain. The ache in my chest slowly eases as the room fills up with more and more sunlight. People walk down the hallway. Their muffled murmurs and footsteps wake Abby, and she stretches against me. Her nightgown rides up even higher, revealing the bottom of her pink panties on the top of her thigh. I'm amazed I was able to keep my hands off of her last night after seeing her naked. She's absolutely fucking gorgeous, and I don't deserve her.

"Hey, sleepyhead."

I brush her hair out of her face. Her eyes are puffy from crying, but most of the other swelling went down in her face. The bruises have already formed in varying shades of purple and brown. At least I know she'll never have to go through this again. I'll spend every last day I have making her feel cherished and loved.

"Good morning." She yawns. My stomach growls loudly and makes her laugh. "Is it going to eat my leg?"

"If we don't eat soon, maybe." I give her a serious face I manage to hold until she smiles at me.

"Then let's get some food. I don't dig cannibalism."

Abby rolls over and slides her sock on, followed by her prosthetic that I put beside the bed last night. I watch her as she gathers her clothes and vanishes into the bathroom. I love the way her ass sways in that thin nightgown. Reluctantly I crawl out of bed and throw some clothes on. She comes out with a sad look on her face.

"What's wrong?" I ask, ready to pounce on anything.

"I can't go out there like this." She points at her face before turning away from me.

"You'll be okay here, I promise. Do you know why it's called Rainbow Lake Lodge?"

Abby turns her body toward mine. "Because of the lake?"

I take her face in my hands. "Yes and no. This is a place for healing. Rainbows only come after the rain. This place was made for people who are going through a rough patch. Trust me. They won't judge you. I came here after Isabelle died. I was in a really bad place for a while after, and staying here helped me begin to move on and to remember her memory instead of just her death."

"Okay." She sighs and goes back into the bathroom to change.

We enter the dining room, and there's a handful of people at the tables. Some do openly stare at her for a moment before turning away. She doesn't meet any of their eyes but leans into me more as we walk up to the buffet. I wonder if they think I did this to her. If I were them, that would be my first impression. I don't care what they think as long as Abby knows the truth. We load up our plates and take a seat off to the side. This room has floor-to-ceiling windows with an unobstructed view of the lake surrounded by trees.

"It's pretty here," she says quietly.

"Yeah, it is. Would you like to go for a walk around the lake after? The trail is also wheelchair accessible." I thought that was amazing when I came last time. Most resorts have wheelchair-accessible areas, whereas this one has all areas available.

"I'd like that." She cuts another piece of her pancake with her fork.

After finishing our meal, Abby decides she'd like to take the wheelchair. I push her out through a side door and into a large butterfly garden filled with different shades of flowers with a bunch of bees and butterflies fluttering around. The sight of all the butterflies, which I'll always tie with Bella, still hurts, but not as bad as before. She spends several moments admiring our natural surroundings. Continuing on the concrete walking trail, we reach the edge of the water dotted with multiple colored rocks; hence the name Rainbow Lake, and I sit on the wrought iron bench as my nightmare comes at me in full force. Just seeing the water brings it all back up. Watching Frank violently shove her and Abby disappearing into the river. The burning in my chest that took so long to go away this morning fires back up again with a vengeance.

Sensing my rising panic, she leaves her wheelchair and sits on my lap, resting her forehead against mine and rubbing our noses together. "It's okay. I'm right here. I'm not going anywhere." Abby puts her arms around me tightly. Her scent invades all my senses.

"How did you know where my mind was?" I look at her in wonder. I didn't tell her what woke me this morning.

"You were talking in your sleep this morning." She places a gentle kiss on the tip of my nose.

Oh. I can only imagine what she heard me saying. "The nightmare I had felt so real."

"I know. Those are the worst ones, aren't they? The ones that linger on."

"I thought I was going to lose you last night," I whisper.

"But you didn't. You *saved* me, Dawson." She cradles my head in her hands, her thumbs brushing the stubble on my jaw.

"I love you, Abby. I love you more than anything in this world. I should've told you that sooner."

Unshed tears coat my eyes as I search her face to see if I've said too much. If I scared her away. I can't go one more day without her knowing how much I love her. My heart slams hard in my chest, waiting for her to say something, anything.

"I love you more than life itself, Dawson."

She presses her lips to mine, slowly deepening the kiss until she's all I know. The sounds disappear, the breeze vanishes, and all I smell is the lavender bubble bath and her soft flowery perfume. My nightmare is now just a distant memory.

I pull back, remembering the cracks in the sides of her mouth. They look better than they did last night, and they're not bleeding. "Does it hurt to kiss me?"

"Only when you stop," she says in a breathy whisper before taking my mouth again.

She shifts on my lap until she's sitting beside me with her legs across mine. Abby pulls away slowly but not before giving me one last chaste kiss and resting her head on my shoulder. The birds chirp nearby, but other than wildlife, we remain alone out here.

"If you could start over someplace new, where would it be?" she asks quietly.

Is that what she wants to do? I contemplate her question. "It would be a tossup between the mountains or by the ocean. And you?"

"I think I like the sounds of a remote wilderness. A little log cabin like this with a pond." She clasps my hand on her thigh.

"Is that what you want to do? Start over someplace other than Montana?" I try to control the emotion in my voice. She just told me how much she loved me. Does she want to leave now?

Abby takes a deep breath in and out. "I don't know. I love my job, and I'd miss Chloe. But I wouldn't go anywhere unless you came with me."

Thank god. I was worried for a minute there. "If you think that's what you need to do to get past this, then I'll go where you go. I know I only just found you, but I can't imagine a life without you." I wrap my arms around her.

"I don't think I can go back to Dillon," she whispers.

"Then don't. Stay with me," I murmur.

She picks her head up and meets my gaze. I can't read her expression, but it looks like shock.

"I mean it, Abby. I want you to live with me. I want to go to bed with you in my arms every night and wake up with you on my chest every morning."

I can't think of anything better. I don't want to leave East Point, my job, or the shelter. But I would leave everything behind for her. There are other towns and cities and other jobs, and Maggie does an amazing job at Bella's. I could oversee it from afar. I'll make this work for Abby. I'll find a way that all our pieces fit together perfectly.

Abby smiles and leans in closer. When her eyes close and our lips just barely brush, I stop holding back and kiss her hard. When she kisses me back, she makes me forget about everything that's happened in the past. Only she and I remain in this moment. The rest of the world disappears. My Abby, my sunshine, is my everything.

Abby

When we finally untangle from each other out by the lake, I leave the wheelchair behind, take my shoe off and dip my toes in the warm water. I see why they call it Rainbow Lake. The smooth pebbles on the bottom are almost every color and shade you can imagine. I reach down and pick up a few of my favorites to put on my desk at work. I've always been a sucker for colored stones. Just being here feels like everything will be okay again. There really is something healing about this place, whether it's the meaning of the name or the peacefulness it embodies. I just know this is where I need to be.

Dawson went to grab his fishing poles out of his truck, and I opted to stay here. This beautiful lake tucked in by a multitude of trees makes me want to paint again. I haven't felt the urge this strong to pick up a brush in a while. I'll have to take some pictures before we leave so I can paint them when we go back home. Home, that's another question altogether. What will I do about the house I bought with Frank now? I can't go back there, and it holds too much trauma within the walls. I don't ever want to step foot in that place again. I sigh. That's a problem for another day.

Looking up to see Dawson walking down the wide path that stretches around the lake, I smile, remembering him telling me he loves me. It's time to start a new chapter of my life, one filled with happiness and love. I collect the rocks I placed on the bank and tuck them in the pocket of my shorts.

"Are you ready to head to the dock?"

"Yeah, just grabbing the rocks I want," I say as I pull my shorts back up from their weight.

"Which ones? Wait, let me guess, some red, some purple, and blue." He grins.

"I'll have you know I also have a pink and a green one." I plant my hand on my hip.

"Well, I stand corrected." He leans in and brushes his lips against my neck before trailing them up to my mouth and giving me an achingly tender kiss. "Hop on your chariot, sunshine. We have fish to catch."

"I want to walk." He begins to protest about walking close to the water. "I can push the wheelchair to steady me."

We stroll side by side to the end of the dock. I put the locks on the wheelchair and lower myself to the dock to sit. Draping my leg over the end, my toes barely break the surface. The water is cooler this far out. Dawson sets a container of worms beside me as he baits a hook.

"Do you want me to put a worm on yours for you?" he asks while he sets his pole down behind him.

"No, it's okay. I can do it." I remember how.

I poke my finger into the swirling tub of slimy worms and pull a small one out. "Sorry little guy," I tell him before stabbing him with the pointy end of the hook and looping him around. Gross slimy stuff comes out, and I wipe it on the dock. I look up to see Dawson smirking and shaking his head.

"What's so funny?"

"Only you would apologize to the worm."

"He's alive too, and I feel bad." That's not wrong of me to feel.

At this, Dawson laughs before sitting beside me and saying, "I know. Your compassion is one of the many reasons I love you."

I could get used to hearing him say those three little words. I lean over and rest my head against his shoulder, and he demonstrates how to cast the line out. I throw my line out too, and within minutes Dawson yanks his pole back and reels in a large bass.

"Oooh, that's a good one," I tell him. He tosses it back into the water, and I squeal as it splashes lake water all over me.

"You got a bite. Pull up hard."

I do, and I'm not ready for how hard the fish would fight me as I cranked the reel. I'm expecting a huge fish with the amount of struggle he put up. Once it breaks the water, sunlight gleams off the brightly colored yellow and green scales.

"Good job, you got it!" He reaches for the line as the fish slaps around in the air. He takes the hook out and holds it out to me. "Just watch out for these spikes."

"I thought it'd be bigger."

"The truth comes out now," he laughs.

"Oh my god, no. I don't even know how it will fit, to begin with." I cringe. "I meant the fish. How can something so small fight so hard?"

"It's a fighter. The little ones usually are." He gazes down at me lovingly, and the corners of his mouth tilt up. "They have to be to survive in this world."

Now isn't that the truth?

We fish for a while. Dawson catches way more than I do, but I'm happy with what I got. I just enjoyed getting to spend time with him. The temperature starts climbing, and the fish stop biting. We return to our room, and I shower while Dawson leaves for some reason. He's planning something and acting shady. When I get out of the shower, he's back in the room. Dawson's relaxed on the bed, watching an action movie, but his gaze hungrily takes me in as I slowly stroll to the bed in my pj's. I wish I had something sexier than matching sets of t-shirts and shorts. His eyes roaming over me makes my skin heat in anticipation. When he looks at me like that, everything else disappears.

I lower myself onto the bed, and he leans in closer, nuzzling my neck. I place my hand under his shirt, directly over his heart. His skin is burning. He kisses me gently before pulling away too soon.

"I'm going to shower, but dinner will be here soon. If somebody knocks, that's probably it."

I flop back on the bed, clearly sexually frustrated, and he has the nerve to laugh at me. "Is something funny?" I ask him, throwing one of the pillows at him. He dodges it at the last second, letting it fall to the floor.

"Nope. I won't be long." He smirks at me before disappearing into the bathroom and closing the door.

I lay back and stare at the wall. What a clusterfuck my life's become. The water runs in the bathroom as he showers. Dawson says he loves me, but does he love me enough not to break my heart? Not like my heart is much anymore. There have been too many pieces torn away from it for it ever to be whole again. All I can do at this point is take it day by day and live for tomorrow. I know some days will be better than others. I remove my prosthetic and get comfortable on the bed, trying to watch a movie I started.

The water turns off shortly, and Dawson walks out wearing nothing but a white towel tied around his waist. He shrugs. "I forgot my clothes."

"Yeah, I bet you did," I mumble. My body reacts involuntarily to his bare chest, and I still can't pull my eyes off him as he drops the towel into a puddle at his feet. My gaze travels the length of his body and back up to his sexy grin. The movie I started watching is all but forgotten.

The muscles in his arms and back flex as Dawson pulls on a pair of loose-fitting sweatpants and a t-shirt. There's a knock at the door. He checks the peephole and opens the door allowing the resort employee to push the metal cart into our room. After the person leaves, Dawson pushes the cart closer to the bed. There are several dishes with metal covers over them and a bottle of wine sitting in a chilled bucket. After he pours two glasses of merlot, he peeks under one of the lids and closes it quickly. Hmmm. What is he hiding under there?

After removing the top off the other dish, he sets two plates of grilled cheese sandwiches on the bed and sits in front of me.

"I'm onto you, you know."

He tilts his face toward mine and smiles. "Is it wrong that I want to give you your favorite food?"

"Not at all." I take a sip of my wine and pull my plate closer. I'm painfully aware of what sits just beneath his clothes. I saw how hard he was moments ago.

Once finished with our sandwiches, he finally pulls off the final two covers, strawberry ice cream, in small white bowls.

"For somebody that's no good for me, you seem to know what I need." I still really don't get why he would even think that. He's a good guy and an amazing person. He's too hard on himself.

"No, I don't. I want to make you happy, and food is easy to do. But I'm trying to be the man you deserve." He looks away.

"You're all that and more, Dawson." I guide his chin until he looks at me again. "Don't you see that *you* are what I need?"

"I'm just worried I'll screw this up." He rests his forehead against mine and closes his eyes.

"I don't think you could even if you tried." I slide both of my palms to the side of his neck.

He swallows and takes a deep breath. "There are days where my head is a dark place to be."

"Then I guess it's a good thing I'm your sunshine. I can light up your darkness." I press my lips lightly against his. "We'll figure this out together."

I'm not going to let him go, even if he tries to push me away to protect me. Who's there for the strong ones who need a shoulder to lean on? I can be that person for him. Everybody needs somebody on their weak days. We can both lean on each other. There's strength in being together.

He nods, and I sit back against the headboard and eat my slightly melted ice cream. Once we're finished, and the bed is cleared of any dishes, he puts the trolley in the hallway, minus the wine and chiller. He pours himself another glass, tops mine off, and sits beside me. I don't drink alcohol often, but when I do, merlot is the one I choose.

I set my glass on the nightstand and curl my body around his. I slowly glide my hand from his neck to his chest, over his abs and lower still. He grabs my hand by the wrist and holds it away from himself before I reach my destination.

"What are you doing?" He places a gentle kiss on my wrist where the scabs formed from the zip ties cutting into me.

"Nothing." I grin.

"It doesn't seem like nothing." He clears his throat. "I thought we were taking things slow?"

"You wanted to take things slow," I clarify. “I don't.”

"I don't want to trigger you."

I bring his hand that's holding mine and place it on my breast. "You won't."

He sucks in a sharp breath but doesn't move his hand as my nipple hardens beneath the thin bra and even thinner shirt. I lean forward and take his face in my hands. Once our lips meet and he deepens the kiss, he slides his hands down my sides until they're below my ass and pulls me up until I'm straddling him. My balance is off without having my prosthetic on but having my hands on his chest helps. His mouth tastes sweet, like the wine we just drank. Dawson's rough hands slip under my shirt and cup my breasts, lightly pinching my nipples between his fingers. I moan into his mouth as the pleasure and pain mix into something else entirely.

He hardens underneath me as he presses himself against my heat, rocking gently and creating friction. My heart beats frantically in my chest. I trail wet kisses from his jawline and nibble on his ear. I'm rewarded with a gasp, and the sound urges me to continue to kiss his neck. The scent of his woodsy body wash is all I smell. I rub myself against him, and he groans. I'm so horny I think I can get off like this. It wouldn't take much, and it's been ages.

Shifting into a seated position, he tugs my shirt off in one motion and unclasps my bra, letting it fall to the floor. Dawson captures my nipple in his mouth. His tongue is hot as he sucks it into his mouth. I grind against him harder, desperate to find a release. My hands fist in his soft hair as his suction pulls harder against me. He slides his fingers down my belly and just inside the hem of my underwear. He stops and looks up at me. Passion blazes bright in his eyes.

"Are you sure?" he asks, breathing heavily.

I nod and bring my lips down to his, our kiss turning from soft and sensual to rough and needing. His fingers slide along the elastic of my underwear and slip under the material until he's touching skin, and as soon as he brushes my sensitive nub, a moan tears through me. As his thumb works circles, the other hand is pinching and tugging at my nipple. Too many sensations and feelings bubble up as he urges me toward my release. When I think I can't take anymore, an orgasm rockets through me, and I arch my back as I cry out his name. He slows down his pace, but he continues to draw out the euphoria until I'm limp against his chest and struggling to breathe.

He carefully lays me beside him and rips off his shirt and pants before pulling my shorts down and tossing them to the floor. He settles his weight in between my thighs and kisses me softly. My fingers fumble down his chest in the small gap between us until I stroke his length, and he tenses above me, pulling his lips from mine.

"Fuck. I don't have a condom," he says quietly.

Too many internal wars flare up inside me at his simple words. Might as well state the truth. "I'm clean, and I can't get pregnant anyway."

Sorrow finds purchase in the way his eyes look right through me. "I'm sorry, I didn't mean to-"

"It's okay." I try to kiss his worries away. He kisses me back but not with the same amount of vigor he held before. Is it because I can't have a baby, or does he think he hurt my feelings? Kids are something we need to talk about sooner rather than later. But damn it. He needs to make love to me now.

I once again wrap my hands around him and stroke his length from the base to the tip a few times before I angle him to my entrance. He stiffens as I slowly push myself against him, making him barely penetrate me. I dig my heel into his ass cheeks to encourage him to keep going. He finally snaps out of it, slowly pushes himself deeper, and then back out until I feel empty. Dawson gently works himself in and out until he's fully inside me. I hold my breath. Holy shit, does it hurt. He retakes my mouth and kisses me tenderly as my body adjusts to his size.

Edging backward, he searches my face and asks in a strained voice, "You okay?"

I nod. The pain is starting to dissipate, but I don't dare move yet.

"I need to hear you, Abby."

The movie playing in the background seems too loud for the moment. "I'm okay, just hurts a little."

"Do you want me to stop?" He holds himself up on his forearms.

I shake my head. At his frown, I say, "No. Just go slow at first."

"Okay. If it's too much, you need to tell me."

"I will." But he'll never be too much for me to deny him. I haven't had sex in over six months, and he's fairly large. I knew the first few times would be painful.

He gently rocks in and out, and I scrunch my face up. I'm thankful he glides in smooth because of how wet I am for him. A few tears leak out, and I have to remind myself to breathe. Dawson kisses my neck as his fingers burn a trail down to my folds. I'm still sensitive from the last orgasm. Pressure begins to build with both pain and pleasure, blending into an intoxicating concoction. My fingernails dig into his back, and he moans a guttural sound against my throat. A cold sweat begins to coat my skin as he ramps up his pace. The pain is more of a delicious sting at this point. Each time he pulls back, I hate the emptiness that follows. That's what my heart will feel like if he ever leaves me, a hollow shell. I try not to think about the what-ifs.

"Come on, sunshine, give me one more," he growls while still pounding into me.

His deft fingers work me faster and harder. My toes curl on my good leg, and electricity shoots through my limbs as his name falls from my lips in a strangled moan.

"Fuck. Abby." His body tenses above me as he reaches his own climax.

The breaths shuddering out of him tickle my shoulder, and I squirm. His lazy smile turns down when he sees the tears in my eyes.

"I hurt you, didn't I?" His forehead wrinkles as he tries to pull away, but I stop him from moving by gripping his back.

"Dawson, I'm okay. More than okay, actually." I place a kiss on his collarbone. "It was a good pain, I promise."

I hold my pinky up for him, and he pretends to bite it. His teeth lightly graze it before he links his own finger with mine. He kisses my face from my eyes, nose, jaw, and lips before rolling off me and walking to the bathroom. The light flickering from the television highlights the red marks on his back. I didn't think I scratched him that badly. He seemed to like it, though. The sound he made, mmm. I loved it.

He returns to the bed with a warm wet washcloth and carefully cleans me and returns the towel to the bathroom. The bed sinks down as he puts his weight on it and drapes an arm over me. I roll onto my side and put my head on his chest, hearing the steady beat of his heart beneath me.

"Dawson, does it bother you that I can't have kids?" Worry eats away at me; I think won't be enough for him. That I can't make him whole.

"Sweetheart, I wasn't thinking when I said that. All that was on my mind was needing to be inside of you." His arms tighten around me.

"That's not an answer." I hold my breath waiting for him to say more. Childbearing will always be something that hangs over my head.

He exhales before answering, "No. It doesn't bother me. Don't get me wrong. I'd love to have biological kids. But there are other ways to have children." He kisses the crown of my head.

I snuggle in as close as I can and pull the covers over us. A new emotion comes over me as his breaths slow. Guilt. Even though I left Frank a week ago. I feel like I'm horrible for sleeping with Dawson the day after he died. Maybe I should be grieving and planning a funeral instead of sleeping with another man. I've grieved Frank several times already while he was still alive. I can't, in good faith, plan his funeral after what led to his death. He intended to kill Dawson, and I believe once he got the baby he wanted from me, I'd be dead too. I don't feel I'm the right person to celebrate his life. Not when his life nearly ruined mine.

Chapter Twenty-One

Dawson

Sunlight dances across Abby's skin with the first morning rays. I've been awake for a while. I didn't have another nightmare but felt her stirring earlier, and having her like this in my arms after last night feels perfect. I never thought of myself as a lucky man before, but now? I've lost a lot in this life, but what I gained with Abby fills that ache in my chest. When we're together, I don't feel alone. I feel like I really have found my so-called tribe, as Isabelle put it. I'm not sure what I believe in when it comes to a higher power, but what I do believe is my sister had a hand in helping me find my way to Abby.

I'll forever be grateful to Isabelle for that. I wish she could be here to meet her. She would love Abby like a sister. I know she would. The part of my soul I thought I'd lost when Bella died is slowly coming back to life again. I didn't know how bleak my life was until it wasn't anymore. I need Abby as much as she needs me. I still don't think I deserve her. But damn it, I'll do everything I can to change that. I will be a better man for her. I'll make her the priority in my life.

Abby stretches against me and rubs at the sleep in her eyes. Once she pulls her hands away and rests on my chest, I brush her hair back and kiss the top of her head.

"Hey, sleeping beauty," I mumble against her hair.

"Good morning," she yawns.

We lie together in silence for a few minutes until she rolls away and tosses the covers off her. She sits up and uses the crutches to make her way to the bathroom, slowly and with an unnatural gait. Shutting herself in the bathroom before emerging a few minutes later.

"Are you okay?" I already have a feeling she's sore from last night's excursions. I feel bad. I tried to be as easy as I could be, but I lost control.

She groans as she hobbles over to the bed and sits back down. "I can still feel you down there. You ruined me for any other man. I hope you know that."

Pride swells in my chest. Mission accomplished. I never want another man anywhere near what's mine. I held back a lot last night because I knew it had been a while for her, and she was so fucking tight. I'm getting hard again just thinking about it.

"I warned you that you'd only ever remember me touching you. I'm sorry you're hurting, but I'm glad you can still feel me." I nip at her ear lobe. "And no man will ever touch what's mine," I finish with a growl.

She shivers against me. "Yours?" She raises her eyebrows with a sultry smile.

"Yes. All mine." I take her mouth and nearly devour her. It's almost check-out time, and I hate to bring it up. I feel like we really connected here. As if the rest of the world doesn't exist in this little bubble. "We have to check out soon."

"I know. I wish we didn't have to. I could stay here forever." She lies back against the pillows and shuts her eyes.

I could easily stay here and block out the rest of the world too. But we both have responsibilities back home. My work has been very lenient given the circumstances, but I'm due back tomorrow. I can't keep pushing it off, or I won't have a job to return to. I don't know how much longer her leave of absence is, but I imagine baggage from Frank will soon trickle down to her as well.

There's not much to pack, and it doesn't take us long to check out from a place that will forever hold fond memories for me now. Not just those dark days when I was a wreck after Isabelle's death.

When Abby and I first arrived at Rainbow Lodge, I sent Russell a message asking if he could clean up the kitchen. I don't want to bring Abby back home while there's still evidence of a struggle. We're still about an hour out, but when I stop by the gas station, I can't help but feel uneasy about returning there again. I decide to text Russell when I step out to pump the diesel and Abby uses the restroom.

Me: We're almost home. Is everything all taken care of?

I watched her body sway all the way inside. She's still walking funny from last night. I have to smirk. At least with every step she takes, she'll be reminded of what we did last night. My cell phone vibrates in my pocket.

Russell: Good as new. How is she?

Me: She's okay for now. I don't think everything has set in yet.

I'm terrified of when it does. That will be the biggest test of our relationship whether she can still look at me without remembering that I was the one who killed her husband. What a twisted series of events have unfolded since I met her. When I close my eyes, I still picture his hand wrapped around her throat. What drives a man to do that? To hurt his wife, fiancee, or girlfriend? Russell doesn't reply back right off, and when I start to think he won't, my cell phone buzzes again.

Russell: She'll be okay. So will you. Just give her time if she needs it. I'm here, man.

Me: I know, thank you. I'll be in touch later.

Russell: Safe travels.

Damn, this pump is slow. Abby's blonde head bobs behind another car before she comes fully into view carrying two coffee cups. The sunlight hits her downturned, bruised face, but she grins as soon as she notices me watching her. The ride back is mostly quiet. She folded up the console and sat beside me, her small body bumping into mine on the rough roads. Tension fills the air the closer we get to my place. When I pull in front of the garage and hop out, she hesitates before getting out. As soon as we enter and walk through the mudroom and into the living room, she freezes.

Abby takes in the scene before her. Nothing is amiss, and it's as if nothing ever happened. The window is fixed, the stools picked up where they belong, and the blood from the kitchen is no longer a puddle on the floor. She still sees it all, though. No doubt it's replaying in her mind. She hasn't spoken about what happened besides to the police. I won't ask, and I don't expect her to tell me, not right off anyway. I already plan on reading her statement as soon as I can. I need to know how to ensure her demons don't come back to haunt her.

She slowly walks into the kitchen and then glances back over her shoulder with a slight smile. I stroll in behind her, and my eyes land on the table. Two dozen dahlias in two vases stand proudly in varying shades of pink and purple. She leans her face down into the bouquet and inhales deeply. At this rate, I should just buy her a fucking flower shop, but I don't mind spoiling her with flowers. She deserves so much more than I can ever give her.

I wanted something good for her when she walked into my house. Holding my breath, I wait for her reaction. What if she can't stand being in my home anymore because the place reminds her of that one terrible night? I still have close to a year left on this lease, but I would get out of it for her. If she really can't stay, I'll move.

Walking up behind her, I wrap my arms around her waist and tug her against me. My heart is pounding erratically in my chest. What if she can't be with me anymore? What if I'm too much for her? Does she regret sleeping with me? She swallows thickly as I bury my face in her hair.

"What are you thinking?" I ask her quietly.

She interlocks her fingers with mine. "I was thinking that dahlias are my new favorite flower." She leans her head back until it rests on my shoulder.

I smile against her neck as the tightness in my chest lessens. "If I could give you the world, it would be covered in acres and acres of dahlias."

"What do we do now?"

"We take one step forward. It won't always be this hard, but for now, it's us against the world. Day by day, we'll get through the worst of it and build our new life together one brick at a time."

"How did you get so wise?" she asks, twisting in my arms to face me. Nothing but love shines in her baby-blue eyes.

I smirk. "I've read a lot of fortune cookies in my time."

"I don't think you could find all that in a fortune cookie."

"I've been doing a lot of thinking since I met you. You make me want to be the best version of myself. I want to *let the light in again."* Sadness overcomes me for a moment. This is exactly what Bella wanted for me, and she's not even here to witness it.

"What's wrong?" Abby searches my face as worry wrinkles her light brown eyebrows.

I sigh. "I wish you could've met Isabelle. It feels like I've been robbed of my sister knowing you. You two would've hit it off so well." That all too familiar hollowness starts to fill my chest again.

"Dawson, I could still get to know her. Through you." She cups my cheek in her palm. "Tell me about her?"

I nod, untangling myself from her. Holding her hand in mine, I drag her out to the couch in the living room, and we cuddle so close not even a piece of paper could fit between our bodies. I pull my phone out of my pocket and start scrolling through all the pictures on my cell. I usually scroll too fast by them, so they're all a blur. The picture my finger lands on brings up a well of emotions I wasn't prepared for. It was one of the few double dates we went on. Lexie and I, Bella and Jackson. Hurt flares up from the women, but pure agony rears its head when I look at him.

Abby notices and tells me, "If it's too painful right now, you can tell me some other time." She rests her hand on my thigh.

"She loved gerbera daisies. You know the ones that have all those bright colors?" My finger runs along the edge of my phone case.

"They're beautiful flowers."

"Every time I go to her grave, I bring some. One day I'll plant some there for her."

"I'm sure she'd love that." Abby leans her head against my shoulder.

"This was my first love, Lexie." It wasn't as hard to say those words as I thought. "That's Bella beside her, and next to my sister is...is...." I can't finish the sentence. I still have this picture because I can't bring myself to part with anything to do with my sister.

"It's okay. You don't have to say his name. She's beautiful. Bella had your eyes. You all look happy there."

"We were. Or at least I thought we were. I don't know how long she hid the abuse from us." I frown, wondering if I missed any signs.

"You can be abused yet still be happy. If it was anything like what I experienced, it was slow and confusing." She pauses. "It's hard to walk away when you still love them."

I guess that's something I'll never understand, how you can love somebody who physically assaults you? When you love someone, it shouldn't hurt that bad. Your body shouldn't bear the marks of their love in that way.

Abby leaves the room to use the rest room and I walk back to the kitchen. Flipping through the mail Russ left on the counter, my curiosity spikes when I find a large envelope with my name and nothing else written on it. Tearing it open, I reach my hand in and pull out a folded piece of paper. My blood runs cold as I read the typed letter.

I know what really happened in that warehouse. If you don't give me $500,000, I'll leak the video I have of you. Wait by your cell phone for further instructions.

Fuck! Who the hell could have a video of that night?

Abby

I got everything ready yesterday. My clothes were laid out in the bathroom, and all of my new supplies for the classroom sit in my trunk. I may have gone a little overboard with how much I bought this year.

Using my key card to gain access, I lead Dawson to my class. Dawson followed me in his truck to help me bring all of my stuff in before he heads to work. Chloe left the room just the way I had it. I'm grateful for all of her help and for stepping in when I couldn't be here for the classes. She's been a great friend, one of the few I have. That's on me, though. I kept everyone at a distance. I didn't want people to get too close and expose my relationship with Frank.

"Where would you like this one?" he asks.

Dawson stands beside me, holding a rather heavy box and taking in the room. Several circular tables fill the room, along with their small plastic chairs stacked neatly in the corner. A large, deep metal sink sits at the far wall next to the floor-to-ceiling cabinets to hold everything I need for the year.

"Right on that table is fine." I point to the one closest to the cabinets and scratch at my wrist. The zip ties Frank used left small scars behind on both wrists.

I'm actually nervous about today. It's my first day back at work, and I'm worried about how the kids will react to my missing limb. They're all great kids, but sort of like me, they lack a filter. Whatever pops into their little heads flies out.

"I thought that was you, I saw. I'm so glad to have you back!" Joyce's heels click on the tiles, and she hugs me quickly before taking a step back. "You look good."

"Thanks. It's good to be back. I've missed you guys." It really does feel good to be here. I'm cautious about her; though. I don't trust people as easily as I once did. I know not everybody has a vendetta. Old habits, I guess.

"Is there anything I can help with?" She gestures to the supplies we carried in.

"No. Thank you. It's only two more boxes, and we can get them. This is my boyfriend, Dawson. Dawson, this is Joyce."

It still feels weird to call him my boyfriend. It's too small of a term for what we have. He shakes her hand, but I don't miss how her eyes linger on him for too long.

"Well, alright then. I won't hold you up. We'll talk later." She winks at me.

I hope we don't. It's only been two weeks since Frank died, and I'm not in the mood to talk to people. Well, not adults anyway.

"Okay." No doubt she was just coming in to be nosey anyway.

"This is a nice room you have. Did you paint this?" He points to a vase of wildflowers hanging on the wall.

Dawson's been a little off since the attack. More quiet and distant at times. But can I really blame him?

"I did." Back before all the abuse when I was able to capture the goodness in everything. When my world didn't seem so tainted. Maybe I'm not so different than Dawson.

"It's beautiful." He flashes me that lopsided grin that heats up my core.

"Thank you." I run my fingers nervously through my hair and twirl the ends of it.

We make our final run out to the car and back into the building. I've been slowly building up my stamina since I got my prosthetic almost a month ago. Each day gets a little easier, and I can go further with the treadmill. Things have been going well between Dawson and me. We're still staying at his Condo, and I finally met Ralph. He's a little strange, but I like him. He's funny. We still haven't talked about that horrible night, and I don't want to. The only person I've told everything to are the police and my counselor. I want to move on and stop reliving the past. I try to focus on my future. The future I'll share with Dawson. It still seems unreal.

"Would you like help to unpack them?" Dawson's deep voice drags me out of my thoughts.

"I'm not really sure where I'm putting stuff yet, to be honest." It's kind of overwhelming coming back after so much has changed. I worry I won't be able to be the teacher I was before. What if I can't be good enough for my students?

"Okay, I'll get out of your hair then. I hope you have a good day. I love you, and I'll see you back at home." He leans down and presses his lips against mine, and pulls away far too soon.

I love it when he kisses me. "I hope you have a great day too. I love you, and I'll pick up dinner on the way home."

I watch him walk out of my classroom, and my gaze lingers on where he was just standing. It's the summer and a time for a new me. One that needs to stop looking at the negative side of things. Glass half full, I remind myself.

Joyce reappears in the doorway of my classroom and asks playfully. "Where have you been hiding that one?"

I laugh but don't give her an answer. Instead, I start tackling the boxes before the kids arrive. I only have about twenty minutes before they usually start to arrive. Screw it. I just toss the pads of paper on the bottom. I can always rearrange them later. Boxes and boxes of crayons, markers, and colored pencils fill the next few shelves. I'm putting the last of the bottles of paint and plastic palettes away when I hear the unmistakable pitter-patter of little feet behind me.

"Mrs. Miller!" a squeal snags my attention. It's Grace, a cute little brunette with a wild side.

"Hi, Grace! I missed you so much." I smile broadly as I lean down to give her a hug, and she wraps her little arms around me. My heart melts when she squeezes me tightly. This is what I've been missing these last several months, but I was in no shape to be here, unfortunately.

"We missed you too. Ms. Chloe isn't as fun as you." She shakes her head, swinging her ponytail back and forth.

Other children start to file in the room. I hate that she felt Chloe wasn't as fun, but I'm grateful she missed me so much. Making an impact in their tiny little lives makes all the difference to me. I know some of them don't have the best life back home, so I try my hardest to make every day special for them. I know what it's like to go home and be filled with sadness. If I can give them one good thing to hold on to to get them through the worst, I will.

"I'm so sorry I'm late." Chloe rushes into the room from the hallway. "I really wanted to get here early. My car had a flat when I went out this morning. I had to wake up Tim to fix it."

"That's okay. Dawson helped me bring stuff in." I smile at her and tug her in for a hug.

She groans. "I missed seeing that hunk of a man?"

I can't help but laugh. She's happy with her boyfriend, but she's always had a wandering eye.

"Back off, Chloe. He's mine," I snap jokingly.

"Wow, possessive much?" She giggles as she pokes her finger into my side.

"Maybe a smidge." I pinch my thumb and pointer together and laugh along with her.

Our relationship may have some complications that others don't, but the love Dawson and I share is pure and happy. The kind of love that makes your whole body warm and tingle at the mere thought of them.

"Uh-huh." She sets her purse down and begins rifling through the new paintbrushes. "If I had a man like that, I'd be possessive too. Ooh, I like this one." She pulls out a larger fan brush and runs her finger across the bristles.

"Tim's a hottie too. He's such a sweetheart."

"I know he is. I wouldn't trade him for anything," she beams.

More kids start filtering into the classroom, and each and every one of them runs up to me as soon as they see I'm back. With it being the extra summer program, there won't be a lot of students. I wore pants today instead of my usual dresses. I want to show them I'm able-bodied and not feel like they're staring at my metal prosthetic all day. They know I lost my leg in the car accident, but knowing and seeing are two totally different things. If everything goes right, I should be able to get a more realistic-looking prosthetic next year. I can't wait for that. Some people stare without caring how it makes me feel, and I hate it and how their eyes feel like they burn into my skin.

"Are you sure today's project is a good idea?" Chloe asks quietly beside me.

I've gotten a lot better at managing my pain, maneuvering, and dealing with my trauma. My psychologist says I have PTSD from what I endured with Frank. I didn't realize all of my issues, triggers, and automatic reflexes I used daily until I started to open up to her about it all. I thought PTSD was something only war veterans got. I was wrong about that too, it seems.

I nod. "I think it'll be good for all of us."

Today I plan to teach the kids how to do a self-portrait. This is one project I've avoided because I feel some students will judge themselves too harshly. If there's anything I've learned in the last year, it's that you have to be able to reflect on yourself. You must be okay with the image staring back at you, or you'll never be happy. Each and every one of my students is perfect the way they are, and I need them to understand that. The world we live in judges the perception of others too harshly. We need to love ourselves first if we ever want to be able to love others.

Chapter Twenty-Two

Abby

Chloe helped me to pick out the dress for the charity gala tonight. The charcoal gray mid-calf gown sits on the velvet hanger baiting me. I've never been to a charity event like this before. I know what people will think when seeing me on Dawson's arm—that I'm his new project. That I'm the reason he wants to expand Bella's Safe Haven. They don't know him. They don't know how passionate he is about ensuring all women have a safe place they can escape to.

"Is everything alright?" Dawson may be able to hide the concern in his voice but not in those gorgeous dark eyes.

I've never seen Dawson in a tuxedo before. He looks absolutely stunning in the black and white three-piece suit he's wearing. His tie is the same shade of gray as my dress. He stands against the doorframe with his hands in his pockets. The sight of him steals my breath away, and I must remind myself to breathe.

"Wow, you look handsome." I flash him a smile. "I'm just nervous, that's all."

"Oh sunshine, I told you that you didn't have to speak tonight. Just having you there's enough for me." His dark eyes roam over the light pink pajamas I'm still wearing.

"I know. But I want to. If I can help others like me, it'll be worth it. I just don't like getting up in front of everybody and speaking."

"Isn't that kind of what you do every day with the kids at school?"

"That's different. They're kids. Not adults that are judging me as I try to talk them into donating money for a great cause." I sigh. "I just want everything to be perfect for you tonight. You've worked so hard on the shelter and this gala." I squeeze and twist my fingers in my other hand.

He walks over to where I'm sitting on the tufted bench at the end of the bed and kneels in front of me. Dawson takes both of my hands in his and places kisses across my knuckles, instantly stroking the hunger tightening in my lower belly. To be honest, just the sight of him alone does crazy things to my insides.

"It'll be perfect because you'll be with me. Whether you get up there or not, people will donate." He shrugs. "You don't have to tell your story now or ever if you don't feel comfortable. It's *your* story."

"Thank you." I love how understanding he is about all of this.

"Now, I've been dying to see that sexy ass of yours in that dress. Do you need help dressing?" He wiggles his eyebrows.

I swat playfully at him as he starts kissing my neck. "If you keep that up, we won't make it to the gala." I run my hands up the inside of his coat, desperate to find skin.

"I can make it quick," he murmurs, pushing me back against the bed.

"I can't go with just-fucked hair, Dawson." It's tempting, though. I can never get enough of this man. He presses his body against me. He's already hard as he grinds his erection against my stomach. Even through the clothes, I can feel him pulsing with need.

"Why not? I think it looks sexy as fuck on you," he says before claiming my mouth in a heated kiss that leaves me breathless.

"Later," I mumble, clutching the lapels of his coat and wanting him to go but needing him to stay.

"At least let me fix it for you." He nuzzles my collarbone. "Let me help you relax."

At my nod, he slides his hand below the waistband of my shorts. His thumb circles my clit as he presses two fingers inside me. Thanks to his skilled touch, the pressure inside me begins to build. His mouth finds mine once again as he ruthlessly chases my release. I'm hot and cold all over as I take in short, ragged breaths. My toes curl painfully as my nails dig into his bicep. My back arches as I climax, and I cry out his name. He gives me one more sweet, tender kiss before stepping back and standing in front of me.

Dawson sucks my wetness off his fingers, watching me with hooded eyes. "God, you taste so fucking good."

And if that doesn't make me want him even more. "Your turn," I whisper as I lower myself onto the floor in front of him. Aftershocks still shoot through my limbs, making them tingle.

"No time." He stops me from reaching for his belt. "We'll finish this tonight because you, my love, have to get dressed." He laughs at my pout before standing up and grabbing my dress. "Strip."

I shimmy out of my shorts and pull my shirt over my head. I stand and walk until I'm so close I can feel the heat radiating from him. An appreciative groan escapes his throat as I place an open-mouthed kiss on his adam's apple.

"Are you sure you don't want this?" I stand before him in nothing but my matching bra and thong.

"You know I do, Abby. Get dressed before we really are late." He unzips the back of the garment before pulling the two-inch straps off the hanger and holding it out for me to step into.

Nearly a month and a half have passed since I started using my prosthetic, and I've gotten more used to it. But, in times like this, where I have to balance on it is difficult. I place my hands on his wide shoulders to steady me. Once I'm in, I pull the dress up over my hips and bust and turn my back toward him. His warm hand goes between the dress and my skin as he zips me up.

"Close your eyes," he murmurs as he trails kisses over my right shoulder.

I shut them and try to decipher what he's doing. The drawer to his bureau opens and closes, followed by a shuffling sound. He moves my hair off to the side. A cold metal chain rests against my breastbone as he claps it behind my neck, his gentle fingers tickling the sensitive skin and making a shiver run down my spine.

"Open them."

Looking down, I see a small silver flower with a diamond in the center.

"Every ray of sunshine should have its own flower."

My eyes water at his kindness. It's hard to imagine this hot-headed rough guy being this sweet. "It's beautiful, and I love it."

"And I love you. Now, spin around and let me see if this dress will live up to my fantasies."

"I love you too," I giggle as I twist around in a circle for him.

A loud whistle lets out. "Damn, so much better than any fantasy."

"You have to say that." I tilt my head, letting my hair fall back over my shoulders.

"No, really, you're like a fucking goddess. Every day I wake up, I can't believe you're mine."

"I'm so lucky I found you. I don't know what I'd do without you. And dressed like this?" I wave my hand toward him. "You could grace a magazine cover as the sexiest man alive." I wrap my arms around his neck, feeling at peace in his arms. "I have to fix my hair and my makeup, but it won't take long."

"Take your time. I'll be ready when you are." He sits at the end of the bed and waits for me to finish up in the bathroom.

I would've loved to wear heels with this dress, but unfortunately, my black flats will have to do. I can picture myself falling flat on my ass in front of everybody because I haven't mastered my fake leg yet. Anxiety builds in my chest just thinking about walking in front of everybody. I'm not ready for a more realistic-looking one yet, so the shiny metal always draws people to stare.

Dawson

My cell phone vibrates in my pocket.

Unknown: We need to move up the drop to this week.

Me: I didn't do anything. Wrong place, wrong time, I guess.

Dots appear on the screen letting me know this fucker is typing. I've been going back and forth with this guy for a few weeks now. I keep putting off meeting with him. The blackmailer thinks he'll get money out of me. He claims he has a video of me in the warehouse but hasn't provided proof of said video.

Unknown: This may change your mind.

I tap my foot on the floor while a picture is loading. Abby's in the next room and has no idea about any of this. I didn't want to add extra worry to her. The picture loads.

Ah hell.

I recognize the surroundings and it's the warehouse. I'm front and center, holding my pistol up. I don't recall seeing any cameras there but I was too focused on Abby and Frank. It's definitely me and for sure that night. My pulse pounds into my ears like a freight train.

Me: When?

Unknown: Thursday, 5pm. I'll text you the address. Remember what I said, no police or I forward this to every news outlet in Montana.

Me: I remember.

"Ready?" Abby asks.

I abruptly press the button to turn my screen off and stand. "I am."

The drive to the hotel we're hosting the gala in is quiet. I haven't enjoyed the silence lately. My mind races too much. All the questions of who this prick is sets me off. Of all nights for him to send proof, why tonight? I have a lot riding on this charity event going smoothly to help fund the Sunshine House.

Nearing autumn in Montana always brings a crisp smell to the air. The leaves change color before falling to the ground. It's a season of transformation, giving way to new beginnings in the spring. Abby and I have only been together a couple of months, but it seems much longer. The way our personalities fit together is perfect. I can let this guy send me to jail. My imprisonment would wreck her.

We each have our own baggage and have suffered our own types of trauma, but we get each other. Not a lot of couples have the level of understanding that we do. I hate that she feels like she needs to help tonight. She offered to speak, but I've given her every opportunity to decline. She's not on the list of speakers either, in case she decides to back out. I wouldn't blame her if she does.

That dress she's wearing, though, hot damn. I'll have to keep myself in check tonight, so I don't deck anybody that looks at her too long. I hate to admit it, but I need the donations from them. Bella's insurance money will only go so far, and I'm remodeling another safe house a few towns over. There are other shelters around, but none can match the security I provide.

Since Frank was able to get into Bella's Safe Haven, I've made more adjustments to the current building, including a peephole at every entrance and a thick impenetrable metal door. No more windows to bust through to reach a door handle. The windows I, unfortunately, barred, which makes it seem like a prison to me, but the women appreciate the extra precautions. In the end, it's about them anyway.

I don't want Abby to know just how important tonight is. I'll have to start funding the project myself soon if donors don't come through. I'm well off, and I have plenty of my own money saved, but I wanted that for my future. A house, not just a condo, I share with another roommate besides Abby. I want to buy us a home that's just for us, maybe a few extra bedrooms. We both want kids and have broached the topic of adopting later on. It sucks not being able to have a biological child, but whatever kid we get will be loved fiercely. This whole blackmail shit is going to take all that savings away.

I pull into an open parking spot, slide the truck into park and squeeze Abby's left thigh. "Are you ready to go in?"

"As ready as I'll ever be, I suppose," she says quietly from the passenger seat.

I help her out of the truck, and we walk arm-in-arm into the hotel we booked for the event. Checking in to the reception, I pull Abby into my side. As we move through the crowd, I can feel her back tensing beneath my palm. I know she's uncomfortable with any attention on her since everything happened with Frank.

The story is he was killed when the police raided the compound he held Abby in. Murphy covered for me. If not, I'd be sitting in a jail cell right now. I saved his ass in Afghanistan, so he owed me. Who leaked the intel? Who had cameras? Or more importantly, why have cameras at an abandoned warehouse? What am I missing?

We mingle with the guests for a while before I have to take the stage. I have a hard time making small talk after the messages I received. I leave Abby sitting with the Thompsons at our table. I can feel her gaze on my back the whole walk. As I take the stairs to the elevated platform, the crowd quiets down. I've never been a shy person by any means, but it is uncomfortable having everybody staring at me.

I clear my throat before I take the mic off the stand. "Thank you all for joining me tonight. As many of you know of my work with Bella's Safe Haven, I'll get to the point. I'm remodeling a building in Silver Falls to be like Bella's, but with fourteen rooms available. There's not enough secure places for abused women to turn to when things get bad." I find Abby's eyes and hold her gaze. "The Sunshine house is the first of many I have plans to build. To say domestic abuse has touched my own life would be an understatement."

I pull at the collar around my neck, suddenly way too hot. Flashes of Bella's and Abby's history burst into my mind. Abby's encouraging smile and nod prompt me to go on.

"My sister was a victim of abuse. Isabelle wasn't able to escape in time to save herself. A few dear friends of mine have also been at the mercy of an abuser, and luckily they got away in time. We need to bring more awareness about these issues to the front lines. Victims of abuse need to know they have options, that they have a safe place to stay, and that we will do everything in our power to help them with their transition. Bella's rarely has open beds, which tells me there's a lot more women who need our help. I'm asking all of you in this room to help me make a safer community for these women. What would you do if it were your sister, daughter, or friend who was being abused? Wouldn't you want her to be able to have a safe shelter to call home during the worst time of her life? I think we as a community can do better." I pause. "And now the ones you actually want to hear from....." I pause again as laughs echo through the room. "I give you the manager of Bella's Safe Haven and a good friend of mine, Maggie."

Maggie takes the stage in a long emerald green dress. I hug her briefly before handing her the microphone and stepping aside. I hear her talking to the crowd, but the words don't reach me. I'm transfixed by how Abby looks at me as if she's seeing a side of me she hasn't seen before. Her fingers are wrapped around the flower necklace I gave her earlier. She mouths the words I love you to me, and I do it back. Maggie finishes her speech by calling up one of the first women that Bella's helped. I can't help but scan the faces in the crowd and wonder if the blackmailer is among them.

Kennedy tells her own story of trauma and escape. The crowd gasps as she details the violence she was subjected to. Abby clutches at her throat. I can imagine hearing another woman speak about her own history brings up everything she endured with Frank. Abby hasn't spoken about much of the trauma she went through with him. I don't push her. If she wants to share that with me, she will. I have a pretty good idea of what triggers her now, and I do my best to avoid those actions or situations. Her counseling has been helping her too. She's healing.

Maggie takes the attention back and starts to give her closing speech, but Abby gives me a wave to signal she wants to come up. I hesitate, wondering if she's only doing this for my benefit. I gesture for Maggie to hold off, and I grab the microphone from her. "It seems we have one other guest of honor who would like to speak tonight. Let me present, Abby."

I walk over to the stairs to guide her up them. Everyone is silent as they openly stare at her prosthetic. They're probably thinking the same thing I did about her leg, that it was her abuser's fault. In a way, it was. Once she's in the center of the stage and has the microphone, I take my spot off to the side.

"Hi, everybody. My name is Abby, and I probably wouldn't be able to stand here in front of you if it wasn't for Dawson." She puts the mic on the stand and gives me a wistful smile. "My husband was... well, he..." She fists her hands together and starts to breathe faster. She struggles to speak.

My heart breaks for her. She's been having these panic attacks less and less. They're still a bitch to get through when they're happening. I calmly come up beside her and place my hand gently on her lower back.

"I'm right here. You're safe now, sunshine," I tell her low enough that the microphone doesn't carry my voice.

She takes a deep breath and straightens her shoulders. In a strained voice, she says, "My husband was my abuser. He wasn't always that way. In the last few years, he started drinking heavily. With the drinking came the anger. It was slow at first, the change. I was stubborn and stayed with him because I loved him. I thought he would get better. I had heard about Bella's Safe Haven but never really knew to what extent they offered services until recently." She pauses and clears her throat. "I didn't think there was anywhere I could go that he wouldn't be able to get to me." Abby swallows. "I met Dawson through the P.T. program he does at the hospital. He genuinely cares about each and every woman who has walked through the shelter's doors, and even the ones like me who were too stubborn to seek help." She wipes at her eyes and clears her throat again.

"With the right funding and enough volunteers, Dawson can provide the help that's desperately needed across many towns in the vicinity. I can't think of a better person to be spearheading this operation. I've spent time with the guests at Bella's and what Dawson and Maggie are doing there truly amazes me. The changes I've seen in the women over time leaves me speechless. If only we can get the word out to more victims and have a place for all of them. Thank you for being here tonight. It means a lot to all of us."

She surprises me by leaning into my side and wrapping her arm around my waist. "Good job, sweetheart. I'm so proud of you," I whisper to her and grab the microphone.

"And there you have it. We would be forever grateful if you would consider donating funds or your time to help these ladies out. May you all have a great night."

I lead Abby down the stairs and back to our table. I offer to grab a few drinks at the bar in the back. I know I could really use one right about now, and I'm sure she would too. The etched glass champagne flutes the waitresses have been handing out aren't strong enough for me. I need something much more potent.

With a drink in each hand and on my way back to my seat, I notice Abby's pained expression as a woman I don't recognize stands by her chair. I catch the last bits of the woman's words. "I'm just saying I heard it was all a setup, so you could get his life insurance and continue with your affair."

As Abby blanches, I rush over, setting both drinks down on the table before I'm tempted to throw the contents in the woman's face. "I think you should leave. Now!"

"I'm on my way out, don't expect me to donate anything after that little performance." The auburn-haired bitch in a skin-tight blue dress tosses her hair over her shoulder and stalks away.

"I'm sorry, Abby, come here." I hunch over to wrap an arm around her shoulders, but she pulls away.

"I need to go freshen up." Her voice is raw as she heads straight for the bathrooms.

"Fuck." I run my hands through my hair, debating whether I should follow her. She wouldn't even look at me.

"Is everything okay?" Russell asks as he watches her hurry away.

'Yes, no. I don't fucking know, man. Who the hell was the redhead in the blue dress?" Could she be the one sending me messages?

"I think her last name's Beckett. I could be wrong, though. There were a lot of people checking in."

I roll my shoulders, feeling the need to hit something. "That makes sense. She'd be the heiress to the Beckett hotel chain. She's got the personality to match her father's." They don't need money. It wouldn't be her.

"Well, besides her, I'd say you're doing well tonight. Look at the line of donors at Emmett's table." Emmett is the financial guy, taking care of all the money and the accounts for the shelters.

He does have quite a few people waiting, but at what expense? I don't know what was said before I came over, but I don't like what she was insinuating.

I make small talk with some of Montana's richest, trying to pass the time while she's absent. She's never turned away from me like that. I've always been able to comfort her. Almost an hour passes, and Maggie assures me Abby's still in the restroom. She's checked on her a few times. The rest of the patrons have left, and I send Maggie, Russell, and Emmett home, leaving only Abby and I.

I rap against the white wooden door of the restroom.

"Yeah?" Abby answers.

"It's me. Can I come in?"

She sniffs before answering, "I guess so."

Pushing the door open, I expect to see her by the sinks and counter, but instead, she's in a stall with the door closed. I press my back against the door to the restroom. "I don't know what else she said to you, but I do know this. She's a manipulative spoiled rotten rich-bitch who's known to stir chaos wherever she goes."

"Is that what people really think happened?" she asks quietly before sniffing.

"No, I doubt that. It doesn't matter what they think. You and I know the truth." I close my eyes as a migraine begins to form.

"Yeah, but-"

"But nothing. You don't owe anybody anything. You don't need to fix the narrative that they planted inside their head. You can talk to these people and tell them about all the trauma you suffered until you're blue in the face. In the end, their opinion of you may or may not change. As I said, you don't owe anybody an explanation. You only owe it to yourself to live your life with the happiness you deserve. Fuck everybody else."

She's quiet for a minute. "How is it you always know the right thing to say?"

"Because sunshine, I was made for you just like you were made for me. You're the sun, and I'm the moon. We were written in the stars, my love."

The lock on the stall clicks, and she steps out. Her dress is wrinkled, and black mascara trails down her red blotchy face. I open my arms for her, and she doesn't hesitate this time. I hold her tight and nuzzle my face in her hair. This is what she should have done earlier instead of running from me. I'll always do everything I can to make it right for her.

"I'm sorry if I ruined the charity event." She sniffs again and lets out a shaky breath.

"Far from, in fact, you're my good luck charm. We raised close to three hundred thousand tonight. It's the most we've ever received."

She pulls away slightly. "Wow, really?"

"Yup. Most of it is thanks to you and the others who spoke tonight. It's one thing to hear about women like you, but it's another to see them and hear their stories." I run my hands up and down her back.

"I'm so happy for you, Dawson. You really don't give yourself enough credit, though. All of this is because of you. You started Bella's." She trails her hand down my face and rests it on my cheek. "I love what you chose to name the new place."

"Good, because you're the main reason I wanted to start another. Speaking of which, since this is your namesake. I want the kids at school to make some artwork for the walls." I sweep her hair behind her ear and kiss her softly. "Do you think they're up for it?"

She beams. "They would love that."

"How about we get out of this bathroom? It smells like a high-end perfume boutique." Which only adds to my headache.

"I'll follow you anywhere."

She clasps her small fingers in my hand, and we walk out together. We'll brave whatever the world wants to think of us, hand in hand. Our love is stronger than anything anybody could ever throw at us. Our love has endured what would end most relationships. We came out stronger and united on a level that most only ever dream of.

Chapter Twenty-Three

Dawson

"That wasn't the deal," I bark into the phone.

This guy has some fucking nerve. I'm supposed to meet him tomorrow, and now he springs this on me? I wasn't even expecting a phone call. All of our conversations have been through text messages. It was a trade of cash for the drive that holds the recording.

"Either Abby comes to the meeting or the deals off."

The muscles in my back clench into a knotted ball as I lean against the cold wall.

"Why does she need to be there? This is between us."

I pinch the bridge of my nose. When I saw it was a blocked number, I stepped out of my office to take the call. I cast a glance down the empty hospital corridor to make sure I'm still alone.

"Something's come to light, and she needs to be at the drop," he commands.

I don't like where this is going. I want Abby as far away from this situation as I can get her. I'm silent while I think of what I can say to get her out of the mess. She's going to be angry that I hid this from her.

"Would you rather waste away in prison?" He pauses. "Either way, I'll get what I need. If not from you, I'll get it from Abby when you're locked up."

"You son of a bitch," I growl. Clearly, he forgot what happened to the last asshole who hurt her.

He laughs. "I've been called worse."

"If you hurt one fucking hair-"

"I have no intention of hurting Abby. But she has something I need."

"What could she possibly have that you want?"

"I'll send you the address tomorrow. Don't be late."

Click. The phone goes dead. I stare at the device for a moment, wondering what the hell just happened. I shove my phone in my pocket and walk back into the office but find I can't concentrate on anything other than that phone call.

Luckily there's only a half hour left of my shift. I file the paperwork that can't wait until tomorrow and head home early. Abby should be home around the same time. I nervously tap my hand on the steering wheel, trying to think of what I'm going to say to her.

Once at home, I find the condo empty. I pour a glass of bourbon and sit on the bar stool while I wait. I questioned Russell about the package I received when we came home from Rainbow Lake Lodge. He said it was just sitting in the mailbox with the rest of the mail. That means the fucker knows where I live. My mind reels with the possibilities. Could it be one of the officers at the scene? They would be the only ones besides Abby that knows the truth.

I lean my head into my palms while I try to recall every detail from that night. The phone call, Bella's, the disarray of my place, the insults Frank slung at Abby, the sound of his hand hitting her face. Her crying out in pain. Fuck!

The garage door opens and closes before I hear the door knob twisting free.

"Dawson?" Abby calls out.

"Hey, sunshine."

Abby's soft footsteps patter on the tile. Her face falls when her gaze lands on me. "What's wrong?"

I swallow. "Take a seat." I get up and take the glass of wine I prepared earlier out of the fridge for her. She likes her merlot cold. She'll need it tonight.

"You're scaring me," she says quietly.

I place the stemless glass in front of her and kiss her forehead. "There's something we need to talk about."

"Okay." She sets her bag down on the counter and plops down on the chair, looking at me expectantly.

Sitting on the bar stool beside her, I flex my hand in and out of a fist several times. "Somebody has footage from the warehouse."

Her face pales. "How?"

"I don't know. There must've been cameras I didn't notice." I'm such a fucking idiot. "Up until today, they were using it as leverage to get money out of me."

"What about now?" Abby takes a long drink of wine.

"The blackmailer requested that you come with me tomorrow when I make the exchange." My fingers drum on the countertop.

Her eyes widen. "Why?"

"I don't know. He said something's come to light. Is there anything you can think of that they can get out of you?" I lean forward onto the countertop.

Abby's brows furrow. "I don't have anything. Besides Frank's life insurance. Which will only be about $200,000 after all his debt is paid off." She looks away.

That's what I thought too, but it doesn't make sense. "If they wanted more money, I think they would just demand more from me." I rub the back of my neck. "We must be missing something."

I ponder if Frank could've been into the drug trade or other illegal activities that could make Abby a target. If so, it could be his dealer coming to collect. Frank's job was construction; maybe he saw or took something he wasn't supposed to.

"It's never going to be over, is it?" Abby sighs and runs a hand through her long hair. "Maybe we should just run away to a new country and start over."

It's a tempting thought at this point. When we were all alone at the hotel, I felt like nothing could get to us. Now it seems as though something is always trying to tear us apart.

"We'll get through this." I cover Abby's hand with mine.

"And if we don't go?" she questions.

I meet her gaze. "He'll send the video to every media outlet in Montana."

She takes in a shaky breath. "How do you know he really has a video?"

I grab my phone off the counter and open the message with the picture and hold it up. She covers her mouth.

"What do I need to do?" She schools her expression but holds her arms tightly around her stomach.

I've thought about this. "You'll stand behind me the whole time, and if shit goes sideways, you run."

I hate that she even has to be involved in this and all the variables at play. I don't know who the blackmailer is and what else they want from her. No clue where the meeting is going to take place either.

"I won't leave you." Abby shakes her head.

"If it comes down to it, you need to." I squeeze her hand in mine, hoping she feels how important this is to me.

"I won't," she snaps, yanking her hand out of mine.

"Abby," I warn.

"Would you run and leave me there?" She lifts her chin defiantly, daring me to lie to her.

My jaws clenches. "That's different."

"How is it different, Dawson? Because I'm a sad broken woman?" Her blue eyes narrow.

I rub the back of my neck. "I never said that, and I never would. I'm supposed to protect you, not the other way around."

"What happened to it's us against the world?" She throws my words back in my face.

"Is it that wrong of me to want you to live?" If she dies now, all of this would've been for nothing. I still would have failed her in the end.

"I could say the same thing." Abby takes another sip of her wine. "How long has this been going on?"

The question I've dreaded. "The day we got back from the lodge."

"You hid this from me for weeks?" Her voice raises. Abby shakes her head and stares at the wall. "I can't believe this."

I slide off the bar stool and stand in front of her but she turns her head. "Look at me."

She intakes a breath but doesn't move. I'm going to lose her if I don't fix this right now. I cup her cheek and gently tug her face until I can see the tears glittering in her eyes.

"Yes, I hid this from you. Honestly, I was hoping you would never have to know. It's not that I think you're weak or broken and can't handle the truth. I told you I was going to do everything in my power to make you happy, and if that means I have to shoulder this alone, I will. I didn't want to add any more pain or stress to your life. I'm sorry."

"I don't like it when you hide things from me." Abby's voice wavers.

"I just thought that you could use a break."

"And what about you? When do you get that break?"

Abby

My heart's in my throat while we await the text that tells us where to meet the person whose blackmailing Dawson.

Ding. I swear I just had a mini-stroke at the sound of Dawson's cell phone going off on the counter.

Dawson's face scrunches up. "They want to meet us at East Point Med?"

That's an odd place to have an incognito meeting and pay somebody money to shut the hell up. It's not exactly where I'd think shady business took place. I know for a fact there are cameras on their parking lots.

"Ready?" he asks.

No, I'm not. "Yeah."

I took today off from work because there's no way I could go in like this. I'm too shaken up by what could happen. Once I climb up into Dawson's truck, he turns toward me.

"Abby, I need you to run if I tell you to." All emotion is gone from his face.

"I'm tired of running." I click my seat belt into place.

"Everything I've done up to this point is to make sure you survive. Please do this for me." He rests his forehead against mine.

I press my lips to his so I don't have to lie to him. I can't leave him behind. The thought of losing Dawson is a heartbreak I can't even fathom at this point. He slips his tongue into my mouth and kisses me as if this could be our very last kiss. It almost breaks me how achingly tender he is when our world is burning down all around us.

"Don't make me leave you," I whisper.

Dawson starts the engine and reaches over, and grasps my hand in his.

He doesn't live far from the hospital, and I rack my brain the entire way. I still haven't found out what they could possibly want from me besides Frank's meager life insurance policy. Dawson parks the truck in the back parking lot where he was instructed.

"I love you, Abby. No matter what happens, I want you to know that." His lips brush across my knuckles.

"I love you, too. Please don't talk like that. We'll be back in this truck soon."

His lips pull up on one side as if he doesn't think that's true. What is he not telling me? Before I have a chance to ask, he hops out, slings the black backpack over his shoulder, and comes over to my side of the truck.

Opening my door and holding his pinky up in the air, he once again asks, "Promise me?"

I link my finger with his. "I promise to stay by your side."

Dawson's jaw locks tight as he places his hands on my waist and guides me down to the ground. "At least stay behind me."

"I will." That I can promise him.

Dawson leads me over to a picnic table that sits below a large apple tree. We're five minutes early. He scans the parking lot multiple times in the short span of time we sit there. He tenses, and his grip on my hand tightens. Adrenaline pounds fiercely in my veins.

"I think that's him."

I follow his line of sight. Recognition flashes in my brain. No way. It can't be. "That was Frank's boss, Tony Crawford," I whisper.

Dawson stands up and blocks my view. An impenetrable wall of muscle. My mind runs wild. I've met Tony a handful of times. I never pictured him as the blackmailing type.

"Dawson," Tony says.

"Tony," he replies coldly.

"Did you bring what I asked?"

His deep baritone sends chills down my back. I can't believe I knew the person all along.

"I want to see the video before I hand anything over."

"People can't pull a fast one on you, can they?"

Dawson stiffens. "I know what makes people tick. Greed is one of the main culprits."

"I can assure you, the money isn't for me," Tony scoffs.

Is he working for somebody else? I still can't see Tony. I don't dare move. Dawson asked me to stay behind him.

"The video?" Dawson asks, flexing his fist by his side.

Clothing rustles on the other side of Dawson. Then there's nothing but tense silence surrounding us. I can only imagine he's watching the video by the sharp intake of breath.

"You hand me the cash, and you get the drive."

"How do I know there are no other copies?"

"I'll delete the one on my phone as soon as the money is in my hand. That's the only other copy, I swear."

Dawson's back expands on a deep breath before handing over the bag. "What do you want from Abby?"

Tony's feet step to the side, and Dawson follows, blocking him from my view.

"I'd like to look Abby in the eyes when I talk to her," Tony says exasperatingly.

I freeze. That can't be good.

"Abby?" Dawson asks me without moving.

"Go ahead," I answer.

Dawson takes a step back and to the side, placing him to my right.

"Abby, I really am sorry for everything that's happened. I wish you never had to know the truth. Unfortunately, fate can be cruel. I didn't know until it was too late. Please don't blame Owen."

What the hell is he talking about? I don't even know a person named Owen. I stare straight ahead. I don't want to give Tony whatever it is he needs from me. If he thought telling me how sorry he is for the trauma I've faced would make me vulnerable to whatever he wants, he's dead wrong.

"I'm going to bring my sister out now, okay?" His eyebrows raise.

Dawson narrows his eyes at Tony before glancing at me. I shrug. I really don't know what the hell is going on. This clandestine meeting went from terrifying to bizarre in a matter of seconds.

After Tony nods, a brunette in dark jeans and a white sweatshirt steps out of a small pickup truck. She walks slowly in our direction. Her gaze bounces between the three of us. The first thing I notice is the large dark semi-circles below her eyes. She won't look at me for much more than a second at a time. Goosebumps form on my arms, and I fight the urge to pull them into my stomach.

"Abby, this is my sister, Evelyn."

"And?" I don't recognize her. Should I?

"I think you two should talk alone," Tony comments.

Dawson scoffs. "I'm not going anywhere."

"Whatever Evelyn has to say, she can say in front of him," I say. Tony's crazy if he thinks I'd want Dawson to walk away from me right now.

"I'm sorry for what you've been-," she begins in a quiet voice.

I cut her off. "What do you want from me?"

Her shoulders hunch. "No matter what I say, you'll hate me. But please keep an open mind."

Was Frank having an affair? "How can I hate somebody I don't know?"

Tony leans against the other end of the wooden table. His brow furrows and his lips pull into a tight line.

"Frank and I...." She pauses and swallows thickly. "We were together, and we had a son."

A vise grips my heart. *Frank had a son?* I've never been more thankful for a piece of patio furniture than I am now. This bench is the only thing holding me up. Dawson steps closer as if he could shield me from the devastating news.

"Owen's sick. He has a very rare form of Sickle Cell Disease." Evelyn's head tilts down at her feet as she speaks in a shaky voice, "He'll need multiple bone marrow transplants."

Yeah, it's sad. But what does that have to do with me? "Your point?"

"There's no match for him in the database. Our only hope would be to come from a sibling." Evelyn picks at a stray thread on the cuff of her sweatshirt.

No. The breath rushes from my lungs. I can't form the words. Frank wouldn't have done that to me. I'm vaguely aware of Dawson placing his hand on my knee. The air feels as if it's been sucked out of my lungs.

"What are you getting at?" Dawson speaks for me.

"I only just found out that Frank's sperm was frozen." Evelyn meets my gaze with watery hazel eyes. "I'm asking for you to release it to me, that way I can have a chance to save my son."

Am I understanding this right? She wants to have another baby just so that child can be a chronic living donor to her current son.

"How old is Owen?" I blurt out.

A painful expression flashes across her face as she says, "Three."

A knife stabs me through the heart. He was having an affair nearly four years ago? I thought our marriage was good up until we tried to start our own family....

A horrible feeling settles in my gut. "When did you find out he was sick?"

"When he was a newborn." She bites her thumbnail.

Bile rises up my throat. Oh my god. That's around the time we began trying for a child. "Was he only trying to have a baby with me to save yours?" I whisper. "Nevermind, I don't want to know. Why didn't you two just have another kid then, since you didn't mind fucking my husband behind my back?"

Evelyn shifts uncomfortably on her feet. "Because I can't." She bites the inside of her cheek. "I almost died during childbirth. I hemorrhaged bad enough that they had to give me a hysterectomy."

And there's the answer to the question I didn't want to know. Frank never wanted to have a baby with me. He only wanted a bone marrow factory for his and his mistress's child. That's why he was so angry I couldn't get pregnant. How could I not know he was cheating on me all these years? Why was I that stupid? I gave everything I had to Frank. It was never enough.

My vision becomes cloudy, and my head feels weightless. I can't breathe. Every ragged breath I draw in does nothing to satisfy my lungs. My erratic heartbeat is thumping against my sternum.

"Abby, I'm right here." Dawson's arms wrap around and shield me from the onslaught of her words.

I rest my head against his chest for a few moments. I feel like I'm stuck in some horrible nightmare. Every time I think I've reached the end, another monster crawls out from beneath my bed trying to drag me down to hell.

"How do I know you're telling the truth?" I finally manage to say.

She pulls out her cell phone from the back pocket of her jeans and shows it to me. Sure enough, there's Frank with a broad smile holding a newborn, and she's beside him on the hospital bed. The photo cuts deep. He was happy there. No remorse showed that he was being unfaithful to me.

Evelyn won't meet my eyes as she informs me, "He also signed the birth certificate."

"How did you know he had his sperm frozen?"

"Jack and Layla."

I intake a sharp breath as my heart refuses to pump blood. Frank's parents? "They knew about you and Owen?"

"Yes."

That whole family betrayed me. I close my eyes tightly to keep the tears in. "I'll sign it over on one condition."

"Anything."

The hopeful shine in her eyes almost makes me regret it. I shouldn't give this woman anything. She's a home wrecker. If it weren't for a child suffering, I would tell the place that holds his sperm to discard of it all. It's one thing for two consenting adults to agree to what they were planning to do with a second child but to blindside me like that? When was Frank even going to tell me?

"I don't ever want to see or hear from any of you ever again."

"I understand. Thank you."

"Take me home, please." I stand abruptly on trembling legs and walk away from Tony and Evelyn.

Dawson doesn't say a word until we're back on the highway. "I don't know what to say. Sorry doesn't do shit."

"How do I know you're not using me too?" I close my fists tightly as I fight to stay calm.

"I know this is fucking hurting you but don't you ever compare me to Frank again. I am nothing like him," Dawson says quietly.

"I never thought he was this way either," I whisper.

Dawson doesn't reply. I clench my fingers tightly as waves of anger roll through me. I was wrong before about not being capable of hating somebody. Every last shattered piece of me is burning with a hatred for Frank so fierce I wonder if there's any room left over for any other emotion.

The truck rumbles to a stop in front of the garage door and Dawson takes a deep breath before turning in his seat.

"I don't know how I can prove to you that I love you and I'm with you for no other reason than because I want to be with you. I'll spend the rest of my life making sure you feel cherished. You accept me as I am, flaws and all. I know there are things I need to work on, and I will. I'll be the man you deserve. When I told you I'd never hurt you, I meant every word."

Chapter Twenty-Four

Abby

Two months later.

I stifle another yawn as the students file out of the classroom. Their voices are unusually high, and their little bodies are in constant motion.

"Hey Abby, are you okay?" Chloe asks once the chaos dies down.

I rub at my temples. "Yeah, I just haven't been feeling well the past few weeks."

"What's been going on?" She adjusts in her chair until she faces me.

"I'm just so tired lately, and my coffee's been messing with my stomach. I haven't been able to drink a full cup in a while without getting nauseous. I think just everything with Frank, selling the house, and being back to work, I'm exhausted. Mentally and physically." I lean back in my chair, feeling drained. This fall has been rough for me.

"Oh." She crosses her arms with a hint of a smile.

"What does "oh" mean?" I narrow my eyes at her.

"Could be nothing," she says in a sing-song voice.

"What are you implying, Chloe?" The thought never crossed my mind until now.

"It sounds to me like you could be pregnant. When was your last period?" She looks away and fiddles with the zipper to her fleece coat.

"That's not even remotely funny." I look away. I know she's not trying to hurt my feelings, but there's no way I'd be pregnant.

"I wasn't trying to be funny. When was it?" she asks in a serious tone, opening her calendar app on her cell phone.

"I don't know. I haven't tracked them since, well, you know when." With Frank, my life revolved around my cycle, but with him gone, I've stopped thinking about it. When my period comes, it comes.

"I'll pick up a test on my way home tonight and first thing tomorrow before the students come in, you're taking it," Chloe commands with a half-smile and raised eyebrows.

I roll my eyes and shake my head. "It's a waste of your money and our time. You know damn well I can't be."

"Strangers things have happened. Your symptoms are like classic early pregnancy." Her eyebrows lift even higher.

Chattering children thankfully interrupt our conversation. She wants me to pee on a damn stick? Fine, I will. Then she can sit there and wait for the negative result while I ready the classroom. She doesn't mention the possibility again for the rest of the day, and I do my best to block out the idea. I won't allow thoughts of pregnancies and babies to invade my mind again. With how exhausted I've been, luckily, dreamless sleep comes fast.

Beep, beep, beep. The shrill sound of my alarm goes off. I slap the snooze button and snuggle in closer to Dawson's warmth. Resting my face against his back and breathing in his spicy, woodsy scent, I almost drift off again before the annoying clock alerts me again. I kiss him between his shoulder blades and get out of bed.

After dressing and brushing my hair and teeth, I quietly walk down the hall to the kitchen. I fire up the coffee maker even though I probably won't be able to drink it. Pregnant? Yeah, not in a million years, but whatever, I'll humor her. More likely, it's just stress. I hired a moving crew to pack up everything from my old house and put it in storage besides the furniture. That can stay. I know at some point, I have to go through all of our belongings, but I just can't bring myself to do it yet. I'm not ready. I'm not sure I'll ever be ready for the tsunami of memories and emotions that act will bring.

I couldn't go to the funeral Frank's parents arranged for him. Can't go to the cemetery or see the gravestone either. I just can't. I'm heartbroken his life ended in such violence. At the rate he was going, he would've killed me. That's the sad truth, and I know that now. Dawson has saved me in more ways than one. I can't help that even in my anger toward Frank and everything he's done. I still miss my best friend. The one who would help me through all this, but he left me years ago. It's up to me to pick up the shattered pieces now.

A few sips of my coffee, and it's already turning my stomach. I sigh, pouring yet another full cup of coffee down the drain. I crunch on a granola bar as I grab my purse and lock the side door behind me. My heart feels like it's taken up residence in my throat. I'm already dreading the pregnancy test. I never thought I'd have to do this again. Chloe's helped me through a lot. If this is all she asks of me, then I'll oblige. Not happily, though.

Pulling into the nearly empty parking lot at the school, I park beside her white Camry. I kill the engine and step out into the howling, bitter wind. Tugging my thick winter coat tighter around me as I walk briskly to the entrance. Winter's here, and you can smell it in the air.

It's a crisp, clean scent. Sliding my badge through, the soft clicking of the lock rewards me. The wind nearly rips the door out of my hands as I step through, and I have all I can do to pull it closed.

I barely have the time to set my bag down on my desk when she comes up behind me. Her soft footsteps gave her away. "Are you ready?"

"Do I have a choice?" I roll my eyes and fight the urge to stomp like the children do in our class when they don't want to do something.

"Nope." She smiles and grabs my hand, pulling me out of my room. "Let's go."

I shuffle my feet behind her dramatically into the bathroom when she hands me the little blue and white box. "All I'm doing is peeing on it. You can stand guard. When it's negative, I won't even tell you I told you so."

"Deal." She holds her hand out, and we shake on it.

I go into the first stall of the teacher's restroom and drop my pants and underwear. Ripping the box open and tearing open the foil wrapper, I pull out the stupid piece of plastic that once controlled my life. I hesitate before taking the cover off and exposing the tip. The fear once again gripping me so tight I can't breathe. He's gone, and this is for Chloe. Nobody else. It's just for her. I can do this. No punishments are waiting for me after. I won't be blamed for a negative result. Frank won't get to use the baby if I were....

I quickly get it over with and cover the stick back up. I hand it over to her, desperate to get away from it. "Five minutes. I'll be in the classroom getting ready." I walk out of the bathroom, and I don't look back.

I'd be lying if I said my eyes didn't stray to the clock hanging on the wall as I place materials at every table in my class. I'm almost done bringing the paint trays to the tables when Chloe returns. I hear her, but I don't look up. I don't want to see the look of disappointment on her face. She looked so excited yesterday at the possibility.

"Abby?" she says quietly.

My shoulders sag, and I look up at the ceiling. I know I can't get pregnant, so why does this hurt so bad? Why does it feel like another piece of me is crumbling and breaking into tiny little shards of rubble? I know what she's going to say. The same thing I've heard for well over three years now.

"Yeah, Chloe?"

"It's positive."

"What? No. It can't be. Let me see." I dart toward her. Sure enough, there's a little blue plus sign in the result window. My mouth runs dry. "It's just a false positive."

"Take one again at lunch, then?"

"I don't want to do this." I cross my arms over my chest and rub my sides. The walls feel as if they're moving closer and closer.

"Come on, Abby. What if you really are pregnant? One more test won't hurt." She peers up at me through her long eyelashes.

"Are you serious right now? You don't know how much I went through with Frank trying to get pregnant, and now this?"

"I know. I'm sorry." She deflates in front of me.

"No. You don't know because I've spared you most of the horrible details. All the mental and physical abuse I would get after a negative result? My mind knows he's gone, but my body is still living in fear of these." I chuck the offending test into the trash can and cover it up with the trash already in there.

"What about Dawson?" She points to my stomach. "And that baby you may or may not be carrying? If you are indeed pregnant, you must see a doctor and ensure everything is good because of your history."

Shit. She's right. If I am, and that's a huge if, I need to be careful of my health. I run my hands through my hair, slightly tugging on the ends. I don't want hope; she's a ruthless bitch. The second I think this could be real, she'll take it away like she always does. If I've learned anything, it's that hope is a dangerous thing. I can't allow it to bloom. Not about a baby, at least.

"Then you'll drop this and never say a word?" I say between clenched teeth. She nods. "Fine, lunch it is then."

The day drags on and on. I find myself counting down until our lunch period. I try to distract myself with as much student instruction as I can until then. Ding, the bell sounds, signaling a change of classes, and all the children in the room scatter to line up at the exit.

Once all the kids leave the room, I repeat the same thing I did earlier, but this time I stand there with Chloe. I need to watch and make sure it doesn't get dropped or tipped or whatever could've caused a false reading like before. I lean against the wall with my eyes closed, waiting for the alarm Chloe set on her phone to go off. I can almost hear each second ticking in my head. Tick, tick, tick. It's begging me to peek at the test, but I won't. I refuse to do it.

The high-pitched alarm echoes off the concrete walls, and we both lean over the sink where the test is sitting, and I freeze. Another plus sign. Unbelievable, two duds in one box or am I really pregnant?

"You need to call your doctor Abby." She rests her hand on my back between my shoulder blades.

"I know." Thoughts race through my head so fast that I can't latch on to a single one. There's no way it's real. This can't be happening. My pulse thunders like a freight train in my ears. Each heartbeat is louder than the previous.

"We're gonna have a baby!" She wraps her arms around me and squeezes. I barely hold her back. I can't think straight.

"I don't want to get excited yet. I can't. Please just wait until I can see Dr. Soloman before we get our hopes up?"

"Well, then, what are you waiting for? Go call her." She gently nudges me out of the bathroom.

Back in the classroom, I pull out my phone and dial Dr. Soloman's office. She agrees to see me after I get out of work Friday. I just have to keep telling myself it's not real until then. But what if it is? Could I really be pregnant after all this time? Oh no. What will Dawson think? He wants kids. I know that. But we haven't been together all that long yet. I don't even know if this would even be a viable pregnancy anyway. I can't tell him yet. I won't allow hope to destroy him too. Not like he'd ever hit me. But look at what hope has done to me. I'll keep it to myself until then. I can't and won't hurt him.

Dawson

I've texted Abby a few times today, but she has yet to reply. That's not like her. I pull my cell phone out and check my messages.

Me: Good morning, sunshine. How's your day going?

Two hours later, still no response.

Me: I miss you.

Another hour goes by with no response. I hate the avenue my brain decides to take. There's no way Frank could've taken her. He's dead. All the anxiety and terror from that night come back in an instant. Everything in me tells me to find her, but that's ridiculous. She's at work. She must be too busy to answer me. I bite down on the panic that continues to bubble through me.

"That virus going around is taking out all my patients. I had my next one cancel on me also." Sandra's voice breaks through my thoughts.

I look up at her as I set my phone face down on the desk. "One of mine canceled too."

"Is everything alright? You seem off today." She pulls her chair closer and sits next to me.

I sigh and shake my head. "It sounds stupid. Abby's not answering my texts, and my first thought is Frank took her."

She nods as her eyes soften with sympathy. "That's understandable after what you two have been through. I'll take your next patient. Go home."

"No. Sandra, really I'm fine."

"I won't take no for an answer. Abby should be getting home soon, and you should be there," she says sternly.

I look back at my computer screen before answering, "Thank you."

I scoop my cell phone into my pocket and snatch my keys. It's almost four. Abby should be home around the same time I am. I pull into our condo's driveway, still not knowing if she's home. She parks her car in the garage now. Walking into the garage and seeing her car, I'm relieved but confused about why she still wouldn't have replied to me. Ralph's vehicle is gone. She's alone.

I unlock the door to the house and call out her name. She doesn't answer. Panic seizes my breath as I quickly walk through the house.

Water running filters through the closed bathroom door. I knock gently.

"Yeah?" she answers.

Relief floods through me at hearing her voice. "Can I come in?"

"Sure."

I slowly open the door and am greeted by the sight of her taking a bubble bath. I kneel on the tile next to her and rest my arms on the side of the tub.

"You're home early. Is everything okay?" she asks, sitting up and sloshing water inside the tub. Her eyebrows scrunch together, and her lips narrow.

"I could ask you the same thing." I search her face for any clue that something's wrong between us.

"What do you mean? This is the time I usually get home." She reaches over and twists the faucet until the water stops running.

"Are you okay? When you didn't answer my texts, I got worried." I put my elbow on the tub's side and rest my chin in my palm.

Realization dawns on her features. "I'm sorry, I forgot to text you back. It's been one of those days."

"Is everything okay between us?" I ask quietly. I couldn't bare to lose her after all we've been through. Her walking away from me would leave me nothing but a broken man.

She smiles at me and gives me a peck on the lips. "Of course, it is. I have a lot on my mind right now, but you are the one solid thing in my life. Us isn't something I question."

"What's going on then?" She usually comes to me when she's struggling.

"It's not something I'm ready to talk about yet." She tucks her hair behind her ears, clearly uncomfortable.

"Is there anything I can do?" I hate feeling helpless. It's like that night at the gala all over again. As much as she claims we're okay. I feel like we're not. There's a crack in our foundation, and I can't help but feel like it's widening the space between us. Creating a canyon we can't cross.

She shakes her head but won't meet my gaze.

"When you are ready, I'm here." I hate this feeling like she's hiding something from me.

"I know you are." She smiles at me warmly and rests her wet hand on my forearm.

"I'll let you enjoy your bath then. I love you." I kiss her briefly on the lips before standing.

"I love you too."

I walk out and close the door. Something's obviously really bothering her. If I'm the one solid thing in her life, what is she questioning? I know selling her old house and dealing with the aftermath of Frank's death, and infidelity hasn't been easy on her. Ever since she found out Frank had an affair and a child, she's been quieter. I know what Evelyn said to her upset her, but this seems like something more.

I'm sitting on the couch when she appears in the hall a short time later wearing black yoga pants and one of my t-shirts, the gray cotton skimming the tops of her thighs.

"Can I join you?"

"Of course."

Abby sits beside me and rests her head on my lap, and her arms wrap over my legs. Her eyes close as I stroke her hair, my fingers running through the soft blonde strands. I don't dare say anything. I don't know what's happening right now. Is she leaving me? My heart is on fire, burning up inside me, choking me. I fight the urge to drop to my knees and beg her to stay. I have her diamond ring hidden in my dresser. I could propose now if it means she'd stay. Christmas is just over two weeks away. That's when I planned on asking her. My big long speech of why we're perfect for each other is written down beside the small velvet box.

"Are you leaving me?" My voice cracks, betraying me.

She whips her head up off my lap. "What? No. Why would you think that?"

She pulls herself up and straddles my legs, and takes my face in her hands. Her eyebrows draw together, and wrinkles fan from her baby blues.

"It feels like you've been pulling away from me." I clear my throat. "Ever since the gala."

She kisses the tip of my nose. "I'm sorry it seems that way. I don't mean to. I've just had a lot going on. It's been hard to process everything, but I swear, Dawson. Leaving you has never crossed my mind. I love you with all my heart, and there's nowhere else I'd rather be than with you."

I exhale my relief. "You *are* my heart, sunshine."

She nestles her body closer to mine and says against my neck, "I just have to work through this on my own for a little while. I'll tell you when the time is right. You're stuck with me, though."

"There's nobody else in this world I'd rather be stuck with. I'm here for you, always," I murmur against her hair.

My hand rubs her back. I don't like that I automatically thought she was leaving me. I've never been insecure before, and that's the flaw I hate the most about myself. That's the power this tiny blonde woman holds over me. I need her more than I need air to breathe or blood in my veins. The thought of a life without her is a very dark place I shouldn't let my mind wander to. I know there are things she has to do on her own, but it kills me she isn't confiding in me. I want to be the one to shoulder all the problems for her.

Chapter Twenty-Five

Abby

Waiting in Dr. Soloman's office brings back all the fear and grief from all of the previous visits. I haven't stepped foot in here since the day of the accident. Nothing in this room has changed. I shiver recalling how desperate I felt to please Frank. All I ever wanted was to make him happy. The guilt gnaws at me for moving on this fast with Dawson, but Frank moved on while he was still sleeping in our bed. Some days are better than others. I know I deserve to be happy, and I am with Dawson. The looks some people slide me when they see us together cuts deep. They don't know how bad it was with Frank, and how could they? I kept it to myself.

I was good at wearing the mask. I was good at making people think I was okay when deep down; I was falling apart, spiraling into the darkness of despair. That's the thing these days. Everybody is too worried about their image and how they're perceived by others that if we ask for help, we're weak. Everybody has things that they hide, their own darkness they swallow.

The incident with Frank didn't get publicity, and the police helped on that front. Once they knew all the baggage my marriage had, and what I'd lived through, they thought it was best not to publicly announce the person who actually killed him. I could only imagine what people would think of me then, sleeping with my late husband's killer. They'd never understand the direness of the situation Dawson walked into. All they know is that we were separated at the time because of domestic abuse and Frank was killed when the police raided the abandoned warehouse. That's all they need to know. The rest is our baggage to handle.

My only regret is that I let it get that bad with Frank before leaving him and that Dawson had to be the one to pull the trigger. I wish it were anyone else. I don't blame Dawson for anything or hold it against him. It was him or Frank that night, and if I had to choose who deserved to live, it would be Dawson. He wasn't the one beating women and kidnapping them, not to mention living a second life with another woman and child. I tap my foot on the floor to cover up the sound of the clock ticking on the wall behind me. Tick, tick, tick. A few more minutes pass before a knock jerks me upright. Damn, I hate this.

"Mrs. Miller, how are you, dear?"

I keep meaning to change my name back to my maiden name. Maybe someday I will.

"I'm well, and you?" Get to the point, lady.

She beams. "I'm ecstatic that I finally get to tell you that your urine and blood work indeed shows you're pregnant."

Thump. Thump. Thump goes my heart. Don't get your hopes up yet. "Can we do an ultrasound to make sure?"

"Yes, I was already planning on it. If you'll follow me?" She gestures toward the open doorway, her stilettos clicking along the tiled floor.

Zombie-like, I stand and follow her out of her office and into the exam room next door. I try to relax and hide how excited I am after all these years to hear those words finally. I freeze once I see the equipment she'll use. I'm starting to regret my decision of not telling Dawson, and I wish he were here with me. He should be here. He'd hold my hand and tell me exactly what I need to hear. He has a right to know, and I've hidden it from him. Guilts sinks its sharp teeth into me.

"If you can lie back and lift your shirt." She pats the bed next to the machine. I do as I'm told, my breathing starting to come in shallow pants as she puts the gel on the wand. "Just try to relax, Abby," she says kindly.

Easy for her to say. She's not the one on the table with everything to lose or possibly everything to gain. The cold gel touches my skin, and my eyes close. I don't want to look at a blank monitor. I don't want to see my empty womb. She swirls the wand around on my lower abdomen and applies gentle pressure here and there. I tighten my lids down and breathe deeply.

"Abby, look." At her prompt, I open my eyes and look at her. She points to the screen. "It doesn't look like much right now, but there's the fetus." She clacks away at the keys while she takes measurements.

Time stands still. I'm really pregnant. I can see my little peanut on the screen. I involuntarily let out a sob as tears of joy threaten to escape my eyes. I can't believe it's real.

"Are you ready to hear the heartbeat?" she asks giddily.

"I thought you'd never ask!" I tell her, bubbling with excitement.

Then I hear the most amazing thing in the world. A weird sound resembling a galloping horse comes through the tiny speakers. "Can you record that?" I want to be able to show Dawson. Now I feel even guiltier about not having him here. Damn it.

"I can put them all on a drive for you, but I'll also print you out some pictures." She continues moving the wand and typing on the keyboard.

I hate to break the moment, but I have to ask, "Does the baby look okay? Like is he or she where they should be?" I haven't been able to pull my eyes from the screen. That's my baby.

"From my measurements, you're six weeks along, which puts your due date at August sixth. But to answer your question, the baby looks as healthy as can be."

I slowly exhale. This is really happening. I pinch my other arm to make sure I'm awake.

"Will the baby's last name be the same as yours?" No doubt she'd heard about Frank's passing as well as me transferring his sperm to another woman.

"No. It'll be Connelly." I'm having a baby with Dawson! How am I going to tell him? Will he be as excited as I am about this?

"Okay, you're all set. Here are the pictures, and I'll send in a prescription for prenatal vitamins to your pharmacy. I want to see you back here in two weeks for a check-up."

I take the thumb drive and the little black and white picture from her. "How am I pregnant after all this time of trying?" I don't understand. We weren't even trying. We weren't tracking my ovulation or anything like that. We just had sex without a condom many, many times.

She thinks for a moment, "I like to believe that everything in this world happens for a reason. The timing just wasn't right for you then, but it is now. I'm so happy for you, Abby."

I wrap her in a hug and squeeze. "Me too."

Out in my car, I can't stop staring at the picture. As much as I wish certain circumstances would be different. I wouldn't change what I went through. Every bad thing that's happened in my life led me to this point, and to Dawson. Sometimes you have to endure the hard things to be able to get to where you're meant to be. I wouldn't have lost my leg if we didn't crash. We wouldn't have crashed if he didn't hit me. He wouldn't have hit me if I was able to carry a child back then. Every cause has an effect. Dawson and this baby were the only good things to come out of that tragedy.

Christmas is in two weeks, and our little miracle baby is the best present I could've ever hoped for. That's when it dawns on me, Christmas will be the perfect day to tell Dawson he's going to be a father. Now to figure out how I'm going to tell him. I don't want to just put the ultrasound picture in a present. He missed the build-up of excitement from the beginning when I first thought there was a chance I could be carrying. I only get one shot at this surprise, and it has to be perfect. He deserves for it to be perfect.

Putting the picture into a small notebook in the zippered compartment of my purse, I head back to Dawson's condo. I feel the urge to paint, and I know exactly what I want to do. I think Dawson will love it.

Dawson

Abby hasn't been to the Sunshine House yet. I'm nervous about bringing her there. I named this one after her, and I want it to hold up to whatever she's imagined in that beautiful head of hers. Today's Sunday, and we're both off. I'm taking her out to breakfast on the way there. There's a new diner everybody's been raving about.

Since we had that talk on the couch when I thought she was leaving me, she's been better. More so when I came home from work on Friday. It was like everything shifted between us. Whatever was bothering her didn't seem to affect her as much. She's been smiling more, and I know it's not the fake smile she sometimes puts on. She truly is happier. It seems she worked through whatever was troubling her on her own.

I'm beyond nervous about next weekend. It's Christmas, and I'm going to ask her to marry me. I don't need more time to know she's the one. I've known for a long while. Since the first time I kissed her, I knew my life would never be the same again. The words my parents spewed at me about never being good enough for a woman are just echoes. Sometimes they linger in my mind and make me have doubts, but then I think about the letter Bella wrote me, and their voices disappear. Bella's the one who knew me best, and if she thought I was deserving of love, then I am.

I squeeze Abby's hand as I continue driving. Silver Falls comes into view. The small town center is beautifully decorated with wreaths on every lamp post and twinkling lights strung up on the small trees that line the road. She takes it all in with a smile. Christmas has always been my favorite time of year. We park in front of the diner and join the line to be seated. The delicious scent of the food wafts over to us.

"That smells amazing," she says, inhaling deeply.

"Yes. It does." I leave my hand on the small of her back. I can't go anywhere without having a part of me touching her. Sometimes I wonder if she's just a hallucination of my fucked up mind.

An older brunette with wire-rimmed glasses seats us close to the window and takes our orders. Abby wanted waffles topped with strawberries and powdered sugar after seeing the table next to us. I have to admit they looked so good I ordered them as well. Snow falls like glitter outside and dusts the ground.

"I can't wait to see the new building."

"I'm excited to show it to you. Do you have any plans over Christmas break?" The clinic is closed for five days, and I plan on getting my fill of Abby every single day.

"Other than Saturdays with Chloe and stopping by my parents on Christmas, I don't have any plans." She bites her lip and turns away to look out the window.

She's hiding something. The way she's biting her lip to smother a grin is a sure sign. She's also been guarding a box in the bedroom closet like a pit bull. I wonder if one of my Christmas presents will translate into some of our plans over her break. I can't help baiting her.

"What are you hiding in that box in our closet?" I take a sip of my coffee while I watch her squirm in her seat.

"You didn't peek, did you?" Her eyes widen in alarm.

"No. I'm dying to know what's in there, though." I smirk.

"You have no idea." She grins, sparking my curiosity.

"Will you tell me?" I ask, my voice going low, the way she likes.

A flush creeps up her face, and she shakes her head. She blows across her cup before taking a drink. That's another thing I've noticed. She doesn't drink coffee anymore. Instead, she opts for cocoa.

"Oh. It's that kind of present, huh?" Images flash before my eyes of sexy lingerie or toys she could be bringing into the bedroom for us to use. My foot rubs hers under the table. "Spicing things up?"

"Stop." She holds her hand up. "Please, I want this to be a surprise for you."

As much as I enjoy watching her squirm under my inquisition, I do as she asks, only because I have a surprise for her as well. The food was as good as it looked. The new shelter is only a few miles down the road. It's not too cold, and we could walk if we wanted to. She's built up her stamina a lot between her work and the treadmill at the gym. We sometimes go together, and I stare at her ass the whole time she's on it. Needless to say, I don't get much of a workout at the gym when she goes. I make up for it when I get her home. I debate on walking there before she shivers when we exit out the front doors. I'll drive.

I put the same security fence around the property as the other shelter. I don't have to swipe my badge and type in my code for the gate to open. There are no women here yet, and with the construction crew coming and going, I don't want them to have any passcodes to anything. For now, the gate remains open. Not that I didn't personally vet every single one of them with a background check first. I didn't want anybody working on this place that could use it to gain access later.

The large two-story yellow building comes into view. "It was used as a bed and breakfast before I bought it." The large wraparound porch looks out of place with the bars on the windows and the steel entrance door.

"It's beautiful." She runs her hand up the railing of the steps after climbing out of the truck.

"I'll change this to a pin code before we open." I slide my key into the lock and open the front door.

I hold my breath as she walks in, her boots muffled on the tile flooring. She looks around at the freshly painted walls and the original coffered ceilings. My gaze never wavers from her face. I never wanted somebody's approval before, but her opinion means the world to me. I want her to like it.

"I don't think I've ever seen a more gorgeously detailed ceiling," she murmurs.

I relax slightly. "Do you want to see the rest?"

"Absolutely." She holds her hand out for me to take, and I intertwine our fingers.

"This is the kitchen and dining room. We didn't do anything other than new paint and a backsplash." All the appliances were still in good working condition. "This will be the manager's room."

I open a door just down the hall from the kitchen. It's a spacious room with a bed, a dresser, and two nightstands. Which is the standard that the rest of the rooms have. The nice thing about this purchase is all the furniture came with it. I plan on changing out the old bedding soon. The walls used to have old peeling wallpaper on them that I had the crew tear down and paint. It's coming together.

"It's really nice, Dawson."

Pride fills my chest. "Would you like to help me pick out the bedding and curtains?"

"I'd love that."

As soon as my lease is up next year, I want to get into a house that is just ours. I'm excited to house hunt with her and can imagine it would be something similar to what we're doing here. I don't want a huge house, but large enough so she can have her library again, and we can have a few spare bedrooms. I want a big yard that our kids will be able to play in someday—one big thing at a time. House comes first.

I lead her through the rest of the house and the other fourteen bedrooms with similar layouts. It's not a hotel, but it's fourteen more beds. Fourteen more women at a time, we can help. That's twenty between the two shelters. The construction crew is ahead of schedule by the looks of things.

"Grand opening is in May, right?" she asks.

"Suppose to be, but if the construction is finished before, I may open it up early."

"Has Kennedy given you an answer yet?" Her beautiful blues meet mine.

"No. She's still thinking about it. Others have inquired about the position, but I really want her to have it." I kiss her knuckles lightly.

"I do too. I think she'd be the best fit. But if she doesn't want to, you'll have to interview the rest." She tilts her head. Abby knows how I feel about that.

"I know." I rub the back of my neck.

I have difficulty telling prospective employees that they can't run my shelter unless they've been abused. That's one thing I'm adamant about. I need them to be able to understand the needs of the women who will be staying here. Everybody's situations may be different, but a lot of the feelings are similar to one another.

"Wait till you see the panic room." I practically drag her back to the kitchen.

"Okay," she giggles as she follows dutifully behind.

"They finished this part two weeks ago." I open the pantry to the side of the room and walk in. The large dry goods storage is lined with white shelving. I pull on the small bins that hang on the left side of the wall, and the door swings open, revealing a vault door.

"That's sneaky. I would've never noticed it." She shakes her head.

I punch in the code and open the large ballistic door. The inside dimensions are ten by fifteen and lined with benches and a large cabinet to hold emergency supplies.

"This one's huge compared to the other one." She sits on the bench closest to us. "And comfier."

"Wanna break it in?" After sinking down on the bench beside her, I dip my head and nip at her earlobe.

"Dawson," she warns.

"That's not a no." I suck the delicate skin of her neck in between my lips. Her hand fists in my shirt, tugging me closer.

"Not here. I would feel too uncomfortable looking the women in the face having slept with you in this room." She gently pushes me away with her hands on my chest.

"I guess I have to get you back home then." I watch as her eyes take on that fuck-me sheen I love so much.

"What are you waiting for?" Her lips brush over mine.

I stand up in one fluid motion and pick her up so her thighs wrap around me and press her back against the other wall. "Don't tease me, or I'll take you right here," I growl against her lips before licking at her seam until she opens for me.

She pulls away breathlessly. "Take me home, Dawson. Let's spend the rest of the day in bed."

"You don't have to tell me twice." I kiss her once more before deciding I should put her down or I'll go through with my promise of fucking her up against the wall.

She deserves a bed, not a wall or a bench. The way her eyes are begging me to take her, I don't think she'd object to either. I lock up on my way out and realize I forgot to show her the gardens. There's always next time, plus there's not much to see yet because of the winter. The bed and breakfast has a large vegetable garden plot I wanted to keep for the shelter. If we can provide fresh vegetables for the meals that will help with costs. Plus, the act of gardening alone can be therapeutic for them.

I have one thing on my mind, and it's not gardening. It's making love to my hopefully soon-to-be wife. Wife, just the word brings a wave of happiness through me. I pray that she says yes.

Chapter Twenty-Six

Abby

Dawson's still asleep beside me in our bed, but I've been awake for a while because of nerves. Just watching him softly snore in the quiet house. I know he'll be happy, and he'll be the best dad. I can feel it. Our child will be cherished like nothing before. I bite my lip, fighting the need to wake him up when he starts to stir.

"Good morning, my sunshine." His groggy morning voice is sexy. Dawson stretches his arms above his head, making those muscles stretch taut under his skin.

"Good morning, my love." I lean down and kiss him on the forehead.

"You're up early." He rubs his fingers over his eyes.

"It's Christmas!" My hands splay over his broad naked chest.

He smiles as he pulls me in closer and drapes an arm around my waist. "I know. Merry Christmas."

"Merry Christmas to you too. Are you ready to get up?" Anticipation is a horrible thing. I usually love staying in bed with him and having morning snuggles, but I can't today.

"Really, woman? I just popped my eyes open. You're like a kid trying to get their parents to get up." He laughs.

If only he knew.

"Well, I have to pee, and I'm counting on that famous hot chocolate you promised me." Keep it together, Abby, don't say too much. The words are right there on the tip of my tongue. Revealing I'm pregnant would be easy to accidentally blurt out.

"I can think of something better than hot chocolate." He nuzzles my neck, placing open-mouthed kisses down to my collarbone.

"After," I say breathlessly. I can't think about having sex right now, no matter how gorgeous he is with that look in his eye. The one he gets before he pounces on me.

"Fine. You just want me for my hot chocolate now." He pouts but still trails his hands down my curves to the back of my thigh.

"Well, we can come back in here before we go to my parents." I wiggle my eyebrows at him.

Ralph is away with his family back in Tennessee, leaving the house to us, and my parents aren't expecting us until around one. This will be the first time they've met Dawson. They're going to love him. I can't wait to tell them they're going to be grandparents too. The only people that know are Chloe, Dr. Soloman, and my counselor. I can't wait to go shopping. I've strolled through the baby store in the mall with Chloe and oohed and awed at all the stuff. The first baby item we buy, I want Dawson and I to be together.

He flops me onto my back and kisses me roughly, running his hands down my thin nightgown. My breath hitches as I gently push him away before scooting to the edge of the bed to put my prosthetic on.

He sighs dramatically as he climbs out of bed and gets dressed. I'm just too excited to see his face when he finds out we're expecting to think of anything else right now. I really don't think I can hold this secret any longer. That would be a horrible time to blurt it out while in the throes of passion.

Once dressed and out in the kitchen, he busies himself with making the mugs while I turn on the lights on the Christmas tree. It's a nice-looking tree sparsely decorated with garland and some ornaments. We cut it down together a few weekends ago. The lovely pine scent fills the house. A few gifts sit below the flashing white lights. I bite my lip thinking about next Christmas. We'll have a little one to buy for. I can see it now; our child won't even be a year old and will have too many presents under the tree.

Dawson comes up from behind and wraps his arms around me, resting his mouth just above my ear. His hot breath fans the side of my face. "Cocoa's ready."

We sit on the loveseat together, quietly sipping our cocoa. I've never had a cup that tasted so good. The whipped cream on top has several lines of rich caramel drizzle and is topped with a few mini marshmallows. Dawson's made me a few of these so far, but I swear each one gets better. I've been craving them badly, and now I know why. His baby wants them.

Exchanging a few gifts, we promised we wouldn't get each other a lot. He bought me some paint supplies and several books, while I bought him new boxing gloves and a speed bag. It's down to two small gifts under the tree. Anxiety grips me as I set my mug down on the coffee table and hand him the last one from me, wrapped in blue paper with a large white satin bow. My heart thuds in my chest, and my palms sweat. For two weeks I've been waiting for this moment.

He slowly tugs the ribbon, which releases the bow, and rips the wrapping paper off. I squeeze my hands together in my lap, awaiting his response.

"You're up to something," he says with a mischievous twinkle in his eye and that lopsided grin I adore.

"Me? Never." I rest my chin on my shaking hands to stop myself from freaking out. Almost there. I hope our child has his smile.

The lid comes off, and he reads the message I painted on the inside of the cover, "And then there were three." He looks at me confused but sets the lid beside him on the cushion and pulls the white tissue paper off the top of the box. Inside is one of those log slices I painted with a picture of me standing in front of him. He's on his knees kissing my large swollen belly.

Dawson's eyebrows draw together, and he swallows thickly, licking his lips as he pulls out the wood and examines it. My fists are painfully tight beneath my chin. My lungs can't take in a breath until he sees the last thing inside.

His eyes search mine beside me on the couch. "I don't understand."

"There's another one in there," I croak, barely able to speak. God, just get this over with, Dawson. I'm freaking dying here.

He reaches back into the box and removes more tissue paper. His whole body freezes as his gaze roams over the framed sonogram at the bottom. My first ultrasound picture with the words baby Connelly written at the top. He gently picks it up as if it'll shatter with too much pressure. His eyes flash to mine with a grin plastered across his handsome face.

"Is this real?" His voice shakes, letting me know just how much this baby means to him too.

I nod. He moves so fast I don't even have time to prepare. Dawson lifts me up off the cushions and spins me around, laughing as he places kisses all over me.

"I can't believe it. This is the best Christmas present ever." His eyes water as he sets me back down to stand. He kneels before me, lifts my shirt up, and places his hands on my belly like in the painting. He places a gentle kiss just below my belly button. "I can't wait to meet you, little one."

Happy tears stream down my face as I run my fingers through his hair. I never thought I could ever be this happy. Once I can find my voice again, I tell him, "We're eight weeks today. The due date is August sixth."

"How?" He still hasn't removed his hands from my lower belly, and he continues placing soft kisses on it.

I shrug. "I don't know. The doctor said he or she looks like a healthy little peanut." I pause as worry seeps in. "It's not the best timing, and I know we said later on and-"

"-No. It's perfect. Our little miracle baby." He looks over at the last present under the tree, and his eyes flick back to me with a slow grin spreading across his handsome face. "I have something for you too. I had this big long speech all planned out, but you got me too excited. Now all I can think about is ten little fingers and toes."

He reaches under the tree to a slightly smaller box wrapped in red and white snowflakes and hands it to me. I can't help but feel this small box is just as important as the news I just delivered.

"What is it?" I ask, peering down at him. My mouth going dry. I think I know what's in there.

"Open it." His intense gaze doesn't give anything away.

I tear off the wrapping and pull the box open. When I pull the tissue paper out, I still. There's a ring box nestled inside a coffee mug. My impossibly fast heart rate beats even faster as I look at him. Dawson's still on his knees in front of me, but now a worried expression forms on his face. His Adam's apple rolls up and down as he works a swallow.

"Abby, I love you and our life together. You're my better half, and you're more than anything I could've ever hoped for. You've already made me the luckiest man in the world. Will you marry me and forever be the sunshine that chases away the darkness?"

Without a doubt in my mind, and before I even see the ring he chose, I blurt out, "Yes."

I lower myself to the floor and take his face in my hands as I kiss him with everything I have. He deepens the kiss but then suddenly draws away.

"You didn't even open the box," he says, smiling at me.

"It could be a ring from a gumball machine, and I'd still marry you."

He reaches over and grabs the box that still holds the mug I didn't look at yet, either. Grabbing the small ring box from inside, he opens the small velvet container and holds it out to me. A beautiful square princess-cut diamond shimmers in the blinking lights of the Christmas tree. The silver band the stone rests on shines brightly. I gently tug the ring out and slide it on my finger—a perfect fit. I beam at him as he sets the ring box on the floor and pulls out a mug with pink and purple dahlias, my favorite. The words in the middle of the flowers are a light purple, "Future Mrs. Connelly."

Dawson bites down on his lip, and I lean in and kiss him again. He wraps his arms around me and drags me down to the floor until I'm lying just in front of the tree. He kisses me deeply, running his hands up my shirt to my breast and squeezes gently. He trails his mouth down my throat and to where my flower necklace sits between my breasts before returning to my lips.

Once we break free, he asks in a low timber, "What do you think, future Mrs. Connelly?"

I whisper, "Best Christmas ever."

The end.

Although Bella's Safe Haven and the Sunshine House are fictional women's shelters in fictional towns, there are several shelters and resources for the abused across the United States. This book was made solely for entertainment purposes and should not be used in any other manner.

The number to the United States National Domestic Violence Hotline at the time of this publication is 1-800-799-7233

The web address of the United States National Domestic Violence Hotline as the time of this publication is: https://www.thehotline.org

The first novel of the Destiny Of Graystone Series, a young adult fantasy romance.

The second novel of the Destiny Of Graystone Series, a young adult fantasy romance.

Katie lives in Vermont with her husband and their children. When she's not working or spending time with her family, she enjoys getting lost in a good book. Her favorite hobby is gardening, whether it's edible or decorative. In her opinion, one can never have too many flowers! She may have a slight addiction to creating things in Canva and Procreate. Visit http://www.katierichard.com for more information and be sure to sign up for her newsletter to stay informed.

CPSIA information can be obtained
at www.ICGtesting.com
Printed in the USA
JSHW030913280223
38294JS00001B/2